"In *The Road before Us*, Rosche ta[kes] ... [the] broken pasts of down Route 66, artfully weaving to... charming and nuanced characters who will have you rooting for their redemption from the get-go. This dual-time journey along the Mother Road is not to be missed."

Amanda Cox, Christy Award–winning author of *The Secret Keepers of Old Depot Grocery* and *He Should Have Told the Bees*

"Janine Rosche takes readers on an unforgettable ride complete with twists and turns that make this book into a beautiful journey. This novel is a soundtrack for the history of Route 66. Rosche's writing draws readers into her characters' lives, leaving them invested in the outcome of each one. I'll be thinking about this book for a long time to come. Thank you for taking me on this trip."

Christina Suzann Nelson, Christy Award–winning author

"Janine Rosche gets to the heart of family, friendship, and love once more in *The Road before Us*. She takes us on not only a literal journey down Route 66—which comes alive through the pages—but a figurative one of belonging and overcoming one's past."

Toni Shiloh, Christy Award–winning author

"Janine Rosche has an incredible way with words! In *The Road Before Us*, she's crafted real and relatable characters I couldn't help but love. This is a road trip you don't want to miss. I call shotgun!"

Liz Johnson, bestselling author of *The Red Door Inn* and *Summer in the Spotlight*

The Road
before Us

Books by Janine Rosche

With Every Memory
The Road before Us

The Road before Us

A NOVEL

JANINE ROSCHE

Revell

a division of Baker Publishing Group
Grand Rapids, Michigan

© 2024 by Janine Rosche

Published by Revell
a division of Baker Publishing Group
Grand Rapids, Michigan
RevellBooks.com

Printed in the United States of America

Library of Congress Cataloging-in-Publication Data

Names: Rosche, Janine, author.
Title: The road before us : a novel / Janine Rosche.
Description: Grand Rapids, Michigan : Revell, a division of Baker Publishing Group, 2024.
Identifiers: LCCN 2023040297 | ISBN 9780800742966 (paperback) | ISBN 9780800745943 (casebound) | ISBN 9781493445622 (ebook)
Subjects: LCGFT: Christian fiction. | Novels.
Classification: LCC PS3618.O78237 R63 2024 | DDC 813/.6—dc23/eng/20231002
LC record available at https://lccn.loc.gov/2023040297

Cover design by Mumtaz Mustafa

On page 236, the lyrics to the hymn "For the Beauty of the Earth" by Folliott S. Pierpoint (1864) are in the public domain.

Baker Publishing Group publications use paper produced from sustainable forestry practices and postconsumer waste whenever possible.

24 25 26 27 28 29 30   7 6 5 4 3 2 1

For Mom and Dad

Thanks to Route 66,
you found each other once.
I pray you'll find each other again,
this time on streets paved with gold.

Afoot and light-hearted I take to the open road,

Healthy, free, the world before me,

The long brown path before me leading wherever
I choose.

Walt Whitman, "Song of the Open Road"

Prologue

Miles from any high-rise, the generations-old asphalt crumbles beneath the soles of my borrowed boots, and I wish my story would fall through the hot cracks of Route 66 along with it.

Ahead of me, a sports car ignores the twenty-five-miles-an-hour speed limit through town. Before he's able to get a one-of-a-kind Jade Jessup hood ornament, I step off the road into the brush. The sound of the engine rumbles up my spine as it passes. This trip was supposed to help, not compound, my troubles. Only now do I hear "Take It Easy" by the Eagles blaring from the speakers. When the tires squeal, I pivot to look back at the Tecoma Springs Motel where the car whips into the same spot I parked in yesterday, only yards from my room. Will the Newtons let me stay gratis until everything gets sorted out? Even the kindest people have their limits.

The town of Tecoma is merely a rest stop on Route 66, otherwise undiscernible and undesirable for lingering, not like the tourist traps we've grown used to seeing. Perhaps that's why Dad chose it decades ago. One can hide here.

I pass the sole lamppost, which sits in the geographical center of town. Considering the amount of aged adhesive crisscrossing its pole, it likely still serves as Tecoma's news central. It was at that post that I learned I was a missing child. Where the seams in my world ripped apart for the first time.

Another vehicle approaches from behind me. A glance over my shoulder reveals an older model Chevy 1500 creeping at my walking pace. A man—check that, a boy—wearing an ASU ball cap practically hangs out his driver window. His left hand slaps the door panel, and he rolls his bottom lip between his teeth. "Hey, baby, where are you going?"

Swatting my hand in his direction like he is a pesky mosquito, I focus on the roadside bar up ahead, the scene of last night's crime, or at least one of last night's crimes. What Tecoma lacks in entertainment, it makes up for in criminal activity.

"Aw, don't be like that," he went on. "It's too hot for a girl like you to be out here. You'll melt the asphalt."

I take a deep pull of Arizona air and shift my focus away from the road. The side entrance of the bar is propped open. Or should I say side exit? After all, that's the door the short man with a big attitude barreled out from last night with a bloody nose and, likely, a solid case of regret. I rub the tender place on my arm where he grabbed me so violently. Glynda, the bar owner, steps through the door now, carrying a large black floor mat. She promptly smacks it against the place's brick wall, releasing a cloud of Arizona dirt into the air.

The truck's engine revs to my right. "This AC feels real nice in here. I have some other ideas of what else might feel real nice if you're up for it."

Glynda looks up from her task and, upon seeing me, glares in a way that would intimidate Medusa.

My twenty-nine-year-old self pulls my shoulders back, lifts my chin high, and latches my sights on the western horizon, where the famous road vanishes behind hills and buttes. Yet my eight-year-old self, with whom I've only just begun to reconcile, yearns to stick out my tongue at Glynda. I could just as easily blame her for what happened to my father that August day twenty-one years ago. Glynda was a grown woman when she did what she did. I was a little girl—a foolish, desperate-for-love little girl who made one haunting mistake. That fact is inescapable, no matter how many miles I've driven—from Chicago to Santa Monica and beyond.

"Come on, baby," College Boy drones on. "You're not a tease, are you?"

I pause, my gaze shifting between the livid bar owner and this bum. I saunter—at least I think I'm sauntering, never done it before—to the front bumper.

"Well, all right," the guy says, shifting the truck into Park.

"Is this a '92?" Carefully, I reach between the grille and the hood, searching for the latch.

"Uh, yeah. Why? What are you doing?"

I lift the hood with one hand and disconnect the coil wire from the distributor cap. The engine stutters and dies, and I let the hood slam closed.

"What'd you do to my truck?" he yells while scrambling from the driver's seat.

With my best softball pitch, I send the wire into the desert flora. Ignoring the litany of sexist slurs he lets loose, I resume my trek to the last building in sight. With each step, my nausea increases, but I have no choice in this matter.

I aim the toes of Sandy's boots in the direction of the small jail that looks to be more tourist attraction than serious confinement. But I have no doubt those bars and locks are as real as the small cactus rising through the crack in the road. To think I was a split second away from landing there myself. But Bridger.

Always Bridger.

Before I can take hold of the knob, the old door lurches open with a groan, revealing an older man with as jolly a face as Santa Claus and a beard just as long.

"Well, well, well. Mighty Miss Jade. I heard you'd come back to visit us. Been a long time." The light from the singular bulb reflects off the too-shiny, blushed skin on his round cheeks and even rounder nose.

Familiarity, along with a striking resemblance to his deputy son, make a peek at his name tag unnecessary. "Sheriff Samson, hello."

"How're you doing? Folks 'round here wonder about you all the time."

"I'm . . . okay." There's no sense in sugarcoating it. "I'm here to see—"

"Me. She's here to see me." Bridger's voice holds more gravel than normal, and it scrapes over me like sandpaper.

My eyes move from Sheriff Samson to the direction of Bridger's voice. I push the door farther open until a cell comes into view. No. Two cells, sharing a wall of bars. In the nearest one, Bridger's lengthy form stretches across the concrete from one end to the other in one of his yoga poses. A shiver courses over my skin when I see his nose brushing the floor that probably hasn't seen a mop in some time. "How is she?" he asks me.

"Good. The hospital's going to keep her for one more night, but that's simply for observation."

The sound of his exhale carries over to me.

"Bridge? Are you okay?" A foolish question, if I've ever asked one.

"Peachy," he says, straightening his arms and lifting his hips upward until he achieves a downward dog position, although he looks less like a dog and more like a grizzly.

"Gotta say, this is the first time I seen someone do that in there." Sheriff Samson laughs heartily. "Been doing it all afternoon though."

"He's a unique one, all right," I say. "I'm here to post bail." Bridger's attention cuts to me. Beneath a heavier than usual brow, his dark eyes are rimmed by red. Even if he was able to fit on the narrow, thinly cushioned cot, he couldn't have gotten much sleep. At once, he looks away and drops his knees to the concrete. "How'd you get money for that?"

"It's not important. All you need to know is I'm getting you out of here." I slide the bank envelope out of the back pocket of the Daisy Dukes I would never be caught wearing if I had any other real choice—which I do not—and hand it to the sheriff. As the man takes to counting the money that would likely cover this jail's entire operating cost for the month, I approach the cell with the enthusiasm of an accused witch to a pyre. I grip the bars, waiting for Bridger to look at me the way he did not so long ago.

He stands but never quite reaches his full six-foot-five height before sitting on the edge of the cot. As he scrubs his hands over his face and then back through his wavy shoulder-length locks, the dull ache that has plagued me since Chicago stretches across my chest and sinks into my bones. Finally, his gaze meets mine. I lean my forehead against the clammy steel and mouth, "I'm sorry."

"Me too," he says. And in his eyes, I see that somewhere, some part of him still cares about me.

"Twelve hundred," Sheriff Samson says. "It's all there. Pardon, Miss Jade." After I step aside, the sheriff fits the key into the door lock and turns it until the click releases my long-held breath. "Mr. Rosenblum, I'll grab your belongings and then you're free to go. And take that yogi stuff with you, will ya, big fella? If I tried any of them poses, I'd never get back up."

Bridger pulls a blanket off the cot as he stands. He folds it with care and hands it to Sheriff Samson. "Thank you for the extra blanket, Gill."

"It's not every day we have a celebrity in here."

"You'd have done it for anyone." Bridger claps his hand on the sheriff's shoulder, and before I can think too long on any of it, I make my exit.

When I walk outside, the Arizona sun sinks deep into my

skin like it somehow missed the flipping of the calendar page to September. College Boy's truck remains trapped in Route 66's westbound lane with its owner out in the dirt, kicking the brush and cacti in search of the coil. He doesn't see me. Probably good, lest Bridger decide to defend my honor again. I don't have another twelve hundred dollars to spare.

"I guess I should thank you," Bridger says, sidling up to me as I stare down the highway—close but not as close as he would've been even yesterday.

"You know it's the least I could do. Bridger, I'm so sorry—"

"Jade, you don't have to do this."

"But I do. Now we're stuck in the middle of nowhere without a car, without clothes, without—"

Bridger steps in front of me. "There will be time to figure things out. For now, only one thing matters."

I nod and force myself to swallow the tumbleweed that seems to have wedged in my throat. "Benny."

Chapter 1

One Year Earlier
Jade

As I near the intersection of Adams and Lamar, I maneuver around tourists posing for a photo in front of Chicago's "Route 66 Begins" sign. April through October I've grown used to the crowd of twentysomething wanderers, retired road warriors, and international adventure-seekers amassing on this sidewalk. A couple in their matching leather jackets and windblown hair hold a neatly groomed bichon frisc between them for their picture, kissing each side of the dog's muzzle as a young bohemian woman counts to three.

Later in the day, a smaller group will congregate here—the eastbound crowd, a travel-weary yet appreciative bunch who have been living out of their cars for the past twenty-five hundred miles and have finally reached the end of their journey. They're quieter, and the smiles they sport in their pictures seem more contemplative than the excited westbounders just starting their drive. I can never help but wonder if they found what they were looking for.

With my focus over my left shoulder, something plows into

my right, and I toddle on my heels before a hand grips my elbow, steadying me.

"Watch it, jerk." Gregory glares at a man wearing a cowboy hat who never pays him or me any mind. "Promise me we won't be like these people on our honeymoon. Blocking traffic and running into people so they can get the perfect picture. A picture, I might add, that can easily be photoshopped without ever having to go to the place." He deftly withdraws his phone from his pocket and snaps a selfie of us before I can plaster on my usual smile. "There. Now give me five minutes, and I can put you and me in front of the Parthenon before we even get to Greece."

I survey his face for meaning. He's been busy since he and his father bought out Mendenhall Wealth Management's Chicago branch. In just two years, they've succeeded where others have not, yet my fiancé always makes time to enjoy his newfound wealth with me at his side. With our wedding only two weeks away, he isn't about to change that now, is he? "That takes the fun out of it," I tell him as my gaze flickers back to the ambitious travelers. "The idea is to say 'I was here, standing in the same place others have once stood, twenty, forty, one hundred years ago.' It connects us to places, to people, to the past. It's romantic, I think."

Gregory laughs. "You? Thinking something's romantic? That's rich. I tell you what. Just for that, I won't call the city and ask them to move the sign out of the Loop."

"Call the city? Why would you even consider that? They aren't doing anything wrong."

"But they're a nuisance. I heard this isn't even the original place where Route 66 began. It's symbolic. Which means the sign can go anywhere, and the tourists will follow and not block the entrance to our office anymore. Maybe they'll take the homeless with them."

I follow his line of sight, squinting as the morning sun reflects off the windows of the coffee shop that Gregory has deemed his own. A man dressed in all black—an interesting choice for August—hunches on the ground, his head so low, the dark tendrils of his hair cover his face. After living in downtown Chicago for the last two years, I'm no longer surprised at the homelessness. But I haven't become calloused to it the way Gregory has, so I nudge him. Even though he rolls his eyes, he releases my arm, reaches into his pants pocket, and withdraws two bills from his wallet. A twenty and a hundred. I point to the larger bill. Gregory grins before crumpling the bigger bill and dropping it into the lidless cup sitting on the bistro table next to the man. "Get yourself a haircut, will ya?"

"Gregory!" My toes curl inside my shoes, and I'm not sure if I'm embarrassed or disgusted. "What's gotten into you? Insulting a stranger?"

Only then does the man lift his chin. When we lock eyes, dread seeps inside me. Not a stranger. Before I can untangle the thoughts going through my head, Gregory presses his hand against the small of my back and pushes me toward the entrance of Hyrem & Hyrem Financial.

"I'm grabbing coffee," Gregory says. "I'll see you up there."

My fiancé disappears inside the shop but I pause. What can I possibly say after insulting this man who is most certainly not homeless? That fact is made clear as he gives a final tug to the shoestrings of his combat boot that was probably made by Alexander McQueen, Christian Louboutin, or some other shoe designer who caters to the Los Angeles crowd. He stands and for a moment I can imagine how David might have felt seeing Goliath for the first time. Then the man's gaze moves from me to the coffee cup at his side. I scuttle past a few more people as well as the door attendant of my office building.

At the bank of elevators, I press the up button three times in rapid succession, then feign a casual stance as I wait. Although my reflection looks good in the mirrored doors of the center elevator, I comb my straightened hair anyway. Finally, the doors part in front of me. Coolly, I stride into the elevator, press the number 12, and settle myself against the back wall. *Close*, I will the doors.

And they do . . . until a large hand, its bronze color far deeper than my Casper-light skin, juts between them, daring them to shut completely. But as I imagine most people would when confronted with a force stronger than them, the doors surrender, opening wide so the man whose hair has inspired at least one Instagram fan account can enter. His scrutinous gaze travels down to my toes and back up to my face. Then he holds out the coffee cup. Its silky liquid washes over the floating hundred-dollar bill in a gentle wave. "Can you hold this?"

Without permission from my brain, my hand folds around the warm cup. "Twelfth floor?" I ask in a meeker voice than normal. Of course he's heading up to the same floor as me because, according to my scheduling app, he's here to accompany my first client of the day.

Instead of answering me, he bends over, placing his palms on the inlaid marble of the elevator floor. Then he kicks up his legs and freezes in a perfectly balanced handstand.

I tilt my head. "What are you doing?"

"It's a great workout." His voice isn't even strained. Good for him. Gymnastics is certainly a healthier hobby for him than the last one I witnessed back in Los Angeles.

The doors close and as we rise, I become more aware of the downward force pressing through my legs. I sneak a peek at his forearms as they hold his body weight plus the additional pressure. Yep. Much healthier. We stop on the fifth floor to let in a tan-suited man who only takes his eyes off his phone to press the button for floor 7, never acknowledging me or the acrobat in our company.

We ride in silence to the seventh floor, then the twelfth. Finally, a ding signals our arrival.

"This is us." I wince at my wording. *Us* isn't a thing. I made sure of that during our first meeting as well. Does he even remember? Goodness knows he wasn't all there that day. Still, I straddle the gap at the threshold to keep the doors from closing before the man can right himself.

He does. With a shake of his head, his hair falls behind his shoulders. He stops in front of me, and a scent wafts past my nose—the sweet soapy smell of a hair salon mixed with the California surf.

"Serious question," he says. "Do I look homeless?"

"No." But it sounds more like a question than an answer. "I'm sorry about that."

"This T-shirt used to belong to Mick Jagger. I bought it at auction for eighty-three hundred dollars."

My focus falls to the solid black cotton stretching across his shoulders until the fabric appears gray. In a Who Wore It Best? comparison between the man before me and Mick Jagger, there was no question.

I narrow my eyes, knowing whose bank account paid for that one. "Really?"

He gleams. "Not really. It came in a pack. Six for eighteen. Plus, I had a coupon."

The elevator door bumps my backside. He reaches over my shoulder and pushes the door back into its pocket for another ten seconds or so. "My name's Bridger."

"I know." As I take in the man before me, I recall his face when it was bloated, his eyes when they were bloodshot. Of course, he wouldn't remember meeting me. "I'm Jade Jessup. I met you at Mr. and Mrs. Alderidge's home years ago."

"Oh." He looks away. Just as his cheeks bloom a rosier shade, he takes his coffee cup back, and with his free hand, motions me into the hall. "After you."

His voice curls around me, its graveled texture grating my nerves, though not in a bad way. I don't often pay attention to celebrity culture, but Bridger Rosenblum was at one time ubiquitous. Gossip rags, social media, even my local radio station kept me up to date on what young Hollywood was up to circa 2010.

While I was working to get into an excellent business school for my undergrad, this guy was riding around with the who's who of actresses, pop stars, and heiresses. Although that was then, when he had short hair and the wardrobe of the *Twilight* cast.

Back then, I didn't waste time thinking about him. I had my own problems.

Who was I to care how and with whom someone spent their time? It wasn't my money he was blowing through. It was Berenice and Paul Alderidge's money; America's favorite classic Hollywood couple had taken the wild teenager in as their foster child, despite the wide age gap.

But ever since the Alderidges put their fortune in my hands, I care a great deal about how he spends their money. "I'm sorry your coffee is ruined. I can send for another one."

"Nah, it's not ruined." He brings the cup to his lips. Instantly, my mind jumps to every germy surface Gregory's hand may have touched prior to passing Bridger that money, and my stomach heaves. Bridger lowers the spoiled coffee as his boisterous laugh turns every head in the office our way. "Jade Jessup, I get the feeling you need more laughter in your life."

I have to work to keep my face from showing the offense I've taken. "You say that like you know me."

"You say that like you know you." His retort stops me in my place as he heads toward the lady seated in the chair outside my office.

Berenice Alderidge, although petite in size, is large in presence. Nicknamed Hollywood's Swiss Miss, she is instantly recognizable with the same barrel-curled bob she's sported since her first movie role in the fifties. Understandably, at eighty-eight, her hair is now white instead of blond, thin instead of full, and frames pale, wrinkled skin with faint age spots instead of sun-kissed freckles. Yet she still smiles as brightly as ever, even after losing her husband last summer.

"Miss Benny, how are you?"

"I'm feeling quite old with all this Miss Benny business." She reaches for me, and I clasp her hand in both of mine. "It's Benny. Simply Benny. Don't you dare go back to saying Mrs. Alderidge either. It took ages to break that habit of yours. I won't live long enough to do it again." She motions toward the man at her side. "You probably remember my Bridger?"

"Yes, I do. And we took the same elevator."

Her attention flashes to him. "You didn't do the handstand trick, did you? She has a fiancé, honey. No need to impress her."

He shrugs. "I don't see a ring."

"Um, Gregory wanted stones added to it before the wedding."

"When is that?" he asks. One thing that hasn't changed since he sobered up? The intensity of his stare. It still unfurls me more than it should.

"Twelve days. Why?"

"Just curious. Not that it matters to me." He plays it off coolly with a heavy sigh. "I'm celibate now."

I somehow choke on my own saliva and begin to cough.

"Jade, don't pay him any mind. I merely brought him for the muscle. Now, Bridger dear, could you help me up?"

While I attempt to get back any air of professionalism, Bridger quicksteps to Benny, offering his arm as she rises from the seat.

Was she this frail the last time we met face-to-face? No, but it has been some time since then. Before the pandemic, when Paul had been all the "muscle" she needed.

After I unlock my office door, I hold it open so Bridger can escort her to the chairs by my desk.

Benny's focus falls to his coffee cup as she lowers herself into the seat. "What is that in there?"

"What? This?" He reaches two thick fingers into his cup and withdraws a slimy bill, liquid dripping from Benjamin Franklin's face.

"Oh, honey." Benny forages in her purse, then pulls out a travel pack of tissues. My face beams hotter and hotter with every second it takes her to unfold the Kleenex and wrap the cash inside. "Didn't I get you a new wallet for your birthday?"

"My bad, Benny. I forgot." Bridger's dark eyes pinch with humor.

I take my place behind my desk. Angling my knees toward my computer screen, I turn away from his antics and log into my firm's system where I can see the Alderidge's entire portfolio, from their savings to their IRAs and 401(K)s. "Benny, what can I do to help you today?"

Her smile drops, and she begins to wring her hands. "Well, uh . . ."

My stomach sinks a bit, and I quickly scan the numbers in each account. No problem there. The totals are even higher than I expected them to be. "Whatever it is, you can tell me. I'm here to make your money work for you."

"I'm getting older, and my health isn't what it once was."

Bridger frowns as the sobering reality of her words thickens the air in my office.

"I've been praying a lot lately about what kind of legacy I want Paul and I to leave behind. I'd like to withdraw money from the market."

"All right. There was no need to come all the way out to Chicago to do that. A simple transfer to your bank account—"

"I need to withdraw a great deal of money. Enough that it may require adjustments to our portfolio. I don't want you to think I don't appreciate your hard work."

I wave my hand and offer what I hope is a reassuring smile.

"The reason I became a money manager is to help people like you and Paul achieve your financial goals. From the looks of it, you've met those goals and then some. So, what would you like to do?"

"There are five charities that are dear to my family. I want to donate ten million dollars to each one."

"That's amazing," My heart swells. How many forms had Paul and Benny's shared generosity taken in my years knowing them? Financially, sure. After all, we first met at a fundraiser for the Joliet Children's Home. And although they were being honored for their years of dedicated giving, they treated me like I was the most important person in the room. With each call and visit since, they have been exceedingly generous with their kindness, their words, and their affection—all things I've treasured more than words can say.

Still, unease seeps through my veins. The Alderidge account is by far Hyrem & Hyrem's largest. Not only that but Gregory and his father have often dropped the Alderidge name to land dozens of other high-roller accounts over the past two years. What if the others get wind that Benny is pulling most of her funds? Even if the reasoning is pure, it could spark panic in this touchy financial climate. Will others follow suit?

"I should be able to sell enough shares well above where you bought them so you'll still have substantial holdings with us," I say. "Let me type up the sales order and send it over to our broker."

Bridger offers Benny a forced smile, then returns his focus to my hands as they type on the keyboard. I hit send, then quickly write up an email explaining the decision to my almost-father-in-law, Walter, in case he gives me trouble again. Lately, he's been on edge whenever I send him an order.

"Are you staying in town long?" I ask Benny, filling time until Walter's confirmation comes through.

"Two more days. The Rialto Square Theater is playing *Casablanca* tomorrow. Bridger has never been to the place where

Paul and I used to work. He's agreed to let me give him a tour before the picture starts."

I relax back in my chair and cross one ankle over the other. "In Joliet? I knew that place had history, but I didn't know it had so much significance for your family."

Bridger's brow hikes mischievously. "Come with us," I blink several times. "I'll have to ask Gregory if he'd like to go." My desk phone rings, and I welcome the break in conversation. "Jade Jessup," I answer.

"Change her mind." Walter's harsh tone chills me.

I sit up straight and swivel my chair away from Benny and Bridger. "Excuse me?" Through the window, the cityscape yields to sky and quickly encroaching clouds.

"You have to change her mind. Get her to sell fewer shares."

"Why is that, exactly?"

"You think you're such a hotshot when it comes to dealing with these idiots. Prove that you can be a valuable asset to this company and to this family."

Idiots. Walter, I've learned, doesn't reserve that term for people with a low intelligence quotient, not that anyone should be called such a name. The man calls everyone an idiot simply for not being him. What's the saying? It's Walter's world. I'm just living in it? Or should I say marrying into it? Which is fine, only because Gregory promised he'll never become his father. I glance at Bridger who is finger-combing the long hair Gregory mocked. I grit my teeth.

As the pit in my stomach grows, I search the computer screen for some clue, any clue that would explain Walter's response. "I don't understand why—"

A click is followed by a dial tone. I fight off a sneer, opting for a pursed grin instead. Benny isn't just any "idiot" client. She's always regarded me with dignity, despite knowing my past. And Paul, before he died, seemed to recognize something in me. While everyone else sees a successful financial whiz, Paul

Alderidge seemed to see the lost and lonely eight-year-old girl I've tried so hard to bury.

"Got it," I say to the dead phone line. "Sure. Give me a minute." I hang up and log out of the computer before turning to Benny and Bridger. "Walter Hyrem is working on selling those shares right now. Would you like something while you wait? Water? Coffee with or without money floating in it?"

They exchange glances, then shake their heads in unison. While I take my leave, possible explanations for Walter's angry words swirl in my mind. I pull my office door closed behind me, catching Bridger's eye just before I do. In the hallway, I hear only the shrill whistle of wind outside. Where the hall ends in a floor-to-ceiling view of Millenium Park, darkness looms. I cover the distance to Walter's office quickly, stepping as softly as possible, until I hear hushed voices on the opposite side of the door. I strain to make out the words, but I'm failing, so I try the handle. Locked. I knock instead.

"Walter, what's going on?" I call out. Faintly, a siren whines on the street below, and my worry spreads to the travelers out there, exposed in the swift-moving storm. I can't think of them now. My focus needs to be on my clients. They're counting on me.

The lock clicks. The moment the door gives way a smidge, I push it wide only to find Gregory blocking my path into his father's office. His eyes, normally hazel, are near black, and his skin has a pale, waxy appearance.

"Gregory?" I take his hand, wincing at its icy feel. My fiancé's bottom lip quivers a touch, and he sets his jaw crookedly to still it. Then, saying nothing, Gregory shuts the door in my face.

Chapter 2

Present Day
Jade

Staring down at my hands, I rub the base of my finger where the imprint still remains, despite not wearing my engagement ring for nearly a year. I release a shaky breath between pursed lips and raise my eyes to the judge.

"Mr. Gregory Hyrem, you pleaded guilty to six counts of securities fraud, investment advisor fraud, wire fraud, money laundering, falsifying documents with the Securities and Exchange Commission, and bribery. You are here this morning to be sentenced for those crimes. Have you discussed the pre-sentence report with your lawyers?"

Gregory nods, looking sheepish despite his Armani suit.

"Yes, Your Honor."

The judge addresses Gregory's lawyers and the prosecutors about the same report and the possible range of sentences in a case like this, then he turns back to Gregory. "Before I impose a sentence, we will hear from the victims."

One by one, family by family, those clients, many of whom trusted me with their financial security, voice what life has been like since they've been informed of Walter and Gregory

Hyrem's crimes—the largest Ponzi scheme in the state of Illinois in the post–Bernie Madoff years. Almost every victim pins me with a glare at some point in their speech. If I had released my own victim statement, to the media perhaps, they might believe I'm only guilty of ignoring my instinct and operating in ignorant trust. And my sentence? Becoming recklessly unemployable.

The last victim statement is the one I've been dreading the most. Roland Alderidge approaches the microphone gripping a pad of paper with white knuckles. Although the man inherited his father's boyish good looks, his face shows only hatred—hard, gut-punching hatred—in everything from his steel blue eyes to his scowling lips.

"Hyrem, I'm here to carve into your cold, dead heart what you took from my mother, Berenice Alderidge, and the estate of my father, Paul Alderidge, who, thankfully, died two years ago. Why do I say thankfully? Because Paul Alderidge learned from his parents not to trust financial institutions to protect his life savings, but you and your employees convinced him to go against his instincts and put everything into your accounts. It would've killed him to learn how he'd been swindled out of the fortune he made as Hollywood's most beloved actor."

A lump climbs so high in my throat, I struggle to breathe. My eyes burn as I fight back tears. Those would only cue more resentment, I learned, from the victims and the media. The only thing worse than a perceived criminal is a perceived criminal who asks for pity. What if I scream at the top of my lungs though? What if I release all the anger I've felt, knowing my own fiancé used the trust I'd gained to harm my clients?

"I know you took a cowardly plea deal to get a shorter sentence, so let me add one. I wish you sixty-five million reminders that you are the scum of the earth. One reminder for every dollar you stole from an eighty-nine-year-old woman. Sixty-five million showings of her and Dad's movies so you'll never forget how hard they worked through the years and how quickly your greed ripped it all away."

Chills rack my body, but I refuse to look away. I have no right to look away. Even if the investigation found me faultless in the scheme, I still benefited from it. Unknowingly, of course. But I'd allowed Gregory to spoil me with lavish vacations, a high-rise apartment in the heart of the city, and that gawdy ring. All on the dime of these clients whom I thought I was helping navigate the stock market quite successfully. My clenched fists burn with the strain. I could easily hop the barrier between Gregory and me and get at least one good crack at him before the bailiff intervenes.

Just when I think I might do it, the judge mercifully speaks. "Mr. Gregory Hyrem, if you would like to say anything, now is the time."

My ex-fiancé avoids eye contact with the victims, choosing to meet my glare instead. The man I loved—the one who pursued me relentlessly until I agreed to a date, the one who filled every hole I'd been peppered with since childhood—does not exist. Now, it's my disdain that keeps me warm at night as I lay awake searching the ceiling for something, anything to make things right.

"Your Honor," Gregory says, facing forward once again, "I have nothing to say."

After the judge reviews the greatest elements of the case, drawing fresh blood from the wounds inside me that had just recently scabbed over, he directs his words to the victims. "I understand that a trustee has been tasked with recovering some assets in clawback proceedings. I truly hope that recovery is substantial for your sake. Now, Mr. Hyrem, please stand."

Gregory rises but never seems to reach his full height. Maybe it's how he's holding his shoulders, slumped and almost curving around his chest.

"It is the judgment of this court that the defendant, Gregory

Walter Hyrem, shall be and hereby is sentenced to a term of imprisonment of twelve years. Three years each for counts 1, 2, and 6. One year each for counts 3, 4, and 5, all to run consecutively."

Gasps from the victims precede a crude, curse-filled holler that curdles my blood. He's getting off way too easy. I know that. Even Gregory knows. I can see it in his lengthening stature. He won't even be forty-five-years old when he is released. He'll still have half a century to live, while many of his victims continue to struggle. I tug at the high neckline of my blouse, but the hot, thick air in the courtroom still stifles me.

Immediately after the judge reminds Gregory of his right to appeal, he adjourns the court, and I bolt from my seat. Half-blind with panic, I push through the spectators lining the back wall. My name is shouted multiple times, and the sound hits me like arrows from every direction. I don't run but rather speed walk past media lining the courthouse steps. This isn't the direction of my apartment or even the L. It's simply away, and that's all I need in this moment.

I glance over my shoulder, and while I see nothing besides the typical Chicagoans, I can't shake this nagging feeling. Something or someone is closing in on me. I cut across one road, then another. It does no good, so I duck between two buildings. It's dark in this alley without the direct light, but that's all right. I need the cool air to soothe my lungs. I lean back against one of the brick walls and rest my head against it, not minding the slight catching of my hair on the rough surface.

Take it easy, I hear a voice from the past croon. *Take it easy.* I allow my lips to move silently with the lyrics that follow. In a strange way that I never quite understood, my breathing slows, and my vision clears enough to see the hulking giant of a man blocking my exit.

"Oh!" I jolt, catching my heel on something and stumbling. I throw my hand against the wall to keep myself from falling.

"Don't be scared," he stammers, stretching a hand toward me. I shirk away, but it does no good.

The man steps nearer. "It's Bridger. Please don't be scared. That better?"

"I'm not scared," I lie. Not that I'm afraid of his size. At five foot nine, I'm not small by any means. Big men don't scare me. Angry men scare me. And like Roland, he probably blames me for losing the Alderidge family fortune.

"I saw you rush out. You good?"

"You're asking if I'm okay?"

"Yeah. Your fiancé got sentenced to prison. Probably puts a wrinkle in the whole life plan you got."

I swipe a stray hair out of my eyes, nearly slapping myself in the process. "Not my fiancé. I broke up with him the day I reported him to the SEC. And I'm fine." Thinking it may help convince him, I straighten up and tug at the cuffs of my suit jacket.

He heaves a breath. "You should really give honesty a try. It's, like, way better."

"I wasn't a part of the deception. Gregory deceived me too."

"I meant you should be honest when someone asks you how you're doing. What's the harm in saying, 'Yo, Bridge, that sentencing date was whack. And all those victims' statements? It was killer'?" He pretended to stab himself in the heart and twist the knife.

Oh, no. I'm not walking into that one. Honest answers are great until they give your enemies ammunition to use against you. Rather, I turn the question on him. "Are you all right?"

"I'm a little hungry." He rubs a circle over the belly of his T-shirt. Yes, the guy wore a suit jacket over a T-shirt and jeans to a sentencing hearing, but that's neither here nor there. He runs his hand over the back of his thigh. "I also overexerted my right hamstring at the yoga studio this morning."

I tilt my head and deaden my eyes.

"You didn't let me finish." He pats the side of his neck where the muscle stretches nearly from his jawline to his clavicle. "I'm holding a ton of anxiety right here."

I nod, knowing the knotted feeling well. "Because of your foster mom."

"A little because my fist keeps begging me to introduce him to your ex-fiancé's nose, and I'm like, I don't think that's a good idea. First you meet a nose, then you meet a pair of handcuffs, then a fellow inmate named Sweet Pete. The whole thing goes downhill." He smirks and—is that a twinkle in his eye? "But, yeah," he continues, "mostly because the best person I've ever known is now house poor and is relying on me to keep my head."

"That's pretty honest." That day, after I literally got locked out by Gregory and Walter, I began to question what our in-house computer system was telling me about all our accounts. It took several days and many calculations before I discovered how Gregory and Walter falsified reports while draining money from our trusting clients. The morning before my wedding, I blew the whistle.

"That brings me to the other reason I chased you halfway across the city," Bridger says. "I need help."

"Help?" What possible scenario would lead this guy from that family at this moment in time to come to me for help?

"Benny and I are driving back to California starting next week."

"Driving?"

"Do I need to speak up, because you keep repeating every-thing I say? Sometimes I try to lower my voice so I don't scare people and I end up whispering, which is actually way scarier if you think about—"

"Wouldn't it be better for someone Benny's age to fly that distance?"

"Probably, but this was her idea. You see, all her money is

31

wrapped up in her house in Los Angeles. The rest of her accounts were drained. She needs to earn some money or she'll have to sell the house she and Paul have lived in since 1961. She loves that house."

"I recall." Although it's been years since my visit, I can still smell the sweet scent of the passionflower vines scaling the Alderidges' quaint Holmby Hills ranch, a mere stone's throw from Audrey Hepburn's home. "And what does this have to do with a cross-country trip?"

"I'm not sure how much you know about Benny and Paul's story, but they drove out to LA from Chicago together in the fifties. Benny proposed I use my USC film school degree and make a documentary where she shares their love story and I weave the history of Route 66 into it."

More questions pop into my mind, but my tongue feels stuck to the roof of my mouth. When he gives me a questioning look, I realize I'm shaking my head, and I don't even know what he's asking me yet.

"So I need you to come with us."

"With you?"

"Yes, us."

"Down Route 66?" I ask.

"Down Route 66," he repeats matter-of-factly.

"Why would I hate you?"

I cross my arms over my stomach. "You don't hate me?"

A half laugh escapes my lips. "Everyone thinks I was in on the scheme that stole your family's fortune."

"The investigators found no evidence that you were knowledgeable. You said you weren't, and I believe in taking people at their word. It's why I love documentaries. I like truth."

"My word doesn't matter to anyone else. Roland doesn't believe it."

"Roland believes the worst in everyone. I know that more than anyone. But if it matters that much to you, I'll simply ask." Bridger takes a big step forward into my space. He's so close, I can see the amber flecks in his eyes. "Did you know what he was doing?"

Although the man's closeness messes with my nerves, I give my answer without even the slightest hesitation. "No."

His serious demeanor cracks, allowing a grin to slip through. He doesn't move back though. "I still believe you. So will you help us out with this trip?"

I worry my lip a few seconds before stepping back from him. "I can't. I work. I'm a server at Lou Mitchell's." Not to mention my five-point plan to recover my finance career, but since that is stalled on point one, I keep that to myself.

"Lou Mitchell's? Their coffee cake is delicious."

"I agree."

"Jade, listen. Men and women in the service industry don't get nearly enough credit or pay for putting up with the rest of us. I'm sure your job is fantastic, but it's not the job you're called to, is it?"

I blink involuntarily. He's right. I graduated summa cum laude from the University of Colorado with a finance degree, not hospitality. For me, numbers are easier to calculate than people's needs, be it a fresh fork for an omelet or a welcoming hello. Of course, no one trusts me with numbers anymore. The only money I've been trusted to handle are my customers' bills, and that's only because my boss at Lou's believes in second chances. Still, it paid enough for me to remain in the city until today, when the trial ended. "No, it isn't my calling, but neither is road-tripping. Of all people, why would you want me to join you on this trip?"

"On a practical level, I need someone to help with the driving. And Benny, although she won't admit this, needs a lot of care. I can handle ninety-nine percent of it, but I can't be at her side every second. Like, what if I have to use the bathroom? Not to be crass but Pampers doesn't make diapers in my size."

"Have you tried Huggies?"

"Those give me a not-so-fresh feeling," he says with a wink.

I laugh despite it all. "But that doesn't explain why you're asking me? We've only met twice before. You don't know me at all."

"You're right. But Benny does." He meets my eyes and I detect sincerity in his expression. "She didn't see you as just her financial advisor. She trusted you. More than that, Paul trusted you, and Paul didn't trust just anyone."

And look where that got them. I shake my head. "Bridger, maybe you've forgiven me for being a foolish bystander to this scheme, but your family certainly has not."

"Who? Roland? That's exactly why you need to join us on this trip. Benny wants other people to see you're faultless here. I think it's like a whole Jesus with Zacchaeus thing." Bridger bites his bottom lip hard. "She thinks if everyone sees you helping with this documentary, it will help you get back on your feet." Despite his words, he's no longer looking me in the eye. Even he knows this plan is naive.

I readjust my purse strap on my shoulder. "I'm sorry. I will continue to help the trustee recoup as much of the stolen money as possible, but it's probably for the best that I stay as far from your family as I can."

34

Chapter 3

"You're wiping down that syrup bottle like you're expecting a genie to pop out and grant some wishes." Trish takes the washrag from my hand and picks up another bottle with a stream of syrup glued to its side.

"Oops. I was lost in thought."

"Still thinking about your eviction notice?" she asks. "I wouldn't worry too much. That apartment building should have been condemned years ago. You'll find somewhere else to live."

"I don't think I can afford anywhere else. At least not in Chicago." I shift my weight onto my left foot to give my right a rest. Even after eight hours on my feet at Lou's, I don't make enough to pay for eight hours of life in this city, let alone twenty-four. It would be nice if the syrup genie was a real thing.

I help myself to a glass of cool water and gulp some down. The water at Lou Mitchell's tastes much better than what comes out of the faucet at my apartment. My days drinking expensive bottled water with my one hundred percent organic vegan diet ended the moment I was forced out of the high-rise Gregory purchased for me. It was the first of many reclaimed assets the trustee gathered to pay back the victims. I bet the water at Gregory's white-collar prison doesn't taste as bad.

Trish rinses out the rag, then picks up another sticky jug. "Who says you have to stay in Chicago? The trial's over. Wasn't that what you were staying for? You could head back to Colorado."

"Maybe." If my plan to rebuild my business here doesn't work, I could return to Colorado. My old boss, Michael, might take me, his protégé, back. It would be humbling, for sure. He expected so much good from me here in the Windy City. Instead, I convinced him to sell his company's Chicago branch to Gregory and Walter. At least that move saved the Mendenhall name. Still, I can't beg at Michael's feet, even if I know he and his wife, Lori, would have mercy on me. He was like an older brother to me. Maybe even a father figure. Goodness knows I no longer have that in my life.

Lyrics to "Desperado" carry me back decades, and I can smell gasoline. My hands are suddenly those of a child with dirt beneath her fingernails and grease stains along her cuticles. The lengthy, lonesome notes streaming from the CD player are nearly drowned out by my off-key singing voice as I try to match the volume of my daddy's baritone. He tosses an empty bottle of motor oil into the trash can, wipes his hands on his jeans, then scoops me off the counter and into his arms. I giggle but continue singing the refrain while we two-step around the mechanic's shop, my feet never touching the ground.

As that song ends, my father locks his eyes with mine and a sour look puckers his lips. "Listen real close. You're a smart girl, and you're a good girl. You ain't an outlaw like me. You've done nothing wrong. Nothing. You're a real good girl. And you sure aren't a desperado either. Got it?"

"Earth to Jade." Trish waves a hand in front of my face, shocking me back to the present.

I blink until my eyes no longer burn from the memory. "I'm sorry, Trish. What were you saying?"

"Your conversation will have to wait." Ajay, another Lou

Mitchell's server, hikes his thumb over his shoulder. "There's a guest seated in my section that specifically asked for you. Do you mind? I may be wrong, but I think it's that old actress Benny Alderidge."

Sure enough, a little lady with a white bob sits in a booth near the front door with her hands clasped atop the table.

I wipe my hands on my apron, then grab the freshest pot of coffee and make my way toward her. "Benny, it's good to see you again."

"Jade, you are as pretty as ever." She tries to scoot out of the booth.

"Oh, please don't get up."

"Well, then, give me a hug here." She motions me near, and my chest tightens. After not seeing her since that fateful day in my office—she avoided the trial altogether—it doesn't seem right that I should still receive the gift of her hug. "Don't make me wait, dear. I'm old, remember? I could arrive at the heavenly gates any moment."

Careful to keep the coffee pot steady and a full arm's length away from the sweet woman, I lean down for a quick hug. Benny sneaks a kiss onto my cheek before I pull away. Tears prick my eyes, and I distract myself by filling her mug with coffee she hasn't even requested.

"I hope you don't mind me stopping by your work, honey."

"Not at all." I scan the restaurant. "Did you come by yourself?"

"Bridger told me you refused the offer. For the trip to California." The sound of her voice is elegant, the way older stars blended British sounds into their American accents. Although now, there's a soft rasp to Benny's tone that beckons me closer so I don't miss a word.

"You heard correctly," I say. "I don't think that's a good idea. With the publicity of the case——"

"The truth is we need you."

Not this again. "Let me put this coffee pot down. Would you like anything else to drink?"

"An ice water would be nice. I'm parched."

As I return to the beverage station, I take another glance at the front door, hoping a large group will suddenly appear, requiring my attention. I'm not so fortunate. With a knot in my stomach, I return to her table, knowing she will be harder to say no to than Bridger. "Here's that ice water. Why exactly do you need me?"

"We need you to drive."

"I don't own a car."

"We'll supply the car. I haven't driven in years, and Bridger can only drive for short periods under certain conditions. He might be too embarrassed to say, but he has some visual impairment."

I wipe my hand on my apron. "Oh, I didn't know that. Couldn't you hire a driver?" Instantly, I regret my words. Hiring a driver would cost money she no longer has.

"Did he tell you why we need *you*?" Benny pours cream into her coffee with hands so delicate, the skin appears translucent. She has aged far more than a year since we last met. No wonder Bridger is so concerned. "Jade, we've seen how the media's treated you throughout the trial. Nasty beasts, some of them. Perhaps if they see us together, they'll forgive you."

Zacchaeus. Right. "I didn't—"

"I know you didn't." Her dainty hand takes mine and gently pulls me into the booth next to her. "You forget that I knew you before you came to Chicago. That girl we met was full of promise and oh so smart. After you confided in us about your childhood, we knew you just needed someone to believe in you. We believed in you then and we believe in you now. I want the world to know that. If we hold no ill will, they won't either."

The knot in my stomach seems to have climbed into my throat. Sure, I shared a bit about my past with her and Paul

38

over the years, but she doesn't know the worst of it. "How can you know that?"

"Because I know my public, my fans. They've been with me a long time, and they will follow my lead."

"My job—" A crack in my voice shortens my sentence to those two words. I can't afford to take off work. Not since authorities confiscated all of Gregory's assets . . . and mine since we'd already begun merging our lives, our homes, our bank accounts ahead of the wedding.

"I'm sure Lou Mitchell's is a lovely place to work. I used to work the concession stand at the Rialto Square Theater in Joliet. Did you know that?" She waves off the question before I can answer. "That's neither here nor there. It's not what you want to be doing, is it?"

My heart drops. What I want is to salvage my career, but so far, I can't get a single bank interview, even for a teller position. "I can't."

Benny reaches into her purse, retrieves a wallet-size photo, and hands it to me. In it, Bridger, not more than fifteen or sixteen, glares into the camera. "When Bridger came to live with us, he was every bit a lost boy. He hasn't had an easy life. Right before Paul passed away, I promised him I would stay behind long enough to make sure Bridger would be all right. Finally, he is in a good place and ready to make something of himself. If I can help him succeed as a documentarian, then when my time comes, I can die in peace, and Paul and I can be together once again. Please, Jade."

Wow. Talk about pressure. How can I deny this woman her dying wish after all she's gone through? And who knows? Maybe the public will finally believe my innocence.

I could make up for all the damage that was done. Even the damage I caused my father. I can almost hear him saying, *"You're a good girl."* Maybe, just maybe, if we're already on Route 66, I might finally get to hear those words again.

Benny nods until I do the same. Then she places the photo of Bridger back in her wallet and withdraws a tissue. She dabs my cheeks, and I smile in response to her care.

Heavy footsteps yank my attention to Bridger coming to a standstill above me. "Did she say yes?" he asks, rocking a Dolly Parton T-shirt. He rests his hands on his waist, Peter Pan–style. I meet his eyes, and he grins, even before I can answer.

Dragging my largest suitcase behind me, I navigate the busy sidewalk on Adams Street. I should've had my rideshare drop me directly in front of the sign, but the car and foot traffic made that near impossible. As I think about where Bridger might've parked his car, I grow concerned. How far can Benny walk anyway? The closest meters are a couple blocks away. Unless . . .

Parked next to the sign in the clearly marked tow-away zone, a crisp red-and-white Chevrolet Bel Air Convertible is surrounded by an ogling crowd. A '55? I inhale sharply, realizing the beauty has taken my breath away. Fantastic doesn't begin to describe it. Somewhere in my memories, I hear my father's appreciative whistle, which lifts my lips into a smile.

In the front seat, Benny holds up a hand in a wave fit for a queen while someone snaps a picture on their phone. *This is the car we'll be driving across the country for the next three and a half weeks?* I'm not sure, but a feeling a lot like love presses on my heart. Can a person truly love a car? I think so. At the car's front bumper, Bridger towers above a cop and a parking enforcement officer. The three are cutting up, laughing like old friends at a Cubs game. In the past I might've assumed he paid them off to keep the tow truck at bay—such is the life of the rich. But their family assets these days aren't landing them on any *Forbes* lists. No, this is pure Bridger charm.

When I get closer, I notice a camera in his hand. A large video camera. He shushes the two men at his side and begins filming my approach. Do I smile? Wave? Freeze like a shy second grader at a choir assembly? So maybe I have experience with that last one.

"Nice Chevy. 1955?" I ask.

"Good guess." Bridger lowers the camera, revealing a mischievous grin. "Jade Jessup is in the vicinity, ladies and gentlemen."

I shoot him a warning glare, which he laughs off. Immediately I feel the scowls of onlookers searing through my blazer. The back of my neck warms, making me wish a ponytail holder would magically appear on my wrist.

Benny extends her hand to me and I oblige the reach, giving her fingers a gentle squeeze and admiring the delicate lace of her gloves—probably hand-darned. "I was afraid you'd changed your mind," she says.

"Of course not." A lie. I've gone back and forth over this decision at least ten times in the three days since Benny came to Lou Mitchell's. She doesn't need to know that though.

"Give me that suitcase," Bridger says after placing the camera on the back seat next to some other electronic equipment.

"It's heavy."

He snorts in reply, then lifts it by the top strap and does one, two, three bicep curls. I shake my head, but one of the young female observers fakes a swoon.

"Is he showing off again?" Benny asks. "That's something you'll have to get used to. Just be glad he's not using you as the dumbbell."

"Believe me, I am," I say. "Have you been here long?" Dropping my meager belongings at the storage facility had taken a few minutes longer than I planned. By the time this trip ends, my apartment building will be condemned, and I'll be officially unhoused. What does it say in the book of Matthew? About the birds not needing to worry about the future because God will care for them? *Are you not much more valuable than they?*

Then again, it also says not to worry about what to wear. I tug down on the waistline of my blazer. *It's fine. I'm fine. Everything is fine.*

"We've only been here a little while. Bridger wanted to get some footage of the car with the sign." She smooths her hand over her hair. "I must look a fright."

"Not at all. So this is the car you were talking about?"

The Chevy rocks as Bridger closes the trunk. My, my, it is a magnificent vehicle. And meticulously maintained. I press the back of my hand to both corners of my mouth in case I am drooling.

"Paul's father bought this car for him brand-new. It's the same car he and I took on our trip out to California. It was his baby. It's Bridger's now. However, he doesn't drive much because of his vision problems."

"How did it get here? Shouldn't it be in Los Angeles?"

"Shipping it here is in the budget Bridger gave to the documentary's investors. Bridger said it was important for authenticity to use the same car Paul and I drove."

"And there's no better vehicle in the entire world," he says while making his way to the passenger side. "We've already got what we need for the documentary here. Maybe one group picture though?"

He helps Benny out of the car and escorts her to the sign. The parking enforcement officer, who has seemingly forgotten the Chevy is illegally parked, offers to take our picture. Bridger places his arm around Benny's waist loosely. Next to me, Benny does the same, reaching her arm behind me. I'm fully aware of the whispers of onlookers as the officer begins counting down. If they recognize me from the news stories, they're probably wondering why I'm here. Three. I take a step away from Benny, letting the lakeshore breeze separate us. Two. She reaches for me again, her hand grasping the loose fabric of my slacks. The muscles around my mouth tense into who knows what expression. One. With the awkward moment captured in pixels for all time, we look to the car.

"Jade, you take the wheel," Bridger says. "Benny, I'd prefer you in the passenger seat so I can get some over-the-shoulder shots of you as we drive through Chicago."

"You? In the back seat? With all that equipment?" Can he even fit in the car? It wasn't exactly designed for men of his stature.

"I assure you, I'm quite the nimble fella." Bridger walks Benny back to her seat, never taking his eyes off mine.

I settle onto the bench seat behind the wheel, wondering how much of this beauty is original and how much is restored. My father could tell with a glance. I did not take after him. At least, not in that way.

With Benny seated next to me, Bridger gingerly—or should I say nimbly—climbs into the back.

"What are we working with here?" I study the controls at my helm. "A three-speed automatic? Cool. Should we put the top back up?"

Benny slowly ties a scarf beneath her chin, trapping her hair beneath. She then slides a pair of sunglasses up the bridge of her nose—the kind that might better be described as goggles since they fit all the way to the skin below, to the sides, and above the eyes. She's ready for this adventure, that is obvious. Meanwhile, I check my reflection in the rearview mirror. The dark hair I'd straightened into a classic, sleek style that fell far past my shoulders—the hair that Gregory had loved to run his hands through—won't stand a chance once we get on the open road. Ready, I am not.

"Where are we stopping first?" I ask.

Beaming, Benny faces me. "We're heading down to Rialto Square Theater in Joliet. For this documentary to get the story right, it has to start there. Jade, if you think Bridger is charming, just wait until I tell you about Paul when he was young,"

Behind me, Bridger gives me his best smolder, which I brush off with an eye roll. That only seems to encourage him because he dangles the keys between Benny and me and then drops them into my curled palm with a wink. "Ladies, adventure awaits."

Chapter 4

1956
Benny

One popcorn kernel. Then another. I'd wait until Paul turned his back to sweep one off the floor, then I'd toss another one. Oh, he must have traced fifteen circles across the lobby floor before he caught on to my game.

Even that didn't get him to speak.

"If you don't say anything, I'll start throwing the Raisinets." I stuck my hand into the concession stand's display case, precisely over the yellow box.

The theater door opened, and a boy I recognized from the American Legion approached me, jingling change in his pocket.

"May I help you?" I emphasized each word with a bat of my eyelashes. Too bad Paul Alderidge was too busy sweeping the already clean floors to notice.

"Hmm. I want something sweet. Say, you aren't available, are you?" the boy teased, peeking over the counter at my legs.

"You've got a real classy chassis."

"Oh, aren't you a smooth talker. If you want something sweet, how about some Raisinets?"

"If I can't have you, I'll take a box of Jujyfruits."

"Thirty-nine cents, please."

I deposited the boy's coins into the cash register. Paul glanced my way only once during the entire exchange. I leaned forward, placing my elbows on the counter. With a sigh so loud they might've heard it on the shores of Lake Michigan, I rested my chin in my hands and turned my attention to the "Currently Showing" sign featuring the poster for *Heaven's Long Road*. Every few minutes I heard the sound of the gunfights as missionaries fought off robbers in the Old West. On the poster, Claire Pendleton stared triumphantly into the distance with a baby in her arms and Clyde Irving at her side.

I tugged at one of my pin curls, wishing I could wear my hair the same wild way Claire wore hers after she saved her family and reached their promised land.

"I wish I had a promised land."

Paul stopped his sweeping for a moment, but a moment was all it was.

After the film had ended and the customers had left, I grabbed my sweater and prepared to head home to my jam-packed house to hear my siblings whine and fight while my parents fretted over keeping food on the table and clothes on our backs. But something stopped me. All the ushers had left, along with the ticket takers, yet one door to the theater remained open. The projectionist was always the last to leave, but he usually stayed upstairs. That left Paul. I'd been looking forward to the cool night air, in hopes it might calm my racing thoughts. In one month, I'd celebrate two years as the Rialto Square Theater's concession stand girl. Still in the same town I was born in twenty years ago. I loved Joliet and my family but not enough to never leave them.

I looked to the open door. The calming air would have to wait a few minutes.

Inside, the house lights were low, yet I could still see the back of a man's head in the front row of the mezzanine. "Paul?"

He didn't respond. If it was anyone else, I might have been frightened. Except I'd known Paul as long as I could remember. Growing up, he and my brother Louie were always in the front yard tossing a ball while I was out twirling my baton or playing hopscotch. He hadn't always been so withdrawn. The war changed him, just like it changed my brother.

I moseyed down the aisle. He didn't look my way until I reached his row. "May I join you for the show?" With a wave of my hand, I gestured to the dark screen ahead of us. He nodded softly. I jumped at the chance, taking the seat next to him.

"What's it like outside Illinois?" I asked.

The question registered. I knew because his chin turned the slightest bit my way. He was only twenty-three, but the last few years had aged him a great deal. Louie too. Neither of them had spoken a single word to me about what they'd endured, but words weren't necessary when I had eyes to see the toll it had taken on them.

"Some things are different. Some things aren't," he said.

"Momma and Daddy took Louie and me to Tennessee once to attend my cousin's wedding. I was too young to remember. Can you believe I've never seen a mountain? For all I know, they could be like those Sno-Cap candies. Sprinkles on top and chocolate on the bottom."

A tick worked his cheek. Not enough to be a smile. However, it was enough to make his dimple appear for the briefest of moments. "It's safer to stay home."

Sure. I could marry someone who works at the jail, have lots of babies, and pass a cup of sugar to my neighbor. That was fine for some people. Not me.

"I don't want to be safe. I want adventure, beauty, and excitement. I want to be like Claire Pendleton, following a dream into the wilderness."

"Did you watch *Heaven's Long Road?*"

"Four times," I stated proudly.

"Then you saw what she faced. Danger around every bend."

"That was the Old West, Paul. It's 1956."

"Danger still exists. Bad people still exist. Trust me."

Why I chose that moment to wrap my hand around the crook of his arm, I'll never know. The instant warmth spread through my fingers, surprising me. He'd been so cold in my presence since he returned from Panmunjom two years ago.

"That was across the world. I'm talking about other places in the United States. Rivers, mountains, deserts, oceans . . . Paul, I've made plans."

He cocked his head, making eye contact and holding it for the first time since before the war. "What plans?"

Oh, to see skies as blue as his eyes . . . *Soon*, I told myself. "I've been saving every paycheck, and I'm finally ready to head out to California. Hollywood, to be exact."

His body tensed, crushing my fingers between his ribs and his arm. "To do what?"

He worked his jaw back and forth. And what a handsome jaw it was.

"No."

Again, I gestured to the silver screen before us. "To be up there. I want to be on that screen, living a hundred different lives in a hundred different times in a hundred different places. Can't you see it, Paul? Can't you see me up there?"

Slowly, I slipped my hand free from his side and settled deep into my own seat. "Am I not pretty enough?" Besides my widow's peak, I'd always been fairly confident with my appearance. I'd taken after my Swiss-born mother not much more than my father. But one had to be beautiful, breathtakingly beautiful, to adorn the same screen as Elizabeth Taylor, Audrey Hepburn, and Marilyn Monroe.

"Of course you're pretty enough." He focused on the railing separating the mezzanine from the orchestra seating. "I said no because you won't make it to Hollywood. It's not safe out

48

there. You're young. You believe everyone is good, but they're not. What do your parents have to say?"

"They're busy with my little sisters. Between you and me, I think they're hoping I'll go. It would certainly free up some room at home." It was only half-true. In Hollywood, Momma believed I'd either become the next Black Dahlia or I'd go the mattress route to become famous and lose my salvation. I smoothed my skirt against my legs to steady my bouncing knee.

Paul swallowed hard, his Adam's apple moving up and down. "Have you spoken to Louie about this?"

"I tried but he's so busy with his work. He's impossible to get on the phone. Not that I blame him. It's the military. I'm sure you understand."

Paul's body shuddered. It was something I'd seen him do often. Every time it happened, I'd wanted to throw my arms around him and hold him until he stopped shaking.

"When are you leaving?" The words came out broken, and for a few seconds, I questioned myself. Was he worried because it was somehow his duty to protect me while my brother was away? Dare I believe Paul might feel something more? What if he did ever allow someone in, and I was too far away for it to be me? That was a big what-if.

"As soon as I can find a reliable enough car."

I wanted him to grab me by the shoulders and beg me not to go. Maybe confess his undying love for me. There weren't any pleas or passionate embraces though. He remained still and silent for quite some time, long enough for me to steady my focus on the dream of the silver screen. I stood and made myself as tall as I could. "I've made up my mind."

Following my lead, he rose from his seat. Silly as it was, I pictured him kissing me like they do in the movies, where the woman presses herself against the man's chest, drops her head back, and lets him find her lips. If only . . .

Paul shook his head. "If there's no changing your mind and all you need is a car, I might be able to help you with that."

Present Day
Jade

"So he just showed up in the Bel Air and off you went?" I ask, wishing I had a bag of popcorn right now. It would only be fitting since I'm standing in the grand historic Rialto Square Theater.

"Yes, he did. Only a week later." Benny removes her lace gloves, then slides her fingers over the wooden armrest. "I was tickled pink he chose to accompany me."

"And these were the exact seats you sat in when you had that conversation?" Having already recorded Benny's story about the genesis of her and Paul's Route 66 trip, Bridger appears satisfied. In fact, he's adamant Benny speaks in short sessions only so she won't get too tired. For a man who might strike others as intimidating, he sure is loving toward his foster mom.

Although Benny nods, our tour guide clarifies in a soft whisper. "During the remodel, they replaced all the lower seats with near replicas from another theater."

Bridger clucks his tongue in understanding. "If it's okay with you all, I'm going to get some B-roll footage of the place."

The guide agrees, and as Bridger begins his wandering, Benny shoos me away. "You'll never see a more beautiful theater, Jade. Go on and look around. I'd like to sit here a bit."

Not wanting to upset her—does Benny even get upset?—I obey. What harm can come to her here anyway?

I intentionally head the opposite direction than Bridger and quickly lose myself in the splendor. Built in 1926, this auditorium screams opulence. Red velvet chairs, ornate gold and faux marble detailing, and original paintings that mimic old-world rococo design. The desire to touch everything keeps my hands pinned to my breastbone. I exit the auditorium through the lower rotunda and walk beneath the enormous chandelier named Duchess. No wonder Benny was inspired to go into the entertainment industry after working here. How shy, quiet Paul Alderidge also became a movie star is a mystery though.

I pass under the arch, styled after the Arc de Triomphe. Earlier the tour guide explained that the esplanade is a replica of the Palace of Versailles's Hall of Mirrors. I'm instantly transported back to when Gregory and I visited the actual palace on our trip to Paris.

A sour taste hits my tongue. Benny and Paul, without knowing, had paid for that trip. To make matters worse, I only learned of Paul's brief illness and passing after I returned to the States. If I'd known, I would have cut our trip short to attend his memorial service. Looking back, it should have been a red flag that Gregory didn't understand why I was so upset since they were, in his words, "only clients."

That's when I stumble upon the plaque with the names of prominent donors. At the very top, I read Paul and Berenice Alderidge.

"They never forgot their roots." Bridger sidles up to me. "It was important to them that this theater never get torn down. They donated money for the restoration in 1980 and 1981, and every year since. In fact . . . nah. Never mind."

"Was this one of the five causes Benny wanted to leave their fortune to?" I ask, already knowing the answer. The look in Bridger's eyes affirms my belief. "Ten million would've kept this place alive for generations to come."

"Yep."

With balled fists, I squeeze my eyes closed. "I wish I'd never let Gregory convince me to move back to Chicago. I should've stayed in Denver. I should've listened to my gut when Gregory and Walter first suggested buying the branch office. Then your family's money would be safe and sound."

"Yep." Bridger has the same nonchalant expression on his face as if I were to ask if Illinois has two *L*s.

Without intention, I growl. "Don't you have anything else to say on this topic? Doesn't it make you angry?"

"Sure it does. But there's no way I'm going to carry that hatred in my body all the time. Do you know what carrying that does to you? It hurts your heart, makes your hair fall out, makes those little wrinkles appear between your brows." He tucks his hands under his chin and presents a cheesy smile. "Sorry, I don't want to harm this pretty face."

"Cute," I say. "What do you do with it? Just forget it exists?"

"I can't forget it exists. It's my face."

I snort-laugh, then shake my head. "What do you do with the *anger*?"

Bridger scrubs a hand over his beard. "Well, no. Actually, I keep it here." He pats his backside.

I'm not sure if my expression shows more confusion or disgust, but Bridger snickers.

"I keep it in my back pocket, so if I ever need to pull it out, I can."

Skeptical, I ask how that works.

"Okay, obviously that Ponzi scheme was the work of a ruthless sociopath. I can assume that because he targeted Benny—my Benny—who is the kindest, gentlest, most loving person on God's green earth, and Paul, who basically had the best traits of all the Avengers and none of the flaws. That makes me angry. More than angry. That makes me hostile." Considering the fire blazing in the man's eyes, I believe him. "If I carry that inside me every hour of every day, I'm done for. I'd be no good to anyone. So, what do I do? I keep it tucked in my back pocket so I'm free from the harm it causes my soul, but I can access it in a jiffy. Like, if that jerk suddenly showed up in this lobby with a get out of jail free card, I could use that anger to protect Benny from any more damage by him."

I rock back on my heels and let my gaze roam over the intricate details of the esplanade. "And do you only do this with anger and hatred? What other things do you keep in that pocket?"

"Pretty much everything negative. Social injustice, racism, violence against women. Those things can eat you up from the inside out if you think about how common they are. I fight those evils when I can through volunteering or raising money and voting, but, man, I couldn't live if I pondered all that twenty-four hours a day."

"What happens when you take one of those emotions out of your pocket?"

"Bad stuff." He offers a laugh. "When I first came to the US, I was adopted by this couple, Rick and Dina Rosenblum. That's where I got the name Bridger. Total White kid name, right? Well, Rick was a bad guy. He'd slap Dina around right in front of us kids. Right after I turned thirteen, I got tired of it. One day, I reached into that back pocket and played my ace."

"You hit him, didn't you?"

"Oh yeah. Not that it did any good. He hit me harder. The next day, they called the social worker, and off I went to foster care. Before that, I didn't even know you could be *un*adopted."

"Dina didn't try to keep you with her?"

"Nah. She chose him over me. But I tell ya, I'd play that card again if I saw a man raise a hand against a woman." He sucks in a big breath and then releases it.

There's so much I want to know about this man. Questions have circled my mind ever since our first encounter at the Alderidge home. That curiosity only grows with every conversation. What right do I have to ask him to share more about his life? Heaven knows I want to. I feel a twinge in the center of my chest, and I realize I'm staring at him. He realizes it too, and his eyes crinkle. "Serious question," he says. "What's going on with your hair?"

I slap my hands to my scalp. "You both wanted to drive with the top down. I didn't have a ponytail holder."

He pushes up his sleeve to show a black hair tie around his wrist. He removes it, then walks behind me. "May I? I'm pretty good with hair, if you haven't noticed."

Is he going to style it? Without a brush? Though I don't understand why, I nod my permission. Somehow this man's giant hands finger-comb my windblown, tangled, rats' nest so tenderly I nearly fall asleep on my feet. After a few minutes and a lot of patience on his part, I'm sure, he begins to French braid my hair.

By the time he finishes, I can't speak. I can't think of the last instance someone treated me so affectionately. If I'm honest, it messes with my heart, and I don't like it. Yet I follow him back into the auditorium to Benny's seat. She appears to be in a trance of some sort.

"Hey Benny, are you ready to get back on the road?" he asks. She doesn't respond. When Bridger kneels and touches her hand, she jerks away. Her stare transfers to Bridger's face, and for a moment, she seems frightened of him. He sinks back until he's kneeling in the aisle. "It's me, Benny. It's Bridger."

Recognition dawns and she smiles. "Did you get all the footage you need?"

He looks to me, sorrow weighing on his brow. "I sure did."

Chapter 5

"I can see why you've planned for this trip to take three weeks," I say that afternoon as I return the gas nozzle to its cradle on the pump. The Chevy only gets about eleven miles per gallon, so we'll have to fuel up every ninety miles. "Most people would want a bigger gas tank. Why did Paul put in a smaller one?"

Bridger takes the receipt from the pump and places it in his wallet. He keeps careful tabs on our spending so the film's investors know their money isn't being wasted. I respect that.

"At some point," Bridger says, "the original tank got a crack in it. He couldn't find a normal-size one so he settled for a smaller one. He always talked about getting the right size on there. I guess he ran out of time." He presses his lips into a hard line and sniffles. Everything about this car links to memories of Paul for Benny and Bridger. It truly is a privilege to drive it, and I realize how much trust they've placed in me. I refuse to let them down.

With each mile down Route 66, I relax a bit more. Between Benny's memories and Bridger's extensive research, we find all the popular landmarks. Sometimes we pull over so he can capture still photos for use in the documentary. Sometimes we slow to a crawl so he can get a moving shot of the Blues Brothers dancing atop the Rich & Creamy ice cream stand or the Gemini Giant in front of the Launching Pad restaurant.

Slow going doesn't describe our rate of progress down the Mother Road. But that's all right. Driving a 1955 Chevrolet Bel Air is a dream. Even more so now that my hair isn't whipping me in the face—thank you, Bridger. I've never known a man who could French braid. I can only imagine what other surprising facts I might learn about him.

Like that he sings to every song that comes on the radio. Every song. Even the ones that require his falsetto. Of all his serenades I've heard so far, "Ol' 55" is my favorite. In the rearview mirror, Bridger catches my eye and double hikes his brows.

"I'm surprised you know this song," I say loud enough for him to hear. "Most people our age only know a few Eagles songs. 'Hotel California.' 'Life in the Fast Lane.' The popular ones."

"How could I own an American car manufactured in 1955 and not know that song? How do you know it?"

I shrug my shoulders. "My dad played Eagles albums constantly when I was with him. I can't tell you why," I nearly laugh at my unintentional joke.

Bridger stays quiet for fifteen or twenty seconds before speaking. "'Get Over It,' 'Witchy Woman.'"

I respond in kind. "Hey, 'After the Thrill Is Gone,' 'Take It Easy.'"

"I'm 'Running on Empty' here."

"Nice try. That's Jackson Browne, but he cowrote some of their songs, so I'll cut you some slack."

"James Dean," Benny adds, understanding the assignment. Then I see what she's pointing to. In front of the Polk-a-Dot Drive-In, several statues of celebrities, including James Dean, greet us. According to Benny, the restaurant had just opened when she and Paul stopped for dinner in 1956. The sun is already falling when we park the car next to the line of figures. While Bridger films Benny with the statues of Elvis, Marilyn

Monroe, and James Dean, she shares her real-life memories of the first two. Elvis, she recalls, was "the kindest man who ever tried to bed her," except for Paul, of course. Marilyn was someone she felt great pity for, even as the young starlet offered Benny advice on how to withstand the glare of celebrity life.

"And boy, was she funny! She had this intelligent, sly humor. She was nothing like the dumb flibbertigibbet she often played in films." Benny turns her solemn expression toward James Dean's replica. "I never did get to meet him. The poor soul died one year before I headed west."

Once inside the perfectly preserved retro diner, Benny and Bridger claim a table while I excuse myself to use the restroom. Upon opening the door, I'm greeted by dozens and dozens of Elvises staring directly at me. All I can think is that the King needs to mind his own business as I tend to mine.

Once I finish, I walk past a few whispering groups, all gawking at Benny and Bridger. A middle-aged woman has her phone camera aimed at them. I hear her tell her male companion to move out of the shot. Tentatively, I slide into the booth behind Benny and Bridger.

"What are you doing?" he asks.

I glance at our fellow diners. "Giving you privacy."

"Jade, I don't want you to eat all alone," he says. "Besides, your food's over here."

I leave my seat and scoot into the spot next to Benny. "You ordered for me?"

Benny nudges a disposable plate holding a chili dog my way. "If you don't want this, we can get something else."

My stomach cinches. A quick perusal of the menu board shows typical diner fare. Nothing I find would fit into my clean, mostly vegan diet. "It's fine. This is fine."

"I take it you're not a big fan?" Bridger makes half of his chili dog disappear with a single bite.

"Um, I just haven't had one in decades. I'm not exactly sure how to pick it up." After a few adjustments to my strategy, I finally decide to dive in, grimacing as the chili and cheese ooze over my hand. The savory bite trumps everything I've eaten in the past ten years. I moan. I actually moan, which cracks up Bridger. His overly loud, throaty laugh does nothing to decrease focus on us.

"I can't help it. It's so good," I say through a mouthful.

"Right?" Bridger hands me a napkin. "Chili dogs taste the way Neil Diamond sounds. I can't explain that."

"No need. I get it. I can hear him singing 'America' in my head."

And I see fireworks when I take a sip from my chocolate malt. Oh, it is worth every calorie. Nectar from heaven.

Once the chili dogs and onion rings are gone, we head back outside where a man is taking a picture of a woman in front of the Chevy.

"Would you like a picture of both of you?" Bridger asks.

The man turns, looking slightly embarrassed. "Is this your Chevy? Sorry. We think your car is beautiful."

"Thank you," Benny says. "You don't have to apologize. I'm glad young people like you can appreciate a classic."

Young, I realize, is subjective, as the couple looks to be at least twenty years older than me. I recognize their friendly faces immediately. "You toured the Rialto Square Theater after we did," I say.

"That's right," the woman replies. "I take it you're also traveling Route 66?"

"You got it." Bridger moves in front of me, thrusting his hand out to the couple. "My name's Bridger." He signals over his shoulder. "This is Jade, and that classy lady is Benny."

But he doesn't step aside to let them see me. I have to peek around him to see the man accept the handshake.

"Oh, we know who you are. We watched *When I See You Again* on our first date. I'm Tim. This is my lovely wife, Sandy,"

Sandy nods. "We're big fans of yours, Mrs. Alderidge. And of your husband too. We were sorry to hear about his passing." Benny touches her fingers to her throat. "Thank you for your kind words. Paul loved greeting his fans. I don't like to think of him as gone. Rather, I see him just up the road, slightly ahead of me in the journey."

We pause—an unofficial moment of silence for Paul and one of America's great love stories. It's Sandy who finally finds words to speak. "That's a beautiful way of looking at it."

We all nod in agreement before Tim asks, "How's the food in there?"

"It's fire," Bridger answers, once again sidestepping to cut me out of the group.

At Tim's raised brows, Benny interprets. "He means that it's very good."

Feeling a bit in my head, I self-soothe with one last sip from my to-go cup. The straw makes an embarrassingly loud slurping noise.

"That speaks for itself." Sandy's warm laugh is enough to make me crack a smile. We spend the next few minutes chatting. The nice couple are schoolteachers from Ohio who are celebrating their recent retirement with this long-awaited trip. They snap some pictures. A couple of only Bridger and Benny. One of Bridger, getting his flirt on with the Betty Boop statue right before he breaks her heart by informing her he's celibate. When Tim asks if we want a picture of the three of us, Bridger shakes his head. "We're good with what we've got."

So much for all the talk about wanting people to know there were no hard feelings.

After we wish Tim and Sandy well on the rest of their journey, we help Benny back into the car. I chew my lip till it hurts as I round the back bumper. Bridger catches my hand before I reach the driver's side.

"Jade, are you upset?"

I pull my arm away. "Nope."

He surveys the other travelers who mill about the parking lot. Then he speaks, just above a whisper. "I asked for honesty, remember?"

"What should I say? That I'm upset that you guys claim I'm part of this trio but then you keep butting me out of the conversation?"

"Jade."

"If I'm just your chauffeur, that's fine." If spit-whispering is a thing, I'm doing it, trying to keep my voice down while also getting my point across.

"Jade, you—"

"I've spent the last year alone. I can keep going."

"Jade, you have chili on your shirt."

What? I look down and see a quarter-size brown smudge in the center of my ribs.

"I didn't want others to see it. I was literally trying to shield you from embarrassment." He motions to the length of me. "Considering you're wearing a pantsuit and high heels on a road trip, I figured you care a lot about your appearance."

"Oh." My mind can't seem to wrap around a man shielding me from anything. Gregory certainly hadn't. Dad though . . . I wince before looking back into Bridger's eyes. "Thank you, I guess."

"I got you, girl." He raises his fist between us. For a fist bump?

I oblige, making this my first fist bump since college. As I stand there with Bridger, my stomach ties itself in a knot, either because of the chili dog or the thought that a fist bump is likely not the only discomforting custom I may face on this trip.

At the driver's side door, Bridger pauses with his hand on the handle. He stares back into the restaurant where Tim and Sandy were visible through the window. "Have you ever been to Ohio?"

I scour my memory. "A few times. Never for long. Why?"

"I don't know. Ohio seems like a cool place. Like the kind of place where you can settle down with a wife, a couple kids, and a Labrador named Wyatt J. Earp. Maybe you get a house with a front porch swing and a pond. And in the pond, there's a turtle named—"

"Doc J. Holliday?"

Bridger taps his temple, then points at me. "Great minds."

"I wouldn't have figured you to be such a family man." Then again, most of my knowledge about him was gained over a decade ago, when he was constantly making headlines for his rebel-without-a-cause behavior around Los Angeles. Not to mention the women the paparazzi always caught him with.

"What can I say? I try not to let my past define me." He boops the tip of my nose, just like Dad used to do. "You shouldn't either."

A few miles down the road, our first hotel, in all its neon-lit glory, appears on the left. The Mother Road Motor Court. At least that's what I think the sign says, but every third letter is burned out.

"This is it?" Benny leans forward in her seat. She points to the first spot in a mostly vacant parking lot. "Paul parked the car right there. I remember clear as day."

I happily oblige her reminiscence and steer the Bel Air into the spot. The hooded headlights shine brilliantly against a plain brown door marked 1 and a large glass window that gives a view to the furnishings inside.

So it's slightly different from the luxury hotels Gregory would book for us on our trips. That's fine. I'm sure it's clean, and after living in my shabby apartment, that alone would be a step-up.

Bridger and I take our luggage out of the trunk and walk with Benny into the motel's lobby. The stench hits me immediately, and I feel that chocolate malt churning in my stomach. I press the back of my free hand to my nose, only to catch Bridger glaring my way.

What is his problem? I'm not the one who scared a skunk inside the lobby, beat it to death, let it rot, and poured pickle juice all over the carpet before smoking a thousand cigarettes.

I turn away as he steps up to the counter and checks us in. A flashing sign points toward a dark, closed-off room. The notice on the door reads "Jacuzzi: 21 and up ONLY." No thank you.

Done with check-in, Bridger leads us back outside to door 1. While I inhale the fresh air, he unlocks the first door and ushers Benny inside along with the suitcases.

We never discussed the sleeping arrangements for this trip. I hoped I'd have my own room, but honestly, who am I to demand anything? It would feel strange to share a room with Benny. She's about as royal as Americans get. Would I feel right sharing a room with Queen Camilla? Certainly not, especially when I'm wearing half my dinner on my blouse.

Clearly Bridger and I won't be rooming together. Yet, as he leaves Benny's room, he pulls the door shut, walks to the next door, and unlocks it.

I follow him inside and flick on a light switch. Unsure whether the tears in my eyes are from the hideously outdated bedding or being reunited with the same horrendous smell from the lobby, I slip past him on a search for tissues. Finding none, I opt for toilet paper, but the moment I turn on the bathroom light, I recoil. "There's mold in the bathtub. And I have no idea what is on the floor by the toilet. I'm not staying here."

"And go where? I don't know if you noticed, but this town isn't exactly hotel central. Besides, this is where Benny and Paul stayed."

"She should stay somewhere better than this."

Bridger takes a single, rather large step to close the distance between us. At my height, I never feel short. Next to him, though, I may as well be a munchkin from *The Wizard of Oz*.

"Jade, I need you to listen to me." The sternness of his voice chills me. "Ever since Paul passed away, Benny has been lost without him. The only place she sees him is in old movies and memories in places like this. So this place hasn't been kept up for the last sixty-eight years. There are so few businesses still around from the time Route 66 was decommissioned. We should be thankful for every single one. In fact, one of the ways Benny planned to distribute her wealth was for the restoration of places like this."

I shrink away. "You're right. You probably think I'm a terrible person."

He cups his hand around my wrist, cradling it. "You're not terrible. Just your sense of style."

I tilt my head and glare, a combo that brings out his goofy grin.

He pulls his hand back and runs it through his hair. "If you really want to, you can drive ahead to Pontiac or Springfield."

"No, no." I wave off the notion. "I can handle one night here."

"That's my girl," he says casually. A throwaway comment that I should not read into.

I know myself too well though.

"If you want me to share the room with Benny, I can."

"I appreciate that. The thing is, Benny has started wandering a bit at night. I want to keep an eye on her. And there are two beds, so I don't have to worry about steamrolling her in my sleep." He shudders. "It would be like one of those tragic news stories about a mother and baby panda. Anyway, have a great night. I'll be next door if you need anything." With a wink, he's gone.

Chapter 6

1956
Benny

"You only have one vacancy?" I asked the front desk manager at the Mother Road Motor Court. A blush heated my cheeks, and I refused to look at Paul. "Are there any other motels nearby?"

"How far are you willing to drive?" The squirrely man righted the glasses on the bridge of his nose.

Abandoning his place by the cigarette machine, Paul stepped forward and rested his clasped hands on the desk. "We'll take the room."

"All right, then." He picked up his ledger and pressed the tip of his pencil to it. "Mr. and Mrs. . . . ?"

I opened my mouth to correct him only to realize he may not give us the room if he knew the truth.

Paul stood straight and tall, pulling his shoulders back and lifting his chin. "Alderidge. Mr. and Mrs. Paul Alderidge. Joliet, Illinois." For a moment, I saw in him that confident eighteen-year-old boy so proud of himself for signing with the Air Force.

To complete the facade, I curled my hand around his arm and gazed up at him in adoration. It was the easiest part of the lie. With the key in hand, we waltzed out of the lobby. I wanted to unleash a chuckle. Positively scandalous, our lie. Unfortunately, my nerves got the better of me. Paul didn't expect us to share a single room, did he? What alternative was there? We moved the car in front of the door to room 1. He was quick to leave his seat and retrieve my travel case from the trunk. For my part, I unlocked and opened the door, breathing a sigh of relief when I saw two separate beds. Paul, once again nursing his solemn demeanor, entered the room and began checking it for something. Was he worried someone might be hiding behind the door or shower curtain?

In a most unladylike fashion, I cleared my throat. "Should we hang a sheet? A wall of Jericho like in *It Happened One Night*?"

He lifted his eyes to mine, the seriousness of his thoughts pooling beneath his furrowed brow. "I'll sleep in the car."

"That won't be comfortable. What if it gets cold? I won't have it. Sheet, it is."

"I won't stay in your room. It wouldn't be right."

In my best Scarlett O'Hara impression, I fanned my face. "My dear sir, are you trying to save my honor? How kind of you!" Then I dropped the act and placed my hands on my hips like a strong fifties woman. "You're being foolish. Now, we'll need some rope." The drawer of the bedside table only held the Holy Bible. That was when I heard the motel door shut.

"Well, fiddle-dee-dee, Mr. Alderidge," I said, before stripping the bedspread and stealing the pillow. If he was set on protecting my honor, he could at least have a pillow and blanket while doing it.

I rose early the next morning and peered into the car window. Curled up on the back seat, Paul looked perfectly angelic as he slept. And handsome beyond understanding. He shifted his positioning. As he pulled his knee closer to his chest, the leg of his trousers exposed the skin near his ankle. Scarred lines crossed the back of his leg. The sight made me stumble into the Cadillac behind me.

Paul jerked upright at the noise. He clambered out of the car and placed both hands on my shoulders. "Are you all right?"

I placed my palm gently on his cheek, so cold to my touch. "Yes, I'm all right."

Was he?

Present Day

Jade

Benny presses her hand against the stone wall of Gardner's historic two-cell jail. Built in 1906, the structure is now a photo opportunity for travelers on the route. Bridger saw the value in it as a backdrop to the next part of Benny's story.

"Paul was captured by the North Koreans in September of 1952," Benny says. "He served in the Air Force as a ground controller, giving information about locations to bombers. One day their position was attacked. He tried to flee to the mountains, but he was caught. He was taken as a prisoner of war and sent to Koje Island Camp. My brother, Louie, was already there. He was a pilot, captured in December of 1951."

She moves to the middle of the small room and grasps one of the bars. "I've seen pictures of the cages they were kept in. Paul never told me specifics, but I know they were both beaten, slashed, starved, confined in sweat boxes, and subjected to endless anti-American propaganda. Louie especially, Pilots were believed to know more information than others, so they were treated worse."

From where I stand, I see Bridger's bearded chin quiver. Did he know this about his foster father? Paul Alderidge was a POW during the Korean War. That knowledge was public. The details, though, put skin on the experience.

"Bridge," Benny says, holding her arm out to him. "I'm done sharing for now."

Bridger stops recording to help her out of the jail and back down the brick walkway to the Bel Air. We both wait as she relaxes onto the bench seat, searches her purse for a tissue, and wipes her eyes.

Knowing what Paul endured, believing he was fighting evil and protecting the people at home and abroad, and how, without hesitation, Gregory stole millions from him, only fuels my anger. If anything good came out of this horrible crime, it was that I didn't end up marrying him. There's no telling what else he's capable of. One thing is for sure—I will do anything I can to make it right. Turning over our shared possessions and helping with this documentary doesn't seem like nearly enough.

A knuckle lifts my chin out of my wallowing until the clear blue sky and Bridger's face come into view. His gaze holds mine, but I don't know what he's trying to communicate to me. Maybe it's nothing at all. No. There's meaning behind those eyes.

They haunt me for the next hour as Route 66 crosses the stunning countryside along railroad tracks and fields of wildflowers. The Chevy cuts through the warm morning air as Bridger films Benny's profile. It will make for a beautiful shot, and I can already see the documentary coming together under Bridger's artful eye. I pull the car to a stop as we reach a fork in the road. Yet, when I glance over my shoulder for a break in traffic, I find the camera aimed at me.

I jerk toward the door. My role is meant to be a shadow. The black-dressed stagehand that makes changes to the set. Not a main character.

"Sorry. Didn't mean to scare you." A sheepish Bridger puts the camera down. "It's so pretty here, I wanted to capture you in it. Sorry. Again."

"I was surprised. That's all."

We soon roll into Pontiac, passing by a treasure trove of murals all dedicated to the Mother Road and its place in history.

We wander through the Route 66 Museum as Benny spins more tales about life in the 1940s and '50s, leading up to her life-changing decision to move cross-country. Firecracker doesn't begin to describe young Benny.

"Louie was in charge of keeping me out of trouble and, boy oh boy, I kept him on his toes. Whether it was pocketing penny candies at the general store or sneaking into the public pool, I was always up for an adventure. It about broke my heart when he enlisted. I rode my bicycle straight to the Alderidge home and begged Paul to make him change his mind."

With a shaky hand, she fidgets with her hair. I take the bottled water I just purchased out of my bag, open the cap, and offer it up. She mouths a thank-you and takes a few sips.

"Paul found me later to tell me the worst news I could ever imagine. When he failed to change my brother's mind, Paul enlisted alongside him so he could keep him safe. I was young, only fifteen, so I didn't handle it well. I felt abandoned by them both."

I fight the urge to pull out my phone and research Louie. Before this trip, I'd never heard of him, let alone what happened to him after the war.

Benny steps toward the retro kitchen tableau. "Jade, Bridge, if you don't mind, may I stay here for a few minutes?"

"Sure," we both agree before heading upstairs to the photo gallery.

On the top floor of the museum, photographs from Chicago to Santa Monica grace the walls, and we move from one to another in step.

"I bet Benny was a great mom to you," I say while perusing a shot of the iconic Twin Arrows from Coconino County in Arizona. I groan when I realize my mistake. "Foster mom, I mean. Sorry."

"No apology necessary. I consider her my mom. I have since I was fifteen years old."

"Why didn't she ever adopt you?" I shake my head. "If that's too personal—"

"We've seen each other eat chili dogs. Nothing is too personal anymore," Bridger teases me with a lopsided grin. "As far as adoption goes, Benny tried. Paul too. I wouldn't let them."

"Why? Because of the age difference, or what?"

"Nah." He peers closely at a pic of the Adams Street Route 66 Begins sign. "See, I was born in Samoa on Upolu Island. The oldest of five children. We didn't have a lot, but I was happy. One day this man and woman came to our village and told us about their adoption agency. They offered to take me to America, give me an education, and then bring me back home when I was eighteen. That's not what the contract, written in English, said though. My parents were deceived into signing me away."

Straightening up, I run my hands over my arms, but the gooseflesh persists. "Oh, Bridger. That's terrible."

He swallows hard and nods.

"How old were you?"

"Eight."

My focus drops to my shoes. "Eight. That's a rough age to be taken from your parents, let alone your homeland."

"True. But none of the kids at the New Zealand nanny home I was taken to had it easy, no matter the age. We were all deprived of food, health care, and sanitary conditions. I developed trachoma—an eye infection—and they left it untreated. By the time I was brought to my adoptive home in California, the scarring had left me mostly blind."

"No . . ."

"I couldn't see my new world. I couldn't speak my new language. I was alone and just . . . scared." He exhales loudly.

"What—I mean, how did you make it through that?"

"'Tu leova i lo Tatua Va.' It's a hymn my mother taught me after my grandmother died. It means 'God be with you till we meet again.' It was also the last thing my mama said to me."

With the heel of his hand, Bridger massages the left side of his chest. "I sang it again and again in my head. And I prayed the way my father taught me to."

I ache. My fingertips burn to sweep away the loose curl that has fallen in front of his eyelashes. I remain still though, unable to trust I'd be comforting him as much as hoping to relieve the weight crushing my own chest.

Bridger presses his wrist to his nose and blinks hard. "Anyway, I got corneal implants right before I turned ten. The surgery restored my sight completely. After that, I wasn't scared so much as angry. Angry at God, angry at everyone, including the Rosenblums."

"So they gave you up." I bite my bottom lip. "Why couldn't they at least send you back home?"

"They should've, especially after those agency people were arrested for a whole host of crimes. I don't know. No one cared enough to take me back. Foster care sucked. I bounced from place to place until I landed with Roland." He sidesteps to another photo, and I follow his lead.

"Benny and Paul's son?"

"Yes, and his wife, Amie. Again, they had good intentions. Things had changed though. I was experimenting with drugs and alcohol, getting in fights, getting taken in by the cops. When I was fifteen, they were ready to turn me loose."

"But Benny stepped in?"

"Paul, actually. He saw something in me besides all the trauma and misbehavior. He and Benny became my foster parents, and they were amazing, even when I didn't deserve it. They even tried to find my birth parents."

"They did?"

Bridger turns silent as he stares at a picture of the Santa Monica Pier. "There was a tsunami in Samoa on September 29, 2009. My village and my whole family were gone." A tear slides down his cheek, and he doesn't try to catch it before it soaks into his beard.

"Bridge, I'm sorry."

"Yeah. Me too. I think everyone in the country knows what I was like in my late teens and my early twenties. There were always photographers happy to share my worst moments with the world. Even through all that, Benny and Paul always welcomed me back home."

He faces me. "With this documentary, I want people to know that even though the world has its share of bad people, there are good ones trying to fix the wrong done by others."

"I can certainly respect that." We share a moment where we stare too long and stand too close. Deep within, my nerves tizzy, and I don't know if I should back away or move closer. Good or bad, I never felt this with Gregory. Dating him was a logical conclusion to months and months of dinner invitations. I didn't have to chase him. He was right there. And he stayed there for six years. And while I loved him, the feelings were lukewarm, even in our best moments.

"What is your name?" I ask. When he gives me a funny look, I clarify. "Your Samoan name. Your birth name. You said you became Bridger when you came to the US."

"Oh." He looks surprised. "No one besides Benny and Paul have ever asked me that. It's, uh, Emanuelu."

"Emanuelu," I let the name roll off my tongue. "I like it. Have you ever considered going back to that?"

"Nah."

"Why not?"

"Um . . . Well, I guess I'd be worried that if I did start using my Samoan name, spoke the language, or embraced other parts of my heritage, it would make Benny think I'm not grateful for all she's done for me."

I chew my words before responding. "Have you two spoken about that? I'm sure Benny would never keep you from connecting with your past. She loves you."

"Yes, she loves me more than anyone else in my life, which

is why I won't risk hurting her feelings. I know she'd support me, but at what cost?"

I get it. Between losing Paul then losing everything she and Paul worked for, Benny has been through enough the past few years. I understand Bridger's need to protect her feelings, even at his own expense.

"Besides," Bridger continues, "I have bigger things to deal with on this trip. We should get back to her."

Chapter 7

1956
Benny

Pontiac. Lexington. Normal. Bloomington. Atlanta. Elkhart. Paul traversed each small town with caution and patience. He even indulged my curiosity at the Cozy Dog Drive In. Who wouldn't want to try a battered hot dog on a stick? Paul, that's who. I thought it was delicious, and the Cozy Dog would always have a place in my heart.

The sun was dipping low in the sky when I saw a sign that made my heart leap.

"There's a drive-in! Up ahead. Paul, we should go."

"A drive-in? You and I?"

I checked the back seat with exaggerated theatricality. "We're the only ones in the car, right? Please, please, please?"

"Do you even know what's playing?"

"Does it matter?"

"I guess not."

One hour later, we sat in the front row of the drive-in, watching *Attack of the Killer Swamp Frog*. After one particularly slimy scene where the giant frog grabbed a girl with his tongue and slowly reeled her into his mouth while she screamed, I turned to face Paul.

"Just imagine, if things in Hollywood go the way I hope, I could star in the sequel to this. Would you come and watch it?"

He thought for a moment. "I'll see everything you star in. Even if you play the part of the swamp frog."

"One can only hope," I said with a smile. A scream pierced through the in-car speaker, but rather than grab onto Paul's arm like I'd seen in movies, I lurched away, hitting my back against the door. "Ouch, ouch, ouch."

"Benny!" He slid across the seat and placed a hand around my back. He was so close. Closer than he'd ever been before.

How often had I kissed my pillow pretending it was him? Now, he was there, right in front of me. I couldn't control myself. I pressed my lips against his. And he didn't pull away until several moments later. Which was fine because I felt woozy and needed to breathe.

Although I had imagined my first kiss since I was ten years old, I never thought that the boy would look as sad as Paul did then afterward. "I . . . I think I'll go get us some snacks." With that he left me alone in the car to think about what a silly girl I was. How could I think that Paul Alderidge might like me? I was Louie's pain-in-the-neck little sister. Plus, he was probably appalled with me for kissing him. What kind of girl did that make me? He didn't know that was my first kiss. That I'd been hoping and praying it would be with him. What if he decided enough was enough and headed north instead of south? Or worse. What if he left me on my own to finish the trip by myself?

No. Paul wouldn't do that. He was honorable. More than likely, he was standing in line at the concession stand right now, thinking of how he could gently remind me that he was not, nor would he ever be, my boyfriend.

"My my," said a voice on my right. "Aren't you a pretty thing? Isn't she pretty, Ken?"

I turned to find three boys—no, three men—closing in on me. A tall one with a floppy, dirty hairstyle. One with a thick neck and round middle. The third—the one who'd spoken—had a decently attractive face and average frame, but I didn't like his slick smile.

"Oh, she's mighty fine," Floppy Hair said.

Thick Neck placed a hand on the Chevy's hood and leaned over the windshield. "What's your name, sweetheart?"

He had a frightening look on his face. Like he was hungry for something. His crooked nose flushed red. I'd learned what that meant when my uncle came back from Europe, and I knew it sometimes made men violent.

"Aren't you going to answer?" As he spoke, Sly Guy angled his head as if to peep down my top.

To be safe, I smoothed the neckline of my cardigan against the base of my throat, feeling the fast thrumming of my heart, and fixed an expression of annoyance on my face. "Mrs. Paul Alderidge. Now, if you boys will excuse me, I'm trying to watch the movie."

"No one should watch a flick by themselves. We'd be happy to join you." Sly Guy leered at me as he inched closer.

I pounded my palm on the door lock, which only made them laugh, then I scrambled to the driver's side of the bench seat. "Boo!"

I recoiled from the hot, putrid breath on my neck and slid back to the center of the car. I was surrounded. Floppy Hair on the left. Thick Neck and Sly Guy on the right. Echoes of Paul's words clanged in my head. *"There are bad people everywhere."* I didn't want to believe him. But then, Thick Neck hopped over the passenger side door and slid into my seat. With no other option, I grabbed for the Cozy Dog stick I'd placed on the floorboard and forgotten to throw away. I jabbed it at the man's face. All it did was break in half against his forehead. His beady eyes turned black.

I was about to scream for help from the cars around me, but I heard a scuffle, and Sly Guy's face hit the windshield along with a dozen popcorn kernels. Thick Neck reached for me, but before he made contact, he was lifted up and over the side of the car and thrown to the ground. Paul, facing away from me, fought off a tackle by Floppy Hair only to be shoved to his hands and knees by Sly Guy.

I yanked up the door lock, then saw Thick Neck trying to stand. With all my strength, I opened the heavy door right into his face, forcing him back to the gravel. Paul and Sly Guy were rolling, one on top, then the other. Around us, other moviegoers exited their cars and gathered to watch the fight.

"Help him!" I cried. No one moved so I ran toward Paul. Yet before I reached him, scrawny arms surrounded me from behind, pinning my hands to my chest and lifting me off my feet until we were back against the car door. "Paul!"

A young boy, sixteen or seventeen, pushed Sly Guy off Paul, allowing him the chance to land a punch that left Sly Guy rolling in the dirt and clutching his nose. Paul turned toward me with a fury in his eyes I'd never seen before. I elbowed my captor, Floppy Hair, in the gut, only to be thrown down to the dirt. Someone helped me up, a woman whose lips formed words I couldn't hear over my own heartbeat.

Paul was slamming the back of Floppy Hair's head against the hood again and again. Floppy Hair's legs dangled loosely by the front wheel.

"You'll kill him," someone yelled.

Still, Paul fought.

Until I tugged his arm. "Paul, that's enough. Let's go." He was in a spell though. I placed my hands on either side of his neck, finally managing to twist his face to see me. "Please. Let's leave. I want to leave."

Understanding dawned, and he let the man fall to the ground. He scooped me up and placed me onto the front seat. I watched the three men, all in various stages of injury, moving around and yelling threats toward us. Paul hopped into his seat and revved the engine to life as Sly Guy got to his feet. He charged at us but was left in our dust as Paul fled down the row. Soon, we were back on Route 66, our headlights cutting through the night. Paul focused intently on the road ahead, his chest still rising and falling rapidly.

I erased the distance between us, placed my palm over his heart, and rested my head on his shoulder.

Chapter 8

2003
Jade

"Have you ever seen the Mississippi River, Baby Jade?" Daddy asked as he drove his truck down the highway.

"I don't think so. Where is it?" I pushed the chest strap of my seat belt out of my way, pulled my knees underneath me, and pressed my hands against the window.

"You can't see it yet. Sit right, please. We've gotta keep you safe."

I listened, sitting like a good girl with my hands in my lap. I still searched out the window though. "My teacher says the Mississippi River is the biggest river in the whole country."

"She's right."

"Daddy, Mr. Lowell is a boy, not a girl."

"Silly me."

"Can I swim in the river?"

"We can't, Baby Jade. We don't have time."

I groaned. "Yeah, Mom gets mad if I'm not in bed by 7:30."

"Isn't 7:30 a little early for an eight-year-old?"

"Mom says after that it's time for her and Hank." I pointed ahead. "Is it under that bridge?"

"It sure is. Hey, uh, back at that gas station, I called your mom. There's been a change of plans. You're going to stay with me for a bit so your mom and Hank can go on a trip."

"Really?" I squealed, unbuckling so I could hug Daddy's arm.

"I'm glad you're excited, but remember, you gotta stay buckled. I can't have anything bad happen to you ever, ever, ever."

"Okay, okay, okay. But we don't cross the river to go to your house."

"You're one smart cookie. I bet you make your teacher proud. You're right. We aren't going to my old house. We're going to a new one, but it's gonna take a few days to get there. Is that all right with you?"

I bounced in my seat. "More than all right!"

"I've got some tunes for the road. Do you like the Eagles?"

"Like bald ones?"

Daddy started cracking up. I laughed, too, even though I didn't know what was so funny.

⁓

Present Day
Jade

I pocket my phone, pretending I never saw the two missed calls from Rockville Penitentiary, and return my focus to the Mississippi River flowing beneath me. When will Gregory take the hint that I'll never speak to him again? I remove my suit jacket and allow the sunlight peeking through the trusses of the Old Chain of Rocks Bridge to kiss the skin on my arms. I press my stomach against the handrail and lean forward. With my eyes closed, I give myself over to elements beyond my control. The sun, the river, the breeze licking my face and rustling the leaves of trees on the western bank.

"Enjoying the scenery?"

I open my eyes and find Bridger on my left. Today he's wearing his hair in a ponytail, and heaven help me, it looks good. "Where's Benny?"

"At the car." He holds up the camera he's carrying. "We're done getting our stuff."

"Great." I fold my suit jacket over my forearm and cradle it in front of me as we begin our walk back to the parking lot.

"Serious question. Does Hillary Clinton know you stole all your clothes from her closet?"

"That's what you call a serious question?"

"Call it desperate curiosity. I didn't know if you had real arms before I saw you at Lou Mitchell's. I'm still not sure about your legs. They could be pegs."

I roll my eyes. "These suits were expensive. And before you ask how many I have, I'll tell you that I have quite a few. I've worked six days a week since college, trying to excel. I had no need for a lot of other clothes. Even when I traveled with Gregory, I either wore a suit or a bathing suit, depending on where we went."

"Are your wooden pegs waterproof?"

I smack his arm. "You and Benny are my clients. I see this as a job, so I want to dress professionally."

"We've been together almost every moment of the last three days and you still feel like we're your clients? Man, my game is way off. Now, what's the real reason?"

We round the twenty-two degree bend in the bridge that had to be a traffic nightmare back when it was open to cars. While I would be perfectly happy to ignore Bridger's probing, his constant stare demands an answer. "Fine. Gregory used to tease me about the state of everything I owned. I was with him for six years, so over that time, all my possessions turned over. Long gone were the thrift store finds and hand-me-downs. I was frugal, you see. He was not."

On the bridge's concrete deck, our stubby late-afternoon

shadows walk nearly hand in hand. Although this part of historic Route 66 has a sordid history, including a few horrific murders, I feel safe with the man at my side.

"I gotta admit," Bridger said, "when I first heard how much they reclaimed from your apartment after the trial, I figured you were a total snob. Benny insisted otherwise. But that's why I turned all Dorothy Zbornak on you at the motor court. Sorry about that."

"It's fine. I'm glad you called me out. The furniture in my apartment, the artwork, my car, my jewelry, even the kitchen appliances were either gifts from Gregory or joint purchases he convinced me to buy. So when the court's trustee came to my apartment to claw back as much of the stolen money as they could, I relinquished it all. All except these suits because I knew I paid for them myself."

"Okay, I see the attachment. In a way, it's like how I feel about the Bel Air. Not that I paid for it myself, but Paul left it to me in his will. Except I can barely drive it. I had that corneal implantation, but over time, it's normal for vision to become reduced again. I have trouble seeing in the bright sunlight and at night. Still, I'll never give it up. It's my pantsuit."

As we traverse the easternmost side of the bridge, our conversation and the roar of the river give way to birdsong. Trees, taller than the highest steel beams, form curtains of foliage on both sides of us, replacing the expansive view up and down the mighty Mississippi.

"Serious question," I say. "Did you make a *Golden Girls* reference back there?"

"Why, yes. Yes, I did." He shrugs. "The real question you should be asking is how did we make it three hundred miles into this trip without a *Golden Girls* reference?"

"True. You know Dorothy's last name and everything." We walk a few yards farther, and the car comes more into view. Bridger stiffens.

"What's wrong?"

"Do you see her?" He doesn't wait for my response. He jogs—no, runs—to the car. After looking inside, he turns in a circle. "Benny!" "Benny!"

"Benny!" I call out as I trot toward him as fast as my heels will let me.

"You check the woods leading to the riverbank. I'll check the road."

Following Bridger's instructions and repeating Benny's name, I step through the trees. Panic grips my throat, straining my voice as I yell. "Benny!" *God, please let her be safe. Please, please, please. I'll do anything you want. Just help us find her.*

Bridger sounds farther and farther away. Did someone take her? The young faces of the two murdered Kerry sisters flash through my mind. Would Benny meet the same terrible fate on this bridge as they did? No, God, no.

I stumble out of the brush and onto a smooth dirt trail. Maybe she went to the woods to relieve herself but fell. Unlikely. A lady like her wouldn't do such a thing. So where is she? I follow the trail to the river, and I'm about to call her name again when I spot her yellow blouse. She's alive, standing at the edge of the river where sand forms a beach area.

"Benny!" I reach her side and take her hand. "We were worried about you."

She turns, yanking her arm out of my grasp. Spite flashes over her normally soft expression. "Who are you?"

I stammer but eventually get my first name out. Even then, she eyes me suspiciously so I add, "I'm a friend."

"Well, Jane, Paul left his fishing pole around here somewhere. He took Roland here this morning and forgot to bring it home. Have you seen it?"

I'm speechless as Benny's eyes scan the bank. I've noticed how often she repeats herself, but that never worried me much. Most of my elderly clients did that. This talk, though, is different.

"When did you say they went fishing?"

"This morning. Roland begged him all weekend to go." Benny looks to the right, then the left, up, then down. She raises her trembling fingertips to her lips. The lace of her glove is torn along her knuckles.

"Benny," I say as calmly as I can, unsure if I'll make whatever is happening worse, "let's have a look in the car. It might be in there."

"No, I already looked."

"I bet Bridger can help us find it. Let's go back to Bridger." Confusion twists her expression, until finally, she relaxes. "Where is Bridger?"

"He's up by the car. Come with me. I'll take you to him."

Five minutes later, we emerge from the trailhead I'd missed earlier. Bridger sprints toward us speaking a language I don't know. Samoan? His ponytail is loose and his hair hangs wildly around his sweat- and dirt-covered face. He's been crying.

I let them embrace while I sort through the questions swirling in my mind.

Chapter 9

1956

Benny

With a bucket under my arm, I returned to room 6 at the Coral Court Motel. "Knock, knock," I said before opening the door. On the end of the bed, Paul sat staring down at his bloody knuckles.

"I got you some ice. Here." I took a seat next to him and placed the ice bucket between us. "Put your hands in."

He obeyed, wincing the moment his wounds touched the icy water.

"Thank you, by the way," I said. "For saving me from those goons. I'm sorry you got hurt." Considering he was outnumbered three to one, he didn't look too bad, knuckles aside. A swollen, red cheekbone, a cut on his chin, and a rash of missing skin on his elbow from where he fell on the gravel.

Paul's brows pinched tight above his narrowed eyes. "Do you believe me now?"

"About what?"

"I told you this plan of yours was too dangerous. You don't know the world like I do. Everywhere you go, there are people looking to lie, cheat, steal, or kill."

"Maybe you're correct. Yet everywhere we go, there are also good people. People trying to help. Back at the drive-in, the other moviegoers were helping us in all the ways they could. Even in Korea, for every person against you, there were people for you."

"It didn't feel like that. The civilians didn't want us there."

"That doesn't necessarily mean they were bad people. Besides, I know there were good people because you were there and Louie was there, and you two are the best men I know."

Paul stuck his hands deeper into the ice so that a few pieces teetered on the edge of the bucket, threatening to spill out.

"You just need to see the sunshine instead of the gloom."

"Benny, if you focus on the sunshine, you can't see anything else. And that makes you vulnerable."

I lost myself in the mirror above the dresser directly in front of us. I wanted to say that if we stayed side by side, nothing could hurt us. We could make it through the worst threats the same way we made it through tonight. And considering the way we appeared in the mirror, we'd look good doing it.

"What do you think California will be like?" I asked. "Do you think Sunset Boulevard is just like it is in the pictures—blue skies and palm trees? And the ocean—do you think it's cold like Lake Michigan or warm like a summer rain?" My attention falls to his lips, and I want so badly to remember what they felt like during our kiss. "When we get to the ocean, will you hold my hand the first time I dip my toes in?"

His answer was hesitant. "If you want me to."

"And what if I'm so busy becoming a movie star that it takes me a while to get to the beach?" I studied his face. With his gaze almost entirely kept low—without doubt a survival mechanism from his time as a POW—I could take a splendidly long account of every feature. The light freckles that dusted his pale skin, just like mine. His lashes, which had once been blond, had darkened to an ashen brown along with his hair, and they swept down to cover his Technicolor blue eyes far too often. Then there were his full, smooth lips. They'd once tipped in smiles more times a day than the flutter of a hummingbird's wings. They rarely moved now. Not to smile and not to talk. My heart held tight to the secret I'd discovered mere hours before—those terrible scars were reminders that someone once wanted him in pain. They might even have wanted him dead. Yet he survived and he had a full life ahead of him. One I hoped to be a part of.

"What are your plans once we arrive in California?"

"To stay until I know you'll be safe."

"And then what? Will you return to Joliet and work for your father?" I hated to admit it, but Paul's safest bet for a steady, secure livelihood was to work for Alderidge Tire and Rubber Company, a thriving business his grandfather had started in 1905. He'd already been working there during the day and making a good living. He didn't need to work evenings at the Rialto. He chose to.

"I'm not positive what I'll do."

"Have you considered acting? You used to love it. When you were Puck in *A Midsummer Night's Dream* in high school, you had me believing in fairies."

The corner of his lips ticked up briefly only to fall again.

"There's not much use for Shakespearean actors unless you're Howard Keel or Laurence Olivier."

"What about your impression of Clark Gable? William Holden? Leon Ford? You have great range. Moreover, you love acting."

"Used to. Playing pretend is child's play."

I stiffened. "Oh, is that right? I regret to inform you that some people, including yours truly, believe film to be a glorious way to bring new ideas, revelation, and hope to the masses. Is *On the Waterfront* child's play? What about *The Best Years of Our Lives*?"

"Benny—"

"And where would we be without *Singin' in the Rain* and *Marty*? Movies that remind us that people can be good and kind and genuine. That love can be pure and—"

Paul yanked his hands out of the bucket and rose to his feet. Facing away from me, he stood with his arms hanging at his sides, red-tinged drips of water falling from his fingertips. "I should walk you to your room."

"Paul? Is this about"—I swallowed hard—"about the kiss? I know it was untoward and you likely find me to be a woman of loose morals, but I grew tired of waiting for you to do it."

"Why would I kiss you? You're young."

I huffed as I raised my chin. "I'm twenty."

"You're Louie's sister."

"And you're his friend. What does that matter?"

"It matters a great deal." He slinked to the door and opened it without so much as a glance at me. "We have a long day of driving tomorrow. You should get some sleep."

I hopped up from the bed. The movement must have rocked the bucket because it tipped over, the cold water splashing my ankles as it sloshed across the carpet. I didn't bother to help clean it up because if I stayed even ten seconds more, Paul would have seen the hot tears streaking down my face. Instead, I ran out the door, into the path of a car driving down the court. Fortunately, they were crawling at the speed of an inchworm and stopped on a dime. I unlocked the door to my room with trembling hands as Paul called out my name. I ignored him though. Once I got inside, I slammed the door behind me, threw myself onto the bed, and let the pillow catch my tears.

Chapter *10*

Present Day
Jade

Outside Ted Drewes Frozen Custard, Bridger holds a cup of vanilla mixed with peanut butter cups and bits of banana upside down over his head. "I told ya. That's why they call it a concrete. And now, you owe me a chili dog."

I shake my head and try the upside-down trick with my strawberry shortcake concrete. It stays in the cup, spoon and all. "We never shook on it."

"You arched a brow. It's basically the same thing."

"That's not what that means."

"Yes, it is."

"No, it isn't." I wave my spoon to emphasize each word. Bridger lunges forward and bites the spoon out of my hand.

"Hey!" I stare wide-eyed at the nerve of him.

He grins with it secured between his teeth. His perfectly straight, bright white teeth.

"Mmm," he says, pulling the cleaned-off spoon out of his mouth. "I should've gotten that one."

A spark ignites in me, and I grasp the spoon in his cup, except when I yank, I take a monster heap of custard with it. It doesn't fit cleanly into my mouth though, and the cold swathes my lips and chin. I try unsuccessfully to chew, but the custard just presses against the roof of my mouth.

"Get ready for it," Bridger says, his eyes shining with pure mischief.

Blinding pain shoots up into my forehead, and it's half a minute or more until I'm able to swallow the lump. When the pain fades, I finally open my eyes and find Bridger doubled over in a fit of laughter.

"What's gotten into him?" Benny steps out of the restroom and gives Bridger a look I can only describe as motherly suspicion.

"I got an ice cream headache, and he found it hilarious," I explain, using the back of my hand to wipe the excess custard off my face.

"I'm afraid he learned that from me. I remember when Paul got a brain freeze here. I laughed about that hard."

"Did he get mad?" For emphasis, I elbow Bridger in his side.

"Oh, no. Paul never did get mad at me. Even at my absolute worst. Like when I threw a hissy fit over something silly like the time he surprised me by painting our family room a putrid green. Or when I accidentally put his watch in the laundry."

"It sounds like he was an amazing husband."

She pats my arm. "The best one God ever made, dear. I pray you'll find a man just like him."

"I don't know, Benny," I say. "I think men like Paul are a dying breed."

"Or maybe," Bridger cuts in, "you surround yourself with criminals."

While I work on not swallowing my tongue, Benny gives Bridger a stern look. "You apologize right now, young man."

"What for? It's an honest fact. She was engaged to an embezzler."

I lean close to Bridger and speak low. "I'm reminded of that fact every minute of every day. Every time I look at you or Benny. Every time I see the indent on my ring finger that won't go away no matter what I try. I don't need a reminder from you." I straighten my posture. "I'll be in the car." No longer craving sweets, I dump my remaining custard into the trash bin.

We're quiet as we continue down Missouri's Route 66. When we stop at the Meramec Caverns, Bridger and Benny set up for an interview beneath a large shade tree. Excusing myself to explore the grounds, or more accurately, to put some distance between us, I move toward the caverns entrance only to have Bridger thrust his smaller Canon camera in my hand. "Will you get some footage underground?"

"I don't know how."

"It's simple. Turn it on, press record."

"What if I don't want to?"

He cocks his head, and his eyes glaze over for several moments like he was searching for a proper answer. Finally, he shrugs. "You don't have to. I can get some shots after the interview. I'd do it all at once, but Benny can't go down in the caverns, and I can't leave her alone after . . ."

Although I wait for him to finish his sentence, he never does.

"Fine. I'll do it."

A half hour later, I'm under seven stories of earth, gathering the most amateur videography of all time. I swoop slowly right. I swoop slowly left. Here a stalactite. There a stalactite. Everywhere a stalactite. Or stalagmite? Whichever one hangs from the ceiling.

Stalactite has a C, so it hangs from the ceiling. Stalagmite has a G, so it grows up from the ground. It's foolish, but I glance over both shoulders. That's how real Daddy's voice sounds in this moment.

"It's in your mind, Jade," I whisper.

"Do you have a question, miss?" the tour guide asks. When I shake my head, he continues with the history of the caverns. "According to local lore, infamous bandit Jesse James and his brother Frank hid out in these caves to avoid capture."

I learned the same fact in 2003, the only other time I've been down here. Back then, the thought of outlaws hiding from the police was fascinating to me because it was only folklore. If I'd known then what I know now, maybe I wouldn't have asked so many questions.

"Who's Jesse James, Daddy? Did he like caverns? Was he scared of the dark too? Why did he have to hide?"

"Watch out. Don't bump your noggin." Daddy put his hand on my head and steered me away from the low ceiling. "Jesse hid because he was a bad man, and the cops wanted to arrest him for stealing and killing."

"I bet they never caught him down here. If I was a bad guy, this is where I'd hide too."

Daddy pulled me away from the rest of the tour group and kneeled so he could look me in the eye. I expected him to scold me or squeeze my arms like Mom did when I was bad. After all, I'd been bratty in the car, begging and begging to stop and see the caverns, even though Daddy said we needed to keep moving. He didn't hurt me though. He gently tucked my wild, uncombed hair behind my ears. "We're gonna play a game. We'll pretend we're bad guys and we need to hide, just like those James brothers. What do you think we'll need?"

"Disguises!"

"Good idea. What else?"

"New clothes. Oh, and a horse."

Daddy thought for a second. "If we're going to get any of that, we're going to need help."

I come back to the present, realizing I've been filming the same spot on the cave roof for a while. The last of the tour group is exiting through a narrow hallway. Alone in the near-dark, the shadows stretch toward me.

The guide pokes his head back into the cavernous room.

"Miss? We're moving on. You don't want to get lost in here. Trust me."

Chapter 11

2003
Jade

"Daddy, I can't sleep without Monty." I kicked off the scratchy sheets. This motel room was too hot. And it smelled icky too. Daddy pulled the sheets back over me. "Monty?"

"My stuffed manatee. I always sleep with Monty."

"Oh, that's right. We left him behind, huh? I'm sorry, Baby Jade."

I pushed the sheets off again. "I'll get sweaty under covers. Can we go back and get him?"

"I don't think so. We're already on our way. Maybe we can find another Monty at the store tomorrow." He tilted the clock. "It's late. You go to sleep. You want me to sing you a song or something? 'You Are My Sunshine'? You like that one, right?"

"Not anymore. I'm eight, remember?"

"Well, excuse me, little lady. Are you too old for a story?"

A story! "I guess that would be all right." I pointed a finger at him. "But don't make it a baby story, okay?" I didn't like going to sleep. My tummy always felt sick. Without Monty at my side, the sickness was worse. I took two of the pillows and tucked them around me.

"Okay. Let's see," Daddy began. "There was once a pretty little girl with dark curly hair and the greenest eyes anyone in the land ever saw. And every day this little girl would walk to a magical cave where all the food and treasures in the whole land were kept—"

"Like the caverns?"

"Yeah, like the caverns. At the door of the cave, a giant stood watch."

"A Gemini Giant like at the Launching Pad?" I asked.

"Yep. An ugly giant who had done ugly things, so he wasn't welcome in the village. So whenever someone would come looking for food or treasures, the giant would ask them to answer a puzzle of numbers. No one could answer the puzzle correctly, except for this little girl because she was so good at math. Are you following me?"

"Daddy, I know you're just talking about me."

He brushed my hair off my forehead. "And how do you know that?"

"Duh. Because I'm the smartest kid in my class in math."

"Do you want to hear the rest of the story?"

I yawned. "Yes, please."

"There was a very mean dragon who would fly down and try to bite the girl and slap her with his wings. One day the giant saw this happening, and he tried to protect the green-eyed girl. He threw rocks at the dragon. He even grabbed onto the dragon's wing. Up, up, up they flew until the giant scratched a hole in the dragon's wing. They both fell from the sky."

My eyelids got heavy. I tried to keep my eyes open but that made it even worse. "Did they die?"

"Nope. The dragon was never able to fly again though. And the giant landed very hard on the ground. The green-eyed girl hugged his neck and said, 'Thank you for saving me and my village.' But the giant said, 'No, you're the true hero for bringing food and treasure to the villagers every day so they can feed their families and build their homes.'"

"What next?"

"I guess the giant went back to the cave and lived happily ever after knowing he had helped the little girl."

"No." I propped up on my elbow. "The girl should bring him back to the village with her so people can see that he is nice and not ugly."

"I don't know if they would welcome him back."

"That's not nice. If that happened, the little girl and the giant could go off by themselves somewhere new and then they could live happily ever after."

Daddy let out a *hmm*. "What would happen to the villagers if they couldn't get the food from the cave anymore?"

"I don't know. I'm good at math, not stories, remember?" I curled my knees into my chest and wrapped my arms around them. I was safe. With Daddy, I was always safe.

He turned off the light, and I fell asleep. Sometime later, I woke up to see him standing by the window. Talking on the phone? Who would he be talking to in the middle of the night?

"It'll take us a few days," he said super quietly. "No, I don't think she saw anything . . . Yeah, I'll avoid the highway . . . Route 66, I know. You sure you're willing to help us out?"

My nose itched, but I wouldn't move a centimeter.

"Thanks, Glynda. I appreciate it."

I squeezed my eyes shut when he hung up the phone. I heard him walking toward me and I tensed up. But he kissed my hair and plopped down on the other bed. Twenty-two sheep later, he was snoring.

Chapter *12*

Present Day
Jade

The neon lights of the Wagon Wheel Motel are a welcome sight for me, and I can't wait to call it a night. While Bridger checks us in, I browse the gift shop until I find a Route 66 guidebook to thumb through, praying against any more memories of my father. The sound of Bridger chatting away with the owner grates my nerves, so I replace the book on its shelf and head outside.

Before long I'm in a room by myself, lying on the bed and staring at the shadow-striped ceiling. *"You surround yourself with criminals."* I roll onto my side. Still, I can't get comfortable.

Outside the window, a shadow passes. Then it passes back the other way. Now, a third time. The knock on my door jars me, and I bolt upright in bed.

"Jade? It's Bridger."

I contemplate my best course of action. Pretend to be asleep and ignore the jerk. Tell him, through the door, that I'm not feeling well. Open the door, burst into tears, and manipulate him into thinking he's ruined my life, just like I learned from Mom. Or call the cops and claim he's stalking me. After all, he was no stranger to jail in the past. I can still picture his mugshot making the rounds on social media when I was in college. He smiled for it in a most drunk and disorderly way.

But none of those will do. I'll just have to confront him.

I shed the blankets and march to the door. Readying myself with a deep breath, I yank open the door and—

Flowers. Bridger holds out a small bouquet of wildflowers to me. "The Wagon Wheel's owner said I could pick a few."

It takes effort not to look him in the eye, so I focus hard on the assorted blooms and cross my arms over my stomach.

"I'm sorry . . . that I'm bleeding all over these flowers. I didn't expect thorns."

"Goodness, Bridger. Let me take them from you," I say, reaching for them.

"Careful," he warns. "They're attached to my hand."

After a cautious removal, Bridger yips and pulls his pinkie to his mouth.

My nerve falters, and I sigh. "Should I try to find a bandage?"

He inspects his finger. "Nah, I think I'm all right. So I, uh, started a campfire over by the vineyard. I'd like it if you'd join me. Benny's already asleep and we'd have clear sight of her door from there."

"I don't—"

"Come on. I even cleared away the clouds so we could stargaze."

I snort, then play along. "You did that for me, did you?"

"What can I say? I know a guy." He smirks in a way that I probably would have found cute a few hours ago. Not anymore.

I don't want to play nice after what happened earlier, but we have many more states to get through before we part ways. For Benny's sake, I have to at least try to smooth things over. "I guess I can sit out there for a few minutes. Let me change out of my pajamas."

Not long after, I reach the firepit where Bridger is waiting.

He stands and spreads out a blanket branded Wagon Wheel Motel. When I near, he swings it around me like a cape and wraps me in it.

He leans in close. "I'm sorry for what I said at Ted Drewes. It was thoughtless, coarse, uncouth, boorish, scurrilous, and every other synonym for rude I found on Thesaurus.com. I'm sorry. Can you find it in your heart to forgive me?"

His sincere gaze lingers, making my mind race. I've never had anyone apologize for hurting me. Not Gregory. He'd have to admit he was wrong first. Certainly not Mom. Or Hank. Or any other man she brought home after him. Do I dare believe Bridger is different? Again, for Benny's sake . . .

"I guess so." I flash a teasing grin. "But only because you are too big to ignore."

"Too big or too mind-bendingly handsome?"

"You? Handsome? I hadn't noticed." I glance up at the starlit sky, letting my gaze trail from one constellation to the next.

Bridger pulls the blanket—and me—closer until the warmth of his body seeps through my silk blouse. He tips his forehead until it nearly touches mine. "I call your bluff." After my lungs empty themselves of air, he releases the ends of the blanket and turns away. "You can sit in that one."

Blast that charm of his. I decide against giving him a swift kick on his backside for the sake of professionalism. Instead, I wait until he sees my stink-eye, then accept the chair he points to. Our words take a back seat to the crackling of the fire.

The flames mesmerize me, the way they dance with the dark. When I eventually tear my focus away, I find Bridger's eyes locked on me.

"Tell me about your family," he says.

"There's not much to tell. It's just me."

"What happened to your parents?"

I hug my arms to my chest to fight off a shudder. "Oh, uh, my mom's still around. We don't speak or visit though."

"Can I ask why?"

"My choice. When I was finishing high school, my counselor suggested I define some boundaries for my relationships. My mom didn't want to abide by those boundaries."

"How so?"

"She thought it was her right to verbally abuse me, and I didn't agree. I took off for college in Colorado, and that was it."

"That's tough. What about your dad?"

God, keep my voice steady. "He was in jail most of my child-hood."

Bridger leans forward in his chair and places a hand on my knee, which I only now realize is bouncing. "So my comment about you surrounding yourself with criminals makes me friend of the year, huh?"

"You're okay," I say, realizing I'm dangerously close to becoming more pitiful. "I guess I won't unravel the matching friendship bracelets I made us."

"Girl after my own heart." He reclines back. "Hey, instead of bracelets, can you weave us matching friendship vests? Is that a thing?"

My laugh erupts through my nose. "I'm not sure."

"It might be in Ohio. If we run into Tim and Sandy again, we can ask."

"What is the deal with you and Ohio?" I ask too loudly, leading me to clamp my palm over my lips.

"I told you. It's idyllic, man."

"You're too much," I say with a shake of my head.

"Aww, you like it." Bridger picks up a stick and stokes the fire. Near the Wagon Wheel's big neon sign, a camper van pulls into the parking lot. The driver does no less than a ten-point turn, then heads back east on 66, his gravel-spitting tires lending a soundtrack to the night's showing of stars.

"Are you still in touch with him? Your dad?" Bridger asks after a bit.

"No." The word catches in my throat.

"Because he did jailtime?"

"No. That doesn't bother me." I uncross and recross my legs. "I mean, it does, but it's all I've ever known. He was a petty thief when I was young, mostly to fuel his love for alcohol. He was in and out of jail the whole time he and my mom were together."

"Married?"

"Never married. They split when I was five or six. When I was seven, he got sober. I was so happy because it meant I got to visit him every other Saturday. I had this little calendar, and I'd count down the days until I saw him—"

My throat constricts, cutting off my words. Phew. Almost shared too much. I wait for Bridger to make a joke, but he stays silent. Instead, he eyes me thoughtfully.

"What?" I ask.

"Nothing. This"—he motions to the fire—"wasn't some elaborate scheme to get you to tell me your deep, dark secrets. You don't have to share anything you don't want to." Now he's the one staring into the flames. "In fact, it's probably wisest not—"

"It's okay." Maybe it's the depth of his voice or the earnestness in his eyes. Maybe it's that he might be the one person in the world who understands what I experienced, even if only a tiny bit, but I realize I want to tell him my story. So I do.

"On May 17, 2003, he picked me up for our usual visit. We went out for ice cream, and he let me get one of those waffle cones that's partly dipped in chocolate and sprinkles, then he took me back to Mom's. He came back later that day while I was playing outside. I told him Mom wasn't home, but he went in the house anyway. When he came back out, he grabbed me, put me back in his truck, and we began driving—down Route 66, actually. I thought it was a vacation, but the courts called it kidnapping by a non-custodial parent. It was four months before I saw my mother again."

"Jade, that's . . . a lot. That's why you cut communication with him?"

"No. That one wasn't my choice." I press my lips together and curl myself up in the chair, hoping he gets the hint and lets any remaining questions dissipate with the rising smoke. He does. Neither of us speak for a long while. My eyelids grow heavier, and my blinks lengthen. I think I'll retire for the night—

"Benny has dementia."

I snap awake, reconciling Bridger's morose expression with the fear I saw on his face at the bridge this afternoon. His concentration has locked on the closed door to the room he and Benny are sharing tonight. "I was hoping we could make it through this trip without any regression, but it's getting worse."

"I—I was afraid it might be something like that. This must be devastating for you."

He breaks a piece of the stick he's been using as a stoker, then throws it into the fire. "This was a bad idea. This trip. It's better for people with dementia to stay in a familiar place."

I wait for him to go on. When he doesn't, I chance sharing my opinion. "That Chevy is a familiar place to her. Besides, she seems to be enjoying it."

"Yeah, maybe." He sighs deeply. "When we get back to LA, Roland wants to move her into a memory care facility. I believed I could take care of her. That's why the incident at the bridge rocked me so hard. I realized my care may not be enough."

"Have you discussed this with her?"

"Only a bit. It scares her, the thought of being locked up in a place like that. She won't say why. You'd think Paul would've been the one afraid of being locked up, after Korea, but it's Benny that's frightened by it."

I pin the blanket around me under my chin. "She's so excited about your burgeoning career as a documentarian. Maybe you could explain that you could pursue that wholeheartedly if you don't have to be her full-time caregiver?"

"I doubt it. Fear aside, she'd be heartbroken to leave the home she and Paul have lived in since 1961. And quality senior care is expensive. For a high-quality private room in a facility equipped to help Alzheimer's patients in Southern California, it will cost almost seventeen thousand a month."

I drop the blanket. "That's crazy! Is a live-in nurse an option?"

"Maybe," he says. "If this documentary does decently well, we may be able to do that and keep the house for a while. That's a big if."

"Well, I know investors, and they wouldn't put their money into a project they think is a dud. All you have to do is create the brilliant documentary they're expecting and everything will be fine. No pressure though."

I expect him to smile. Instead, he squeezes his eyes closed and exhales forcefully. I don't know why, but I expect the fire to extinguish with the heaviness of his breath. It doesn't, of course, but he still seems far away. I want, perhaps need, him to come back before I can head back to my room for the night.

"I bet high-quality memory care facilities are cheaper in Ohio," I say.

That brings his smile back, and I'm satisfied.

Chapter *13*

I arise to the melody of birdsong outside my window. For years as I toiled in the financial realm, I awakened to a 5:00 a.m. alarm for a Peloton workout, quick breakfast, and early start ahead of the market's opening bell. Admittedly, it is strange to allow my body to dictate my waking rhythm, but not unwelcome. It also gives Bridger time to film during the sunrise hour. My custom over these last few days on the road has been to start my day with a long, hot shower, apply my makeup, dry then straighten my hair, and get dressed. This morning, I open the door to welcome in the cleansing September air and unencumbered sunlight.

Instead, I find myself facing a familiar form performing a tree pose near the vineyard line. After several seconds, he shifts his body into what I believe is a warrior stance, and the movement allows me to see Benny's small frame behind him, molded into a modified version of the same pose.

The sight gives my heart a squeeze. When Bridger notices me, he waves me over. I hesitate, knowing I'm not exactly present-able in my flannel pajamas and unbrushed hair and teeth. Yet, for some reason, I don't care as much as I once would have. I glance at my heels, resting neatly by my suitcase, and forgo even them. Something I regret moments later when the gravel digs into the soles of my bare feet.

Bridger and Benny pause their yoga workout to welcome me.

"Oh, honey, you should at least put on some house shoes so you don't hurt yourself," Benny says, watching me walk gingerly toward them.

"I don't have any."

"Of course you don't," Bridger says with a laugh. "Even your pajamas are formal attire. You love pantsuits more than I first suspected."

Benny swats Bridger's stomach. "Don't listen to him, dear. You look fetching."

"Thank you, Benny." I glare at Bridger, but grin nevertheless.

"What a beautiful morning."

"Fetching, I'd say," Bridger teases, sneaking glances at both Benny and me. "Want to join us?"

"I'm not much of a yoga person."

"Neither was I before I quit alcohol and drugs. This helps me focus on my overall health physically, emotionally, mentally, and spiritually."

"Spiritually?" I ask.

"It's good for meditation or, for me, prayer. It helps me see that there are some things I can control, like my core and my limbs, and other things I can't—those are in God's hands."

Benny clears her throat. "And Bridge is a good teacher, Jade. Look at me."

I don't have a chance to say no. Suddenly, my body is getting molded into what Bridger calls a chair pose. With bent knees, my hips hover above an imaginary seat.

"Keep your weight on your heels." Bridger stands in front of me, takes my hands, and gently lifts my arms overhead, straight in line with my ears. "Pull your core in tight but keep breathing."

I lock eyes with him. There's something new in the way he looks at me, and the warmth of it has a melting effect on my limbs.

"Why are your arms like jelly? Force them to stay straight, just like you do to your hair."

I roll my eyes but still listen. He moves next to me and places steady hands on either side of my rib cage. My eyelids flutter closed without permission. It's been over a year since I allowed anyone this close to me. I've missed affection, and I can feel a craving building in the deepest part of my chest.

Voices rise out of the morning. Bridger's hands release me, and I nearly tip over.

"Tim! Sandy! Good to see you again," he says as I right myself, feeling silly in my pajamas.

"Hey," Tim responds, walking up to shake Bridger's hand. "Are you all having a good trip?"

Bridger spreads his arms wide. "It's been prodigious, man. How's it been for you?"

The couple relays their favorite experiences so far, then their faces sour. "We had an unfortunate incident with some other travelers taking 66 west. We'd much rather cross paths with you all instead of them."

"What kind of incident?" Bridger asks.

Tim takes Sandy's hand. "Two men in a white van, riding our tail, honking, and yelling obscenities out their window for a good ten minutes or so."

"We eventually had to call the police because they wouldn't leave us alone," Sandy says. "Of course, they fled once they saw us on the phone. The police said they were probably a couple hooligans with nothing better to do than taunt travelers."

"Except they had New Mexico plates," Tim says. "We're a bit worried we'll run into them again. I don't know why we thought Route 66 would be different than other places. There are rotten apples everywhere."

"Yeah, we've known a few," Bridger says without elaborating, thank goodness.

"True. I've been debating whether to say this ever since we

spoke outside the Polk-a-Dot," Sandy professes, turning to Benny. "Mrs. Alderidge, we're beyond sorry for what has happened to you. It's a real shame what greed can lead people to do."

I wrap my arms around myself and step back. Only Bridger catches me with an arm around my shoulder. He gently urges me back to his side, back into the circle of good, rather than the otherhood of bad.

"Thank you, dear," Benny says. "I'm fine. No need to worry about me. I have family to love me and faith to sustain me. That's all I need."

"Have they been able to recover any more of the money?" Tim asks.

"Some of it. It gets split between all the families, but we're hopeful," Bridger explains. "Aren't we, Benny?"

"Well," she says, her gaze flickering past mine, "I can't take it with me to heaven. As long as my family has what they need, I'm content."

After a few more pleasantries, Tim and Sandy say goodbye, and Benny excuses herself to freshen up in her room.

"Thank you for that," I say. "Just so you know, I've done everything I can to help the court find the lost money. I told them the names of every investor who profited from the scheme, every asset Gregory and Walter owned, every bank account . . ."

"We know that," Bridger assures me.

"What about Roland?"

Bridger lifts his face to the sun and rakes both hands through his hair. "Roland is . . . Don't listen to Roland. He likes to feel in control. When he has the opportunity to give a soundbite, he feels like he has control. Personally, I admire your integrity. I can't imagine how hard it was to turn in your own fiancé."

I shrug my shoulders. "There has been a lot of hard. But the decision to turn him in was not that hard. When I discovered the extent of his crimes and who his victims were . . . When I think back on how he changed during our relationship and how he treated people—even how he treated you on the street that day, I realize he was not the man I thought he was. I don't love that man."

"Good. Otherwise, I might question your sanity."

I gesture to my room. "I should finish getting ready so we can hit the road." I take my first slow step onto the gravel but am quickly swept up into Bridger's arms.

"What are you doing?"

"Being the greatest hero your feet have ever seen."

"Is there any point in me fighting you?"

He pauses. "I hope you won't. You deserve to have someone care for you."

And I don't fight him.

An hour later, we leave the Wagon Wheel Motel behind in our trusty Bel Air. Any tension from the first portion of this trip eases with each mile we drive through the Ozarks. Rolling hills, smooth pavement, and sunny skies make it easy to pretend I'm living a different, easy life where the soundtrack is provided by Elvis, Doris Day, and Fats Domino. Other than the tunes, it's quiet in the car, although I sense a certain sadness coming from Benny in the passenger seat.

Nothing cracks her smile, not even giant landmarks like the rocking chair in Fanning, the dripping faucet and big hillbilly in Rolla, Waynesville's frog, or Buckhorn's bowling pin. It doesn't help when I miss a few turns trying to follow the route through the busy streets of Springfield, Missouri, and have to pull over to consult the map. Benny removes her glasses, looks at me with confused disgust, and tries to open her car door. Bridger responds quickly and explains who I am and where we are.

"I need to get home," she says with concern tipping her features. "Paul has an appointment today. I need to help him get ready."

Bridger taps my shoulder and motions for me to switch places with him. Careful of the traffic around us, I step out and take his place in the back seat. Bridger sits behind the wheel and takes Benny's hand in his. "Paul doesn't have an appointment today."

"He does. I wrote it down on the calendar. November 4. Two o'clock."

"Benny, today is September 12, and it's already 2:45. The appointment isn't today."

She looks through the windshield. "Where's Paul? Where is he, Bridger? I miss my Paul."

"I know you do, Benny." Bridger's voice breaks, and his eyes glisten.

Although I'm the outsider here, my heart aches for the mother and son seated in front of me, especially with Bridger's lips moving but unable to find the words to answer her. I place my hand gently on his shoulder and sweep my thumb back and forth in a caress so light he might not even feel it beneath the fabric of his T-shirt. But I can't do nothing.

Benny shifts in her seat and notices me for the first time.

"Who's this?"

"This is Jade. She's helping us with the drive."

"For goodness' sake, Bridger, I thought you stopped bringing girls home."

I press my lips into a tight line and try not to think about how cute Bridger looks when he blushes. *Not the time, Jade.*

"This one's different. You'll like her."

"Doesn't matter if I like her. Do you like her?" Benny attempts to whisper the question, but I hear her loud and clear. I give a light pinch to Bridger's neck. A warning to let him know I'm listening.

"Don't tell her this, but I like her very much. She has a heart like Paul's."

Warmth blankets me, and I can't blame the sun. To be compared in any way to the benevolent, silver-haired man who welcomed me into his home with a kiss on the cheek? The one who refused to discuss money matters until I had something to eat and drink and all my other needs were prayed over? I've never received a better compliment.

Benny looks me over. "Why is she dressed like a lawyer?"

"Because even though she has a good heart, there's something seriously wrong with the rest of her."

I pinch harder, then let go, settling back into the bench seat. Bridger explains to Benny again where we're headed and that he needs to put up the convertible top so he can see well enough to give me a break from driving. She nods her understanding and puts her glasses back on. Crisis averted, I relax and let my eyes roam the back seat where Bridger has some of his recording equipment. When he pulls back out onto the road, a spiral notebook slides off the seat. I place it in his laptop bag but not before I notice the writing on the top of the page:

Father in jail. Rough childhood. Cut off communication with mother.

Why has Bridger been keeping notes about me? I meet his gaze in the rearview mirror. I've been honest with him. Has he been honest with me?

Chapter 14

2003
Jade

I held tight to Daddy's hand as we walked through the junkyard. The jagged, rusted metal of scrapped cars was everywhere. I'd almost scraped my hand when we first got here, and the man in the building yelled at me to be careful. I wanted to stay in the truck, but that was why we came here in the first place. Daddy said the pickup broke down and we needed a new car to finish our trip.

Everything felt wrong though. The truck seemed to be running good. Daddy had it since I was a baby. He loved that truck probably more than he loved me. He saw that truck every day. I only got to see him two days a month. So why did he want to get a new one?

The farther we walked, the more cars we saw that weren't skeletons. They still weren't nice like the new Saturn Hank bought Mom.

"Do you see any that you like?" Daddy asked me.

I shielded my eyes from the sun as I looked over each one. My eyes landed on a bright blue one with four doors. "That one."

"You've got good taste, but we need a car that won't draw as much attention."

"Huh? I don't get it."

"I don't want any speeding tickets," he explained. He pointed ahead to an ugly tan car. "Looks like a late-80s Civic. After-market tinted windows. Needs new tires. Bumper's hanging on by an actual thread." He plucked at the rope tying the bumper to the frame. "As long as it runs, this one might be the ticket."

I scrunched my nose. It was a boring, ugly grandpa car that looked like every other boring, ugly grandpa car on the road. I'd be so embarrassed to ride in this at home. But at least with this one no one could see me in the back seat.

After Daddy argued with the man in the office, we moved on down the road in our new wheels.

~

1956
Benny

"I see another motel up ahead." I pressed forward in the passenger seat and silently prayed this would be our ticket to a good night's sleep. I'd been able to nap in the car, but Paul was fighting to keep his eyes open. Hope diminished, though, when the fourth No Vacancy sign of the night appeared. "Well, I'll be. What do we do now?" I asked.

Paul rubbed the back of his neck. "I don't think I can keep going. Especially not to Tulsa."

"We aren't the only ones." Quite a few cars had pulled over to the side of the road. I pressed down on the bench seat. "If you can sleep in the car, I can."

He shook his head. "No, I—"

"Paul Wayne Alderidge, don't treat me like a doll."

Ten minutes later, with the Chevy safely tucked away in a

111

pocket of trees, I molded my body to the front seat and, using Paul's jacket as a blanket, tried to find sleep.

The wind came in angry fits, each gust whipping the tree branches above us into a fury. I tried to focus on the soft, steady snore resonating from the back seat. Perhaps his time in the military and the POW camp ensured he could sleep anywhere, even when a critter scampered about outside, squeaking and scratching. The slow rumble of a car—no, a truck—grew louder and louder. By the time it overtook us, I could feel the vibrations in the seat beneath me. Though I wrapped Paul's jacket around me tighter, I still felt the panic rising in my chest. I tried to focus on the moonlight filtering through the trees and dancing across the windshield this way and that.

Until a large shadow thumped itself against the hood, hissing and skittering with its claws clacking over the metal. I shrieked and scrambled over the seat, landing in the back seat with a thwack. "Oomph."

"Benny? What are you doing on the floor?"

"I-I got scared."

Paul helped me up, making room for me next to him on the seat. "You don't have to be scared. I'm here. I'll protect you."

I took that as an invitation to snuggle up to his side—something he didn't seem to mind since he put his arms around me and held me close. Matching my breath to his, I felt my fears calm with every rise and fall of his chest. "Paul, what frightens you?"

The wind howled again and again before he finally answered. "Not being there when someone needs me." Paul leaned us forward to grab his jacket off the floor. Settling back, he spread the leather over my curled-up body.

"Someone?" I melted into him, aching to hear one answer only.

He didn't say anything, but he pressed a kiss onto my crown. I savored his affection in every way. Surely, he felt the same.

He had to. "Paul, when you were being held, did you receive any of my letters?"

His chest stilled. "Eight."

Eight? A small percentage of the amount I'd sent. "You never wrote me back."

"I didn't have anything good to say. And you were always so hopeful I'd be released soon, and I'd come back home the same person I'd always been."

"No, Paul." I lifted my chin so I could see at least a glimmer of his eyes in the dark. "I wasn't naive enough to believe anyone could go through war and be unchanged. But my love for you . . . I wanted you to know that wouldn't change." It was true too. I'd loved my brother's best friend for as long as I could remember, although I doubted he would ever see me as anything more than a foolish little girl.

"When I left for the front, you were so young. I loved the innocence you showed in your letters. The way you told me what plants were in bloom around town, what the popular movies were, and how boring your classes were. It reminded me what we were fighting for. For others to live without fear. Then one day you had graduated from school. You sent me a picture, and you'd grown up so pretty."

My breath caught, but the shadowy lines of his face made him look solemn.

My fingertips find the top button of his shirt, and I trace the perimeter of it. "What frightened you then?"

"To be honest?" He breathed the words into my hair. "That I'd never get to do this."

Chapter 15

Present Day
Jade

"That night as we slept, something changed," Benny says. "Like our hearts had found a new rhythm, beating in harmony with each other. I know it's an old-fashioned notion, but he became mine and I became his, even though so little had been said. It was one of those times in life when words weren't needed."

My vision clears when the tears finally drop to the waiting napkin I hold against my cheek. I never felt that way about Gregory or any guy before him. In fact, the only time I felt I belonged to anyone, I was a child. And being independent one hundred percent of the time has its negatives.

The ache stretching my heart overwhelms me as I sit at the back table of Waylan's Ku-Ku Burger, the route's cuckoo clock–themed restaurant. My grilled chicken breast has grown cold as I listened to more of Benny and Paul's love story. And for the millionth time, I'm reminded how Gregory preyed on them, using their trust in me against them. It burns me up inside. If only I paid attention to all the signs that Gregory wasn't the honorable guy I thought he was . . .

114

Father in jail. Rough childhood. Cut off communication with mother. For two days Bridger's notes about my life have echoed in my mind. As much as I've tried to rationalize his need for taking such notes, it's been chipping away at me. *Am I being deceived again?*

While Benny continues with her story and Bridger films, I sneak away. Outside by the car, I tear off my blazer and place it on the hooded headlight. It slips to the pavement, but I don't care. I place my hands on my head and gulp for breath. Yet the stagnant Oklahoma air evades me.

The more I strain to breathe, the more my throat constricts. My pacing does nothing to relieve my growing concern, especially when it leads me directly into Bridger's chest.

"Hey, hey, hey," he says with concern streaking his face. He places his camera on the trunk of the Chevy and settles his hands just above my elbows with enough tenderness to make me doubt my reality all over again. "Jade, it's okay."

"No, it's not."

"Talk to me. What's not okay?"

"You, Bridger. You're lying to me."

He takes two steps back, crosses his arms over his stomach, and searches the ground. "Jade——"

"You gave that whole speech about honesty being important to you. You told me to look you in the eye and you asked me if I knew about that Ponzi scheme." The tightness of my throat makes talking difficult, but I press on. "And when I said no, you said you believed me. But you lied. You don't believe me."

Bridger's usual confidence gives way to confusion as he works his jaw back and forth. "I don't understand where this is coming from. I do believe you."

"Then why are you fact-checking me? I saw what you wrote in your notebook. Father in jail. Rough childhood. Cut off communication with mother. Why would I lie about any of that?"

Realization seems to smack Bridger square on the forehead. He drops his arms and squeezes his eyes closed.

I feel abandoned . . . again. A hum steadily grows louder, until the roar overtakes all other sound and the edges of my vision blurs. No. I'm not abandoned. God has not abandoned me. Everyone else might, but he won't. And he knows I wouldn't lie. Not after what happened the last time. I learned my lesson. Dad made sure of it.

Finally, Bridger opens his eyes, his expression warped with sorrow. "Those notes . . . weren't for fact-checking. I believe everything you've told me."

I throw my hands up. "Then what were they for?"

"My memory isn't so good sometimes. I jotted those things down . . . so I wouldn't make another insensitive joke like I did at Ted Drewes. I don't want to hurt you." His brows knit tight, perhaps painfully so. "I don't want to hurt you."

My stomach sinks. "Oh."

Bridger picks up my discarded jacket, shakes it, and neatly folds it. He holds it out to me.

I step forward to accept it, placing my hand on his and holding still. "I'm sorry. I shouldn't have made that assumption. I guess I've developed some trust issues."

"You don't have to apologize. With what I know about your ex-fiancé, and what you've told me about your mom, it's understandable."

I wait for his eyes to find mine. When they do, I have to steady myself against the Chevy. "You should probably get back inside to check on Benny."

Bridger clears his throat. "You're probably right. She's going to eat my chili dog. Are you coming back in?"

"I don't think so. I'll wait out here until you guys are done."

He reclaims his camera. "Okay, then. But don't you start worrying again. I have plans for us tonight, and there's no room for that nonsense."

~

"What in the world is a spook light?" I ask.

"We shall see, won't we?" Bridger says in his Vincent Price voice. He glances down at the paper he found at Waylan Ku-Ku's, using his phone's flashlight to see in the darkness. "Take this next turn."

I ease the Chevy onto another country road. "Now what?"

"I think this is it. Pull the car over and cut the engine."

"What do you think about this, Benny?"

Benny chuckles. "I think this is the exact kind of silliness Bridger has been bringing to my life for the last sixteen years."

"Benny, are you getting out to search for the spook light with us?" I ask.

She shakes her head. "You two have fun. I'll be in here planning your funerals."

Bridger leads the way out of the car. The clouded sky provides zero light so the only break in darkness is the red dots on a far-off cell tower. I stumble. I step in a hole and nearly fall, but I catch myself on Bridger's arm.

"You good?" he asks.

"I'm good. I just rolled my ankle a bit."

Instantly, he drops to the ground. His warm hands envelop my foot, and I steady myself with a hand on his shoulder. "Did you sprain it?"

"No. I'm fine. Really. Never thought I'd be so happy to have cankles."

Bridger scoffs. "Better to have cankles than wooden pegs, I always say."

I laugh. Then, on their own accord, my thumb and forefinger gentle a lock of his hair between them.

He stills, and I clasp my hands in front of me. After several seconds, he stands, takes my right hand, and weaves his fingers through mine. "I should probably hold on to you in case there are any more potholes. I'll need you to catch me if I fall."

"I'll do my best."

Together, we move farther down the road, eventually coming to a stop amid the eerie silence. Even the insects decline to sing their serenade.

"What do we do now?" I whisper.

"We wait for the spook light to appear."

I study the darkness. "What is it exactly? Do we need to hide like it's the great pumpkin, Charlie Brown?"

"No one knows exactly. It could be a ghost or an alien."

I glance up at the clouds. "I don't believe in ghosts or aliens though."

"Neither do I, which makes this even weirder."

I prop my free hand on my hip and wait. "Is this a thing people actually do?"

"Shh! You'll scare it away."

Some kind of animal yips in the distance, and I wrap myself around Bridger's arm.

"Scaredy-cat," he says. Then something shakes the bushes nearby. Bridger freaks and runs back to the car, leaving me alone.

I know I should run too, but my legs freeze like I'm a ditzy starlet in a terrible horror movie. Then I see it. A pinpoint of white light in the distance, hovering in the air closer, closer, closer. I open my mouth to scream, but nothing comes out. So I snap. Only God knows why, but I snap my fingers to get Bridger's attention. But the light disappears. I rush back to the Chevy.

"Did you see it?"

Where he stands by the passenger door, the dashboard lights show his grin. "It's a joke, Jade. There is no spook light."

"No, there is! Come here." I take hold of his hands and, walking backwards, lead him to the approximate spot where I'd been standing. After releasing him, I stand at his side and practically climb up his arm to get as close to his eyeline as possible. I point ahead. "Watch right there."

I feel breath on my cheek. "You're not looking." I step in front of him and square my shoulders to the space where the light had been. "Concentrate out there."

I feel Bridger dismiss the space between us. His hands graze my waist. The tender touch does something to me. We're quiet. So quiet.

All I can think about is how great it would feel to have him surround me with his arms. And what if I dared to turn around? What if he lowered his face to mine and kissed me? Would it be simple and uneventful like Gregory's kisses? Or would I feel it down to my toes? I imagine it would be the latter since just the thought has my skin tingling.

"It's there!" Bridger says.

"It's been there all along," I say softly, still caught up in my daydream.

"What?" he asks.

"What?" I play dumb.

Bridger snickers. "I don't know what you're referring to but I'm talking about the spook light. See it?"

Again, a small light follows the same pattern as before, hovering a bit, moving close, then disappearing. Then another two lights, one after the other, take the same path. I squint. "Wait. That's old Route 66, isn't it? Those are just cars driving the same road we were just on. And you had me believing it was some otherworldly phenomenon." I swat his shoulder.

"How can you be sure? Maybe that's exactly what the spook light wants you to believe so it can sneak up on you and take you off into the night." He lifts me off my feet and carries me on a trot down the road. Then he spins me, and I hold tight to his neck.

"Are you two done with this hullabaloo yet?" I hear Benny call from the direction of the car.

I'm laughing. When had I started laughing? Whenever it was, I won't complain. It's the best I've felt in over a year.

Chapter 16

2003
Jade

"What's that car?" Daddy asked, pointing to the yellow sports car that had just sped past us in the other lane before cutting in front of our slowpoke car. Daddy must have really wanted no tickets because normally he drove much faster than this.

"Um, Corvette?" I guessed.

"No, that's a Pontiac Firebird Trans Am."

"I'm never gonna get these right." I kicked the seat in front of me. Maybe if I learned the car names, Daddy would take me to races and car shows more. I wouldn't have to wait for a big trip to see him.

"It's got a standard 310-horsepower, 5.7-liter V8 engine. That one has screaming chicken graphics on it because it's a special edition. Yep, that one will be worth money one day if they take care of it because 2002 was the last year they made that car."

"So?"

"What do you mean so? The Pontiac Firebird is a classic. It was first made in 1967. My first car was a 1972. Boy, she was pretty. It turned some heads, including your mother's."

"You called it a she, silly."

"Some folks do that—refer to a car or a boat as a she."

I scrunched up my face and flicked the headrest in front of me. "Not this car. This car is a stinky boy that picks his nose."

"Fair enough. But he's brought us this far. We oughta be thanking him."

I watched the Pontiac until she was just a dot on the road. There wasn't much else to look at wherever we were now. Not even those Burma-Shave signs that made Daddy laugh. "Can we get a new car when we get there?"

"That's a good idea, Baby Jade. There's a garage where we're heading, right on this same road. I'll be helping people fix up their cars when they get into trouble on their trip. Maybe one of them will want to trade or sell."

"Is that why you want me to learn about all the cars? So I can be your special helper?"

"You know it." He winked at me in the rearview mirror.

We continued on Route 66, passing a green car getting gas. I recognized the front right away. "That's a Jeep!" I yelled.

"Right! That's my girl!"

Proud of myself for finally getting one correct, I settled into my seat. I would be the best helper in the whole world. Daddy would never want me to go back home to Mom and Hank.

Chapter 17

1956
Benny

We tread the sidewalk away from Tulsa's Spanish Mission–style Casa Loma Hotel where we'd checked in for the night. If the rich and savory smell of seared meat hadn't already beckoned us toward Barker's BBQ, a red neon sign would have. With only a short distance to walk, I took the opportunity to wrap my hand around the crook of Paul's arm. I'd hold his hand, but his knuckles were still tender to the touch from the fight at the drive-in two days ago. "I've never had true barbecue. Have you?"

"I have. But I'd like to try brisket if they have it. I've heard it's tops."

"Whatever they've cooked up, it smells fantastic."

Paul opened the door for me, and I was dazzled by a brass band playing a bright and jubilant tune. The melody made my shoulders rock and my toe tap. At home, Momma and Daddy only played gospel records. I grew still though as something became quite obvious.

"Paul," I whispered, "we're the only Whites in here."

He glanced around. "And?"

123

One of the diners, a teenage boy, caught sight of me. He said something to his friend, and they both stared us down. When the friend's attention drifted down to my purse, I realized how tightly I was holding on to it, and shame pricked at my heart.

"And nothing."

By the jukebox, a woman with Dorothy Dandridge's tousled Italian cut stepped in front of her grade-school daughter as if to shield her. From who? It couldn't be from us. Paul and I could never have been seen as threatening. Or were we?

"Maybe we should go somewhere else."

He imparted a strange look. "Why?"

"Are we even allowed to eat here? They don't—"

"Come on in, young love," a woman called from behind a counter. "Sit anywhere you like."

Paul led me to a table for two next to the dance floor. He didn't seem bothered by all the disapproving stares coming our way. But I was, especially as the whispers gained volume.

"Who let them in?"

"We've got Pat and Shirley Boone making themselves right at home here."

"Watch them. Might be fixing to burn the place down."

The tension in my neck grew painful and with one hand I kneaded the muscle. "I don't think we belong in here."

"Benny, take a breath," Paul said. "I didn't see a sign telling Whites to eat somewhere else. Besides, that woman welcomed us in."

"I know, but I'm not used to this. Mama always told me they don't want to be around us at restaurants or stores or—"

"Can you blame them?" Paul averted his eyes from me.

I shrank into my chair, feeling as tall as a hoptoad—something else Mama used to say.

Paul took my hand. "I'm sorry. I shouldn't have interrupted. I get cross on the subject of Jim Crow, segregation, designated seats . . . Like what's happening down in Montgomery. It shouldn't take a bus boycott or, or photos of a fourteen-year-old boy in a casket to see change." He forced a swallow. "In Korea, we all bled red no matter what color our skin was."

I nodded, too nervous to say anything else.

A man sporting a three-button suit jacket, a crisp blue shirt, and high-waisted trousers neared, towering over Paul. "You all lost?"

"No, sir," Paul said. "We're traveling through Tulsa, and the smell of barbecue drew us in."

"The smell of barbecue. Is that right?" With a tilt of his head, the man eyed Paul, then me, and then Paul again. "White folk don't always have the best intentions at establishments like this."

I scooted my chair back.

Paul's handhold held strong though. "We don't want trouble," he said. "Only brisket."

The woman who'd first welcomed us in put a hand on the man's shoulder. "Sam, I know you aren't trying to scare off my customers." She playfully swung a dish towel like a pinwheel. "Look. You've got Blondie there scared to death. Now, go on back to your table and I'll bring you another slice of pie."

After a small bow directed toward the hospitable woman, the man—Sam—strolled away, stepping in beat with the band's rendition of "Ain't That a Shame." Then she addressed us. "Don't worry about Sam. Tulsa has a history y'all know nothing about. It's kept some people on edge, but you've got just as much right to this grub as anyone." She raised her voice for the last part, and at that, the other diners turned their attention away from us.

"All the food is listed up there on the menu board. When you're ready to order, just holler for me and I'll take care of you. The name's Miriam."

My nerves settle just a little, and soon I was eating the best meal of my life. Beef brisket with macaroni salad and corn pudding with a bottle of Coca-Cola. At one point, a family of four sat at the table nearest us. The mother held a small book with the cover facing me.

The *Negro Travelers' Green Book*, my nosy self read. I gave Paul a curious look and nodded toward the other table. He shrugged. "I'm stumped."

Miriam, who had been keeping one eye on us throughout our meal, stopped at our table with a stack of dirty plates in her hands. "The Green Book. Our roads aren't safe for every traveler. That's a list of places that cater to folks other places might turn away."

"Like what?" I asked.

"Restaurants, service stations, and motor lodges." Miriam asked. "They should give a list of sundown towns too." She left our table before I could ask more.

Paul placed his silverware on his plate and pushed it away, his food only half eaten. "Sometimes I wonder why I fought for a country that allows towns to kick out people who don't look like George Reeves or Harriet Nelson."

"Ma'am?" the mother next to us said to Miriam. Her little girl couldn't be more than four, and she was a blink away from falling asleep. "We don't see any lodging around here."

"You won't. Not in this part of town. You'll want to head up to Greenwood. I recommend Mr. and Mrs. Small's on Archer Street. And if they're booked up, you can try Del Rio or the Y.W.C.A."

Once their conversation ended, I leaned close to Paul's ear. "Not the Casa Loma? It's not right that we can stay there but they can't. They have children."

"No, it's not right," Paul said. "But it's how it is." I huffed and crossed my arms. "It has to change." Paul stared at me, blinking sparingly so I could swim in those aqua blues. The corners of his lips turned slowly up. "What? Why are you looking at me that way?" I asked.

"I admire you."

Heat climbed my neck, and I pulled a finger curl across my throat to hopefully hide my flush. "I admire you too."

The band began to play "Only You" by The Platters, then called a few couples to the dance floor.

"Hey, Paul, how long has it been since you've danced?"

He scratched his cheek. "The school prom, I guess."

"That's far too long. Even one year without dancing is too long." I stood and held my hand out to him. I expected him to resist the invitation, but to my pleasure, he didn't. In fact, he accepted my hand, then escorted me onto the dance floor. I fell so naturally into his arms, and as the lyrics voiced the feelings we wouldn't admit to having, we swayed back and forth until finally I rested my head against his chest.

"Benny, we shouldn't be doing this," Paul said in a crackly voice. "I'm not good for you."

"Phooey." I tipped my chin up to look him in the eye. "That's not true. You, of all people, deserve to be happy. You deserve to be loved." I released his hand and cupped my palm around the back of his neck, slipping my fingers through his short hair.

With my caress, his eyes fluttered closed, and he dipped his head down to me, touching his forehead to mine. He loved me. I was sure of it, but I couldn't understand why he couldn't admit it.

"Do you want to kiss me?" I asked.

"More than anything."

"Then why don't you?"

He peered down at me, but while I was smiling, he looked pained. Like being around me hurt him. Is that what I was doing to him? Hurting him?

A shattering of glass behind me led to screams. Paul put himself between me and the front of the restaurant. I peeked around him and saw a brick in the middle of the tile. Outside, red taillights shone bright. A slurry of racist curses accompanied the squealing of tires. A couple men, led by Sam, hopped through the broken windowpane to chase down the vandals. Paul moved to follow them.

"Paul, no!"

He turned back to me, and the anger in his eyes scared me. "I can't do nothing. Stay here." Then he was gone. The children at the table neighboring ours cried. Some men and women in the joint hollered in anger while others remained seated or standing in place with weary expressions on their faces. Totally helpless, I stood in the middle of the dance floor, hugging myself as the other customers began cleaning up the mess. Miriam and a tall man in a well-worn apron moved between groups of patrons.

When she got to me, the lump in my throat released as a sob. "We're all right. Ain't nothing but a piece of glass. What about you? Are you okay?" She was worried about me? Maybe that was because I was the only person in Barker's BBQ that was truly shocked by the incident.

"Has anyone called the police?" I asked while swiping tears off my cheeks.

"What good would it do? Let's get you a seat before you take a fall." Miriam guided me to a chair out of the way, then went to help other customers.

It didn't take long before a large community had gathered to comfort the family who owned the place. Paul had yet to return so I sat alone, despite an invitation to join the group in prayer. A local preacher took the helm, asking the Lord for protection against those who meant harm and forgiveness for them for they'd been cursed with evil—the power of which they didn't understand. Was this kind of thing common everywhere and I just hadn't seen it?

An eternity later, Paul returned, trailing the other men through the door this time since people had already begun nailing plywood to cover the window. Were those men soldiers like him? Responding to threats with action? Or were they normal men trying to protect their family and friends?

Sam apologized to the man in the apron that they weren't able to catch the culprits, then shook Paul's hand. Afterward, Paul searched the room. The moment his eyes settled on me, he jogged over, lifted me from the chair, and embraced me for a long, long time, until the band picked their instruments up once again and began playing a faster tune than before——"Long Tall Sally" by Little Richard. When the floor filled up with dozens of folks dancing and singing, Paul and I slid the money for our food under a glass at our table and took our leave.

~

Present Day
Jade

Benny's gaze moves across the black-and-white photos on the wall at Greenwood Rising, the history center that celebrates Black Wall Street and memorializes the victims of the 1921 Tulsa Race Massacre. "Yes," she says. "A very dark history." After a heavy sigh, she turns to Bridger, and he folds her into his arms.

"Do you need to sit down?" he asks above her head.

"Maybe for a few minutes."

I drift toward a display of the businesses that existed before the arsonists' destruction. Knighten's Filling Station, Sister's Grocery, Mrs. Turner's Chili Parlor, and nearly three hundred more. My head begins to fog as I read over each. Then I see Benny reach into her purse and pull out a couple bills. She stands, slowly walks over to a box for donations, then places the cash into the slot. Cause number three, I assume. But instead of ten million, the Greenwood Rising foundation gets only what Benny has in her purse.

I sink my teeth into my bottom lip until it hurts.

"You good?" Bridger sidles up to me. He left his cameras in the trunk of the car for this slight detour. This isn't our story to tell, we realized. But that didn't stop us from wanting to pay our respects to the victims and learn how to best uplift the right storytellers.

I bristle. "Uh, I don't think my well-being matters when we're standing in this place."

Bridger shakes his head. "It does matter. I get it. You weren't one of the victims then and you aren't the most likely person to face racial violence now. But, Jade, if you weren't upset by what happened here, I'd question your humanity. So . . . you good?"

"I'm good. My heart just hurts." The massacre itself is unimaginable. The fact that it was hidden for nearly a century is beyond words. No wonder Benny and Paul were seen as a threat at the Black-owned restaurant in 1956.

"I feel that." He's quiet for several minutes as he, too, reads over the business names. "I wonder if something like this ever happened to my people—the Samoans. I should know that. I hate that I don't know my ancestors' history."

"Seems like a knowable topic. What's keeping you from researching it?"

He glances back at Benny, now perusing a brochure on one of Greenwood Rising's partner foundations.

I blow out a breath as our conversation in Pontiac comes back to me. "You don't want to seem ungrateful. Right."

"Not after she welcomed me into her family."

The feeling of being welcomed is more than I ever felt in my family. Still, something doesn't sit right with me. "She wanted to take you back to Samoa to see your family before you learned about the tsunami. You need to talk to her about exploring your birth culture."

"Like I said before, I won't risk hurting her. She's all I have left in this world." Bridger wipes his forehead with the back of his hand. "It's the same reason I never shared what it was like to be a kid with brown skin at the richest school in Los Angeles. Even when I'd get into fights with guys for what they'd call me and she'd ask why, I would lie." He eyed Benny. "I didn't want to break her heart with those stories. I still don't."

Despite his definitive words, I see the grief in his eyes. "Bridger, she's not oblivious. She knows what our world is like. She lived through the Jim Crow era, the civil rights movement, the LA riots. You wouldn't be telling her something she doesn't know." I take his hand between both of mine. "I think you should talk to her. You owe it to her, and you owe it to yourself."

Chapter *18*

1956
Benny

At the Esso filling station, I pressed my forehead to the Chevy's window and peered up at the falling rain. "I'm going to see if they have a phone," I told Paul. "I promised I'd call Mom once from every state."

"Better take this." Paul reached into the back seat for his jacket. "Don't want your hair to get wet."

"Ever a gentleman." After opening the door, I spread the jacket above me and began singing the title song from *Oklahoma!*—I'd seen that movie at the Rialto the year before—stopping short as I bumped into the attendant.

"I'm terribly sorry," I said. "Fill 'er up. Also, do you have a telephone?"

The young man adjusted his cap. "Not inside. There's a telephone booth over yonder. Be careful crossing the road."

I continued my song and skipped past puddles, ignoring the reddish-brown mud spotting my stockings and soaking into my flatties. I skidded to a stop, letting a farm truck pass by before crossing the street. Once inside the roadside booth, I slid the aluminum and glass door shut.

Lifting the receiver, I dialed the operator.

"Yes, I'd like to call Joliet, Illinois, 5-2598." I recited my parents' home number and fished in my purse for the dollar thirty it cost. "I can't find enough change." I hated to call on Paul for help, but I knew he'd have the extra dime I needed.

I opened the door to the booth and waved him over. Almost immediately, he popped up from behind the car and jogged over to me. He paused outside the booth, and I asked him for a dime. While he dug his hand into his pocket, the rain fell harder and in thick droplets. I gripped his T-shirt and tugged him inside with me.

Why he looked so sheepish then, I'd never understand. We'd been closer than that in the past few days, although not in such tight quarters. I couldn't have him stand in the rain. He deposited the dime in the coin slot, and the operator connected the call.

"Hello, Briner residence."

"Josie?" I asked, recognizing my eleven-year-old sister's voice.

"Berenice! Are you in California yet?"

"Not yet. We're in Oklahoma City."

"Guess what. The neighbors got a puppy. And there was an explosion at the brewing company. It blew out the wall and spilled thousands of gallons of beer into the street!"

"Oh my. Was anyone hurt?"

"I don't think so. How's the dreamboat?"

"Heavens to Betsy, Josie!" I pressed the receiver tight to my ear so Paul couldn't hear my sister's words.

Josie laughed. "You love him. We all know it. Even Momma and Daddy."

"You're aggravating. Is Momma home?"

"Berenice and Paul, sitting in a tree——"

"Josie!"

"Fine. I'll get her." Josie continued the silly rhyme, but her voice faded enough for me to relax.

While I felt my three minutes ticking by, Paul raked his fingers through his hair, which had darkened in the rain. Despite his effort to dry his face on his sleeve, droplets slid down his cheek and fell off his jaw and onto my skirt, so close were we.

"Berenice, where are you?" Momma was out of breath.

"Where the lilacs grow green."

"Oklahoma?"

"Mm-hmm. We're making good time."

"Is Paul treating you good?"

I steady my eyes on his. "Yes, Momma. He's treating me really well."

"Good. You know you can always come back home. Find a nice boy to marry. Maybe that could be Paul. With his family's money, imagine the wedding you could have. You could wear Princess Grace's gown. Would that be so terrible?"

Paul looked away. Momma spoke so loud, he surely heard her proposition. "Of course not. It would be lovely, but not at the expense of my dream."

"Can't you have both?"

Slowly, Paul faced me like he might be wondering the answer to that same question. I brushed the slick of moisture off his brow. Either I swayed toward him or he swayed toward me because we were as close as two people could get. "I'm working on it."

The rain pelted the roof of the telephone booth, causing so much noise I could barely hear Momma ask when we'd be in Albuquerque.

"Two days, probably."

"Call me when you get there. And tell Paul I said hello. And promise you'll stay safe."

"I will. Goodbye, Momma."

Paul took the receiver out of my hand and hung it up. Neither of us moved to leave.

"My mother says hello," I said. "She made me promise to stay safe."

He nodded. "We should stay in here until the storm passes, then."

"Yes. We should." I lifted my shoulder in coy fashion. "Any idea what we could do to pass the time?"

His smile fell. "Benny, this isn't a game."

"I never said it was."

"You asked me if I wanted to kiss you. I do. I have ever since I returned home. But in the POW camp, when I didn't know if Louie would survive, I promised him I'd look out for you if he wasn't around."

"Is that why you took the job at the Rialto?"

"Yes."

I shook my head, trying to comprehend this man. "How is that related to kissing me?"

His gaze dropped to my lips as he wet his own. "I'm not a good enough person for you."

My groan joined with the thunder overhead. Even the heavens knew Paul was wrong. "Paul Alderidge, you're the best person I know."

"You don't know me well enough to say that."

Ugh. This boy made me as mad as a child who spilled their candy. "You know what I think is holding you back? You doubt my goodness."

"Never," he said in an offended tone.

"No, you do. You believe that there's something inside of you that I couldn't accept, forgive, desire . . . You doubt my goodness."

My words seemed to cut straight to his heart. He gripped my upper arms, not enough to hurt or feel threatening. Enough to secure me in this moment, in this place, in front of him. "I don't doubt you, Benny. I love you. Everything about you."

Warmth spread through me, and I brushed the tip of my nose against his. "Prove it."

135

Present Day

Jade

Benny takes a sip of her Route 66–branded root beer. "And, as the song goes, then he kissed me."

Bridger lifts his brow. "Like a single kiss or you guys steamed up the glass in the telephone booth?"

I elbow him in the side and hit him with my most incredulous look.

"What? Don't act like you weren't wondering the same thing."

"They aren't my parents." I meet Benny's gaze. "Plus, a lady doesn't kiss and—"

Benny holds up a stern hand. "Bridger, dear, you've never kissed anyone the way Paul kissed me that day."

"I object." Bridger pounded his Stewart's Orange Crème on the table like a gavel. "I'm a great kisser. Have you noticed my lips?"

Yes.

"Overruled," Benny replies. "You've never loved any of the girls you've kissed. When you do, you'll see the difference."

"You never dated anyone other than Paul, so how could you know that to be true?"

Benny narrows her eyes, yet the smile never leaves her face. "Just consider my list of costars through the years. I kissed Clyde Irving, remember? And he has an entire award show named after him. Paul beat them all."

"Okay, I give. I give." Bridger stands.

Pops 66 Soda Ranch in Arcadia has just about every color and flavor of carbonated beverage one can imagine, including a sixty-six-foot-tall neon-lit one outside. The three of us already taste-tested ten different brands of root beer at our table. A small burp escapes Benny, and she quickly covers her mouth.

"Nice one, Benny," Bridger holds out his hand in my direction. "Take a stroll with me? I want to grab some pop for the road, and I need your help."

Cautiously, I accept the hand up. Bridger answers my hesitancy by whispering, "I'm taller than all these shelves. I can keep her in my sight."

"Fair enough." I help Bridger collect our empty bottles and bring them to the recycling bin. Before I toss the one Bridger drank, I thumb the words on the label and send my memories from the summer of 2003 into a tailspin.

"What's up, Jade? You look the way a clogged sink sounds when you plunge it."

"Wow. Do you charm all the ladies this way?"

"What can I say? If you've got it, you've got it."

I assemble a cardboard bottle carrier as we make our way to an aisle with pop bottles on both sides. We stroll along, every now and then choosing a bottle from its shelf and placing it in the holder.

Although Bridger didn't press the issue on what's bothering me, I open my thoughts to him. "The summer I spent with my dad, we drank Stewart's orange and cream sodas every day—the one you had. I can still taste it."

"Oh, man. I wish you'd said something. I wouldn't have chosen that."

"That's silly. You can drink whatever you want. Any sane person would have moved past this long ago."

"Jade, you were kidnapped. That's an entire level of trauma that few people have experienced. I don't expect you to have moved past it. No way."

"You have. In a way, you were kidnapped too."

"I've never used that word for it, but yeah, I was." Bridger's eye twitches. "I haven't gotten over it. Even though I try to keep the emotions in that back pocket of mine, it doesn't stop trauma from working its way into who I am."

I feel tethered to him in this moment. He feels it too. I can see it in the depth of his eyes as he looks at me now. "I never asked," he says. "Where did you spend that summer? Was it in Oklahoma?"

"No. Arizona. A tiny town called Tecoma. Route 66 cuts through it."

"We'll be seeing it? Is there a chance your father's back there?"

I shrug. "I don't know where he is. The prison let me know when he was released but nothing else. And my dad . . ." I shrug. "If he wanted me in his life, he would have reached out. But he hasn't."

Bridger puts an arm around my shoulder and squeezes me tight against him. "I've got you, girl. We'll get through it together." Then he kisses the top of my head—a friendly, not at all romantic kiss. The kind you might plant on a puppy's snout. We finish loading up assorted bottles of pop into the cardboard carrier, then head back toward where Benny is waiting.

Bridger leans near her ear and whispers. I can't be sure, but I think he says, "You're right."

Chapter 19

2003

Jade

We stopped at a tiny grocery store, and I was ready to jump out of the car. For the last hour, I had been building a list in my mind. Lunchable, fruit snacks, Goldfish crackers, Cherry Coke. All stuff Mom never let me have.

"You gotta stay in here, Baby Jade."

I pouted. "Why?"

"Uh, because it will be easier for me to grab what we need."

"But I'm a good helper. I'll be super quiet, and I won't beg," I promised. "Pretty please with a cherry on top?"

Daddy shook his head. Then he grabbed his baseball cap, put it on, and tucked his shaggy, sandy blond hair into it. "Fine. You got me wrapped around your finger. You know that?"

"What's that mean?" I scrunched my nose as I unbuckled my seat belt. Whatever it meant, I was just glad it wasn't the opposite. Daddy's fingers were always stained with grease from the body shop he worked at, and they smelled gross too. I didn't want to be wrapped around them, but I loved him, so I guess he could be wrapped around mine.

Daddy reached to the back seat and booped my nose, and I

imagined the tip of it smudged with black. "It means that I'd do anything in the world for you because I love you."

"But if you love me, why do I always have to go back to Mom's house? I want to stay with you."

"I don't like it either, but it's what the judge said when your mom and me went to court."

"Make him change it." Didn't Mr. Lowell say that courts and judges are there to help people? This didn't seem too helpful.

"I've tried, Baby Jade. Trust me, I've tried. But they won't change it because of those times I went to jail." Now it was Daddy's turn to pout, I guess, because he looked sadder than ever.

"That don't mean nothin'. Going to jail doesn't make you a bad daddy," I sat up as straight as possible. "What's the judge's phone number? I'm going to call him and tell him to change it."

Daddy laughed. "Maybe later. First, we gotta get some food before your tummy goes from growling to biting."

I hopped out of the car, slammed the door, and then skipped to Daddy. I hugged his arm. "Swing me!"

"All right." He curled his arm around my back. "One, two, three!"

I jumped as he swung his arm. As he lifted me up, my empty tummy flipped. But Daddy grunted.

"You're getting too big for this," he said when my feet touched the ground again.

"Noo!"

"Don't worry. You'll always be my little girl."

I held his hand inside the store. When I saw something I wanted, I'd yank and point. Sometimes he got it. Sometimes he said he couldn't afford it today. After a few minutes of looking at toothpaste and shampoo, I got bored.

"Can I get a coloring book?" I whispered, nodding down the aisle.

He didn't look up from the box with the pretty blond girl

on it. He kept reading the back of it, but he nodded a little, so I walked toward the books and magazines. I made sure to avoid the cracks in the tile because if Mom's back broke, she'd probably blame me.

At the shelf holding the coloring books, I flipped through all my choices. Unicorns, baby animals, or cars. I didn't need to think. Daddy would like my car pictures best, so I chose that one. Two sizes of crayons sat right below the coloring books. I wanted the big, sixty-four-pack box, but it was way more expensive than the one with sixteen. Daddy was broke, Mom always said. She also said I was too smart for my own good. Now I was going to be smart for my good daddy.

In my head, I tried to add the cost of the book and crayons. I closed my eyes and pictured the numbers. Nine plus nine. Carry the one . . . "Three fifty-eight?" I took a step back to him. "Daddy, can I spend three fifty—"

A picture on a newspaper distracted me. The man's face was right on the fold so I could only see the short hair, small eyes, and cartoony nose. But he looked like Hank. Next to the picture were thick letters. I slid my finger under each word and read, "Girl, 8, Missing." I picked up the paper to read the rest of the headline, but Daddy snatched it away. His eyes scanned the article until his face turned white, and his chest started moving in and out super fast. He must have felt bad for the girl's dad since he knew what it's like to be the daddy of an eight-year-old.

"Time to go," he said. He took the whole stack of papers and dropped them in his basket. Then he changed his mind and placed them back on the shelf. Again, he paused before putting a different paper on top of Hank's twin.

"Daddy, there's a missing girl."

He didn't say anything. He pressed his hand to my back and pushed me toward the front of the store so fast I thought I might trip. Lucky for me, he stopped by the checkout, got down on one knee, and dropped three quarters in my hand. He nodded toward the door. "You see those candy dispensers? Go get something while I check out. Wait for me there. Got it?"

"Got it." I booped his nose just like he'd booped mine. Then I charged toward the candy machines. With seventy-five cents I could get Mike and Ikes for me, Hot Tamales for Daddy, and a gumball for the missing girl, just in case we found her on the road.

Chapter 20

Present Day
Jade

Bridger

Hey slowpoke. We're down in the lobby. I'm not saying you need to hurry up but there's a sloth down here that's moving faster than you.

A sloth doesn't have to get ready for the day.

This one does. She's wearing a pantsuit just like yours.

I bet she rocks it better than I do too.

Only because she's more my type.

So she's an heiress with a Dolly Parton figure?

Who thinks I'm the greatest thing since sliced . . . leaves.

Sounds like I'm outdressed and outclassed.

And yet I'm standing here missing YOU. Get down here already!

Missing. The word jumps off the screen and punches me in the jugular. My panicked heart drums at the idea of Bridger having feelings for me, and I can't help but smile. *He's a flirt. That's all. Goodness, Jade. Get yourself together.*

I place my makeup kit in my suitcase and start to close it only to have the zipper catch halfway. I back it up and realize what's in the way—a stuffed replica of the Catoosa Whale we saw two days ago. Bridger found the souvenir at a gas station and presented it to me yesterday.

I pick it up and touch it to my cheek, repeating the kiss the whale gave me under Bridger's control. Would it be so horrible if Bridger did have feelings for me? I've had my own moments where I've imagined more than friendship with the man—but there's an easy explanation for that. Bridger, although not my normal pleated pants–type, is not ugly. And he's got a heart bigger than all of Route 66's Muffler Men combined. Not to mention his loyalty, humor, and strong hair-braiding skills. Plus, it's been a long time since I've been kissed and a great deal longer since I've been well-kissed. It's only natural for me to have an *occasional* thought about him in a romantic sense.

With all my luggage in tow, I exit my room and head down the hall. As I near the lobby, heated words echo off the walls from a voice I recognize. My steps slow, bringing me to a halt at the end of the hallway.

Roland Alderidge stands nose to nose with Bridger. Okay, that's merely an expression, because even though Roland balances on the balls of his loafers, heels in the air, he's still five inches shorter than Bridger. "You know the deal, and you know the stakes."

Bridger's hands are stuffed in the pockets of his jeans in a casual stance, yet I notice the muscles straining in his forearms. "I can't, Roland."

"Get. It. Done." Roland pokes Bridger's chest with each word.

Benny steps between the two men. "I don't know what this is all about, Roland, but you were in favor of this trip, last I recall. Bridger has been taking good care of me on this trip—a trip that was my idea."

Roland scoffs. "Anything to help Bridger. Right, Mom?"

How on earth did Benny and Paul Alderidge raise a jerk like him? At nearly sixty, the man seems to be a version of future Gregory if he'd gotten away with it all. Successful, rich, entitled, and arrogant as can be. From what I've observed, Roland's personal wealth is probably doing just fine as he didn't invest with us. I may be wrong, but his interest in Benny's finances seems self-focused. Maybe the reason he wants Benny put in a home is so he can pocket the money from the sale of her house.

As I'm pondering this, he notices me, and his eyes narrow. "There she is. Still playing the part of sophisticated professional, I see."

I tug the hem of my suitcoat down though what I want to do is use the fabric to absorb the sweat on my palms. Trying my hardest not to be intimidated, I march forward and extend my hand. "Hello, Roland. I didn't expect you to join us for the trip."

Roland's stare never leaves my face, and he doesn't acknowledge my outstretched hand so I drop it. "I thought it wise to check up on my mother, given her present company. Can't have anyone taking advantage of her any more than they already have." I expect him to laser me with that jab. I do not expect him to also face down Bridger. "And since my friends are the ones bankrolling this documentary, I'm invested in making sure it stays on track and tells the story the people want to see."

Roland's behind this? He found the investors? Who is he to Bridger anyway? A former foster dad? A current foster brother? Whatever it is, there isn't much love, let alone trust that Bridger can succeed without micromanagement.

"That's nice of you. Benny, this must be quite a surprise," I say.

Benny shows a sad smile. "It is. I love spending time with both of my boys."

"Who do you think you are? Calling her Benny?" Roland is radiating hatred I haven't felt in the two weeks since the sentencing hearing.

I clench my jaw, refusing to shirk away.

"That's enough, Roland. Jade has been in our life for several years. Your father and I were always fond of her. She was more than our financial advisor." Benny pushes her way between her sons and takes my hands. "Sweetheart, will you help me make some coffee for the road?"

"Absolutely." With the hotel's coffee bar mere yards away, I half listen to Benny nervously describing the best cup of coffee she's ever had and half listen to the tense conversation pulsing between her two sons. Although they speak low, I catch bits and pieces.

"I know you, Bridger . . . distracted by a pair of legs . . . don't care how."

Bridger fumes. " . . . wrong about her . . . talk about it." He steps past Roland and says, "I'm handling it, okay?" Once he approaches us, he turns to Benny. "Guess what? Roland's going to come along with us, at least until Amarillo. He's offered to help me edit parts of the film."

Benny frowns, glancing between them. "Oh dear. Please don't get him riled up, Bridger."

"That's never my intent."

We head out to the car. Roland leads with Benny on his arm, walking much slower than she needs. Bridger trails me, hauling Benny's suitcase as well as his own. I pull the keys from my purse, unlock the Chevy's trunk, and help him store the luggage, careful not to crush any of the camera equipment or his laptop bag.

Bridger mouths "I'm sorry," and I nod in acknowledgment. Acknowledgment of what, I'm not sure. Is he apologizing that

146

his brother randomly showed up to echo everything that's already been said about me? Everything I've had to combat with the truth. I'm innocent. I'm whole. I'm accepted and loved by God, and he isn't done with me yet. Still, it seems I'm the birdie in a not-so-friendly game of family badminton. Oh well. Better me than Benny.

Cool as I can pretend to be, I stride to the passenger door and use the keys to open it. Bridger, per usual, climbs in the back, and Roland unnecessarily helps Benny lower herself into the front seat. As I hold the door, my phone vibrates in my purse. I take it out only to see Rockville Penitentiary on the screen. I hit the ignore button, but not before Roland catches sight of my screen.

"Still in cahoots with him, eh?"

"Not at all. I ignore his calls."

He leans closer to me—close enough for his stale, coffee-tinged breath to turn my stomach. "You may have them fooled, but I see you. We both know who you really are."

A shiver climbs my spine.

He holds out his open palm. "I'll drive."

"Let me ask Bridger first. It's his car."

"It was my father's before it was his. I'm driving."

With hesitation, I hand over the keys. Soon I'm sitting in the back with Bridger at my side. His fist flexes even as it rests on his thigh. I lay a soft hand over his white knuckles, and his body relaxes a touch. From beneath those dark lashes, he peers at me, and I offer my best reassuring smile.

Until a duffel bag lands squarely on my wrist.

"Keep that back there for me, would you?"

Although I'm tempted to tell him where he can put that bag, for Benny's sake, I remain quiet. It makes me wonder how often Bridger speaks up for himself, if at all, when she's around.

"Where to?" Roland asks.

"The Oklahoma City National Memorial. I'll text you the address." Bridger types on his phone.

"What does that have to do with my parents' story or Route 66?"

Bridger lowers his phone. "There. I sent you the map. To answer your question, it doesn't. Jade wants to see it."

"Did you know someone who died in the bombing?"

I shake my head.

"Were you even born when it happened?"

Yes, I don't say.

Roland stares me down in the rearview mirror, but I don't back down. If he's such an expert on my life, then he knows I have experience with bullies like him. I spent my entire adolescence perfecting my staring contest game so my mom would know she hadn't broken me with her barbs and lies.

"You know, I read an article about people like you, Jade." Roland searches stations on the radio, jabbing the buttons. "Morbid tourism—visiting sites where death or tragedy occurred. Paying an entry fee so some greedy tourism association can milk the macabre, as it were. If you didn't personally know anyone impacted by it, why do you care? Wait. It's not for social media content, is it? Are you and Bridger going to do yoga in front of the reflecting pool for likes and comments?"

"Maybe if you gave someone else a chance to speak, you'd get your answers," Bridger says.

Roland turns the ignition but never takes his eyes off me.

"Well? We're waiting."

"I drove by it once, a long time ago. My father told me what happened here."

"Your father, huh?" Roland sneers.

"We didn't have time to stop though. I told myself that if I ever came by again, I would stop and pay my respects."

Benny's hand loosely grips Roland's wrist. "Son, where is this coming from? You didn't have a problem visiting Pearl Harbor or that volcano . . ." She closes her eyes in thought.

"Mount St. Helens. In fact, you were fascinated by both.

Jade, no explanation is necessary. I'd like to see the memorial too."

"Then we'll go." Roland takes his mother's hand and kisses it. "I'm only looking out for you, Mom."

"I know, dear. But Jade's a good girl. Your worry is as necessary as a snow cone at the North Pole. And I should know because I played Mrs. Claus in 1997." Benny sends a wink my direction, and I realize again where Bridger gets it.

Thankfully, once we arrive at the memorial, Roland has finally hushed. Not that this fact makes me feel any more comfortable in his presence. I finagle a reason to skip ahead of the group so I can be alone.

After I finish touring the museum, I head outside to the Field of Chairs, taking time to read the names of all 168 people who perished—171 when you include the babies who died in their mothers' womb that day. Just when I don't think my heart can take any more, I'm drawn to the chain-link fence where tributes, flowers, and stuffed animals line the path. A photo of toddler brothers breaks my heart wide open.

They should be here, with careers and families, bringing joy to those around them. I've had decades to live, yet I can't say I've brought more good than harm to the world. Not for my mom. Not for Hank. Not for my dad. Certainly not in dollars. I can't do anything to change what happened to my family. But if I can get my career back, I can change the last part.

"Gone before they had the chance to live. It seems unfair I've gotten eighty-nine years." Benny holds out a pack of tissues to me. I accept, removing two. I've only begun reading the tributes, and my eyes are already swollen with tears.

"I was thinking the same thing. Where are your boys?"

"Back at the car. I wanted to join you." Benny stroked the fur of a teddy bear that had become matted in the elements, fluffing it a bit. "Not many people know this, but Paul and I lost our first child on July 3, 1961. A little girl we named Charity. She was born without a heartbeat.

A pang resonates through my chest. "Oh, Benny. How tragic."

"Yes, losing a child is the hardest thing in life."

"I bet you were happy when Roland came along."

"Oh, yes. So happy. We indulged him quite a bit. He's never lacked for anything." She sighs. "And it shows. It isn't his fault. Paul and I are to blame."

I force a swallow, remembering the oft-repeated advice of my counselor. People get to choose who they want to be and how they act. We aren't responsible for adults' choices. "I don't know. You raised Bridger, and he seems pretty great."

Benny brushes her fingers along her brow. "I do so wish they could get along. Bridger resents Roland and Amie for bringing him into their home only to kick him out. Roland resents Bridger because we then took him in—much like the older brother in the story of the prodigal son. He hated that we loved him despite his poor behavior. That Bridger got as much love and gifts as he did even though he wasn't born to us. And don't get me started about the argument over the Chevy."

I offer a wan smile. "You and Paul are wonderful parents." I'd felt their love myself—at every shared dinner, on every phone call, in every meeting with them.

"And Bridger is a wonderful son. He's had too many people give up on him. He fought us and fought us until he realized it was no use. He was stuck with us. It's silly he never let us adopt him knowing how short life is."

"So you would want to officially adopt him? And have him take your last name?"

"Oh my, yes. Paul and I have been begging him for years. He's still fighting our love in a way. Adoption, though it begins with loss, is a beautiful, even biblical act. The notion has been tainted in Bridger's mind. What happened to him was criminal, and the people responsible were never truly held accountable for what they did to those children and those families. And now he believes he must prove his worth to be part of our family, hence the documentary. Nothing I've said can convince him otherwise."

At the end of the fence, Benny and I pause for a quick prayer for those who ache for their loved ones as well as for people who face terror in various parts of the world still. We turn back to where we'd left the Chevy. Bridger stands at the back bumper, looking our way with his arms crossed. A small child pauses on the sidewalk staring up at him. Bridger gives a little wave, which the kid returns. My broken heart gets one small mending stitch. Maybe this is how we go on in a harsh world that tries to tear us apart. By reminding each other of the good. From what I've seen on this trip, Bridger is the king of silver linings.

"Jade?" Benny takes my hand in hers. "I won't always be here. Bridger looks tough, but after I'm gone, he's going to need someone to love him." She gives my hand a soft squeeze, letting the sentence hang. I don't mind. In fact, it's an honor that despite everything in my past, she believes I could be good enough for her son.

Chapter 21

1956
Benny

"Welcome to Hamons Station. I'm Lucille. What can I do you for? Gas, tires, cold drinks? I can even change headlights if needed." The woman wore a sunny yellow day dress as she stocked a cooler with pop bottles. The sound of the clinking glasses clashed with the same few measures played repeatedly on a trumpet on the second floor of the service station.

"We'd like to stay in your motel if there are any vacancies." I touched the stacks of maps on display. One for each of the states the highway passed through.

"Fortunately for you, we have one available room."

"Only one?" Paul asked.

"Yes, the one on the end. Cheryl Ann?" Lucille snagged the attention of a grade-school girl playing with—

"Is that a monkey?" I asked.

Lucille chuckled. "I never know what animals Carl or the kids will bring into our family. A monkey, orphaned sheep, stray horses. Cheryl Ann, will you and Delpha Dene turn over room 5? Tell her she can practice her trumpet after."

"Yes, ma'am." The girl held out her hands, and the small

primate leaped into her embrace. Paul and I exchanged a glance as quick footsteps pounded up the stairs.

"You're in luck. Normally, we're filled up on fair weekend, but one of the families left a day early."

I tugged Paul's arm excitedly. "Oh, Paul, please can we go to the fair? I haven't been to one since high school."

He grinned. In fact, the man had hardly stopped grinning since our time in the telephone booth. As it turned out, Paul's joy could be found quite easily, although perhaps that was because his mind was occupied. When Paul thought of me, his mind wasn't trapped in the war. If it were up to me, I would never stop kissing him if it kept him away from that awful place.

After we checked into the single motel room—Paul planned to sleep in the car once again—we rode out to nearby Hydro where the fair was already underway. The crowd was the largest we'd seen since we left Joliet. Excursion trains brought fairgoers from all the neighboring towns.

I didn't mind all the people because Paul held my hand when we walked through the crowd. And he tossed rings onto milk jugs and won me a caramel apple. Actually, we shared the caramel apple. His kiss was even sweeter after that. We rode the carousel and the kiddie train, ate popcorn, and watched a magic show.

We returned to the service station later that night—me, with an angel food cake on my lap that we'd purchased from the Andy's Bakery booth. Paul opened my door for me, and for a moment, I was afraid this was our good night. The good Lord knew I didn't want it to be, but he also knew Paul shouldn't join me in that motel room.

While Paul hemmed and hawed about enjoying the evening and the weather being so perfect for a fair, I placed the cake on the Chevy's hood, my arms around Paul's neck, and my lips against his.

Oh, I relished the feel of his fingertips skimming the sides of my rib cage, then clutching fistfuls of my sweater at the small of my back.

Breathless, he pulled back, and although I was tempted to follow, I created an invitation instead. "It's a beautiful night for stargazing. What do you say?"

He said yes. We spread a blanket across the grass and sat with the angel food cake between us. Taking turns, we tore bits off and let the sweetness melt in our mouths.

I held a sticky piece between my thumb and forefinger. "It's not often I get to eat cake. Even after the war rations ended, Momma and Daddy haven't been able to afford sugar. A cake on each of our birthdays is all we've ever had."

Paul looked at the blanket, too reminiscent of his countenance weeks ago.

"What's wrong?" I asked.

"Nothing's wrong. I . . ."

"Go on," I commanded.

"I wanted to say . . . if you were mine, I'd make sure there was always cake in our home."

I laughed.

"Why are you laughing? I would. We'd have a crystal cake stand as a centerpiece on our kitchen table. Chocolate cake, cherry, coconut, pineapple upside down . . ."

"Crystal? I never imagined we'd be so fancy. I'd be content with one made of glass," I breathed in deep. "Sounds like a great life, although we might also need to have Jack LaLanne and his trimnastics in our home as well."

"Hmm. I'm not sure I'd like having another man in our home. I don't need anyone else. Only you," I admitted.

Paul dragged the remains of the cake off the blanket, then scooted closer to me.

A pair of headlights broke through the darkness and painted

a ghostly trail down Route 66, growing larger with the hum of an engine. The distraction was good because I was ready to go awaken a preacher and get married right there with Lucille and the monkey as witnesses.

"I heard that it's a tradition for a couple to get married at the fair every year. I wonder who it was this year."

"Is that what we are? A couple. Are you my girl?"

I nodded excitedly. "And you're my guy."

We sealed it with a kiss. Several, actually. By the time I opened my eyes again, the car had long since passed.

"I heard something else at the fair," Paul said. "It's a local legend."

I beamed. "Paul Alderidge, are you about to tell me a story?"

He jumped to his feet, then standing in front of me, he stilled as if to get into character the way he used to on the high school stage. When I reclined back on the blanket, propped up on my elbows, he looked larger than life.

"Once upon a time on a night just like this," he began in a theatrical voice, "a lone driver was traveling west down Route 66 when he spotted a man in the middle of the road. His car screeched to a halt, inches away from the stranger. He leaned against the steering wheel, peering through the windshield. The stranger was hunched over with one shoulder higher than the other."

Paul adjusted his tall-drink-of-water frame and became the mysterious man. He craned his neck and morphed his facial features, creating a masklike and spooky effect.

"He was old with gray, crepey skin that hung off his cheekbones, nose, and jaw. His stringy hair was partially covered by a Bogey hat pulled down low to hide his eyes. He also wore a brown trench coat, but Humphrey he was not. He walked to the passenger door. The driver rolled down the window. 'Hey fella, you want yourself a ride?'" Paul asked in an exaggerated Southern accent. Then he straightened himself. "The driver was from Georgia, you see, and even though he was unsure who this stranger was, he practiced Southern hospitality and offered a ride."

"Of course he did," I affirmed.

Paul scrunched down. "The little man said nothing. He merely opened the door and climbed in. He shut the door and sat very still. The Georgian noticed the man's hands. The yellow-streaked nails curled over the tips of his fingers. The nailbeds were stained. With mud perhaps. The same mud that was caked on the little man's trousers but disappeared beneath the coat."

I perked up and sat cross-legged. "I bet he was a gravedigger. No! He crawled out of his own grave."

"Are you telling the story, or am I?"

I pulled an imaginary zipper across my lips.

"The Georgian, he was nervous, without a doubt regretting his decision to offer this man a ride. He asked the man where he's from." Paul froze. "No answer. He asked him where he's going. No answer. He asked him his name. The man removed his hat and slowly turned to face the driver. 'My name' he said, 'is Richard J. Calhoun the third.' The Georgian's face went slack. He gawked at the little man, but where there should have been teeth, there were only worms. Where there should have been eyes, there were only two black, abysmal hollows. The driver slammed on the brakes and the car skidded to a halt. The passenger door flew open, and the little man jumped out of the car. The Georgian checked every mirror, but there was no sign of the strange ghoul. He leaned across the seat and pulled the door shut. He hit the gas, driving faster than he'd ever driven before."

Paul checked to see if I was still listening, which I absolutely was.

"Then, several miles down the road, the Georgian saw the same man standing on the center line, and he had to swerve to avoid hitting him. For a moment, he wondered if he had imagined it all or plain gone mad. He looked at the mud on the passenger seat, still wet. The little man had been real. So the Georgian, Richard J. Calhoun the third, sped down the Mother Road and didn't stop until he reached the state line."

"So it was his own ghost?" I squealed in excitement more than fear. I never did believe in any ghost other than the Holy Ghost.

Paul hiked his brows. He crept toward me, hunched over. "And to this day, Richard J. Calhoun the third lurks along Route 66 . . ."

I laid back on the blanket as Paul crawled over me.

". . . between Hydro and Weatherford . . ." He laid on his side and lowered his face to mine. " . . . looking for someone to give him a ride."

"You made that up."

"I promise I didn't. A man told me while you were at the bakery's booth. I mean, I might have added a bit to make it more interesting."

I gave him a peck, which turned into more than a peck. I couldn't help it with the way he was coming back to life in front of my eyes. "Paul, you're amazing. You're the one who should be heading to Hollywood for a career in television and movies."

"Nah." He shook his head. "That's your dream."

"We can share the dream. We can do this together. We could be there for each other when it gets tough." I studied his face—his gorgeous face. He might actually have been the most handsome man in the world. "That could be our life. I want it to be our life. Can you see it too?"

"Yes, I can." A shadow fell over his features. "I haven't always though. There were hard times when I couldn't see the future at all."

I caressed his cheek.

"In the darkness, I held tight to that picture you sent. You

157

weren't a girl anymore. You were a woman, and not merely with your appearance. On the back of the photo, you wrote something. 'A moon and star in the night, as far as one horizon to the other, yet in time, we'll meet again when my path crosses yours and yours mine.' I prayed every day that we'd end up on the same road. It was that prayer that kept me alive. It gave me hope. A simple prayer that, Lord willing, I may hold you like this. So yes, I can see it."

Chapter 22

2003
Jade

Daddy steered our ugly car off the paved road and parked behind a boarded-up building. It was scary dark outside, but Daddy still could unlock the door to the room on the end. I followed him inside, carrying the grocery bag with my dinner. The smell of the room turned my stomach. It looked like a swamp, and the shadows inside began to morph into a monster.

"Daddy, turn on the light, please."

"There ain't any light."

"What hotel has no lights?"

"See, this place hasn't had any guests for a while. But Lucille, she said we could stay here anyway."

"I don't like it. Where are the beds?"

"Well, we're going to camp."

"We don't have a tent."

"Lucille said we can use the stuff we find in her store. Let's put all this down, and we'll head over there."

The store was part of a gas station. The old metal pumps still stood outside, but everything else made me think this place wasn't open. The sign was super hard to read. "Historic Highway?"

"That faded part says Lucille's. And the place we're staying used to be called Hamons Court. It's all vintage. Do you know what that means?"

"Smelly?"

He laughed, but I was serious.

Vines covered the front part of the building, hanging down. I jumped to touch a leaf, but I was too short. "It's like we're in a rainforest."

"Yeah, it feels like that, don't it?" Daddy held something metal in his hand. He pressed it into the doorjamb. Then, noticing I was watching, he moved his body so I couldn't see what he was doing. After a loud creak, the door popped open, leaving splinters of wood all around it.

"Uh-oh."

"I'll fix that later. Chin up, all right?"

The store was empty and dark. "Are we at the right place?" I asked.

He didn't answer, so I just followed him through another door, holding tight to his belt loop. This room was bigger but still had no furniture. It smelled nice though. Maybe Lucille wouldn't let us sleep here tonight instead of the hotel room. Daddy went straight to the small kitchen and flicked on the faucet. Water sputtered out at first, but then flowed easily.

"Good." He turned off the water, then reached into our grocery bag and pulled out two boxes. One had a dark-haired man on the front. The other had a blond-haired woman on it. Daddy took a deep breath. "Remember our game about hiding out—Jesse James and all them?"

I nodded slowly.

"We need disguises too. You ever wanted blond hair?"

Chapter 23

Present Day
Jade

I stay in the Chevy when we arrive at Lucille's service station. Fortunately for Benny—and all other Route 66 travelers—someone in recent years restored the building and even the motor court as a historic site. The roof has been refinished, a porch added, and the doors and windows replaced.

After fifty-six years of helping travelers on 66, Lucille Hammons, known as the Mother of the Mother Road passed away in 2000—three years before my father and I broke in to find shelter. Having her permission had been another lie he'd created that summer so I wouldn't know what was really happening.

I catch my reflection in the rearview mirror. I smooth down the flyaways that had come loose from the French braid Bridger styled for me that morning. Mahogany strands that appear amber in the sun. Not the awful orange color my father turned my hair at this very place. He used school scissors to crudely cut my hair to my shoulders and chop uneven bangs. The only positive from that day was how my father comforted me as I cried myself to sleep on the floor of the building in front of me. Bridger appears from behind the shop trudging toward the car, but when we make eye contact and I smile, he starts to stroll like he's simply out to enjoy the sunshine. "They'll be here in a minute," he says. "Roland wanted to talk to Benny alone." Bridger scoffs then goes about loading his gear into the trunk.

"Any idea what about?" I ask.

Bridger drops to the ground, and I peek over the side of the car. With his forearms flattened against the grass, he lifts his hips until he forms an inverted V. "Honestly, I have no clue." He lifts one leg, then the other into the sky. His T-shirt slides down to his armpits and covers his face.

"Um, do you need help?"

"Nope. I'm good." He bends his legs and arches his back until his toes aren't too terribly far from his head. "Scorpion pose."

I consider applauding, yet I can only gawk at him. I turn my entire body away and instead attempt to watch the semitrucks traveling by on I-40 not too far away.

Footsteps near, and I look back in time to see Roland try to push Bridger over—*try* being the operative word because Bridger holds firm.

"Young man," Benny scolds, "don't you dare hurt your brother."

"He's not my brother."

"Psh," I accidentally let out. How much longer must I deal with Roland? I've had it with his passive aggression. No, there's nothing passive about it. Just aggressive. And the worst part is that Benny is the one who suffers when he gets going. While Roland gives his full attention to every tiny movement his mother makes like she's a toddler just learning to walk, Bridger rights himself, tossing his hair back in an absolute Little Mermaid move. But the happy-go-lucky side of him is gone.

Once we're back on the road, we drive to the Route 66 Museum in Clinton where Bridger already worked it out for us to film more of Benny's story. We set up in the room resembling a

1950s diner. Benny sits on one of the stools at the counter and, at the insufferable urging of Roland, I sit one stool away. Not in the shot but close enough to hear every word Benny says.

Bridger looks at Benny. "Can you tell the camera why you believe preservation of Route 66 is important?"

"Without preservation efforts, so many places on Route 66 have fallen into disrepair. The road itself has fallen into disrepair in some places. Yet for so many of us, this road and the people we met along the way, changed us. The Mother Road accepted us, sheltered us, carried us, and challenged us to dream big. When I visit these locations that played such a significant role in my life and relationship, it gives me hope that perhaps others have gotten to experience the joy I felt there. Whenever you feel something that others have felt, a connection is made. I've never claimed to be the wisest gal, but in this world, we need more of those links because where there are connections, there is compassion and empathy. Paul always said compassion and empathy are the two most underutilized values in society. And Paul? He was a wise man."

Bridger and Benny seem to share a moment. Roland notices as well and rolls his eyes. So Benny's only half right. Roland may be jealous of everything Bridger was given despite his troubled past, but I think he's also jealous of the bond between him and Benny.

"It's difficult to see the remnants of places. The skeletal remains of hotels and cafés where we once stayed. It's sad to know that they had no one to save them, to keep them, and to preserve them. In a way, it reminds me of how some people age—without anyone by their side, helping them through their mistakes."

Somewhere in the back of my mind, the memory of my father and I singing "Desperado" zings me. Who does Dad have now that he's out of prison? Does he miss me? Does he wish he hadn't pushed me away? Has he forgiven me yet?

"I have a question," Roland says.

Bridger shoots him a glare, but Roland keeps on. "Can you explain how traveling 66 was different then and now? I mean, back then, Dad had a lot of money because of Granddad's business, but you were pretty much broke. And now you've had almost all your money stolen from you, so once again you're . . ."

I'm not sure if Roland realizes the awfulness of what he is saying and that's why he stops short or if God strikes him temporarily mute.

The air feels thick, so thick, I can't seem to raise my chin or my eyelids to look at anyone.

"What are you getting at?" Bridger asks.

"The point, Bridger. The reason we're all here." The louder and more shrill Roland's voice gets, the more I struggle to fully expand my lungs.

"All that money ever did was allow me to give you boys anything you asked for. One of you asked for a great deal more than the other. I can be content with five dollars or five million."

"Mom, you need money to live. You deserve to use the money you and Dad worked for to enjoy your last years on earth. Thanks to Jade, you have no money. The trustee is struggling to find all that was taken from you. Where is it, Jade? Where's the unaccounted-for eighteen million?"

"I don't know," I stammer. "If I did, I would have reported it already."

Bridger seethes. "Jade is innocent."

Roland turns to him. "How well do you really know her? I'll answer that. You don't. You know why? Because she's gone to great lengths to hide who she really is, son." What should be a term of affection sounds like a slur from Roland's lips.

"Don't call me son." Bridger steps back from the camera.

My gut twists and a wave of nausea induces a cool sweat across my forehead. *Lord, help me. And help Bridger and Benny too.*

"Roland," Benny interrupts, "I told you not to bring this up."

"Mom, with Dad gone, it's up to me to look out for you. Besides, we all know documentaries are about truth."

Bridger widens his stance and crosses his arms. There's fire in his eyes, which only heaps guilt on me. I hate, and I mean hate, how the subject of me and my past can turn this gentle man into a threatening one.

I meet those eyes and pray I can somehow extinguish the blaze. "It's okay, Bridge, Benny."

"The truth is that Jade Jessup is imaginary. She changed her name in 2013."

My heel slips off the stool's footrest, and I nearly fall.

"Roland Irving Alderidge." Each name drips off Benny's tongue with the gentleness of falling icicles. "I told you not to say anything about that nonsense."

"It's not nonsense. When I couldn't find anything about the past of the woman who lured you into a Ponzi scheme, I hired a private investigator. Jade Jessup's real name is Julianna Talbot."

How much did Roland learn beyond that? Where did the trail lead him?

Benny began to climb off the stool, distaste in her expression. I place a hand on her knee. "Benny, it's true." Maybe if I own up to part of it, they'll never learn the whole. "I changed my name because I was——"

"Kidnapped," Benny finishes my sentence, awareness finding its place. "I remember the news story. You were kidnapped by——"

"My father. After a visitation, he drove me from Illinois to Arizona. It was such a big news story that it promised to follow me everywhere. That's why I changed my name when I turned eighteen."

"Oh, come on," Roland says. "You're leaving out a big part of the story, Julianna."

I clench my teeth until my jaw aches, exhaling through my

nose. A shiver wracks my body, and I convulse. "There's no point in trying to hide it. My father got into an altercation with my stepfather after our scheduled visit. My father . . . hit him . . . several times." I meet Roland's glare straight on. "Hank had an underlying condition that led to a cardiac dysrhythmia—a heart attack resulting from the assault."

Roland clears his throat. "In 2003, Edward 'Eddie' Talbot pleaded guilty to aggravated kidnapping, unlawful transportation of a minor across state lines, and second-degree murder. He served seventeen years in jail for those charges."

I set my jaw and grip the counter as my vision clouds, and my pulse throbs violently in my ears.

"But before that, in the 1980s, Eddie was in and out of prison for petty theft, burglary, motor vehicle theft, and grand larceny." Roland looks between Benny and Bridger. "And you actually believe Julianna had nothing to do with the scheme that ruined our family?"

The stinging behind my eyes becomes too much. "Benny, I . . ." My words catch in my throat, and I can no longer explain myself or my familial ties without the doll I'd sewn, Jade Jessup, coming apart at the seams.

Bridger steps in front of the camera and reaches for me. I hop off my stool, evading his grasp, and then head into the final room of the museum, which unironically, shows the destruction of Route 66 in the sixties and seventies. I burst through the gift shop and out the exit doors. I find the refuge I need behind the relic of a Valentine Diner at the far end of the parking lot.

I sink to the ground and bury my face in my hands.

A filmstrip of awful memories flips through my mind, its soundtrack the rhythmic beat of my sobs. My parents fighting, my father leaving, my mother bringing man after man into our home, her decision to marry Hank, that fateful visit with my father, the frenzied trip down Route 66. Then building a new life in Arizona and feeling happy for the first time only to have the police rip me away.

The wall behind me shakes a bit. Then arms pull me against a warm body. Although I can't smell anything thanks to my runny nose, I know that this person smells like a combination of a hair salon and the ocean. He tucks my head under his chin, and his beard tickles my forehead and brow. Bridger holds me so tightly, I wonder if his embrace is the only thing keeping my pieces in place.

I don't know how long we remain like this. Long enough to hear Bridger say "I've got you" a dozen times or more. Long enough for me to stop shaking my head after each of his repetitions. Long enough for my tears to run dry. Long enough for my breathing to align with his.

"I should have told you." My words come out in wheezes and puffs.

"No. You could have told me. I would have listened. I would have understood. But that was your story to share if you wanted to. There's no *should* with me. I hoped you'd know that by now."

"I'm so ashamed." I feel him shake his head slightly.

With a knuckle beneath my chin, he gently lifts my face, and I see the sincerity in his eyes. "What your father did . . . it wasn't your fault."

My chin puckers as my lips bend into a painful frown. "But it is." A fresh tear slips down my cheek, and he brushes it away with his thumb.

I try to swallow the lump filling my throat, but I fail. "My mother was not the nurturing type. But my father was, and I loved him more than anyone in this world. In the custody battle, my mom used his drinking and criminal history against him, and then I rarely got to see him. Of course, I only learned that later. My mom told me the reason he didn't often visit was because he didn't love me. When he got sober, I got to see him every other Saturday. I was young, but I'd already learned from my mom how to use words to get people to do what I want. And I wanted to see my dad more." I hang my head. "I told him that Hank was mean to me—that he hit me and such—so that he'd fight for more custody; I didn't think he'd confront Hank about it."

Bridger worries his bottom lip.

"But it was a lie." My voice breaks, and it takes several moments before I can resume. "Hank never hit me."

I can't look at Bridger as the silence stretches between us.

"Did your dad ever find out it was a lie?"

I nod. "I admitted that I lied the same day the cops found us in Tecoma."

"How did he react?"

"It broke him." I shrug my shoulders. "We both knew that if I'd never lied to him about Hank, he never would have confronted him. He never would've beat him like that. My dad had cleaned himself up by then. He'd left his criminal life behind. He thought he was protecting me."

"Did your mom know?"

"Yes. I tried to get her to tell the police and the lawyers that it was my fault. She wouldn't because she said my father deserved to rot in jail. At home, though, she blamed me for Hank's death. There wasn't a day from when the police reunited us to when I left for college that she didn't tell me what a monster my father was and how I'm just like him."

Looking up at the sky, I release a breath. "When I was old enough to use the internet, I looked up my dad's lawyer, called him, and told him about the lie. He said that he'd consider including that in the appeal, but nothing ever happened."

"Were you able to visit your dad at all?"

"Not when I was young. My mom wouldn't let me have any contact with him. I mean, I found a way to sneak letters to him, but she never gave me any of the letters he sent back. Finally, when I was sixteen, I borrowed my boyfriend's car and drove the hour to his prison. He looked so different. He just kept saying I needed to stop blaming myself for what happened. That I was a child. That just fueled me all the more.

"I visited probably once a month. Between visits, I wrote to the Illinois Supreme Court, the governor, the parole board. I was obsessed with fixing the mess I'd made. Then one day, he refused to see me. And the next time and the next."

"Why?"

I shrug. "I guess the longer he was in prison, the more he realized I ruined his life? I should've kept my mouth shut."

Bridger cradles my face in his hands. "You were a kid," he whispers while looking deep into my eyes.

"I know," I say. "I tell myself that all the time. Counselors have told me that. When I pray, God reminds me. But then something will happen, and all I can hear is my mom's voice telling me I'm a bad person."

"And do you believe her?"

"No, but my dad might."

"No way." Eyes narrowed, he concentrates on my face. "You know, Jade, we can stop in Tecoma if you want to find out some answers."

My heartbeat picks up at the thought. "I don't know if he'd even be there. I have no idea where he is."

"Well, maybe someone there does. It might be worth a shot, especially if we're already driving through."

I will my voice not to crack. "What if he doesn't want to see me?" It cracks anyway.

Bridger gives a half smile. "I was in drug and alcohol rehab three times, so I feel I can speak with some authority on this. Your dad battled addiction and got sober so he could spend time with you. That takes a commitment and fierce love—the kind that doesn't just go away. He'll want to see you."

Chapter 24

2003
Jade

"I'm awful sorry about your hair. You're still pretty," Daddy had apologized every mile since we left Lucille's.

Apology, schmapology. I pulled his baseball cap onto my head and covered the rest of my splotchy, carrot-colored hair with my hands. "I look like Chuckie."

"The killer doll?"

"No! From *Rugrats*."

"Oh, gotcha. You don't have glasses though."

I groaned and pressed my nose against the window.

"I know someone who can fix it as soon as we get where we're going."

"I'm not getting out of the car."

"What if you get hungry?"

"Drive-thru," I grumbled.

"What if you have to use the bathroom?"

"I'll make a puddle on this seat. It won't matter because it's already grosser than gross. This trip isn't fun anymore. I want to go home."

Daddy got quiet and stared down the road. "Do you really mean that?"

No. Not for a million reasons, one of which was I'd get teased by all the boys in Mr. Lowell's class.

"Hey, that color orange makes your eyes look even more green, my Baby Jade. Do you know why I call you that?"

Duh. "Because my eyes are green."

"Not just green—the prettiest green in the entire rainbow."

"The boys at school say my eyes are Shrek-green."

"What? No way. Shrek is more of a lime green. Your eyes are British Racing Green. I have an idea. Remember our hiding game? Maybe we should come up with some new names. Is there a name you like better than Julianna?"

"Um, Jade? But not the baby part. I'm eight now."

"Deal. How about you're Jade and I'm James?"

"Like Jesse James?" I asked.

"Hmm. That might turn heads. How about . . . Jessup? Jimmy Jessup. And Jade Jessup. How's that?"

"Sounds kinda dumb but it's okay, I guess." I thunked my forehead against the glass. "How much farther till we get there?"

"Well, we're about to cross the state line into Texas. We've gotta go through New Mexico and most of Arizona. Why?"

I squirmed in my seat. "Because I have to go to the bathroom."

Chapter 25

Present Day
Jade

I can barely breathe. The steam from my long, hot shower makes it nearly impossible, yet I continue to stand under the showerhead, letting the water pummel my back. Strange comfort, but it's what I need after an extremely awkward drive from the museum to this motel outside Amarillo. Bridger had spent the entire time trying to lift my spirits. First by giving me the most amazing hand massage of all time. The guy's talents don't ever seem to cease. Then by performing a medley of Jackson 5 songs, finishing with a serenade of "I'll Be There" that he sang to Benny. And if you think Bridger can't sing like young Michael Jackson, you are right.

Yet even his best efforts can't bury the truth that had purged itself all over this trip. Because of me, one man's life ended literally, and another man's life ended figuratively. All the emotional work I've done in the counseling office and all my time seeking solace in Scripture seems to have been scratched in Roland's presence.

With sufficiently puckered fingertips, I step out of the shower and get ready for bed. I search my suitcase for my hair dryer and

172

unwind the cord. A hard knock at the door makes me pause then check out my reflection in the mirror to ensure I'm visitor-ready. Of course I am. These modest pajamas could never be considered sexy or revealing. The only problem is my wet, unruly hair. The idea of Bridger seeing it doesn't worry me though.

"Jade, it's Roland," the visitor calls through the door.

I clench my teeth. What are the chances he'll go away on his own? Not high.

"Coming." I prepare myself for whatever insult the man has prepared for me. He's a bitter, spoiled, angry old man. *If anyone tells you you're a bad person, don't believe it,* I tell myself. A lot of good that advice has done for me.

Except when I open the door, it's Bridger I see.

"Ha! Did I scare ya?"

I give his shoulder a shove. "You're a punk."

He bats his thick, dark eyelashes my way. "Admit it—you love me. Can I come in?"

"Mi Casa Del Sueno es su Casa Del Sueno," I say, referring to the name of the motel.

"Ah, I see what you did there. Hey, your hair is the bomb. Maybe I'm just saying that because it looks like mine. Twinsies!"

"Oh yeah," I say, tugging a handful of it. "I prefer it straight. It's more professional."

"At the risk of sounding like a Neanderthal giving a woman advice on how she looks prettiest, I think you should wear it like this sometimes. Messy is underrated, if you ask me. If you want, you can share my hair product."

"Aren't you sweet."

Bridger, with a gleam in his eye, leans against the doorframe all suave-like. "What can I say? I'm a romantic."

"Did you come over to give me hair advice or . . . ?"

His grin grows wider. "Roland found a flight out of Amarillo tomorrow morning."

Oh, thank you, Lord. "Bridge, if you want him to stay—"

"I booked it for him."

I press my lips into a hard line to keep from smiling before realizing it's no use. "Thank you."

We stare at each other. Maybe it should be awkward, but it isn't. In fact, I search my mind for something to say so he'll stay longer. "Did you and Roland get some editing done?"

His demeanor hardens. "Yeah. He's always happy to give input." He lowers his chin and coughs. "Jade, about the documentary. I haven't been entirely truthful about it."

My heart aches for him. "Bridger, I know. Benny told me."

He retreats a step, but I follow him and place both of my palms on his upper chest, my fingers curling over his shoulders.

"She says the reason you're doing this documentary is to earn the Alderidge name so you'll finally consent to an adoption. I think it's sweet, but Benny is already proud of the man you've become whether this film ever sees a screen or not."

Tears well in his eyes, and he shakes his head slightly; I lift up on my toes and press my lips to his cheek, holding the kiss long enough for yearning to sweep through me.

A shattering sound pierces the quiet. His body bows protectively around me, but only for a moment. By the time I've regained my breath, he's already at the door to his family's motel room. I follow.

"Get out!" Benny, in her nightgown, presses herself against the wall next to one of the beds. The mirror across the room had lost several shards from the cracked web in its center, probably courtesy of Bridger's boots—one of which lays in the middle of the floor. The other remains in Benny's hand, poised to be thrown.

Roland's wide-eyed stare lands on Bridger. "I didn't do anything."

Bridger ignores him. "Benny, it's me, Bridger."

"You get out of here now. My husband will be back soon, and he'll slug you right in your ugly face."

"We won't hurt you," he says in a velvety voice. "You're safe with us."

Benny points a shaky finger at Roland. "Who is he? Who is she? Where have you taken me?"

"That's your son, Roland. I'm your foster son, Bridger, and this is our friend Jade. We're on vacation." Bridger slides into a seated position on the bed farthest from Benny. I take the cue and lower myself into the chair by the door.

Her chin trembles. "I don't know you. I don't know any of you. When Paul gets back, he'll wallop all of you." She looks at me. "I'm not your prisoner. You can't keep me here. I'm leaving and you can't stop me."

"You can't leave, Mom," Roland says.

"Stop calling me that." She throws the boot toward Roland, but Bridger intercepts and calmly places it on the floor. "What have you done with Paul?"

"Paul asked us to watch over you for a bit." Bridger leans forward to peer out the door where the Chevy is parked. "Would you like to wait for Paul in the Bel Air?"

Her frantic eyes search left, then right, then left again. "Yes. It's certainly better than being trapped in here with you. He said we wouldn't be apart long."

Bridger agrees. "Let me clean up this glass first. Then you can wait in the car."

He and I make quick work of the cleanup. Roland holds out the trash bin for us to deposit the sharp fragments. I meet his eyes once, and the sadness on his face makes my heart grow heavy.

"I'll go find a vacuum," he says before disappearing.

A few minutes later, Benny sits in the passenger seat in her nightgown, believing her beloved is on his way to her. For the first hour, she rambles, piecing together shreds of memories about her life with Paul. The second hour she's mostly quiet, occasionally looking around for Paul.

Bridger and I sit in the back seat, and I watch him shatter just like that mirror every minute Benny doesn't return to the present. We wait until she dozes off and her breaths deepen, then we sneak out of the car. Coming around the passenger side, I open the door and Bridger leans down to her ear. Softly, he says, "Benny, it's Bridger. I'm going to carry you to your bed now."

Her eyes flutter open briefly, "I can walk, honey."

"Nah. I've got you."

I help guide him into the room. Roland sits up in the second bed, and I'm glad he wasn't able to simply fall asleep after this episode. He must have a heart in there somewhere. Then I notice the pillow and blanket forming a bed on the floor by the bathroom. So that's where Bridger is expected to sleep. Maybe I'm wrong about that heart, after all.

I fold back the sheets so Bridger can lay Benny's spindly form down. In her nightgown, she's even more frail. He tucks her in, even taking the blanket off the floor and adding it to her covers. He kisses her forehead. "I love you, Mama," he whispers. "Sleep well."

Before my tears get the better of me, I head back to my room, but before I get entirely inside, Bridger's hand stops me from closing my door.

"You good?" Inwardly, I cringe at my question. I'm beginning to speak like him now.

"No." He wipes one eye, then the other. "I was wondering . . . can I get a hug?"

"Absolutely."

My arms encircle his waist, and I rest my cheek against his collar. It's a good feeling. It makes me almost forget that I'm supposed to be comforting him until he dispels a hefty breath into my hair.

His love and concern for Benny is evident in so many ways

even as he shudders slightly with each exhale now. Jealousy shoots a pang into my chest. What would it feel like to love someone so much that the idea of losing them makes you emotionally and physically ill? Or is Bridger reacting to losing the one person who loves *him* that way?

The melody for "Desperado" plucks its notes in my head, and I cling tighter to the man, rubbing his back all the while. Through the thin fabric of his shirt, my fingers map each muscle. Minutes pass. I'm not sure how many.

"Are you feeling better now?" I ask.

"Yeah, thanks." He steps back, offering a nod of gratitude.

"You're welcome."

Before he turns away completely, he gives me a sideways glance. "Serious question. Were you copping a feel just then? Because, in case you forgot, I'm celibate."

With all my might, I shove him back toward his room.

Roland barely speaks as the Chevy heads toward the airport the next morning. I allow him the space for contemplation and keep to myself in the back seat. But after we come to a stop in the short-term parking lot at the Amarillo airport, it's Benny who breaks the silence.

"Roland, before you leave, I need to say something." She pulls off her sunglasses, then looks at Roland and then at me. "Jade told us about her father several years ago when he was released from jail. Not everything, mind you, but about her father's criminal history."

My lips part but fail to form words as I remember how anxious I'd been to admit such a thing to the two clients I admired most.

"She felt we should know. Your father didn't put his trust in any Tom, Dick, or Mary, in this case, but when we first met, he saw Jade's pure heart. He saw a young girl who had to raise herself and had done a fine job of it at that." Benny winks at me. "Any distrust your father had would have been directed at the Hyrem family, not Jade. So no more ugliness toward her, do you hear me, son?"

He stares at his hands a moment, then nods. He gets out of the car, holding the seat forward so I can extricate myself from the back. Once out, I wait by the back wheel for him to step aside. Instead, he walks straight toward me, forcing me backward until the back of my leg catches on the rear fender.

"Jade," Roland grumbles, "may I speak to you a moment?"

"I guess so." As I follow him ten or so yards away, near the terminal's entrance, I steel myself for whatever he is about to say.

It's unnecessary though, because the man standing before me is anything but intimidating. Downtrodden and broken with eyes that clearly found no sleep in the aftermath of last night's event. With his bleeding heart on display, all I can summon is empathy.

"I want to apologize for my behavior these past few days." He looks anywhere but at me. "Mom's right. My father didn't trust many people, and he loved a good charity case. Bridger's proof of that."

I button my lips.

"It doesn't matter how I feel about you. It was my mother's money your firm took. If she chooses to let you into her world, then so be it." He huffs. "But, for what it's worth, thank you for helping look after her."

"I'm glad to help." I wait until he meets my eye. "Roland, there's something I keep asking myself. It's clear that you want the best for your mom. I see how careful and protective you are." I force a swallow. "But in all this talk about money and the cost of care, why haven't you stepped forward to help? If you want to see your parents' story documented, why have you only recruited your friends to invest? Why not open your own wallet?"

Multiple emotions seem to war on his face, twisting his mouth and rippling his brows. In the end, shame appears to conquer the rest. "The long and short of it is I don't have it. I've made mistakes. Trusted the wrong people. Followed the wrong gut instinct."

"We aren't so different, then," I say.

"Guess not."

I extend my hand.

Roland eyes it for several seconds before accepting. "If there's any chance you can get Gregory Hyrem to open up about where that missing money is, I suggest you start answering his calls."

Something about climbing back into the Chevy's driver seat feels right. I reacclimate my hands to the cool sleekness of the steering wheel while Roland retrieves his bag and bids goodbye to his mother. Once Benny gets her kiss and a final wave, I steer us toward the exit. At first sight of the iconic Route 66 sign, I relax. "Well, keeper of the maps, where to next?"

"Now?" Bridger's cheek twitches in that mischievous way of his. "Now it's time for some fun."

Chapter 26

"What on Route 66 is the Big Texan?" I ask that evening as I park by a vintage police car and a cow statue the size of a small house.

"Whoo!" Bridger pounds the back seat with his fist three times. "The home of the seventy-two-ounce steak challenge, baby!"

My laugh comes out as a snort. "You're not."

Bridger pokes his head between Benny and me. "Oh yes I am." He kisses Benny's cheek, then mine. "What else are we going to do in the beef capital of the world?" He hops out of the car, then opens the door for me. "Do you doubt my ability, Miss Jessup?"

I pat his stomach. "Not for one second."

He grabs my hand as I pull away. "Wait. I wasn't flexing. Do that again. Unless you're worried about hurting your hand."

I simply shake my head. In the pocket of my purse, my phone chimes. I fetch it and cringe at the incoming call from Rockville Penitentiary. Roland's suggestion keeps my forefinger hovering over the screen until my hesitation makes it too late.

After some obligatory shots of Benny with the big bovine, iconic cowboy sign, and the random dinosaur in cowboy boots, we head inside the Big Texan Steak Ranch to the hostess stand where a pretty girl in twin braids and a cowboy hat might have fallen in love with Bridger at first sight.

"I spoke with your manager about doing the challenge this afternoon," Bridger tells her.

"Yes, he told me that Bridger Rosenblum would be here." Between batting her eyelashes and twirling the end of a braid, the girl couldn't be any more obvious about her crush. "Will your mom and your, uh, assistant be doing the challenge too, or will they need menus?"

He grins but lets her assumption stand. "They'll need menus."

Does he see me as his assistant? Or is he trying to work that Bridger magic with this girl who is, let's face it, probably exactly his type?

Either way, it gets under my skin. How else can I explain what comes out of my mouth next? "I will be doing the challenge as well."

That gets his attention away from Elly May Clampett. "Really?"

I shrug. "If you can do it, I can do it."

"We have another couple that wants to do the challenge as well. Would you mind sharing the table?" the hostess asks.

"The more the merrier," Bridger says.

"Here they come now."

Bridger looks behind me and does a double take. "Ohio! We meet again!"

I turn to see Tim's and Sandy's familiar faces. The five of us exchange greetings and hugs, quipping about seeing the same people stop after stop along the route, before heading into the Western-style dining room together. One table sits on a stage in the center. Behind it, a countdown clock reads sixty minutes—the time we have to complete the challenge.

"We have to do this on a stage?" I ask, feeling a touch of stage fright.

"Yep," Tim says. "There's a livestream on their website too."

"Great. I've always wanted to vomit live on the internet." I get no response, so I glance over my shoulder to find Bridger in conversation with the hostess again, giving her the same flirty smiles he gives me. My ears turn poker-hot. I undo my convertible-friendly French braid and comb my hair to cover them.

After we've settled into our seats and Benny and Sandy have ordered one of the reasonable meals on the menu, I ask our Ohio friends how the trip has been going. Not going to lie, it's mostly to distract myself from Bridger and Elly May's googly eyes.

"We've been having the best time," Tim says. "We saw the Museum of Pioneer History, Arcadia's Round Barn . . . Oh, and Sandy got her Route 66 guidebook signed by the author Jerry McClanahan. And every time we see replicas of the characters from *Cars*, we stop to take a picture for our grandkids."

"Ka-chow," Bridger says in true Lightning McQueen–style.

"What about you?" Sandy asks. "How's your trip going?"

"Benny's son, Roland, met up with us in Oklahoma City, which was a real nice surprise." I feign as much enthusiasm as I can muster.

Benny chuckles. "It was a surprise, all right. I'm not sure how nice though. He's nearly sixty, but he can still be a handful."

"My mother would probably say the same thing about me. Blessed be the mothers." Tim raises his glass of water in a mock toast.

Bridger lifts his as well. "Hear, hear."

Our meals arrive, along with a waiver for us to sign that states the rules. After sixty minutes, if we haven't eaten the seventy-two-ounce sirloin, baked potato, side salad, shrimp cocktail, and dinner roll, we'll be required to pay the cost of the meal, which is about the size of my grocery store bill for two weeks.

As we begin the challenge, Bridger hypes up the crowd in the dining room. And although he said this has nothing to do with the documentary, he props his phone on the edge of the table to get a time-lapse video.

I move through the meal the same way I approached college, graduate school, and my career—systematically. I dissect the food into six portions. If I eat one portion every nine and a half minutes, I will have time to rest my chewing muscles and stretch in between. Everyone else at the table jokes around, but I buckle down and focus on the task at hand. Before I know it, twenty minutes have gone by.

"Hey, Bridger," one of two men seated at a nearby table yells. "Is it true you were raised by wolves?"

I pin the man with a glare, which only seems to goad him more.

"You've gotta be kidding me," Tim says. "Remember when we told you about the two men that were harassing us back in Missouri? That's them."

That convinces Bridger and I to take a long, hard look at the hooligans, as Sandy had called them. One man sits a head taller than the other and wears a baseball cap. The shorter one is sporting a mullet—one of the trendy hipster ones.

"Hey, Mowgli, didn't you hear me?" the short one yells.

A flash fire burns through my veins, and I slam my fists on the table.

"Ignore them," Bridger says to me. "They don't know me."

"It doesn't matter. It's racist and not even geographically accurate."

Bridger laughs. "If I got upset every time someone called me Mexican, Indian, Hawaiian, Aleutian, or Black, I'd never be happy. Let it go, Jade, and eat up."

Letting it go isn't in my wheelhouse. I'm ready to yank that racism card out of Bridger's back pocket and shove it down the man's throat. Luckily, two guitarists intercept, playing the first few notes of "Get Your Kicks on Route 66."

Trying to take a page out of Bridger's book, I move onto my third portion. I'm doing well in the challenge, but I'm full already. I'm not accustomed to eating big meals, or meat in general. Certainly I'm not ready to give up, especially with the cost of this meal hanging over my head.

"Jade, Bridger," Sandy says, "how long have you two been dating?"

"We're not." My words come out far more curt than I intend.

"I'm sorry. I didn't mean to assume."

"No worries," Bridger says.

Tim puts down his fork like this is a great excuse for a break between bites. "You two would be cute together. Have you ever considered it?"

"I'm celibate."

"He's celibate," I say at the exact same time.

Boy, did that get them laughing. I'm not in the mood though. I bury my face in my baked potato. Eventually, Tim stacks his plates, signaling that the Big Texan was too big for him. But I can see the finish line, and I won't stop for anything.

Not even a roll hitting me in the forehead. The two hecklers hoot and clap. "Sorry, toots. I was aiming for the last Mohican there," the one in the hat says. "Hey, Bridger, seen any good rehabs lately?"

Bridger's face turns an almost blistering shade of red, and a vein throbs at his temple. Still, he sits.

Until the mulleted man invites me to do something quite vulgar with him and his buddy in the parking lot.

Bridger stands, knocking over his chair, making the crowd gasp. The men aren't intimidated though. In fact, they appear revved up for a fight. And as much as I would love to walk over and projectile vomit on the men, I know how these stories

184

end—with a lawsuit that neither me nor Bridger can afford. I take his hand.

"Let it go, remember? Besides, we can't afford this food. Let's get back to it."

Tim rises from his seat. "I'll handle it."

And he does. Calmly, he explains to the men, who can't be much younger than me, that this is a family restaurant and none of the guests want to hear offensive jokes or see two men get their hides tanned by Bridger. It's enough to stall until Elly May Hostess can bring the manager over to escort the men out the door.

I let the applause from the crowd fuel me. I check the clock as I stuff two cold, mushy shrimp into my mouth. Yuck. Crustaceans should not be food. The last bites of steak aren't as delicious as the first, but that's only because my jaw hurts and I've somehow outgrown my pants in fifty-two minutes.

"That's all I got." Bridger's fork is loaded with salad greens when he drops it back onto his plate.

I pause my chewing of the third shrimp to urge him on. "You can do it. You only have the salad and a bit more steak."

"I know." He stretches his arms above his head, dropping his napkin in the process—a white flag if I ever saw one.

Elly May comes onto the stage twirling that braid again. "I can't believe those men. What nerve!" She looks at me. "I would have died of embarrassment if I was hit in the face by a roll on a livestream."

"I've been through worse." I stuff the final bite of steak in my mouth and shove my plate away triumphantly.

The clock reads less than two minutes left in the hour-long challenge. As the manager grabs a microphone and begins announcing that I've finished all the food, Elly May slips a piece of paper into Bridger's hand. He opens it and peers at a scrawled social media handle. Then he glances at the girl and winks.

The owner asks my name, but I swat the microphone out

of the way so I can pick up Bridger's fork and salad plate. While I finish off Bridger's meal, the audience cheers and the guitarists play "Life in the Fast Lane" so loud I can't hear the owner's words.

I won't sit by while the Alderidge family loses more money if I have it in my power to stop it. Not even the amount of this steak dinner.

I stand as I swallow the last bite of Bridger's steak with ten seconds remaining. Although I try to bow, my torso refuses.

"Talk about teamwork!" the owner says. "Unfortunately, the rules of the challenge state that each individual must finish on their own, but hey, you can pat yourself on the back. Just don't do it too hard. But there's a trash can right beside you, just in case."

I'm still in my zone minutes later as we, once again, say good-bye to Tim and Sandy on the porch of the Big Texan. Bridger keeps close tabs on me as we walk to the car. "Why'd you do that—finish my food?"

"Because if you didn't finish it, you'd have to pay for it. I wanted to save you money. I didn't think about that dumb rule."

"I thought it was quite admirable," Benny says.

"Admirable, yes. But unnecessary," Bridger rubs the back of his neck. "I hate to tell you this, but I spoke to the owners. We were going to be comped no matter what. Because, you know, the celebrity thing."

"Are you serious?" If my stomach could drop, it would.

"I am. I should've told you, champ." Bridger motions to my stomach, which is distended quite visibly. "On a scale of one to ten, how uncomfortable are you?"

Since we first arrived, clouds have rolled in, tamping down the bright Texas sunlight—the only weather Bridger feels truly comfortable driving in. "Whatever number lets you drive for a bit so I can lie down on the back seat."

"I think I can handle that. I gotta admit, I was proud of

you up there." So maybe my worry about the hostess wasn't warranted.

"What happened here?" Benny's fingers touch the back panel over the driver's side rear wheel where dark scratches form shapes. No, letters. After I read what has been keyed into the paint of this vintage beauty, I retch on the pavement.

Chapter 27

1956
Benny

"One milkshake. Two straws," I said.

"Sure, hon." The waitress tapped the eraser of her pencil on her notepad. "Anything else?"

"Just the check when you get a chance." Paul sat across from me at Tucumcari's newest diner, Del's Restaurant, which would make sharing a milkshake tricky. "You are a funny girl, Berenice Briner."

I patted the spot on the booth next to me, and he took the cue. He put his arm around me and held me close. "So, how long do you think it will take us to break into the movies?" I asked.

"Probably a while, if ever."

I took hold of his shirt and tugged his collar. "You have to believe, Paul Alderidge."

"And what will we do before we become the next Lauren Bacall and Humphrey Bogart?"

"We can work as extras and audition for the different studios. For money, I can work as a waitress and bring milkshakes to young couples at a café on Sunset Boulevard. You can build sets, don't you think?"

"I can do that. The most important thing to me is that I support your dreams. Anything beyond that is . . . is . . . "

"One strawberry milkshake with two straws," the waitress said. She placed the milkshake topped with whipped cream and a cherry between us, then left to welcome another customer.

"Anything beyond that is a cherry on top," he said.

After we finished, we walked back toward the neon lights of the Blue Swallow Motel hand in hand. However, before we could get there, thunder rolled. The clouds opened up, and plump raindrops splattered against the pavement. One hit me on the tip of my nose and, shrieking, I started running. Paul quickly caught up with me, and together we ran through the heavy rain. We were soaked to the bone by the time we got to my motel room door, but rather than seeking shelter, Paul kissed me. Oh, and it was a good kiss. So good that I said, "If we were married, you could join me inside. No more sleeping in the car."

"That's true." He placed a kiss on my throat.

"And once we get to California, we could get one apartment instead of two. One stove, one sofa, one bed."

"Mm-hmm." Another kiss. This one on my jaw.

"We should do it. Let's get married, Paul."

The kisses stopped. He froze entirely, and I began to panic.

"I know it's soon. Too soon," I stammered. "Don't pay me any mind. I'm acting foolish."

"It's not foolish at all." He finally met my eyes. "You should head inside and get changed into dry clothes. Your mother will be upset if you catch a cold on account of me."

"What about you? The lightning is getting closer."

"I'll be fine in the car. Good night."

Except it wasn't a good night. Just after one, I was awakened by a pounding on the door. "Benny, are you there? Benny?" Paul's voice pitched with terror.

No less than a dozen possible scenarios ran through my mind. A tornado? Mudslide? A communist invasion? I threw the door open, and Paul nearly tackled me with an embrace. Then he put a hand on each side of my face and studied me. "You're okay. They didn't take you."

"Who? Who didn't take me?"

His body shook and tears streaked his cheeks, but then he came to. He stepped back from me and wiped his sleeve across his jaw. He stuttered, then paused. "No one, I suppose." Something warm trickled down my neck. "Paul, your hand is bleeding."

"You folks in some kind of trouble?" a man with a thick Southern accent and pinstriped pajamas asked from the door.

"No, sir. Thank you for checking. We're fine. An injury, is all." I ushered the man out and closed the door.

"I must've punched the car window." Paul stared down at his blood-soaked hand.

After a quick examination, I found a towel in the bathroom and wrapped his hand in it. "You'll likely need stitches tomorrow if we can find a doctor or a hospital. Why did you punch the window?"

"It was a nightmare. He took you away from me, then locked me in the sweatbox."

"Who did? One of the North Korean soldiers?"

Still trembling, he gave no answer. "It was a nightmare."

"You aren't going back out to the car. Don't you dare protest. You aren't sleeping on the floor either. I'll do that."

"Benny, be serious."

"Oh, I am serious. You are sleeping in that bed so that whenever you feel yourself slipping back to the dark place, you'll have every feather in that pillow and every stitch in that quilt to remind you that you're safe." I forced him onto the mattress and under the covers. I propped up his hand to hopefully stop the bleeding, then I slid down to the floor with my back against the nightstand and gazed into his eyes. "You're safe, Paul. And you're loved. I'm not going anywhere."

I didn't rest my head against the side of the mattress until his tortured soul found peaceful sleep. *It will all be better tomorrow*, I told myself. My surprise would make it better. After all, it couldn't get worse, could it?

~

Present Day
Jade

Dirty Orphan. The words carved into the Chevy's side earlier that day still nauseate me. Why would anyone do such a thing? Bridger didn't do anything to them. Not that any deed deserves this. And what really gets me is that if those men ran into trouble, Bridger would still give them the shirt off his back. He'd probably offer his pants too, and it would get awkward in true Bridger style. Then we'd all come together for a yoga session.

Outside the Blue Swallow Motel in Tucumcari, I run the back of my fingernail over the *D* scratched into the car. "It went down to the bare metal. We can temporarily cover it with duct tape. My dad always said there's nothing on a car you can't fix with duct tape or WD-40."

Bridger rubs the back of his neck. "You want me to put duct tape on my Chevy '55? Won't that ruin the rest of the paint?"

"It might leave adhesive, but it shouldn't lift any paint. Even if it does, we'll have to prime and repaint that panel anyway."

"How much will that cost?" He looks more tired than I've ever seen him. Benny took it hard too. That's why she chose to head to bed early.

"If I had the equipment, I could do it for the cost of the paint, 400 grit sandpaper, and a bucket of water. It should be easy to find the right white for her since she's a Tri-Five Chevy."

"How do you know this?"

"The summer I spent with my father, I worked beside him

at a garage. He was a genius when it came to cars—a real gear-head." I don't want memories of that summer lingering in my mind, so I change the subject. "It's supposed to rain tonight. I'm going to see if the motel office has some tape so we can keep this from rusting."

"I'll join you."

We stroll through the parking lot, smiling and nodding to some other motorists sitting around a small firepit. It was busy today. So busy I had to get a room across the road and a few dozen yards down at the Motel Safari—another vintage motor court. The real definition of vintage. Not my eight-year-old definition. Neither of us speak until we see the manager working the desk. After we've attained the tape—black, not white unfortunately, we head back out into the evening's thick air.

"You haven't said anything about how you're feeling," I say.

"There's not much to say now, is there? After all, I am an orphan. That much is true."

"Benny would disagree with that statement."

"I appreciate you wanting to help me, but this isn't something others can understand."

"I might. I haven't had any contact with my parents in years."

I pick at the end of the tape where it has adhered to itself.

"That doesn't make you an orphan," he states matter-of-factly. "You can't understand. Your parents might have hurt you—for years, decades even—but they aren't dead. They're still your parents. You could call your mother and try to patch things up. God willing, you'll find your father one day and reconnect."

My heart drums against my sternum until it begins to ache. I press my hand against my breastbone. "And you have a woman who desperately wants to be your mom in the legal sense as much as she already is in the emotional sense. You're dragging your feet, waiting to become someone else, even though she loves you as you are. You're choosing to remain an orphan."

He rips the tape roll out of my hand. With one quick motion, he stretches a length of it and cuts it with his teeth. "Even if Benny adopts me, it won't change what I've been through." He spreads the tape across the top half of the words.

"I didn't say it would. What you've been through is part of your story. But if you think about it, everything has worked out. Even you getting adopted by American parents, as awful as that was. You got your sight back, and it kept you from being killed in that tsunami."

His hands still, and he stares directly at the section of letters not yet covered. "Am I supposed to thank God I was taken from my family?"

"Bridger, I didn't mean that."

"Am I supposed to be thankful I got kicked out of house after house so I could end up on Benny and Paul's pity list?"

While he pulls a second strip of tape to apply to the car, I take a mental step back. My lungs struggle to fill, giving me an all-around lightheaded feeling. What happened to the always positive, always calm man I've come to know over the past two weeks? "I'm not trying to minimize what you've been through. I'm sorry if that's how it came across." I reach for him.

His shoulders tense and his fists clench. "It's been a long day. You should probably go to your motel."

I withdraw my hand, searching for pockets these slacks don't have. He isn't wrong. My words have cost me loved ones before. If I keep trying to fix this, I'll probably make it worse.

Chapter 28

2003
Jade

By the time we pulled into the parking lot of a dark wood building with neon signs hanging in the windows, I was hungry again. "Can we get food here?"

"Probably. At least some pretzels or something to tide you over."

I stared at one of the signs. "Bud . . . wees . . ." I tried to sound out.

"It's a brand of beer. This is my friend Glynda's bar, Tecoma Tavern." Daddy turned to the back seat where I'd created my own little world with coloring pages. A sports car, a pickup truck, and a van for a family. I wished I had a big enough family for a van. Maybe one day Daddy would meet a new lady—someone nicer than Mom—and they'd give me lots of little brothers and sisters I could help take care of.

A piece of my hair fell in front of my face. I quickly tucked it behind my ear. "I don't want to see anybody. I look ugly."

"Glynda used to be a hairstylist." Daddy helped me out of the car. "She said she can fix your hair and make it look pretty again."

Then a lady with red hair—the pretty kind—came out the door, wiping her hands on her apron. "Is this her? Your daughter?" She kneeled in front of me. "Aren't you the prettiest thing? My name is Glynda, and you and I are going to be good friends, Julianna."

I looked over at Daddy.

"Her name is Jade now. And I'm Jimmy."

Glynda stood and went to him. When she pressed her face against his, I squeezed my eyes closed. I hope they don't do the things men and women do in the yucky videos Hank watched on the big TV. I didn't open my eyes until a gentle hand touched my shoulder.

"Come on inside, sweet girl. I can make you look like you were born to be in the Southwest. And I bet you're hungry too. I just got the best tamales in the country delivered, and one of them has your name on it."

"It has my name on it, for real?" I asked.

Daddy and Glynda both laughed. I don't know why because it was a lie. My name wasn't on it. And as I soon learned, lies aren't funny.

~

Present Day
Jade

Light and shadows creep across the ceiling of my room as I lie awake, hour after hour. I blame the rain for my insomnia. Lightning and thunder do a number on my nerves no matter where I am or how safe it is. But the storm has long since passed, the only sign of its existence the tinkling of water spilling down the roof and into the gutter. Yet here I lie, still unable to find peace, hours after that wretched argument with Bridger.

I check the clock. A few minutes after two in the morning and my legs are restless. At this rate, I'll never conk out.

Maybe fresh air and stretching my legs will get me out of this headspace so I can come back inside for three or four hours of sleep. I climb out of bed and stand next to the luggage rack. Seems silly to change into dress clothes for only a few minutes outside. Instead, I grab the cuffs of my pajama sleeves and slide my arms into my tan dress jacket. I won't be winning any outfits of the year with this ensemble, but what are the chances I see anyone in this sleepy little town this time of night.

I slip my feet into my most comfortable heels—I really need to get some sandals or something—and pocket my room key. As quietly as I can, I exit my room, making sure the door softly clicks closed. Just because I can't sleep doesn't mean I should wake up anyone else.

First, I walk a circle around the parking lot but soon find that to be as enclosed as my beautiful but small room. Instead of doing another loop, I direct my steps to the large Motel Safari sign. Its neon bulbs and that of the Blue Swallow are the only sources of light nearby. Like a moth, I'm drawn to the purple, blue, and red. There's a strange feeling of home that accompanies it. Just like that silly Budweiser sign at the Tecoma Tavern, a place I once grew to love.

Route 66 is a ghost road in the midnight hours, especially after a storm. There aren't any headlights in either direction.

With my toes on the edge line, I get the urge to do one of Bridger's yoga stretches. He said it helps settle his mind and emotions, which is exactly what I need, so I try it—warrior pose or something like it. Keeping one leg straight, I step forward with the other, bending my knee and leaning over it with my arms wide. This body I can control. What I can't control is . . .

"Open your body to the side." The voice comes from the overhang at the Blue Swallow. Bridger emerges from behind a late-50s Hudson Hornet. Also in his pajamas, he strolls toward me, and I toward him. We meet on the broken yellow line in the middle of the road.

"Why am I not surprised that you're ready for a business meeting at two in the morning?" Twin lines dig into his forehead, between his brows.

"I couldn't sleep," I say. "I feel sick over how I treated you earlier. I overstepped and shouldn't have made assumptions about what you've experienced or how you feel. I'm very sorry, Bridge."

"I'm sorry too. I had no right to dismiss your experience or assume it was any less traumatic than mine. It might even be worse, knowing your parents are somewhere out there and you can't talk to them."

I frown. "Good thing we're not in a trauma pageant. The judges would be in a pickle."

"A hundred percent. But what I should do is say thank you. You've been a sanity-saver on this trip." He waves back toward his motel room door, which is in both our peripheries. "Helping with Benny, doing all the driving, putting up with Roland."

Warmth blooms in my chest. "I'm happy to do it. This past year has been so lonely. I can never thank you enough for welcoming me, trusting me."

"I have a confession," he says shyly. "At first, I didn't want you to come with us. That was all Benny. She's pretty intuitive. Sometimes I wonder if she saw something in you that might fit something in me."

I tuck a curl behind my ear as I drag the toe of my shoe over the loose gravel between us. "Whatever the reason, I'm glad I'm here with you."

"I'm glad I'm here with you too." He palms the back of his neck. "I like you, Jade. Like, I like like you in a way I've never liked anyone."

Suddenly I can breathe deeper than before. Something's still off though. "What about the hostess from the Big Texan? You seemed to like her. And she's your usual type."

In the otherwise quiet night, his laugh resounds through the air. "I was only talking to her to make you jealous. It seems to have worked."

My heartbeat kicks up a notch. "Why would you want to make me jealous?"

"Maybe I wanted to fuel you for the challenge. Maybe because I'm incredibly immature."

I cross my arms and purse my lips.

"Or maybe because if you got jealous, then it would mean you must like me too."

"Like you?" I scoff. "I just hoped you weren't going to bring her along on the rest of this trip."

He lowers his chin and peers deep in my eyes. "Remember. I can tell whether someone is telling the truth or not. I already know you like me because, well, everyone does, Roland excluded. But do you like like me?"

There are so many answers to that question, but which one should I give to the handsome man in front of me? The hard truth or a much easier lie? "No," I finally say.

For several seconds, Bridger keeps reading me, until finally, he sings the title line of "Lyin' Eyes."

My cheeks flood with heat. I rock back on my heels, then forward on my toes, bringing me closer to him.

He slips one arm around my waist to keep me from rocking back again. "That's what I thought. Now, if only there was a way to stamp this big moment in time as we stand in the center of Route 66, the Mother Road, the Road of Flight, the Road of Dreams, where generations of Americans have traveled to—"

I kiss him to shut him up. It doesn't work though because his groan sends shivers down my spine, and I'm grateful when his hands press against my back to keep me from trembling any more. It's a sweet kiss, tender and light, the exact opposite of what I expected from a man of his stature.

Then I pull back and look into his half-lidded eyes. "Wait. Is this going to jeopardize your celibacy pledge?"

"Kissing's allowed," he whispers against my lips before capturing them with his own.

This. This is the kiss I'd always hoped to get. The toe-tingling, mind-bending, time-and-space altering kind. As soon as I'm dreamingly invested in the way his mouth moves over mine, he stops.

My heartbeat feels like it comes to a screeching halt. "What's wrong?"

"You know if we do this," he says, a bit breathless—something I take as a compliment, "if we really do this, it might get messy."

I slide both hands up the sides of his neck and into his long hair. "Messy is underrated, if you ask me."

Chapter *29*

1956
Benny

It was here! The day I'd been waiting for was finally here, and even better, I had Paul by my side. I tapped my foot anxiously on the floorboard with each mile we drove closer to Albuquerque. In Moriarty, we stopped at a doctor's office for some stitches on Paul's hand. Then, we headed to the Whiting Brothers service station for a fill-up. Leaving the Chevy in the hands of the attendant, Paul came around to my side of the car. He tucked one of my curls under my scarf. "How about a Coca-Cola? It looks like they've got some cold ones inside."

"Yes, please."

Paul lifted my hand to his lips and kissed my knuckles. I sighed happily. To think that in only forty miles, I'd have my two favorite men in the world before me.

It had been more than two years since I'd seen Louie. Not since he'd left for his assignment at the Pentagon. He hadn't come home between that assignment and the one he'd recently accepted at an Air Force base in Albuquerque.

I'd always struggled to keep secrets. In my excitement, my mouth often moved faster than my brain and I ended up spilling the beans. Not this time. I'd held my tongue, but I couldn't wait any longer. Paul returned to his seat and handed me my soda pop.

"I think we should toast," I said, holding my drink up.

"Sounds good. To what?" Paul squared his shoulders to face me.

"Cheers to new starts, new love, and old friends."

"Cheers," Paul said, clinking his bottle against mine. Then he raised the bottle to his lips, but I placed a hand on his arm.

"Before you drink, I have something exciting to tell you. You know that the next big city on the road is Albuquerque. Well, Louie was transferred to a base there. We're going to see him!"

Paul's smile fell. So did his bottle of pop. It hit the seat, then tipped backward, spilling into the crack before Paul could retrieve it. The attendant scrambled to find a rag and Paul jumped out of the car. While they worked together to clean the mess, I stared in the side mirror and chewed my thumbnail.

Once Paul finally got back into the car, he sat with his hands clutching the steering wheel.

When he didn't speak, I filled the silence. "Louie told me not to tell you about the transfer. That since it was a promotion, he didn't want you to feel bad because you left the service. That's silly though. I knew you'd be happy for him." I swallowed a sip of pop. "Paul, I don't understand. I thought you'd want to see your best friend."

"An Air Force base in Albuquerque, huh? Kirtland?"

"I'm not sure. I only have an address," I said. He still wasn't smiling though. I could change that. "Maybe it's a secret one. We aren't too far from Roswell. Maybe Louie impressed the right people in Washington and now he's heading up some secret mission out here."

Alas, my enthusiasm wasn't reciprocated. In fact, Paul didn't speak until we entered the Albuquerque city limits. He returned from a corner store with a detailed map of the city, which he spread across the hood of the car. "Kirtland Air Force Base is on the southeast side of the city, but the address he gave you is nowhere near that."

I stomped my foot on the ground, feeling like an angry five-year-old. "Why are you being like this? This is his home address, not his work address. He must live off base. Be honest. Did something happen between you? An argument of some kind?"

His splayed fingers tensed against the map. "We grew apart, that's all."

"Okay. We can fix that with this visit. You can do that, right? For me?"

His Adam's apple bobbed in his throat twice before he faced me again. "I'll do anything for you, Benny."

"Good. Then, on we go. You drive. I'll read the map."

From Route 66, I directed us north on Edith Boulevard, and it may have been my imagination, but Paul drove as if the Chevy's wheels were bogged down in tar. "We should be getting close now. It'll be on the left," I said, trying not to show my frustration.

We crossed Osuna Street, and the address on the paper no longer made sense. I'd expected apartments or perhaps a small neighborhood of Craftsman homes. Not this.

"This can't be right. Maybe he wrote it down wrong."

Paul said nothing. He steered the Chevy onto the drive of the Sandia Ranch Sanatorium with its garden, trees, clay walls, and barred windows. An asylum? Impossible.

"No. Turn around," I said. "We'll find a payphone and, and, and I'll call Momma. She'll have the right address. Go on. Turn around."

He didn't listen to me though. He parked the car in front of the entrance and turned it off. A muscle in his cheek flexed grotesquely.

"Benny—"

"I'm very upset with you right now, Paul Alderidge. The

fact that you might even think that my brother would be here is preposterous."

"I'm happy to drive away if that's what you would like."

My mind raced. Louie had only written one letter since he moved to New Mexico. The letter currently in my hand, with the envelope that held the return address in Louie's penmanship. I skimmed my brother's words. Nothing whatsoever hinted that he was in a place like this. So, without any other idea what to do, I left the car and Paul behind, marched up to the front doors, not knowing who or what I was about to see, and rang the buzzer.

The door swung open at the hand of Mamie Eisenhower's doppelgänger. "May I help you?"

"Yes, hello. This is rather foolish, I know, but I received a letter from my brother. He must have written the return address wrong on the envelope, but I've driven all the way from Chicago to visit him and——"

"May I see the letter?" she asked, holding out her hand.

I handed it over and waited with bated breath as she read the envelope.

"Louie Briner. You said you are his sister?"

"Yes, I am. Berenice Briner."

"Your brother is indeed a patient here. He was admitted two months or so ago."

I shuffled backward, straight into Paul, who caught me before I could tumble down the step. I looked up at him through bleary eyes.

"I'm here with you," he said. "You can count on me."

"Miss Briner, why don't you join me in our office? One of our doctors would be happy to go over your brother's records with you."

Soon thereafter we were sitting across the desk from Dr. John Myers, poring over my brother's thin folder of records. "On the fifth of June, 1956, Louis J. Briner was escorted by two captains in the Air Force. We'd been in contact with his commanding general at the Pentagon. He was admitted under the presumption of schizophrenia and paranoia."

"I don't understand," I stammered. Paul tried to hold my hand, but I tucked it firmly in my lap.

"He isn't the first veteran to need help returning to proper society," Dr. Myers said. "After our initial testing, we believe that Louie's time as a POW led to delusional and sometimes violent thoughts."

Paul's stoic expression added nothing to my understanding. Had he seen signs of this in the POW camp? When they were immersed in pro-Communist, anti-American propaganda? When Louie, a pilot, was tortured worse than the others for what they assumed he knew? Had that sickened my brother's mind?

"Is he beyond help?" Paul asked.

"We don't believe so. We pride ourselves on our use of the latest research and treatments for our patients. He'll have access to insulin therapy, hydrotherapy, electroshock therapy—"

"No! You can't." I bolted forward in my chair.

"It sounds worse than it is, Miss Briner. It can be quite useful in retraining the mind. We also offer therapeutic occupational therapy. When Louis gets roaming privileges, he'll be allowed to choose a job, perhaps as a baker or groundskeeper. We also have social events where he can reengage with a community. We have movies, dances, dominos, and bingo nights. And in our recreation room, we offer pool and Ping-Pong."

As if the promise of good times could allow me to walk out of this building feeling better. "I want the name of his commanding officer—the person who arranged this."

Dr. Myers exchanged looks with the woman who'd initially greeted me. "I'm not sure we can disclose that information."

I stood, stretching myself to my tallest height possible. "I'm not sure I can allow my brother to stay here, then."

Unimpressed, the doctor flipped to another page in the file. "It's not an option. His admittance here was a component of his honorable discharge."

A chill raced over me. "I demand to see him."

Again, the two communicated nonverbally until finally the doctor gave a curt nod.

The woman called upon an orderly—a man about my age dressed in head-to-toe white—and they led Paul and me to a ward labeled "High Risk." Slowly, we approached a door with a small, square viewing window.

Before the orderly unlocked the door, he turned to us. "So as you're not taken aback, he is restrained for his safety as well as others'."

"My brother would never hurt me."

"Even so . . ." The orderly didn't finish his sentence.

The moment the door cracked, I pushed forward, leading the way. But as soon as I saw Louie, all my breath rushed out in a cry. He lay strapped to a bed, his eyes fixed on the single point of interest in the entire room—a barred window.

"Louie?" I sank to my knees by his bedside and laid my arm across his chest.

He turned his head toward me, and his eyes worked to focus on my face. Did he even recognize me? His expression remained blank.

"It's Benny. I came all the way out here to see you." When he still didn't respond, I turned to the orderly. "What did you do to him?"

"He's been sedated, to keep him calm. Without it, he's combative."

"Not him. He's the most gentle brother in the whole wide world." I returned my focus to him. "Don't you worry, Louie. I'm getting you out of here." Finding the closest leather strap, I began to unclasp it.

But the orderly stepped in, pulling my hand away with such

force, one of the metal parts of the clasp scratched my hand, and I recoiled in pain.

"If you try that again, miss, you'll have to leave," the woman scolded.

I scowled and dealt her the only curse word I knew.

"Is he kept sedated twenty-four hours a day?" Paul asked.

"Oh, no. This was a particularly rough day. He attacked one of the other patients."

Louie's lips moved slightly, then a tear slid from the corner of his eye to his temple.

"I'm here, Louie." I placed my palm on his cheek, and he turned into it. "That's it. You recognize your sister Benny. I knew you would. Guess what. I'm on my way to Hollywood. I'm really doing it, but I wanted to visit you on my way west."

He blinked slowly, but I thought he understood me.

"You look good. So handsome. It makes me wonder how many nurses have fallen in love with you already," I chuckled. Louie always had a girl on his arm in high school. Sometimes two, and he couldn't have changed that much. "I have another surprise."

Paul stood back by the door. I went to him, took his arm, and tugged. He didn't move. "I know it's hard to see him like this, but he needs to know he's loved right now more than ever before." I pulled with all my might, and it was enough to get Paul to Louie's bedside.

"Look, Louie. I brought Paul with me."

Their eyes met. Then Louie released a garbled growl and tried to sit up. He fought against his restraints, bucking his body up and down, then back and forth.

"Get them out of here," the orderly commanded the woman. He pinned Louie's body to the bed and called for help.

Between the woman and Paul, I was shoved out of the room, past a cart with needles and vials being pushed by a nurse.

"No! I want my brother," I protested. "Please! I don't want to leave him. Don't make me go." I fought them, but it was futile. Entirely futile. The man I'd brought on this trip for protection and strength was now using it against me. By the time we were back to the car, I didn't like him so much anymore.

Chapter *30*

Present Day
Jade

Benny rests on a boulder, staring at the open field where the Sandia Ranch Sanatorium once stood. She presses a palm against her heart. "I'd like to take a break, if you don't mind. I don't like this part of the story."

"Benny, are you okay?" Bridger asks from behind the camera, concerned lines crossing his forehead.

"Peachy keen, jelly bean," she says with what I guess is a forced smile. "Maybe you can get some footage of the trees while I think of more pleasant things."

I place a hand on Bridger's shoulder, my thumb offering a quick caress. "I'll stay with her."

"All right. I won't be long." He holds our stare a few seconds too long for a platonic relationship, so I'm not surprised by Benny's words when I join her on the boulder.

"You can go with him. It's a nice afternoon for a lovers' stroll." Only Benny can say the word *lover* and not make the listening audience cringe. "You two don't think you can pull one over on me, do you? Keep in mind that I starred in *A Kiss*

208

Between Friends. I know what happens when a man and a woman give in to their feelings."

My mouth goes a smidge dry. Had she been as bold with Bridger when he returned to their room after kissing me until a sedan honked us back to reality?

"Jade, sweetheart, you don't have to play coy with me. I've never heard Bridger whistle a day in my life. And you're looking at him like he painted the moon and stars. I think it's wonderful."

"Really? It doesn't bother you, having me"—I shift my position on the stone—"interfere with your family even more?"

"Is there a new meaning for the word *interfere* that you young people use? Because I don't see you interfering at all. I've been praying for a nice girl for Bridger as long as I've known him. And I've been praying for a Paul Alderidge for you. That's Bridger."

"It was a kiss. That's all." A twinge of guilt hits me at my blatant lie. The truth is it was so much more than a simple kiss. Bridger redefined what a kiss is. The way it felt physically and emotionally. How long a kiss could last. "It's not a big deal."

"Would it be so bad if it was?"

I press my lips into a tight line.

Benny rummages through her purse, eventually pulling out a tube of lipstick and a compact. "You know the best part about being my age? I can speak my mind and if people agree with me, they pat themselves on the back for being on the same side as wisdom." Using the small mirror, she shakily applies the rosy shade to her lips. "And if they disagree with me, they pat me on the head and think, *What a sweet lady with a few screws loose.* Either way, I get to speak my mind."

"I'm listening."

"People think they don't like knight-in-shining-armor, damsel-in-distress fairy tales," she says, depositing the makeup back in her purse. "But what they really don't like is the way the story is told—from a man's perspective. Hans Christian Andersen, the Brothers Grimm, those male studio heads who were the catalyst for the MeToo movement."

I nod, wondering where Benny might be going with this.

"Now this is not a politically correct position, but men—they need women, and they need them more than most of them are willing to admit. Women like men. Sometimes we love them. And though we might think we need them, if you take the men away, we see how strong and independent we are capable of being on our own. We don't often hear about the prince's search for the princess. We don't hear him sing 'Someday my princess will come.' But behind the scenes, he's looking and polishing his armor so that if he finds her, she might find him suitable."

"Are you saying Bridger's polishing his armor?"

"In a way. He's come a long way from that angry, rebellious teenager. A few years ago, he accepted our invitation to join us at church. The sermon sparked a desire in him to live differently. He wanted to live a life of giving, not taking. He wanted to be a good husband one day, just like Paul. So he checked himself into rehab a few days later. Now, Bridger had been to drug and alcohol rehab before, but this was different. He returned home as the Bridger you've gotten to know here—devoted, loving, and at peace with God and humanity."

A breeze rustles the leaves of nearby trees, and Benny lifts her face to the sun. "Before Paul passed away, we were both ill with COVID. There wasn't much hope for either of us once it got into our lungs. However, I knew there were storylines to tie up. If my soul left this earth, Paul wouldn't have been able to survive alone. I could. Even though it would be hard, I could." Benny stares off into the distance where Bridger captures B-roll footage of the vacant lot. Tears pool in her eyes, and her lips pinch until she speaks again. "So the last thing I said to my Paul was that he didn't need to keep fighting. He could rest. He could have peace. I'd finish things up here. I'd disseminate our fortune to the causes for which we'd lived, and I'd see that Bridger was taken care of. Once those two things were done, I'd go looking for Paul."

Her quavering voice adds to the weight pressing down on my shoulders. All this time my focus has been on restoring Benny's finances and thereby, restoring my good name for the sake of my career. A greater purpose, however, is niggling its way into my heart. Perhaps it already has. If, at the end of this trip, Benny feels that Bridger is safe, well, and secure, she can have that sense of peace she seeks. She can find Paul on the golden streets of heaven without remorse. What greater good can I offer than that?

~

2003
Jade

"Keep 'em closed, Baby Jade."

"Daddy!"

"Sorry. Keep 'em closed, Jade. No peeking," Daddy said.

"I'm not," I said in a shaky voice. I stutter-stepped as he pulled my hands forward. "Don't let me fall."

"Never." He released my hands. "Okay, take a look."

I opened my eyes. Dust fairies floated in the sunlight in front of me. I swiped at them. They swirled about but remained. I looked up. Boxes stacked high against the wall. Several trash cans were in the corner, a few tipped over. Two garage doors kept the fresh air out, and I coughed. My tennis shoes stood in a dried puddle of something dark. I backed away, bumping into a counter with a sink.

"This is going to be our garage. We're gonna clean it up and help out all the travelers that come through."

"Um, Daddy? We're gonna need a whole lotta Windex."

Daddy laughed, which made me happy. "Yes. A whole lotta

Windex and Lysol and Mr. Clean. Guess what's behind that door?"

"Skittles?"

"Sorry. No Skittles. Better! Come on." He opened the door to show steps that went up to a second floor. He held my hand as we climbed. "Up here is where we're gonna live. There's two rooms, a bathroom, and a kitchen. You get to choose which room you want."

I wanted to be happy, but my new home was as gross as the garage. The carpet was stained. So were the walls. Old furniture was busted up and flipped over. And it smelled like when the boys in my class pulled each other's fingers. My face got really hot. Big fat tears plopped down my cheeks and onto the floor.

"Oh, Jade."

I shook my head. "I'm trying not to cry, Daddy, I promise I am. I'm sorry." Those tears kept coming even when I pressed my fingertips to my closed eyes and begged them to stop.

"Go ahead and cry if you need to, baby." He picked me up and held me like he used to when I was little. I squeezed his neck tight. "Miss Glynda said she would help us clean this place. We'll tear out this carpet and put in some nice linoleum, maybe. You and me, we can go get some new paint—any color you want. She also said she has an extra mattress we can borrow until I can get you a new one."

"Where are you gonna sleep?"

"I'd rather sleep on the floor. It's good for my back after all that sitting in the car." Daddy brushed my curls off my wet face. "You'll see. We'll make your room perfect. We can put some of those glow-in-the-dark stars on the ceiling. We might could even find a poster with Justin Timberland on it."

I giggled. "Timberlake."

"Isn't that what I said? Anyway, can't you see it? Our new home?"

I squinted until I could only see a little bit. Even that was blurry. I let Daddy's words color in the rest of the room. "I can see it!"

"Good! And first things first, we're gonna need a CD player so we can play some Eagles while we fix this place up. That way we can sing our hearts out."

"And dance!"

"Dance? You mean, like this?" Daddy tightened his hold on me and spun me around super fast.

I squealed and laughed until I was so dizzy I almost puked. Then I begged him to do it again.

Chapter 31

Present Day
Jade

"Serious question," Bridger asks. "Why do you have fingers for toes?"

"What?" I lift my feet out of the water and stare at my bare toes. I bump Bridger's shoulder as we sit at the edge of the motel pool. "I have pretty toes."

"Sure. They are long, dainty, and perfect for peeling a banana or playing the violin."

"I can't believe you're making fun of me when you have enough muscle to account for a high school football team."

"Not true. Psh. A college football team, at least. Maybe pro in the off-season."

"You don't lack for confidence, do you?"

"Not anymore. Not since I got you wrapped around my finger."

Wrapped around his finger. Just like Dad. I release a groan up to the starry sky. The first line from "Seven Bridges Road" runs through my head. I can picture Dad crooning the lyrics loudly as he sweeps the dirt on the garage floor into my dustpan.

"Where'd you go?" Bridger asks.

"Hmm?"

"You did that thing where you kind of left your body for a minute."

"Oh, I didn't know I did a thing." I stare at the small ripples of water before me.

"Cool. Don't answer. We can do this instead." He twists his body, slowly tackling me back on the pavement, and presses his lips to the spot where my neck meets my shoulder.

I squeal as his beard tickles me.

"Shh. You're gonna wake up Benny," he mumbles against my skin, further teasing my nerves.

"Fine, I'll talk. I'll talk."

Just like that he pulls me back up to a seated position.

"I've been having a lot of memories of my father lately, especially now that all these small towns are resembling Tecoma. Like the service station where we bought oil for the Chevy earlier. When my father and I arrived, he rented an old service station, cleaned it up, and started doing business out of it. We'd sing Eagles songs at the top of our lungs while we worked."

"You know, everything you've told me about your father doesn't—"

"Make him sound like a murderer?"

"Uh, that's blunt, but yeah."

"He wasn't a bad man, despite what the newspapers said. He didn't mean to kill Hank. He just wanted to scare him, I think, so he wouldn't hurt me. You know he never did tell the court what I said."

Bridger cocks his head. "Really?"

"He didn't want to drag me through the police investigation or trial, especially since what I'd originally told him wasn't true. And he pled guilty in part to convince me it wasn't my doing. He was a good dad to me."

"Do you think he ever felt guilty for rocking your childhood so hard? Even though his intentions were to protect you, he heaped a pretty big amount of trauma on you at a young age."

"Maybe. I've been thinking. About stopping in Tecoma? I think I'd like to. Or need to. I need to know why he cut me out of his life. I thought I'd moved on, but clearly, I haven't."

Bridger sticks his arm out, and I burrow into his side.

"Even if my father isn't in Tecoma, maybe someone else will know where he is."

"Sounds like a plan."

"You sure it won't mess up your production schedule?"

"I'm not much for schedules, especially if it can help you out."

Already, I feel the fear pulsing in my heart. All the what-ifs. *What if he isn't there? What if he is? What if he died yesterday and I'm too late?* Heat climbs my neck despite the cool night. So much it stifles my breath. Without a word, I slink into the pool, beneath the water's surface, dress clothes and all. I suspend myself in the weightless world, letting my hair swim around my face. Once my lungs burn for new breath, I stand, emerging from the water.

"Belly flop!" Bridger jumps, spreads himself wide in the air, and smacks the surface hard, splashing me in the process.

"Good night, Bridger!" I shove an unimpressive wave of water back at him.

He dives forward, pulling me under before I can protest. Of course, I don't mind so much when he kisses me beneath the surface.

When we come up for air, Bridger nudges my nose with his. "What did I tell you? I've got you, girl."

~

1956
Benny

We stayed in Albuquerque another day so I could visit Louie once more. Paul tried to dissuade me, but I needed to talk to my brother when he wasn't sedated or I wouldn't be able to continue on our trip. Paul understood but chose to wait in the office.

I sat by myself in a small, sterile room with only a table and two chairs. My nerves were on edge simply being in there for five minutes. I couldn't imagine what the patients felt.

After an eternity, the door opened and Louie entered the room in a dark shirt and overalls, followed by a different orderly than yesterday. I rose from my seat with much less energy than I felt and calmly embraced him. Tentatively, he put his arms around me, and I was grateful he wasn't restrained in any way.

"Louie, I've missed you very much."

"I missed you more, sis. I can't believe you're here."

Where my hands rested on his back, my fingers fell into the grooves between his ribs. Still as small and thin as he'd been when he first returned from Korea. How could anyone possibly believe he was a threat? Louie was the most gentle soul. Even if he wanted to hurt someone, he was too weak. I pulled away. "Why didn't you tell me you were here? I would have come earlier."

"That's part of why I didn't tell you." Louie's voice sounded so strained and hoarse, as if he'd been yelling.

"Take a seat, please," the orderly said.

Louie nodded and held my chair for me. Then he sat across from me but reached for my hand, holding it tenderly, even as his trembled against my skin.

"I came yesterday, you may or may not recall. You were . . . tired. I'm driving to California to pursue my dream like I always said I would."

"I'm happy for you. I know you wanted this." Like Paul, Louie struggled to keep eye contact as he spoke and, instead, kept his focus on the table. For the ten thousandth time, I cursed the POW camp in my mind. When I waited to speak, he remained quiet. So he wasn't going to share without prompting. Fine.

"Louie, what happened in Washington? What brought you here?"

He clenched his jaw and his nostrils flared. "Alderidge didn't tell you?"

I stared, not understanding. "What does this have to do with him?"

His eyes grew large and almost . . . wild. "He's the reason I'm in here."

"How?" A sour taste filled my mouth, one I couldn't swallow.

"He was in Joliet with me."

"With you?" Louie tightened his grip on my hand. "With you?"

"Careful, Louie. You're hurting me." I tried to pull my hand away, but he didn't let me.

"Did that no-good traitor defile you?"

The bones in my fingers ground together. If he kept squeezing, he'd break something. "Please, Louie. That hurts."

The orderly stepped behind Louie and put him in a hold that forced him to let me go.

"I'm going to kill him. If he touches you, I'll kill him." He kicked the table so hard, it knocked me out of my chair. I tried to catch myself and pain shot through the heel of my hand, my wrist, and my elbow.

More orderlies came in. The one I recognized from the day before helped me to my feet. He may have asked me if I was hurt, but all I could focus on was the bloodlust in my brother's eyes when they dragged him out of the room.

"I love you, Louie," I called out in my cracked and broken voice. As soon as he was gone, I grabbed my purse and hurried out of Sandia Ranch.

Chapter 32

2003
Jade

"She's over here!" I pointed toward the Junk and Treasure Shop across the street. Okay, so maybe Daddy said it was called the Trunk and Treasure Shop, but the stacks of old shutters and piles of scratched-up spindle chairs and rusty bicycles looked more like junk to me. But Celine, my favorite of the wild burros that live between Tecoma and Oatman, loved that old store because the owner always fed her carrots.

I crouched behind the vintage Coke cooler, shadowed by one of the red, white, and blue flags hanging from the motel's front porch.

Max crept to my side and then raised his gun-shaped saguaro root in front of him, pretending he was a cop like his dad. "We can't let her get away this time."

"No. Not after she robbed that train of old nuns." I peeked over the cooler, checking that no cars were coming from the east or west. "On the count of three. One. Two—"

Max took off. I groaned. What a dummy. He was going to start fifth grade in four days, and he still couldn't count to three. I jumped up and ran across the road. If my legs were only a little longer, I could catch up.

Celine turned her head and her big, lashy eyes stared at us. Max dove onto the dirt and aimed his fake gun at her.

I giggled so hard I almost tripped. "You almost landed on that!" I pointed to the stinky pile Celine had left on the ground just minutes ago.

Max scooted away. "A sheriff's gotta do what a sheriff's gotta do."

With the back of my hand, I wiped the sweat off my forehead. As much as I wanted to see the Newtons' Fourth of July fireworks tonight, I was worried they would make tomorrow even hotter. It would be nice here in fall when it wasn't so hot outside. For Halloween, Daddy and I could go as Shrek and Donkey and not burn up in the costumes.

I sneaked up behind Celine and reached out to pet her. But the junk store's door opened, and Mrs. Henry popped her head out. "You children leave that burro alone. One day she's gonna bite you, and you'll learn the hard way."

"It's Celine's mom. Run!" I kicked up my heels and beat it back to our side of Route 66. But when I glanced back, Max wasn't with me. He stood by the lamppost with a confused look on his face.

"It's called electricity, Max. It starts as lightning, goes through the ground and up the poles, and lights the bulbs."

"This girl kinda looks like you, Jade."

I went numb when I saw the poster he was staring at. *Endangered Missing Child. Julianna Talbot. DOB 4/5/1995. My crooked-tooth second-grade school picture was right next to a smaller picture of Daddy.

"Julianna is believed to have been taken by her non-custodial father after her stepfather was killed," Max read. "Edward Talbot has ties to Illinois, Virginia, and Arizona. Do not approach. Call this number to report any sightings." Max turned his eyes toward me. "Don't you think she looks just like you? And that guy looks like your dad?"

220

Hank was killed? When? How? Was it an accident?

"How can I be missing when I'm right here?" I ripped the poster down. "Don't be stupid. I gotta go help my dad," I said over my shoulder as I walked away. "I'll see you later, Max." Once he was out of sight, I ran to the garage until my chest burned and my throat felt like I'd swallowed a firecracker.

❧

Present Day
Jade

El Rancho Hotel looms large over the parking lot in Gallup, New Mexico. Although dense fog rolled over the desert landscape, the light from the marquee above the entrance cuts through. "Charm of Yesterday . . . Convenience of Tomorrow" is written below the hotel name.

"It looks exactly the same," Benny says without her normal joy. In fact, the corners of her lips turn down. Since we left the former site of the sanatorium yesterday, she's said nothing about what happened after she discovered her brother's whereabouts back in 1956.

I was too curious to wait so I waded through internet sites last night after Bridger and I splashed around in the motel pool. Louis Briner was eventually released from Sandia Ranch in 1957. He moved in with Benny and Paul but never married or made marks worthy of note in any articles. He died in the 1980s and received a military burial in Westwood Village Memorial Park, the same cemetery where Paul was laid to rest.

Bridger didn't want to push her to share. In fact, when he tried to broach the topic this morning, she'd had another erratic episode where she flagged down a police officer, believing she didn't know us. It wrecked Bridger, and nothing I said could put him at ease.

Now we walk through the parking lot, and I'm careful not

to step in puddles. Not that it matters. My shoes at this point are toast. To be honest, I don't care either.

The lobby is two stories high with a lodge feeling—much different from the retro sixties vibe Route 66 has become known for. Double staircases cloaked in red carpet cascade around a tile-and-brick fireplace, accented with mounted, antlered animal heads. The rustic Southwestern style is paired with more celebrity memorabilia than I've ever seen. I peer closer at posters for *The Treasure of the Sierra Madre* and *The Sea of Grass*.

According to Bridger's research, there were many Western films made here in Gallup. This was where all the great stars stayed during the filming: Spencer Tracy, Katharine Hepburn, Gregory Peck. As I stand in the same place those stars once stood, I'm starstruck. Benny is less than impressed. Then again, those names are probably normal people to her.

While Bridger checks us in, she and I peruse the pictures of famous visitors on the second floor. One, in particular, catches my eye. A professional photo of Benny and Paul back in the 1960s, perhaps, with their signatures on the bottom. "Thanks for the memories. Thanks for the love," Benny wrote above hers.

Bridger climbs the steps two at a time and hands me a key. "You, my dear, are staying in Bogey's room, 213. Benny, you and I are staying in the Berenice and Paul Alderidge suite."

"You're kidding," I say.

"I am not. They have a room named after them. And get this. We get it at a fifty percent discount too." Bridger offers his arm to Benny and leads the way down the hall adorned with Navajo-inspired decor. As predicted, each door has a nameplate featuring the name of an actor, actress, or director who frequented this hotel.

I pause at the door marked Humphrey Bogart. "I guess I'll see you downstairs for dinner in a few."

"Yes, sweetheart. I want to powder my nose," Benny says.

"I need to powder mine as well," Bridger says with that

sophisticated mid-Atlantic accent Benny perfected. "I'll come get you when we're ready."

I've barely settled into my, er, Humphrey's room when my phone buzzes on the bedside table, signaling an incoming call. Rockville Penitentiary. Those two words leap off my screen and claw at my skin. This is what I've been waiting for since we left Amarillo. Still, it takes all my willpower to thumb an answering swipe.

I lower myself onto the armchair in my hotel room. "This is Jade."

"This is a call from inmate Gregory Hyrem at the Rockville Penitentiary. All calls are logged and recorded and may be listened to by a member of the prison staff. To accept this call, please stay on the line. If you do not wish to accept this call, please hang up now."

I immediately feel nauseated.

"Jade?" The shock in Gregory's voice would have been comical in any other scenario. "You answered."

"Hi, Gregory. How . . . how are you?"

"I'm surprised. I was beginning to wonder if you'd ever take my calls. I miss you like crazy."

"Mmm." I press the heel of my free hand against my eye socket.

"Do you miss me?"

"I don't know you—not the real you. How can I miss you?"

While I wait for him to respond, I count the stripes on the wallpaper. Finally, he speaks. "About what happened in Chicago . . . I got caught up. That's all."

"Caught up? Gregory, you ruined lives. I'm still upset. Everyone is still upset."

"Completely understandable. If I could, I'd apologize a thousand times for the hurt I caused you and our clients."

"Apologies don't get them their money back."

"I know. I promise, I only did it for us and our future."

There's a long pause. "Do you think there could ever be a future with us?"

Bile burns its way up my throat. "You're in prison for the next twelve years. I've been blocked from the financial industry. I have fifteen hundred dollars to my name."

"What? Why?"

"I couldn't keep anything you'd touched. I gave it all to the trustee. My salary from the firm, my apartment, my car, all the furniture and art." I can feel the edge in my voice scraping my throat, but I welcome it.

"You shouldn't have been forced to give that up."

"I offered." I button my lips to keep from adding, "and I'd do it again."

Gregory sighs. "I wish I could help you somehow."

A knock sounds at my door. Not just any knock. The tune of "Don't Worry, Be Happy." Ideally, I'd cut this call off and open the door to the man who brought happiness into my life, but I answered this call for a reason.

I force a sigh—the kind that Benny always made sound so lovely in her early movies. "I wish I hadn't given it all away. I'm so desperate, Gregory, I had to take a job as a, um, rideshare driver."

"A rideshare driver? I heard something different."

"What do you mean?"

"My lawyer said you're traveling with Berenice Alderidge and that hippie son of hers."

My chest burns. "Yeah, they hired me to drive them down Route 66 while they film a documentary. Like I said, I'm desperate." I tighten my abdominal muscles and pray that strength will enable my next words. "It's a shame there isn't money tucked away somewhere."

The following silence is long. I fan my face to stop the sweat from beading. Again, the knock sounds. No cute tune this time though, only a quick one that matches my racing heart.

"Gregory?"

"Why do I feel baited, Jade?" His tone has shifted. "You know these calls are recorded. There's no hidden money. I've handed over every dime in each account I had, both here and overseas."

"I knew you had it spread all over the place. I was just hoping there was a place you forgot?"

"I have plenty of time to think in here, especially since this is the first call you've answered. If I forgot about an account, I would have remembered it by now."

I stammer over my words, finally forcing out the question I've asked myself time and time again. "What am I supposed to do?"

"I don't know, Jade. You're going to have to be that strong, empowered woman who had no problem calling the regulators the day before our wedding."

As fire flashes through my veins, I prepare a slurry of insults, most of which compare Gregory to the incredible man standing outside my door.

But I don't get a chance because Gregory hangs up on me.

Chapter 33

1956

Benny

The trip to Gallup was long and hot. I didn't want to stop. I wanted to put as much distance between my brother and Paul as I could, though I still didn't know why that was necessary. We found vacancies at the El Rancho Hotel.

I had no appetite, but we went to the restaurant next to the lobby anyway. It was busy, but we found a table in the corner. After we ordered our food, I finally got up the nerve to confront Paul about what Louie said.

"What happened between you and my brother?"

Paul kept his eyes glued to the vase on the center of the table.

"We grew apart."

So help me, I wanted to reach across and force his chin up, force him to look at me when we spoke. I didn't though. "What made you grow apart? And don't say it was because he was a pilot. He would never let such a thing go to his head, and you would never let such a thing bother you enough to forget your best friend."

Paul mumbled something.

"What did you say?"

"I said, please don't keep asking about this."

226

"Why not?"

"Because you want to believe that people are inherently good, but they aren't. Louie isn't and neither am I." Paul stood abruptly. He fumbled to take money from his wallet, eventually dropping two twenty-dollar bills on the table—far more than the cost of our food—and left me there.

Perhaps I should have let it die right then. However, my spiritedness got the best of me. I chased Paul out of the restaurant and up the stairs to his room. I stuck my foot in the door right as he tried to close it. It took one shove, and I was standing in his room, gasping for breath. "What happened . . . in Washington?"

Paul paced near the bed. "I was never in Washington."

"What happened that followed Louie to Washington, then?"

"You don't want to know."

I had half a mind to take off my shoe and throw it at him. "Yes, I do. And if you don't tell me what you did to send my brother to that . . . that . . . place, then we are through, and this trip is through. I'll take a bus to LA, or I'll hitch a ride."

Paul came to a halt in front of me. He pulled his shoulders back, puffing out his chest, but I wouldn't budge on this, even if it was tearing my heart to pieces threatening to leave him. "If you truly want to know, I'll tell you."

"I truly want to know," I said after a hard swallow.

He sat on the edge of the bed, his shoulders lowering as well. "Something happened after we left the POW camp." He paused, reading me, perhaps hoping I might stop him right there. No such luck. "After we left Koje Island, we were released to Panmunjom, a United Nations–run medical camp. I was low in weight with a cough but otherwise in good health. Louie, however, was quite ill, in both body and mind." He took in a deep breath. "The morning we were to get on a plane back home, I went to visit him in the tent. He was there with this look in his eyes."

227

Paul swiped his hand across his mouth and stared at the wall. "Louie stood over the bed of a South Korean man who had also been a POW. Young-soo was his name, and he'd once shared his rice with me on a particularly bad day. He'd been on the mend the day before, saying the name of his wife again and again." A dry cough erupted from his chest. "But he wouldn't get to see his wife. He was dead."

My breathing quickened yet I still felt lightheaded as I tried to comprehend what was being relayed.

"Louie was holding a pillow. He said Young-soo was an infiltrator, planning to kill all of us in our sleep. There were streaks of blood—deep scratches—on Louie's cheek. . . . Young-soo hadn't gone easily."

Nausea ravaged my insides, and I pressed my hand to my mouth to keep from vomiting. I shook my head, refusing to believe Paul's story.

He carried on. "I moved toward Young-soo, but Louie stopped me, shoving me back. I told him I might be able to save him. He said no, that he and the rest of the 'Commies' wanted to finish us off. That was when I heard voices coming near the tent. Two Danish nurses entered and looked from me to Louie to Young-soo."

I stumbled back, catching myself on the dresser. Paul didn't even look my way.

"Louie said, 'He's not breathing,' and watched the nurses attempt to revive the man—but they couldn't. I'll never forget how, after that, Louie said, 'And so close to him going home.'"

I marched over to the bathroom sink to splash cold water on my face. Then I buried my face in a hand towel, wanting none of this to be real. That was it. I returned to the bedroom. To Paul. "You didn't actually see him do it. He might have imagined it or created a story like he used to when we were kids. Louie isn't capable of murder. He used to cry over dead birds we found in our backyard. And he loved the Korean civilians he met at the beginning of his deployment."

"Before he was captured," Paul said. He rose from the bed and met me by the dresser. "His mind was poisoned by the enemy. Add to that news stories of actual North Korean soldiers hiding among civilians, and it created a paranoia." Paul held me by my shoulders. "It wasn't the only time that Louie's paranoia showed, but it was the only time I reported it to our commander."

I jerked away from his touch. "You reported him for acting like a soldier in a wartime environment?"

A muscle ticked near Paul's jaw. "Killing unarmed allies is not acting like a soldier, no matter the environment."

Hot tears stung my cheeks. "There were all kinds of atrocities committed by the North Koreans, Chinese, and Russians. We heard about them on the news all the time."

"Our country committed war crimes as well." Paul lowered his voice. "They've been brushed under our government's rug."

"And Louie's the paranoid one?"

"It's not paranoia. It's facts. Louie isn't the only American whose actions went against the Nuremberg Code. But his was the only one I saw with my own eyes."

"But you didn't see it." The shrill pitch of my voice shocked me, but I didn't care. Louie needed someone to defend him.

"Louie didn't deny what he'd done. Not then, and not when I told him I was making a report."

"When did you report it?"

"After I'd been home for a year or so. I wanted to forget what I saw but I couldn't." Paul crossed his arms over his chest. "Benny, I'd wake up seeing Young-soo lying in that bed. I'd hear his voice when he spoke English words he'd learned from us. I couldn't keep it inside any longer."

"Washington didn't believe you. Louie was discharged honorably."

"You heard the doctor. Upon the agreement that he receive help at the sanatorium. I'm sure this was their way of dealing with the person without dealing with the crime."

I slapped away the tears on my face. *Curse these emotions.* They tempted me to comfort Paul for his ordeal. That would be choosing loyalty to him over my own brother though, wouldn't it? Again, I shook my head. "I can't be with someone who would hand my brother over to the authorities."

Paul took a step back from me. "And I can't be with someone who would expect me to keep such a terrible secret."

A million thoughts muddled my mind including some truly horrid ones that I'd never share. I was equal parts ashamed at my own defense of Louie's crime and angry at Paul's decision. That was positively impossible to reconcile, so I didn't. Without another word, I left Paul's room that night, not knowing what I was going to do next.

Present Day
Jade

"The next morning," Benny says, "I woke up early, got ready for the day, and left my room in search of breakfast. I'd only taken two steps down one of the grand staircases when I saw . . ."

She gazes out where erosion has formed a massive hollow in a rising butte—the perfect backdrop for all the cowboy Westerns that were filmed in Gallup long ago.

"You saw what, Benny?" Bridger's question strains his neck muscles.

I also go on high alert as Benny's hands agitate, and she shifts her weight back and forth in her camping chair.

"I saw a stallion over there. Anne couldn't wrangle it. It ran into the road and almost got hit by a motorist." She looks

Bridger up and down, then waves her hand in front of her. "They all, well, no one told me about this or them or you, with your long hair and tight T-shirt. Does Levi know you're here? I wish this weren't the case, but I wouldn't waste your time. He won't hire people your color."

Bridger leans forward and speaks softly. "We're doing an interview, Benny, about your trip down Route 66 when you stopped in Gallup. Would you like to take a break?" He turns to me. "Jade, can you get her a bottle of water?"

I reach into my bag but before I can withdraw the bottle, Benny stands up, knocking over a light-diffusing umbrella. I let it fall, choosing to come to her side instead.

She searches my face in desperation. "I need to find Paul. I didn't mean to send him away. I was angry. So angry." She peers down the road.

While I exchange glances with Bridger, Benny pulls away from me and walks straight toward Route 66. I hurry to block her path, as does Bridger. Quite a few cars travel the westbound lanes where the speed limit is fifty-five. One tractor trailer approaches eastbound.

"Get out of my way," she yells.

"You can't go in the road, Benny," Bridger says. "You'll get hit by a car."

Benny mumbles something unintelligible and throws herself into my left arm and Bridger's right in an attempt to break through our blockade. We catch her, but she continues to struggle toward the shoulder. In the process, she backhands me. Not hard, but her wedding ring catches the corner of my eye forcing me to fall back. With the pain, my eyelid refuses to open, and tears stream down my cheeks.

"Ow!"

Squinting, I see Bridger's head awkwardly angled. A fistful of his hair is held taut by Benny. Even still, he keeps her from advancing toward the dangerous path of the truck.

She spits in his face. "You won't keep me from him. I'll search for him with my dying breath!" The line of dialogue is from Benny's film *Happier Times*, but the curse word she adds after is not.

Once my vision clears, I help Bridger. Benny is no longer fighting or speaking. She looks lost though. We lead her back to the Chevy. Bridger's short of breath. Nearly hyperventilating. I know then, the choice of where Benny will go after this trip has been made for him.

2003
Jade

When I burst through the door of the garage, I sucked in a big mouthful of motor oil–smelling air and it turned my stomach. I coughed and tasted throw up.

"Hey, hey," Dad left his spot on the far side of a car hood and got to me quick. He held my shoulders as I tried to speak.

I imagined Mom dressed in black and crying over Hank's coffin. Gasp after gasp, I fought to erase the image.

"What's going on? Is Max hurt? Are you hurt?" He patted my arms and legs like he was looking for scrapes and bruises.

I held out the balled-up poster from the lamppost. He took it from me, straightened it, and with a sad look on his face, read the words under my picture. That's when I heard an awful noise, like a strangled cat.

"No, no. Don't cry, Jade. It'll be okay."

"What . . . What did you do, Daddy?"

After dropping the poster, he smoothed my hair back from my face. His eyes, nose, and mouth twisted in an ugly way. "Let me get you something to drink first."

A few minutes later, I sat at our tiny table and stared into my chocolate milk, watching each tiny bubble pop. My crying had softened to some sniffles so I could hear what Daddy was telling me.

"I haven't always made the best choices, Jade, but what happened was an accident," he said. "Hank . . . I think he had a heart attack. I didn't mean—ahem, it's a father's job to . . . to keep his little girl safe."

I picked at the skin around my nails. After a few seconds, blood spread onto the pink nail polish Glynda painted on yesterday. It was my fault Daddy hurt Hank. My fault. New tears dropped down my cheeks. "Mom's going to be so mad at me."

"No, she won't."

"Are we gonna go to jail?" I tried to drink my milk, but it dribbled down my chin.

"No one's going to jail. And no one's gonna separate you and me." He used a napkin to wipe my cheeks and chin. "That's why it's so important that we remember our new names. And we can't tell anybody what happened in Illinois. It's got to be our secret."

My body shook. Keeping secrets felt just as bad as telling lies.

Chapter 34

Present Day
Jade

It was a bad few days. Each time we prepared to film Benny telling the next part of her and Paul's story, her mind would slip back to years past. Since Benny's first film, *Sundown Shootout*, was shot here, Bridger wanted to spend more time capturing footage in New Mexico and hopefully, discovering what happened between her and Paul. Unfortunately, Benny's disease prevented that.

"We need to keep moving west," Bridger says softly as we stand outside El Rancho's Alderidge suite where Benny is resting. "Roland isn't happy with what this is costing. I think I have enough footage of the landscape and the interior of the hotel. I should be able to add her voiceover."

"That's probably the best option." My heart aches seeing him so worn down. "How are you doing?"

He answers with a deep sigh. "I called her doctor. He said we've reached zero hour. I set up an appointment with the team of clinicians at Swallow's Nest Memory Care for two weeks from today."

"Are you prepared for what they'll say?"

Bridger leans against the wall only a couple inches away from me. He trails a fingertip from my temple down over my jaw and then to the nape of my neck. "It's time. I want to be enough for her, but she needs specialized care that I can't provide. Realistically, I can't watch her twenty-four hours a day. Even if we hire a live-in nurse, there's too much of a risk she'd wander away in search of Paul. A memory care facility is the only option, and Swallow's Nest is the best in the country at what they do. It's time."

"At least now you know where her fear of being locked away comes from. From what she said about visiting Louie at Sandia Ranch . . . it sounded awful. Maybe if you talk to her and recognize her fear, you can help her get through it."

"But even then, I'll still have to convince her to sell the house to pay for her care."

Deep within me, I curse Gregory for not telling me where that money went. I take Bridger's hand and give it a squeeze. "Or this documentary will be so good, distribution companies will get into a bidding war and the proceeds will help you keep the house."

Bridger's focus sharpens on me, then he drops his head. "I don't . . . I mean, the film Roland thinks will sell isn't one I can make. Things have changed. Maybe I should throw in the towel."

"You can't quit, especially if you've already gotten backing from investors. Something tells me Roland wouldn't hesitate to bury your burgeoning career with news of a broken contract. Finish the film. Do it for Benny, Bridge. And do it for you. If the film's success will get you to a place where you can accept Benny adopting you, I think it's the right move."

The next morning, I'm navigating the Arizona portion of the route. It isn't easy. The original road crosses I-40 multiple times and then turns to rough pavement and dirt that leads through Querino Canyon. As Bridger points out, it's easy to imagine Steinbeck's 66 in this area. To imagine we are the Joad family, desperately seeking a better life away from dust and destitution only to find hardship after hardship, heartbreak after heartbreak. If Bridger is Tom and Benny is Ma, then who am I in the story? I'm not wise enough to be Casy. Maybe I'm Al, with his knowledge about cars. Or Ruthie or Winfield, with their naivety. Goodness, I hope I'm not Rose of Sharon. Regardless what character I am, by the time the road merges with I-40, I'm grateful for some interstate miles that don't rattle my bones.

As much as the drive is good for me physically, our detour through the Painted Desert is good for me emotionally. As if I've stepped into one of Georgia O'Keeffe's Ghost Ranch canvases, the hills roll from lavender to coral to red, rising above gray-green veins of sagebrush and saltbush.

"For the wonder of each hour, of the day and of the night," Benny sings in her pleasant rasp. "Hill and vale and tree and flow'r, sun and moon, and stars of light. Lord of all, to Thee we raise, this our hymn of grateful praise." I'm not sure in what year her mind is currently living, but it doesn't matter. The hymn is timeless.

From there, we cruise into Petrified Forest National Park, which Bridger rates only a two out of five, stating, "I thought a forest would have actual trees. Bad advertising." But he doesn't complain about the footage he gets, including the stretch of old Route 66 that nature has taken back, with only the rusted skeleton of a 1932 Studebaker and a line of ghostly telephone poles to mark its path.

Before he goes searching for a parking spot, Bridger drops us off at the entrance to the Painted Desert Inn, a Pueblo Revival-style structure with thick walls, earth-tone stucco, and petrified wood beams supporting its flat roof. Inside, the design echoes local culture with Hopi murals and pottery motifs etched into the skylights and Navajo rug patterns engraved in the concrete floor. The sweet and smoky scent of burning sage soothes my soul.

Benny and I find seats at the Harvey House counter in the Tap Room and sip from bottled water. She nods to the *Petrified Forest* movie poster on display. "If you had told me when I was young that I'd be as famous as Claudette Colbert, I'd have said you were crazy. God has indeed blessed my life and career."

"I think so," I reply.

"Not many women get to grow old in this business and keep working."

"Why did you stop?"

"I chose to when Bridger came to live with us. He needed a lot of love and attention. I don't regret that for a moment. He's been a good boy. He would never lock me away." Benny's eyes, normally a soft watery blend of blue and gray, gain a fiery gleam. "Roland tells me I need to live in a hospital, but I know what happens behind locked doors."

I force a swallow. "Benny, memory care facilities aren't like Sandia Ranch or the POW camp on Koje Island. You'd be protected and lovingly cared for."

"Experimented on," she says in a strained voice. "Bridger won't let them take me away. He's a good boy." She stands and trips off the step. I grasp her elbow, but it's a man that catches her before she hits the hard floor.

"Whoa there," he says.

My gaze travels up the blue-jeaned legs to a large belt buckle and tucked-in T-shirt. He grins crookedly at me. "Hey, pretty lady."

"You." My lungs fill with the rank air surrounding one of the men who harassed us at the Big Texan.

"Aww. Call me Dwight. You're Jade, right?"

I stop myself from threatening to call the cops about their hate crime when I see the way his hands grip Benny's arms. It wouldn't take much to hurt her.

"She remembers me, Eli."

The shorter, mulleted man comes up from behind him and places a hand on the back of my stool. "Where's Mowgli, sweets?"

I clench my teeth so hard I think I might break one. I refuse to acknowledge his question. Instead, I shoulder my purse and prepare to get Benny out of there.

"Don't rush out now," the one named Dwight says. "My brother here thinks you're pretty. Not me though. I'm not into manly types."

Thank the Lord for my five-foot-nine, mostly curveless stature. I crane my neck to peer out the back door of the Tap Room. "Come on, Benny." I climb off the stool and push myself between Dwight and Benny, which fortunately, makes him drop his hold on her. Unfortunately, his body presses against me in a perverse way. On instinct, I elbow-strike him in the ribs and hear his breath rush out.

Before he can recover, I usher Benny to the exit. Dwight and Eli follow. Then, God bless him, a park ranger opens the door for us.

"Sir," I say quickly, "these men are harassing us, and they vandalized our car."

The park ranger blocks the doorway after us. Benny and I walk up the steps to the parking area as fast as we can. I remember Tim's description of their van and scan the parking lot. I spot it—a late-nineties Ford Econoline, I believe. They're parked too far away for me to get the license plate number. Then Bridger rounds the corner near the van and sees us. I mime taking a picture and point to the Ford. Thankfully, he gets the picture—pun intended. Finally, I hope, we can make a report.

"Are you all right, Benny?" I ask as we keep shuffling toward the Chevy.

She hums a melody. "For the wonder of each hour, of the day and of the night, hill and vale and tree and flow'r, sun and moon, and stars of light."

"Such a beautiful hymn" is my only response.

Chapter 35

2003
Jade

"Come on, Jade. You need to eat." Daddy pushed my plate closer to me. "I made your favorite."

I squished my face. I liked peanut butter and honey sandwiches the way Mom made them. Daddy used too much peanut butter and always the crunchy kind. It felt like I was chewing on bugs.

"One bite. Please? For me?"

I picked up one half and nibbled the crust.

"You need to eat, sweetheart."

"I'm not hungry," I said, dropping the sandwich on the plate next to the untouched Cheetos. A big yawn stretched my face.

Quick footsteps climbed the stairs to our apartment. "Yoohoo!" Glynda appeared in the doorway holding a big Ziploc bag. "I made cookies. Chocolate chip."

I stood. "I have to go to the bathroom." I held on to the waistband of my shorts so they didn't slip down, then I locked myself behind the bathroom door. Even chocolate chip cookies sounded gross to me. I slid down the wall and sat on the floor.

240

When I heard Dad and Glynda whispering, I laid down on the ground and listened under the door.

"She's still not eating?" Glynda asked.

"What am I going to do? She's getting worse."

"Give it time. That girl's strong. She'll—"

I turned my head to look under the door, but all I saw was the dirty carpet.

"Eddie—Jimmy, don't you even think about it. They'll send her right back to that awful woman, right back to that house where it all happened."

"But she'll get the help she needs. One of them child psychiatrists or something. That's not possible here, and if I do find somebody to help her, she's gonna have to tell them the truth."

"Did you think about where that'll leave me?" Glynda was yelling now, even with Daddy shushing her. "Everyone in town knows you and me have a thing. I'll end up in prison with you."

"Glyn, that's why you've gotta be the one to call in the police."

The police? No. She can't. He can't. I couldn't go back home, even if Mom did make better lunches.

"I won't do it," Glynda said. "I won't."

"You have to. For Jade's sake, you have to."

I jumped up off the ground, opened the door, and ran out of the bathroom. "I'm ready to eat now." While Daddy and Glynda watched, I forced myself to take the biggest bite I could.

Chapter 36

Present Day
Jade

Still shaken from our encounter with the two men, I'm not able to appreciate our scenic journey through Sun Valley. Benny, though, gazes peacefully at the passing desert from the passenger seat. In the back, Bridger hides behind sunglasses and a trendy, wide-brimmed straw hat that would have already blown away without the strap securing it beneath his chin. While he talks a big game about keeping his emotions tucked in his back pocket, I can see his sagging shoulders and clenched jaw in the rearview mirror. Benny and I repeatedly told him not to blame himself for what happened at the Painted Desert Inn, but I can see he does. The possibility of upsetting Benny was the only thing that kept him from confronting the men right there and then. We settled for reporting the license plate information to the local police as well as the National Park Service.

Not even a stop at the Jackrabbit Trading Post can lighten his mood. He doesn't perk up until we start cruising into the next town.

"I have a surprise for you," he says.

While I pin him with my best suspicious look in the mirror, I nearly miss the marker declaring the town limits of Winslow,

Arizona. Immediately, the melody of the Eagles' "Take it Easy" strums its way into my mind. A crowd mills about the upcoming intersection. When I see the reason for it, my eyes mist up.

On the pavement, a massive Route 66 emblem painted white directs my attention to a lamppost with a sign that reads "Standin' on the Corner." A bronze statue of a man and his guitar is flanked by two tourists getting a picture. Behind them, on the side of a brick building, a two-story tall mural perfectly depicts the second verse of my father's favorite song, complete with a girl driving a flatbed Ford. Such a fun way to commemorate a slice of pop culture, and yet, sorrow digs deep into my heart, making my shoulders ache terribly. Maybe it's due to the resemblance my father has to the statue—which only makes sense since my father was the spitting image of songwriter Jackson Browne. It's good that I find a parking spot quickly.

The tears fully unleash when I catch sight of lead singer Glenn Frey, also memorialized in bronze, leaning against another post. Was the rest of this here in 2003? Or was Glenn's statue added after his untimely death in 2016? I'm sure Dad would have wanted to stop, but if this tourist attraction was as popular then as it is now, he wouldn't have risked being recognized, even with his newly dyed and shorn hairstyle.

Although I'm not in a selfie mood, I take pictures of both statues, the mural, the intersection's Route 66 emblem, and the actual red, flatbed Ford truck parked nearby.

"You good?" Bridger asks me as a street musician finishes up his countrified rendition of "Take It Easy."

"The closer we get to Tecoma, the more real it gets. I keep thinking of all the ways it could go terribly wrong."

Bridger puts his arm around me. "Like the song says, we don't know what's ahead of us so we should take it day by day, mile by mile. Let faith do the rest. I'd be wise to follow that advice too."

I roll toward him, soaking in the comfort of his strong arms pinning me securely in his care and protection. Around us, chatter grows, and I open my eyes to see that the interest of the crowd has shifted to Benny and Bridger's celebrity presence. I step out of the way so the fans can get their pictures. Once the people have been more or less appeased, we escape into a bank-turned-café across the street.

"Welcome to The Sipp Shoppe," a tall teenage girl says from behind the counter. Another girl stands beside her, preparing some old-fashioned fountain soda. When her eyes lock on Bridger, her jaw drops, and she overflows the plastic cup in her hand. She jumps back as the liquid spills down her front.

Benny elbows him. "Look at you, causing a distraction. Jade, see what you have to look forward to for the rest of your life?"

I try to catch Bridger's eye so we can share an "isn't it funny she thinks we're going to get married?" look, but he's locked on to the menu and the plethora of choices of what to "sipp." Fortunately, Benny comes to our rescue by offering to order for us. "Three Italian sodas with cherry phosphate." She turns to me. "I figured you were getting tired of chocolate malts."

"I'm not tired of them but my waistline is."

We take all three stools at the counter, and I scan the interior of the small café. Only one thing gives away that it was once a turn-of-the-twentieth-century bank—the imposing vault door that opens to a storage room.

"Diebold Safe & Lock Company," I read. "Bridge, that vault was made in Ohio."

"Are you from there?" the clumsy, starry-eyed employee asks. Bridger perks up. "Nah, but just the other day I was saying that Ohio seems like a great place. And there's the proof. Nothing says safe and secure like a vault."

"I think there are companies in other states that make safes too," the other girl offers.

Benny shakes her head. "It's no use trying to reason with him. To him, Ohio is the promised land."

A few minutes later, they serve us our drinks. Upon her first taste, Benny's eyes fill with tears. "This was Paul's favorite." She dabs her eyes with a napkin, then slowly swivels her stool to face Bridger and me. "I'd like to continue my story now. Would that be all right?"

~

1956
Benny

After a fitful night of sleep, I decided to get myself breakfast downstairs at the restaurant. However, just a few steps down, I noticed a man staring up at me. I knew him from somewhere, yet I couldn't quite place his face. Once the man turned and I saw who he was speaking to, I knew.

Levi Livingston, the award-winning director of 1955's *From Whence We Came*, watched my every move. And he was speaking to Clyde Irving, the king of the silver screen. I nearly lost my footing. Once I regained some feeling in my legs, I continued down the steps.

Levi tipped his Scala hat. "Miss."

I nodded back. As I passed by and made my way toward El Rancho's restaurant, I felt at least one pair of eyes on me. *I must be dreaming,* I thought. Why else would a director of Levi Livingston's caliber show interest in me? Maybe he was picturing me in a future role. Catherine Earnshaw in the next movie version of *Wuthering Heights* or Elizabeth Bennett in another *Pride and Prejudice* adaptation. I'd nearly worked myself into a frenzy by the time I found an empty table by the window next to a beautiful fair-haired woman who sat, cradling a baby.

I perused the menu. I was absolutely famished, but it wouldn't be proper to stuff myself with the largest meal available. So instead, I ordered two meals. One for me, and one for my invisible companion across the table.

The baby next to me began to fuss.

"Hush, hush, darling," the mother cooed against her child's cheek. Then she looked at me. "I hope you don't mind. She's a colicky one."

"Not at all," I said. "My momma had to hold my baby sister in this peculiar way whenever she'd fuss."

"What way? I'm willing to try anything."

I twisted in my chair and tried to model it with my arms. The woman didn't comprehend. "Okay," I said, "stand for me."

She did.

"May I?" I asked, gesturing to the child.

She tentatively handed the little girl to me. The baby couldn't have been more than six months old. And even though she had the prettiest features, she twisted them in obvious pain.

"Okay, bend your arm," I instructed. Then, I placed the baby back into her mother's arms, with her face against the crook of her elbow and her tummy facing down on the forearm. "Now hold her a little tighter against your chest. That should relieve some of the pressure of the gas in her tummy."

"And that's it? Good! I was worried you were going to suggest I put bourbon in her bottle."

"Oh goodness, no." I laughed, retaking my seat.

The woman glanced up from the baby. "I'm Charlotte. People call me Charlie."

"Berenice. People call me Benny."

Charlie grinned. "We must be two peas in a pod. What brings you to Gallup?"

"I'm on my way to Hollywood."

"Oh, an actress, are you? I should have known. You have that look about you. That Princess Grace look. Rumor has it, she's retiring, so there's an opening for a doe-eyed blond."

My blush got the best of me, and I tried to hide the bottom half of my face with my hand.

"Oh dear. You're an innocent one." Charlie swayed left and

right and soon the baby quieted. "Benny, if you want to be an actress, you need to toughen up or people will tear you limb from limb."

I struggled to respond. I was about to ask how she knew that, but my answer came in the form of Clyde Irving. He swooped in and kissed Charlie's cheek, then the baby's crown.

"Clyde, this is Benny," Charlie said. "She's on her way to California to be an actress."

"Is she really?" Clyde studied me, looking at my face from one angle then another.

"It's a pleasure to meet you, sir. Both—all three of you."

The famous actor humphed. "They'll eat you alive."

Discouragement carved a crater in my heart. First, I'd lost Louie. Second, Paul. Now, my dream?

Clyde looked to his wife. "The doctor said it could be a month before Claire's back on her feet. They're hoping the second trimester will bring relief to her morning sickness."

"Even then, she can't very well ride a horse or she'll have that baby before it's time," Charlie said. "I told Levi he needed to replace Claire. Now, it's a week into shooting and you've barely made any progress."

Claire Pendleton? The same actress I'd just seen in *Heaven's Long Road* two weeks ago? She was here and pregnant?

Charlie slid a sideways glance my way. *Lord, please let her be thinking what I'm thinking.* "Levi should give Benny a chance. She may not cut it, but even still, getting advice from the biggest director in film would do her a world of good."

A waitress delivered two plates of food to my table. My stomach growled in celebration.

"That's not the worst idea. Benny, if you don't mind your food getting cold, why don't you come with me?"

Who needed food? I pushed back from the table, but all those times Paul told me about bad people stopped me.

"It's okay, honey," Charlie said. "You can trust Clyde. He'll watch out for you. It's Levi that you should never follow into a hotel room. And I mean that. Seriously. And if you do end up there, remind him that his wife, Angela, will divorce him and take him for all he's worth."

I nodded and followed Clyde toward the front of the restaurant. As he rounded the corner, he bumped into . . . Paul. An unshaven, tired-eyed Paul.

"Pardon me, old chap," Clyde said, sidestepping him.

Paul lifted his gaze, and I could see the awe strike him. But that moment of magic quickly disappeared when he realized I was right behind Clyde. I studied the floor and walked past Paul. What was he saying? Out of sight, out of mind?

"Benny?" My name coming from his broken voice undid my resolve.

"Mr. Irving," I said, praying this wouldn't kill my one chance. "Can we get one minute, please?"

Clyde looked from me to Paul and back until understanding appeared to dawn for him. "Sure, I'll be in the lobby."

Paul and I both watched the Hollywood icon parade past a group of stunned hotel guests. After an uncomfortable few seconds, I fixed my attention on Paul.

"Benny, what's happening?" Based on his facial expression, he was wavering between suspicion of Clyde's motives and pain over our argument. I could certainly understand the last part. Even though I was still angry at him, heaven knew I'd always love him.

"Clyde Irving and Claire Pendleton are filming a movie here. Claire may not be able to continue, so Clyde is taking me to audition for her role in front of Levi Livingston. Isn't that the most?"

Paul's lip turned up ever so briefly before falling. "If you get the part, you'll stay here?"

"I haven't got the part, so I don't know. That would only make sense."

He moved a touch closer. "What does that mean for us?"

I bobbed my shoulders to feign apathy. "It means I'll be here. You're free to return to Joliet if you want."

"I don't want that."

"You made it very clear last night that you can't be with someone—"

"We both said things we shouldn't have last night, but we can work this out. I know we can."

"I'm not so sure, Paul." My trust in him was still broken. Yes, that crime should have been reported, but did it have to be by Paul? And if it did have to be him, he could have, should have, told me about it long ago. Certainly before we started this trip. I wasn't about to let him wait around for me while I worked through that level of forgiveness because I wasn't sure I'd ever be able to move past it.

"Well, I know what I want. And it's to follow Clyde Irving to that audition. I'll always appreciate you driving me out here. Thanks for the memories." I gestured toward Clyde and my golden opportunity. "And thanks for the love. Goodbye, Paul."

Chapter 37

Present Day
Jade

"My review of the Grand Canyon," Bridger says as we stand safely behind a stone wall, "is that I expected to see way more hijinks involving Wile E. Coyote and the Road Runner. Three out of five stars."

I playfully shove his arm. "Hey, blame Warner Brothers for that, not the National Park Service."

Bridger places his arms securely around me. The warmth of his body against my back is the perfect balance to the cool autumn breeze caressing my face. "In case you ever wonder," Bridger says by my ear, "I'd run straight into a tunnel painted on a canyon wall for you."

"You romantic, you." I twist in his arms and catch his wink. Between yesterday's stop in Winslow to see the Eagles memorial, stargazing last night at Flagstaff's Lowell Observatory, and this surprise detour, it's easy to feel quite *in like* with this man. And every moment I spend with him turns the dial one more degree from like to love.

"A rainbow after the storm," I say softly.

"What was that?" Bridger asks, turning me to face him.

I consider telling him how he's a gift from God, a reminder that dawn follows night, good defeats evil, love conquers hate, and every other silly but true cliché out there. But I say nothing because he kisses me, lingering for several heartbeats longer than normal.

"I never did like that Pepé Le Pew."

Bridger and I pull back from each other as Benny's comment jolts us back to reality.

"Someone needed to neuter that skunk," she says. "Putting that behavior in a kids' cartoon? And we wonder why some people in our country don't understand what consent is."

"Amen," Bridger says. "We should've voted you in for president. Our country would be better off."

"I would vote for you," I add.

Benny turns her back to the canyon and sits on the wall. "I'm quite tired. Do you mind if we head back to the train early?"

"You got it. Piggyback ride?" Bridger asks.

"Sure." Benny motions to her back. "Hop on, big fella."

Nearly an hour later, I lean against the back railing of the caboose as our train chugs along the Grand Canyon Railway. Soon, we'll be back in Williams, Arizona, the last town on Route 66 that I-40 bypassed. After one night at the Grand Canyon Hotel, we'll get back in the Chevy and head to Tecoma.

The door to the train car opens, and Bridger ducks through, joining me outside. He takes hold of the bar overhead with one hand and welcomes me against him with the other. We're so rarely alone that it feels a bit indecent. Between the beauty of the northern Arizona forest, the gentle rocking of the train, and the depth of Bridger's kisses, I'm swept. Absolutely swept. I'd be one blessed girl to get my breath routinely taken away by him for a lifetime, whether that's in Los Angeles, Chicago, or even Ohio.

Once we risk overheating our engines, we wisely give each other space on the platform.

"Is she still resting?" I ask.

"Yeah. I wanted to come out and see how you're feeling about tomorrow."

"The million-dollar question, right? I don't know how I'm feeling. I don't know what to expect. Even if he isn't there, I'm sure it will bring up more memories of that time in my life."

Bridger takes my hand, weaving his fingers through mine.

"I'm proud of you for putting yourself out there. After what you've been through, well, most people would build themselves a safe room and never leave."

"I don't know about that, but I appreciate your support. I'd like to say I'm a strong, independent woman who doesn't need a man . . ."

He kisses my knuckles. "You are a strong, independent woman with a tender heart. So of course you could use the support of others on occasion. And even if Tecoma turns out to be a bust, I know you've challenged me to conquer my fears. Just the other night, I told Benny that I'd like to begin exploring my Samoan culture once we get back."

My heart soars higher than the Ponderosa pines. "You did? How did she take it?"

"She started crying, especially when I told her why I never had before. She said her feelings weren't hurt and that it doesn't diminish our relationship if I want to embrace my heritage."

He laughs. "She wants to help me any way she can."

I smile. "That's wonderful, Bridge."

"I'm thinking she and I should get matching tattoos to start."

He winks.

"I mean, why wouldn't you? I suggest anything but Pepé Le Pew."

"Good call."

I chew on my next words carefully. "Do you think that conversation could open the door to the discussion about getting her the help she needs?"

Bridger winces. "I'm not ready for that one."

"Don't you think she deserves to be a part of that decision? I think you and I can both relate to having decisions made for us in life. She deserves better than that."

"You're right." He cracks his neck. "I should talk to her about Swallow's Nest. I—"

"There's no time like the present. She's in a good place, mentally and emotionally. And we have the entire caboose to ourselves."

Bridger looks up at the sky. "God help me." He faces me again. "You're right. There's no time like the present."

The door opens behind us, and Benny pokes her head out. "Hello, you two."

In a blink, Bridger reaches for her arm. "This train rocks too much for you to walk unassisted, Benny."

"What was I supposed to do? Wait for you two to stop necking and come help me?"

With a new flush in my cheeks, I grasp the doorframe. "On that note, I'll give you two some time to talk," I say.

After stopping at the bar for a Diet Coke and some roasted almonds, I return to our table. I pop the top of my drink, then fight to open the stubborn bag of nuts. When the seam finally gives way, I accidentally knock over the pop can. Caramel liquid pools on the table and drips off the side and onto Bridger's bag. As quick as I can, I save the laptop from any worse splatter and use a cocktail napkin to wipe it clean. While the train car's attendant helps with the rest of the spill, I find another napkin and open the laptop to dab the edges.

It lights up. Instead of a lock screen, it awakens to an image I know well. My missing child poster. I survey the back of the train where the windows and door show Bridger and Benny, still outside talking.

With trembling fingers, I use the cursor to minimize the poster image. Text appears on a square in the center of the screen.

Jade's father, theft and larceny, Illinois. Tie that in.

I click on another electronic note, and it expands.

Met Gregory in graduate school in Colorado, dated for six years. Was he faithful? Any dirt from Colorado?

I move the cursor across what appears to be a video clip. I press play and see myself standing on the Chain of Rocks bridge in silent contemplation. I click on another square and watch myself stroll alone through the Pink Elephant Antique Mall in Livingston. "He's been filming me."

"Pardon?" The attendant leans in.

My throat burns. "Can I get a water, please?" I don't sound like myself. I sound weak, childish, naive. It's happening again. I'm being used by someone I thought I knew, someone I care about.

A minute later, the cool water brings little comfort. And worse, my throat tries to reject the water. When I finally manage to swallow, I look up and see Bridger and Benny coming inside. All life drains from Bridger's face when he sees me holding his laptop.

"What is this?" I ask.

He reaches for it. "You shouldn't look at that."

I hold the computer out of his reach. "What is this? Why are there so many questions about me?"

He won't meet my gaze.

"Tell me. You're the one that talks about trust and honesty. What is this about?" I scan the screen again. "Why am I in the documentary?"

"Jade . . ."

I close my eyes and see all the pieces coming together. Roland's impromptu trip to ensure Bridger was doing what he needed to do. Roland asking about my kidnapping and Hank's murder while Bridger just so happened to be filming. Those notes I saw early on about my childhood.

"This isn't a documentary about Benny and Paul's journey, is it? It's a story about how I scammed them out of their life savings. Roland's investors, the production companies . . . they're expecting a film that destroys me even more than the press already has. Am I right?"

Bridger doesn't answer.

"Am I right?" I cry. "Benny, did you know?"

Benny's gaze bounces from me to Bridger, her confusion too real to be an act. Even she couldn't pull that off.

I slam the laptop closed and stand. I shove it against Bridger's stomach. He bobbles it as I turn away. I cross the connecting platform and enter the next car, passing families and couples all enjoying their trip.

I can hear Bridger's footsteps behind me. "Jade."

But I move ahead. He catches up to me before I open the door to the car with the observation dome.

"Jade, please wait."

I stop running away. I've faced a whole lot worse than a terrible boyfriend. Goodness, he isn't even my boyfriend. He's just a guy who's good at kissing—so good at kissing, apparently, that I ignore red flags. Story of my life. I turn on my heel and face him. "What, Bridger? What could you possibly say to explain yourself?"

"Roland set it up. It was all his idea to include you in the story."

"Oh, so you're completely innocent. I see."

"Not innocent at all. I needed the money. I needed someone to take notice of my documentary. It was the only way anyone was interested. I needed to make a name for myself so I could make Benny proud. To not just be a screwup."

I shake my head. "You honestly think she'd be more proud of you if you make a documentary exposing me as a villain?" What dumb logic. Benny loves me. At least I thought she did. Who knows anymore? The lump in my throat threatens to choke me, and I gulp at the air.

"But that was at the beginning." Bridger closes the space between us.

"Let me guess. You got to know me, and you chose to go a different direction with your story. I've seen movies too, Bridger."

"It is what happened though. Jade, I've fallen for you. Completely."

I rear back. *Fallen for me?*

His eyes plead. "I'd throw this whole thing out the window if I had to choose between it and you. I did try to change the focus. You were the one that told me to make the movie people wanted to see."

An attendant opens the door behind me. "You can't be in here. It's not safe."

I ignore him. "You're blaming me?" I say to Bridger. "I thought you were doubting yourself and your abilities. That's why I encouraged you to keep going. I wasn't inviting you to sound off a death knell." I comb my hair back, but my fingers catch on painful tangles. "You know I believed you when you said I wasn't at fault for any of the stuff that's happened in my life. Shame on me for giving you that much power."

Chapter 38

2003
Jade

"Am I doing this right?" I turned the ratchet lefty-loosey, but it took all my muscle.

Daddy put his hand on mine and helped, probably so I wouldn't drop it on my face again. He grinned. I grinned back. Just two mechanics lying under a car, doing mechanic stuff.

"You're a natural," he said. "Now hold it there while I un-screw the oil plug."

"Okay." I pushed the ratchet out from under the PT Cruiser that Daddy and I were doing an oil change on.

"Get the catch can in place," he said.

I did just what he said, scooting over more so I didn't get splattered. "Ready."

Daddy held the oil drain plug between his thumb and pointer finger. "On the count of three. One, two—"

A crashing sound made me cover my ears. It came from the door where black boots—lots of them—came running into the garage. I scurried farther under the car and closer to Daddy.

"Edward Talbot, you're surrounded," an angry man said.

"You're wanted for murder and kidnapping. Come out from under there with your hands spread wide."

Daddy touched my cheek. "It's okay, Baby Jade. You remember what I said? You're a good girl. A real good girl."

I clung to him as tight as I could. There was the strangled cat sound again.

A head peered under the car. Sheriff Samson. "You aren't armed, are you, Jimmy?"

Daddy shook his head a little. "No. I'm not armed. Tell 'em I got my little girl under here with me. I don't want her to get hurt." Then he spoke to me. "You stay here until they take me away. The sheriff will keep you safe."

"Daddy, no. Don't leave me!" I clawed and scratched to get a better hold on him. "It's my fault," I said as loud as I could.

"Julianna," a woman's voice said. "You're safe now. Your mom is here. She wants to take you back home."

"I don't want to. It was my fault, not my dad's." I stared hard at Daddy. "I lied. Hank didn't hit me ever. I told you that so you'd want me to live with you."

His mouth fell open, and his eyes turned watery.

"I'm sorry, Daddy. I'm sorry I lied to you. I'll tell the truth now. I promise."

He tried to speak, but I didn't hear anything except for the sound of him shuffling out from under the car. I curled myself into a ball against the cool garage floor. When my dad was nearly out, he was yanked clear of the car. Then he was slammed down on the ground a couple feet away from me. The cops put handcuffs on him—the real kind, not the kind Max and I played cops and robbers with—and they said a whole bunch of stuff about his rights. The whole time he stared at me, and he was crying.

Chapter 39

Present Day
Jade

In my bed at the Grand Canyon Hotel, I stew in my sorrow, surrounded by a barricade of pillows tucked tightly against my body. Not even a knock on the door can rouse me from my tear-soaked sanctuary.

Jesus, make them go away.

A second knock makes me think even God's love for me is iffy.

"Go away, Bridger!"

When the third, harder knock rattles my nerves, I scramble off the bed and prepare to word vomit all over him. The composure I maintained throughout Gregory and Walter's trial is now roadkill somewhere along Route 66. I unlatch the door while telling myself I won't be anyone's fool. Not even—

"Benny." I peer out the door to the right and left, but she's alone. "What are you doing here?"

"I've come to check on you, dear. May I come in?"

I turn away to wipe any smeared makeup from my puffy eyes. Before I'm finished, my arm gets a tug.

"No need to clean yourself up for me." Benny clings to my arm for support, and I lead her to the desk chair near the window. She's weaker now than she was in Chicago, which reminds me that this trip has taken its toll on someone other than me. Once she's seated, she exhales on a sigh. "That's better. These old bones are giving me fits."

"You didn't have to come down here," I say as I plunk back onto the bed.

"I very well couldn't sit in that room and listen to Bridger blubber like a big, bearded baby, knowing how betrayed you feel."

"You understand why I'm upset?"

"Absolutely, dear. Although, if you take some time to listen to him, it may make a tad more sense why he did what he did, whether that was right or wrong."

"He knows I've been manipulated by people before, and yet he did it anyway. I can't forgive him for that."

"And I'm not asking you to. You need to look out for your own heart. But it may help your heart to know he wasn't trying to bring you pain."

I scoff. "He could have told me about Roland's vision. Trust me, I know all about confused allegiances. He kept it a secret just like he did with the memory care facility for you. I told him to discuss it with you back in St. Louis—"

"What, about Swallow's Nest?" In her lap, Benny wrings her hands. "It's no secret that Roland wants me to go there. But not Bridger. He wants to care for me at home. He knows I'm frightened of what happens in those places. Louie told me what happens when they have you trapped. I saw the terror during his nightmares. Bridger won't put me through that."

A putrid taste settles on my tongue. Of course, Bridger didn't talk to her after he said he would. In the ultimate case of irony, the truth would jeopardize the completion of this documentary. And as I've painfully discovered, this documentary's success is all that matters.

"Bridger has already come to peace with the decision," I

spew despite the unsettling feeling in my gut. "He's spoken with your doctor. Once you get back, you'll meet with the team of clinicians at Swallow's Nest Memory Care, and they'll explain all they can offer you." Even as I speak, I see Benny's nerves agitating. "They want you to feel comfortable and safe. It won't be like what Louie experienced. It's what Paul would have wanted for you."

She is woefully still and quiet for several long moments.

"What will happen with the house?"

I bite my lip. "I'm sorry, Benny. You should ask Bridger about that. I thought he told you on the train."

Benny's deep frown tears me apart. "If they sell the house, that would leave him without a home."

After all this, Benny is still looking out for his best interests. Bridger is the real fool here.

～

"Is it your dad's shop?" Bridger's voice is nearly unrecognizable. He's barely spoken to me since yesterday on the train. Even when he did, I rarely answered. As far as I'm concerned, we needn't ever speak again. The only reason I even got back in the car with him was for Benny. While I don't give two licks what happens with the documentary or Bridger's career, I do care that Benny gets to LA safely.

"This is where it was back then." I cut the engine then fidget with the keys. Jimmy's Garage, including a neon sign I don't remember, fills the rearview mirror.

Benny stills my hand with hers. I haven't been able to look at her, really look at her, all morning and afternoon. I still hear myself spilling the news that wasn't mine to share. It all feels wrong, especially since I don't know if she has brought it up to Bridger yet.

"Jade, sweetheart," she says, "look at me."

I meet her eyes and see only care.

She gently brushes a curl back from my face. "Whether your father is in that building or not, whether he accepts you or not, you are a child of the Lord, chosen and dearly loved. Let him give you the strength and confidence you need."

Thank you, I mouth. Then I get out of the car and cross the lot to the shop's front door. I stop in my tracks.

Be back soon? I focus harder on the sign hanging on the door of the shop like it might make the words form a different message. What does "soon" mean? Lunch? No. It's three thirty. He probably wouldn't take a lunch this late. I peer past the sign to investigate the inside. A black-and-white checkerboard floor pairs with sharp red paint and chrome detailing. Much nicer than it was way back when. Everything about this building is sharp and clean.

If the Jimmy of Jimmy's Garage is still Dad, he must have really gotten his life together in the years since his release. I crane my neck to see the far side of the shop. A late-fifties Ford Fairlane. Maybe an Interceptor. It's hard to tell without the bumpers and the right rear panel. Dad must be in the restoration business. Maybe that works for relationships too.

I don't try to hide my disappointment upon returning to the Chevy.

"No luck?" Benny asks from the passenger seat.

"There's a Be Back Soon sign on the door."

Benny nods. "Well, you can't give up yet."

I peer westward. "There's a tavern down that way. He used to have a thing with the owner. If Glynda's still around, she'll help us out. She was always good to me."

Now fully committed to this plan of finding my father, I drop Bridger and Benny off at the Tecoma Springs Motel to get us rooms for the night. Then I pull into the parking spot closest to the tavern's door. I give myself a once-over in the rearview mirror. I might have my mother's dark hair, but in all other ways, I'm my father's daughter. From my heart-shaped lips to my high forehead and my jade green eyes. How many times did my mother use that against me, telling me I was just like him? What if he hates me like she does? *Lord, if you aren't too busy, I could really use some of that confidence Benny spoke of.*

"Julianna," a voice behind me snarls.

Glynda, carrying a brown grocery bag, rounds the Chevy's fender. Although it's been more than twenty years, she looks the same. Thin with very low-cut, flare-legged jeans and a spaghetti-strap tank top that bares her belly and navel piercing. Her hair, still a pretty sunset-reddish orange. Her face has aged slightly, the passage of time marked by crow's feet and frown lines. Her eyes are the most striking difference though. Where I once saw the love of a surrogate mom, I now see only bitterness.

"Hi, Glynda."

She shifts the bag from one hip to the other, the way a mother might when holding a baby.

"What are you doing back here?" she asks. "Come to destroy more lives, have you?"

There it is. And if Glynda believes it . . .

I could flee. Jesus knows I want to. And isn't that just like me? What happens when I get to the California coast where this road ends? Do I hop on a plane or a ship and keep running?

No. I won't let others determine the path of my life anymore. I flick my wrist and turn off the car. "I was hoping to find my father. I thought you might be able to help."

"I have a business to run." She struts a straight path to the bar's entrance. But after she unlocks and opens it, she presses her back to the door and waits—a most unwelcoming welcome, but I accept.

Once inside, my memories go full tilt. The dark walls and ceiling contrast with the neon signage, the light reflecting off the dozens of liquor bottles lined up behind the bar, creating what I once thought of as a Christmas light effect. It smells different though. Instead of stale cigarette smoke, it's more like the old college library stacks I used to study in.

Glynda goes right to work unloading groceries from the bag on a far counter and making it clear that I am not to interfere with her life in any way, shape, or form. "What do you want to know?"

"Do you know where my father is? I haven't spoken to him since I was eighteen. I was informed by his lawyer that he was released from prison a couple years ago, but I don't have his contact information." I wait for a response but don't get one. "I happen to be driving through, so I thought I'd see if he came back here."

She freezes, a jar of maraschino cherries in her hand. "You destroyed his life only to show up a decade later because you happen to be driving through?" She tsks. "I figured you would have matured a bit since childhood."

Her words slice their way into me, not cleanly.

"I guess I shouldn't have come. I expected . . . I don't know what I expected, but I'm sorry for everything." I pour all my concentration onto the toes of my shoes and hurry to the door. I burst out into the sunlight, heeding the temporary blindness it causes by shielding my tear-filled eyes. The sound of a whistle catches my ear and I prepare to lay into whatever loser would hit on a woman who is clearly crying. Except I'm not the object of said whistle. The Chevy is. And the man walking a slow, appreciative circle around it is Jimmy Jessup.

Chapter 40

1956
Benny

"I'm terribly sorry, but I have to kiss you," Clyde had told me between takes.

We'd been filming for nine weeks, which meant it had been nine weeks since I last saw or spoke to Paul, and now I was about to kiss another man.

"If we get this right, we'll only have to do one take." He lifted his chin so the makeup artist could touch up his fresh-out-of-the-saddle look. "Did Charlie talk to you? She always likes to give my leading ladies permission to kiss me."

"Yes, yes, she did. She also said she'd buy me a bottle of Coca-Cola if I say 'ew' afterward."

Clyde laughed. "That wife of mine loves to keep me humble." Then he looked at me seriously. "Are you sure you're willing to do this? This being your first acting role, I don't want you doing anything that makes you uncomfortable. It's bad enough that I'm nearly twice your age."

"Clyde, I'm fine. I promise. If I'm not willing to kiss someone in a film, I may as well head back to Joliet."

Levi strode toward his director's chair. He snapped his fingers, and his assistant sprang forward with a Lucky Strike and

265

a match. While Levi lit his cigarette, I got into position, sitting on the porch step with my arm around Judy Herron, a fifteen-year-old novice actress who was playing my character's little sister.

Tears. I needed tears. *Buck is dead and I, Grace, will never love again. He took my heart with him when he left that day. I should have stopped him from leaving, but I was too stubborn and angry. What a fool. What an absolute fool.* The first tear rolled down my cheek as soon as Levi called action.

"Men like Buck, well, they're too good for this world," I said. "We'll have to find a way to carry on without him. It won't be easy though."

Judy popped her head up and looked off into the middle distance. "Grace, who's that comin' over the hill?"

"It's Pa," I answered solemnly.

"No, behind him. It's Buck!"

"It can't be. It can't."

"Oh, yes, it can!" Judy jumped up and waved.

Disbelief and confusion battled within my features. At least I hoped they did. Then I let hope find its place as I rose to my feet. I huffed a short breath and smiled. "Go tell Ma they're home. They're all home."

"Aww, do I have to?"

"Yes. Now skedaddle before I give you a swat."

Judy brushed by me in a teenage tantrum, disappearing into the farmhouse facade as the wrangler cued the horse to walk into the shot. In one smooth motion, Clyde swung himself off the horse. He handed the reins to the man playing Pa and jogged to me.

"Oh, Buck." I threw my arms around his neck and hugged him tight for a count of three, then pulled my shoulders away, arching my back so he could keep hold of my waist. "I thought I lost you. Big Roy said—"

"Big Roy has no faith in yours truly."

I shook my head and knitted my brows. "Neither did I. I shouldn't have let my stubbornness keep me from seeing you off."

"Aw, honey," Buck said, removing his cowboy hat. "Didn't I tell you that night at the well? You'll never lose me. Not so long as the stars have light."

It was time. The moment we would kiss. Just a simple, easy kiss. Although I leaned forward and dropped my head back like Debra Paget in *Love Me Tender*, I felt my body tense. I closed my eyes and waited for it to be over. Clyde pressed his lips hard against mine. All I saw behind my lids was Paul standing in the lobby of El Rancho that day. Oh, Paul.

"Cut!" Levi groaned. "Let's do that again. This time, Judy, I want more of a tantrum. Really play it up and make 'em laugh. Benny, I need more passion from you on that kiss."

We went through the scene again . . . and again . . . and again until finally Levi called for a break. "Benny, we need to talk. Meet me in my trailer in ten. Everyone else, be back here in forty-five minutes."

The warning Charlie gave me on the day we met resonated in my head.

Maybe we could settle this right here and now. "Levi, what advice do you have for me? I'm ready to hear it."

"Listen, doll, I've got some notes to make, and I don't have a lot of time. Follow me." He walked quickly off set—a man on a mission—and I struggled to keep up in these uncomfortable boots from wardrobe. He seemed distracted. Was he angry with me? Would he fire me? Could he fire me so close to the end of filming?

I hesitated on the trailer's steps.

"Now, Benny," he demanded.

With a gulp, I listened and stepped inside. I'd never been in his trailer before. For some reason, I hadn't expected a bed since he stayed in the El Rancho like the rest of us.

"Benny, Benny, Benny," he said, scratching his cheek. "You want to make it in Hollywood, but here you are, struggling in Gallup."

"I can do better. Please don't fire me."

"Fire you? We aren't at that point yet. I see your potential. Audiences will too. They'll be begging us for pinups."

My ears flamed. "I'm not that type."

"No one's that type at first. You've got to loosen up. Like in that scene. The moment Clyde goes in for a kiss, you freeze up quicker than an orphaned puppy in a snowstorm."

I cringed. "I didn't realize—"

"Benny, it isn't difficult. Come here." He pointed to the floor in front of him.

Slowly, I met him toe to toe. He grabbed my upper arms and gently shook me back and forth. It was only then that he smiled.

"Loosen up. Pretend you're at a church picnic or something. Relax your shoulders."

I tried my best. Anything to get his focus off me sooner.

His fingers crept up to my neck until his hands encircled it.

"Relax your neck. Don't be so stiff."

I laughed nervously, even as his thumbs caressed the hollow of my throat.

"Now tilt your chin up and close your eyes."

"Levi, I don't—"

"Do you want to be an actress or not?" His words came out fast and harsh. "If you can't give a realistic kiss, no one will want you. Not MGM, Fox, RKO, Paramount. . . . They'll ask me what you bring to the table. Whatever I say is pure gold in the film industry. Got that? I'm trying to help you here, so stop fighting me."

My nerves shook beneath my skin. What would happen if I turned and fled? Was that even possible? Could a man snap a neck with his bare hands? Could Levi strangle me without anyone knowing? Would anyone even care if he did? Paul. Paul

268

would. But what chance would Paul have against someone as powerful as Levi.

So I tilted my chin, closed my eyes, and prayed for courage as his breath heated my lips.

Then an idea popped out of my mouth before I could think twice. "Is this how you kiss Angela? Maybe if I tell her your advice, she could offer me the best resources that money can buy."

Almost immediately, Levi's hands fell. He went to the trailer door and kicked it open, all the while not meeting my gaze. "Hopefully, that was useful so the next take is good to print. Back on set in thirty."

Chapter 41

Present Day
Jade

"Jade? Is that you?"

Why can't I speak? Why can't I move? A strain pulls at my chest, creating a sharp pain. My heart, it seems, can't handle this strain. It might give out at any second, and all I can think is how pathetic the eulogy at my funeral would be.

"Honey?" My father doesn't look a day over fifty. His face and body are fuller than I remember, but in a good way. He moves closer to me until I can see the tears filling his eyes. "My, my . . . Baby Jade, you're all grown up."

A sob collects in my throat, growing so large I think I might choke. "Daddy."

He catches me against him, and while I unleash a decade's worth of tears—for him, for me, for us—he holds me tighter than anyone else ever has. "What are you doing here?"

"I'm helping some, uh, friends drive to California."

"On Route 66?"

I nod against his chest. "All the way from Chicago."

"Is this your car?"

"It's theirs."

270

He pulls back and studies me. "And you stopped in Tecoma? I didn't think you'd remember this town."

"Remember it? That summer was probably the happiest I've ever been. I think about it all the time. I didn't know where you were after you left prison. I had to at least check if you were here." I swipe at my eyes, finding more tears than I expected. Then again, nothing is as I expected anymore, and I've been carrying this pain a long time. "Why did you stop wanting to see me? I had so many ideas of how to get your conviction overturned. I'd have done anything to make things right."

He frowns, and after some time, he takes a few steps away from me. "I know, Jade." He shoves his hands in his pockets.

"How long are you staying?"

"I'm not sure."

"If you need food, there's a café down the road. And there's a motel—"

"That's where we're staying."

"Nice. Nice. The Newtons still own it. Nancy will treat you well." He increases the distance between us. "Look, it's, uh, good to see you."

"What are you doing? Why are you backing away again?"

He stumbles over a curb, barely staying upright. "That summer never should have happened."

No, it shouldn't have. Not in a perfect world. Still, his words feel like a punch to my gut.

"I gotta get back to my shop now. It's good to see you."

"You said that already. I came all this way—"

"And believe me when I say, it's better for you to go on." He starts walking back toward his garage.

Still, I reach for him. "Dad, can't we just talk about . . . everything?"

My father pauses and speaks over his shoulder. "I did my time, Jade. I paid up. Best you go on and best you forget it."

"No, Dad," I call after him. "Why did you stop seeing me? Please tell me. I can handle it."

He doesn't turn around.

❧

Somehow I manage to get the Chevy to the motel. What I can't manage is getting out of it. A door opens a few yards down, and Bridger appears, holding an ice bucket. When he sees me, he places the bucket on the ground and jogs over.

He hops over the passenger door and slides onto the bench seat next to me, concern creasing his forehead. "What happened? Did you figure out anything about your father?"

"Only that he doesn't want me," I eke out. Even in the heat, chill bumps spread over my arms, and I rub my hands over them, up and down, up and down. With Bridger beside me as a reminder of the friend, confidant, and comforter I had—or thought I had—just yesterday, I feel more alone than ever before. A desperado. The only thing I never wanted to be.

"Jade, I want to hold you so badly; I know I've lost your trust, but if you could forgive me—"

"Forgive you? How can I possibly forgive you after what you did?" I give him a cutting glance. "You're the last person I would ever let comfort me right now."

The sound of feet crunching on gravel draws our focus back to the room. Benny has walked straight out into the parking lot. I push open the driver's side door and go to her. She'll understand my pain. She'll give me the comfort I need in this moment. I place my arms around her, but she's distant.

"I need to get home. Tell Roland we need to go."

"Benny, Roland isn't here, but Bridger is."

Bridger exits the Chevy and holds his hands up, palms out. "Roland's at his home in California with Amie," he explains.

"Where's Paul?" She marches back into the motel room, searching and not finding.

I follow her inside and lower myself onto the bed closest to her while Bridger takes a stance in front of the television.

"He's with the Lord in heaven," he says. "But he left me to care for you."

She searches the carpet for answers. "Bridger? Yes. Bridger." She tightens a fist in front of her chest. "You don't care for me. You want to dump me in one of those hospitals, like the one Louie was in. You think I've lost my mind. You want them to shock me and poke me with ice picks."

Bridger tosses a confused glance in my direction, and a rush of nausea floods over me. "No, I don't," he says to Benny. "You and I live together, and I take care of you."

"You want to pawn me off. You want to sell my house and lock me away to wither and die at that Swallow's Nest place." She points an accusing finger at me. "She told me so."

I squeeze my eyes closed. Despite Bridger's betrayal, I can't bear to see the pain my reckless words cause him. But he said he would talk to her about the plan.

"Anything we can do to help?" I recognize the voice immediately. Tim. He and Sandy stand in the doorway, having once again crossed our path. Yes, I recall, that was their Subaru parked on the opposite side of the U-shaped motel.

Bridger advances toward Benny, and she releases a panicked cry as she shields herself from him. She collapses beside me on the bed and turns into my embrace. "Don't let him hurt me! Don't let him lock me away!"

In my periphery, Bridger stands still as can be, except that his chin quivers, and when he sniffles, a tear escapes down his cheekbone. I feel his pain. A knife to the heart would hurt less.

Outside, a familiar engine starts, followed quickly by revving and tires tearing over loose gravel. Tim bolts out the door and Sandy trails him. A thick cloud of dust rolls past our window. Bridger remains in suspended motion, staring at Benny.

Dreading what I'll find, or not find, I feel the pocket on my slacks. Empty. After the tavern, I parked the Chevy. Then I sat for a long while until Bridger came out and then Benny. And the keys . . . never left the ignition. *Jesus, please no.*

But the prayer is of no use because Sandy, out of breath, returns to the room. "The Chevy . . . It's gone."

Chapter 42

1956
Benny

"Hello, Mrs. Alderidge. This is Berenice. Is Paul there?" As I held the receiver to my ear, the fingernails of my free hand dug into the wood of the bedside table. My manicurist wouldn't mind since filming ended this afternoon. All we had left was tonight's wrap party.

"Oh, Berenice. No, Paul isn't here. He never came home after you headed west."

Words eluded me. I'd figured Paul returned to Joliet, to his parents' mansion, even to his job at his grandfather's company or at Rialto Square. Or maybe that was simply what I'd hoped this entire time I was out here toiling for twelve hours a day in the New Mexico heat. That he was safe, secure, and comfortable in a familiar place with familiar people who could help him in all the ways I'd failed.

"Are you there?" His mother's voice brings me back to reality.

"Yes. I apologize. Have you spoken to him? Do you know where he is?"

"Dear me," Mrs. Alderidge said. "I have many times, but he requested I not tell you where he's gone, just that he is safe and paving his future."

"In California?"

There was a brief pause. "I promised him I wouldn't say. I must honor that, though I can tell you, Berenice, that when two people are in love, they'll find their way back to each other under the Lord's providence."

"I believe that too."

After I replaced the receiver, I stood and looked myself over in the mirror. Thanks to the help of my costume designer, I'd ordered the perfect dress for the wrap party. The Lanvin-Castillo gown of white lace created a thin silhouette, not as full as the casual dresses I'd packed for this trip. Its sweetheart neckline was a touch lower than I'd ever worn in the past, and the silken red bow tied at my waist added the same measure of sophistication as my slicked-back bun hairstyle.

Very Princess Grace. Was it me though? What would Paul think if he saw me this way?

I answered my own question with a hand over my heart. Would it ever stop hurting? What I wouldn't do to have him here with me now.

I grabbed my clutch and headed toward the sound of music. The terrace was filled with the cast and crew, as well as a few other famous faces. Clyde introduced me to Ronald and Nancy Reagan at that party—a lovely couple. After Ronald shared his views on the current state of the world, I suggested he run for president. He said he'd consider it.

"Have you seen Judy?" I asked Charlie as she and Clyde prepared to retire to their suite for the night. "I'm leaving in the morning, and I'd like to say goodbye to my 'forever little sister.'"

"You know, I haven't seen her since the toasts." Charlie squeezes both of my hands. "Benny, it's been a joy to get to know you these past months. If you need a place to stay while you get settled in, simply give me a call."

Clyde hooked an arm around my head the same way Louie used to. "I'm going to miss you, kid."

I knuckle-punched his stomach. "My hair. You're messing up my hair!"

He released me, laughing. "You've got a strong uppercut there. That may come in handy when dealing with these Hollywood hotshots. By the way, should you ever find yourself in a tricky situation, you call ol' Clyde."

After I saw them off, I said goodbyes to the other cast and crew, making sure to thank everyone for welcoming me so spectacularly. I'd happily pass on the chance to bid farewell to Levi, but I'd really taken a liking to Judy.

"Last I saw her, she was over by the 49er Lounge," the actor who played Pa said when I inquired about Judy's whereabouts.

I thought it strange that a fifteen-year-old was spending time at the hotel's bar, but I followed the lead anyway. The bartender corroborated, saying he'd served Judy a ginger ale a half hour before.

"She was here with Livingston," he told me. "He tried to get me to add gin to her glass. I did not."

"Thank you for that. Did you see where they went after?"

"If I had to guess, I'd say to his suite."

I considered putting it out of my head. Maybe swallowing a drink or two myself would drown my concerns. In good conscience I couldn't. Not after remembering how frightened I'd been in that trailer with Levi. I hurried to the front lobby and asked the clerk to ring Clyde's room. Nervously, I twisted the cord around my finger as it rang.

When the call connected, I heard a child crying, and not a whimper either. Ruthie was crying so loud I could hear a slight echo of it through the hotel's walls.

"This is Clyde."

"It's Benny."

"Benny, sorry for the noise. Ruthie's tummy is hurting again. We've tried everything, but well, you can hear how well that's worked. Can I help you with something?"

As I began to ask for his help in finding Judy, Ruthie hollered so piercingly, I had to pull the telephone away from my ear. "It's nothing. I can handle it. Thank you. Oh, and try a warm bath. And if you can get some basil or mint leaves from the restaurant or bar, you can add that to the water or use it to make her a tea."

After Clyde ended the call on his end, I kept the receiver to my ear while I thought of a new plan. Then I got an idea.

"Levi has tea leaves in his room?" I said loud enough for the desk clerk to hear. "Oh, yes, I know. He drinks a good deal of tea. Surely? He won't mind? You're right. He wouldn't want baby Ruthie in pain. I'll ask the front desk for a key, I'll get that tea to you as soon as I can."

I handed the receiver back to the clerk. "Could I get the spare key for Levi Livingston's room? Clyde Irving needs some tea from there."

"Sorry, miss. We can't do that. I could call up to his room for you though."

"He's not there. He's still dancing the night away on the terrace. He would trust me to go into his room. And you know, if it would make you feel better, you can come up with me. I'll be in and out real quick."

"It's not possible."

As if on cue, another cry sounded through the lobby. "Do you hear that poor little girl? Are you prepared to field complaints from other guests all night? Or do you want her father, Clyde Irving, to know you've done all you can to help her feel better?"

Five minutes later, the man unlocked the door to Levi's suite, and I gathered all my courage. I opened the door and rushed inside.

Judy sat on the bed with her back to me. Where the fabric of her dress had once come together, skin was now visible. I took another step forward and stepped on something. Glancing down, I realized it was a button. There were at least five or six littering the ground. I peered around the wall to find Levi frozen in the act of either taking off or putting on his pants.

Fortunately, the bed was still neatly made. Thank you, Jesus, I wasn't too late.

"Judy?"

The girl's wide, teary eyes latched on to me, and despite Levi's protests, she ran into my arms.

"How dare you?" I said to the acclaimed director. "She's a child."

He pointed a finger at me quite confidently for a man with his pants around his ankles. "You say anything, and your career is done before it's started."

"I'll take my chances." I led Judy out of the room.

The clerk seemed quite confused. "I thought you came here for tea leaves."

"What can I say? I'm a good actress."

Chapter 43

Present Day

Jade

Although he now wears a police uniform, Max Samson still looks like the ten-year-old boy I crushed on back in 2003. Baby-faced and awkward as ever, even as he takes this stolen vehicle report.

"Besides the duct tape on the back quarter panel, are there any other distinguishing markings on the car?"

"No," I say, "but I don't imagine there are many 1955 Chevy Bel Air convertibles on the road. It's an eye-catcher."

Max moves his stylus on the tablet almost like he's never used the thing before. "And Tim, you said the carjacker was alone, Caucasian, had medium-length brown hair, and full tattoo sleeves. Both arms or one arm?"

"I'm not sure. I only saw his right arm." Tim sits in a patio chair next to Sandy, holding her hand in a way that sends a pang of jealousy straight through my heart.

Max chuckles. "I always think it's strange when there are only tattoos on one side of the body. The person looks like they are going to tip over from all that extra ink."

"Max," I say, trying to keep frustration from my voice, "I

know we were friends once upon a time, but I need you to take this more seriously. That car and its contents are extremely valuable, not to mention my purse and identification, Benny's medications . . . " I pace in front of our room, peeking in on Benny who is trying to rest. Can this trip get any worse? Can life get any worse?

Tim scrubs his hand through his dark hair. "You know, he looked an awful lot like one of the guys who kept heckling us during the steak challenge, but that was back in Texas."

I lurch to a stop. "Dwight and Eli. We had a run-in with them in Petrified Forest National Park," I add. "They're taking the same route west as us. Or maybe, they were following us." I give Max all the details about their van, including the license plate information.

"Wouldn't be the first time criminals target travelers on 66. Back in the nineties, it was the ultimate hideout for 'em. It still happens occasionally."

Don't I know it. "Max, what happens if they've already left Tecoma and are out of your jurisdiction?"

He opens the door of his cruiser and places his tablet on the seat. "I'll head back to the station now and send out an APB to all the surrounding towns. Beyond that, there isn't much I can do. But, Jade, if you need anything at all, you call me. Your father would want to help you too. Does he know you're here?"

"I'd appreciate it if you could get that APB out as soon as possible," I say, ignoring the question. "And if you see our friend, Bridger, could you let us know? He took off on foot a while ago."

"Anything for you, Jade." Max retrieves his tablet from the seat but struggles to turn it on.

"Thanks, Max." He pulls away, and I join Benny inside the room.

From the bed, she reaches out to me. "Could we search for

Bridger now? I'm terribly worried about him." Her eyes, red and swollen, plead with me.

I get it. I feel like crying myself. I kneel next to her. Once again, my actions have inadvertently brought harm to this woman. In time, the money will be replaced. But this car, with all its memories of her trip with Paul, is irreplaceable. And mad as I am at Bridger, I feel my heart aching at the loss of Paul's gift to him. "Of course, Benny. You know him best. Any clue where he might have gone?"

"You said there's a bar, right?" Benny shivers. "We should try that first."

Although it isn't a far walk to the tavern, Tim and Sandy give Benny and me a ride. Tecoma has only one streetlight, so on this moonless night, I didn't want to chance Benny getting hurt on a walk. Plus, her episode exhausted her. She wouldn't dare let me look for Bridger without her, though, so here we are.

As we pull up to the front of the tavern, I touch her shoulder. "Benny, I shouldn't have spoken about Bridger's plans after the trip ends. It wasn't my place. I'm going to tell him the same thing."

"And I should have spoken to him about the options long ago. I let my own fear stand in my way." She squeezes my arm. "Let's go in there and get our boy."

Inside, only a handful of people mingle. A few others have stationed themselves alone at a table or, in Bridger's case, at the bar. He stares hard into a tall, full glass of amber liquid. Benny and I take seats on opposite sides of him.

"How many is that?" I ask, motioning to the glass.

"First one. Still deciding if I want to take a drink or not."

"The police have all the information about the car, and they're sending out an APB. Tim thinks it was stolen by one of the guys from the Big Texan and the Painted Desert Inn."

Bridger nods slowly.

Benny takes one of his hands off the glass and holds it,

tenderly stroking it from wrist to knuckle and back again. "Bridger, dear, Jade told me what I said to you. You know I love you more than life. And I've never once feared you. Do you hear me?"

Again, Bridger nods.

"Jade was only trying to help by talking to me about Swallow's Nest."

"What does it matter? The money's gone. The Chevy's gone. My computer, my cameras, all my filming equipment. No documentary, no money, no Swallow's Nest. It was bad enough I had to rely on Roland's connections to find the money for this trip. I'm not even sure we can keep the house if we have to pay back what we've already spent."

"We'll get the car and all your stuff back," I tell him. "I reported it to the local police."

He laughs bitterly. "The Tecoma Police? How many people are on their force? Five?"

"Two."

"Perfect." Bridger raises the glass and holds it just below his lips. He closes his eyes in a sort of quiet contemplation. Maybe battle is the better term. A surge toward victory occurs when he lowers the glass without taking a sip.

"Did you back up all your work to the Cloud or did you store it all on the hard drive?"

"What's the difference?"

"Months of work. Hundreds of hours of footage."

"Yes, I backed it up along the way."

"Then it's settled," Benny says, her voice clearer and stronger than it's been since Chicago. "You'll take the footage you have and leave everything that isn't true, honorable, and right on the cutting room floor. You'll focus on Route 66. How, on it, I was able to chase my dream of a better future—same as you, Bridge. And Paul was able to flee his nightmare of a past—same as Jade." Benny slides the glass out of Bridger's reach.

"And darn it all if the studios aren't interested in a feel-good story like that."

Bridger sits back and releases a surrendering sigh. He places a little kiss on Benny's cheek. "I love the heart behind it." Bridger stands. "But we all know heart won't pay the bills or bring the car back."

Benny and I watch him disappear into the men's room, then look to each other.

"It really is a beautiful idea for a film," I say.

Someone grabs the glass of beer off the bar. Eli, the shorter of the two tormentors, stands over Benny's shoulder, chugging the drink.

On instinct, I hop off my stool and wedge myself between him and Benny.

"Hey there, sweets." The foul-smelling man slams the drink on the floor, splashing me with beer and shards of glass. He grabs my hips, and his fingers press into my flesh through the fabric of my slacks. I shove against his chest hard, which provides only enough space to make him drop his grabby hands.

"Where you going, beautiful? I just got here."

I move right, and he moves to mirror me.

His wolfish grin makes my skin feel like it's turning inside out.

"Where's our car?" I ask between clenched teeth. Over Eli's shoulder, I see Sandy run toward the men's room. Tim nears, but he's still several yards away.

"What car?" Eli belches in my face, and I turn away from the stench.

When I look back, I see a scuffle between Eli and Tim. Tim falls back just as the jukebox kicks off a new song. "I Love Rock 'n' Roll." Must be time to unleash my inner Joan Jett.

"Bring back the car." I shove Eli, but it doesn't do much. He spins and grips my arm like a vise. "Or what? That's what you get for hanging out with that dirt——"

I kick him in the shin with the pointed toe of my designer heel.

Rather than dousing the man's rage, it fuels the fire in his eyes. He pushes me to the ground and I land hard on my tailbone, my head thwacking against something solid. Neon lights swim before me, doubling then disappearing, before settling in my field of vision. Shouts and footsteps pierce my hearing. Bridger! He throws a heavy punch at the man, knocking him into the bar, his upper body bending backward. Eli takes a clumsy swing, but Bridger blocks it easily and hits him again. He slumps onto the stool. Glynda climbs up and over the bar, and while she spreads her arms wide between the two men, her angry words are aimed squarely at me. I press a palm to my forehead, hoping to stop the throbbing.

Someone takes hold of my arm and lifts. Sandy's face shows concern. Poor Ohioans. All they wanted was a nice trip to celebrate their retirement. Look what I've done now.

"Benny," I don't recognize my voice. I can't see her anywhere. I try to stand but I stick to the floor.

When I do get to my feet, one leg is shorter than the other, and I lean hard into Sandy. The heel of my shoe is laying a few yards in front of me. But I see something else that concerns me much more. Benny is trying to calm Bridger, while Eli regains his footing. He throws himself at Bridger, and Benny falls. That's when Bridger locks his arms around the man and tows him past Sandy and me. The two barrel through the exit followed by Glynda.

Bridger can hold his own outside, so I limp to Benny's side. Tim holds her hand, then looks up. "Sandy, call an ambulance."

Chapter 44

Exhausted doesn't describe the way I feel after spending all night in the hospital waiting for Benny's surgery to be completed. And while she made it through all right, the recovery from a broken hip for someone her age won't be easy.

Tim and Sandy were absolute lifesavers in the figurative and literal sense. They called 911, who arranged for Life Flight to transport Benny to the Western Mountain Medical Center in Bullhead City. They drove me to the hospital, waited with me, and even called around Tecoma to find out what happened to Bridger. After the fight with Eli was broken up, Max brought him to the two-cell jail at the edge of town. His bail was set at an impossible amount for someone with no access to credit, debit, or proof of identification. My bank, while happy to freeze my account and cancel my cards, wouldn't send me the money, so Tim and Sandy, once again proving how nice Ohioans can be, lent me the money on good faith that I'll pay them back.

Not only that, but once we returned to Tecoma, Sandy also lent me a pair of shorts, a screen-printed Route 66 T-shirt, and boots to wear until I could find some other clothes and shoes. I looked myself over in my motel room's mirror before heading out. The shirt is fine, but the jean shorts, which fit Sandy's five-foot-nothing frame well, did not cover enough of my legs to make me comfortable. They barely covered my backside. I looked like I walked straight off the set of *Coyote Ugly*.

Modesty, of course, was the least of my concerns. It was more important for me to spring Bridger and get back up to the hospital. Benny would be awake and ready for visitors this afternoon.

I already said a tearful goodbye to Tim and Sandy. They needed to continue their trip, and they helped more than enough. So how Bridger and I would get back to the hospital was still a mystery. I began my trek to the jail at the edge of the tiny town.

Once I've handed the money to Sheriff Samson and freed Bridger, we stand on the edge of Route 66. The sadness pulls his lips into a taut line. "So what's the plan?"

"Go up and see Benny, I guess. She has to stay in Bullhead City overnight. Then she'll move into a rehab facility for six weeks or more. I called Swallow's Nest. They said they can help her with that recovery."

"Thank you, Jade. I really am sorry about the documentary."

"Yeah. So am I. Not that it matters, but I get it now. I'd do anything for Benny, and she isn't even my mom."

"She's not technically mine either," Bridger says, staring hard at the ground.

"Hey." I nudge his side until he meets my gaze. "Yes, she is. No more of that talk. Got it?"

The smallest trace of a smile lifts his lips. "Got it. So how do we get to the hospital?"

I eye College Boy's stalled pickup. Maybe I should have been nicer. I might have been able to finagle us a ride. Far off, an engine roars to life. A tow truck down by my father's garage pulls up to the road, then turns our way. Dad recognizes me, I know he does, but he looks away. He drives ahead of the pickup and backs up to make a tow possible.

"Wait here." I leave Bridger's side and enter the desert brush. It doesn't take me long to find the coil wire caught in the leaves of a desert spoon, a plant that looks like it belongs in a Dr. Seuss book. When I see my father come around to the open hood, I hold up the wire. The driver squawks about me being a rattlesnake as I toss the coil to my dad. "This is all it is."

"Your work?"

I nod. "He disrespected me."

"Think he learned his lesson?"

"Unlikely," I say as another nasty name flies from the guy's mouth. I leave my dad to reconnect the coil, and soon, College Boy takes off at lightning speed, apparently in quite a rush to leave Tecoma. I wait by the cab of the tow truck until my dad nears.

He jingles his keys in his hand. "I'm shocked you're still here, especially after last night. Glynda told me about it, if you were wondering."

"That woman does not like me."

"She's bitter. That's all," Dad says. "I led her to think we had a future together, then I went to prison for seventeen years."

"And she blames me for that?"

"You did nothing wrong. Nothing."

"Dad, I know you want me gone, but I need help. I'm desperate. My friend Benny broke her hip. She's at the hospital in Bullhead City, and our car was stolen and my purse and our luggage—"

"Hop in."

"Really?"

He nods.

I whisper a thank-you, then I beckon Bridger to join us.

"Dad, this is Bridger. He needs to come with us."

"Fine by me. Nice to meet ya, Bridger."

Bridger's emotions teeter, already at a breaking point. He nods.

I ride between my father and Bridger on the drive to the hospital. Between us, a thousand unspoken words.

My father drops us off at the front door of the medical center.

"I'll stay here."

"You don't have to if you don't want to."

"I want to."

I fight with my own emotions, then finally I climb down from the cab and give an awkward wave. I lead Bridger to Benny's recovery room. She's awake, and when she sees us, her face brightens. At her bedside, Bridger takes her hand and, careful of the IV, bends to kiss her knuckles.

"Honey, I'm all right," she assures him. "The doctors know what they're doing."

"Are you in pain at all?" he asks.

"Just a little."

Bridger sets her hand back on the blanket. "I'll call for more pain reliever."

"Bridge, wait. The nurses are making sure I'm comfortable. I wanted to be lucid when you came to visit so we can talk."

"Benny, it's not—"

"Son, we're talking. We can't avoid it any longer. I need you to unload the burden you've been carrying."

Bridger sighs. He pulls a chair over and sits next to her. "I should have told you about the memory care facility. As much as I hate it, they can care for you way better than I can, especially now that you'll have some physical recovery too."

She motions for her thermos on the table. I bring it to her, holding it while she sips from the straw. When she's finished, I return to the chair in the corner.

"Bridge, I cannot expect you to take care of me any longer. You have a life to live. I'll go to that hospital so you can carry on."

"Benny, listen. The facility and the care you need is . . . expensive. We'll have to sell the house to pay for it."

Benny's eyes fill with tears. "Where will you live?"

"Don't you worry about me. Worst case, I'll shack up with

Roland—take my old room back. You know me. I'll roll with any punch that comes my way. I've done it before."

"And you'll do it again." Benny glances at me. "Both of you will."

Many tears are shed, and my job becomes handing out tissues. When I open the door to flag down a nurse for a new box, I overhear words whispered behind me.

"Have you two made up yet? Don't let this keep you apart." I hold my breath to hear his response but nothing comes.

"Any news about the car?" she asks.

"Not yet," Bridger says. "The sheriff is going to figure it out though."

I slip back into the room and retake my seat.

Benny smiles softly. "Roland has arranged for a medical transport for me to Los Angeles. I'm sorry I won't be able to finish the journey with you, but this story was never about me anyway."

Frowning, Bridger shakes his head.

"Bridge, you needed this road to see that the person you were at the beginning was just as worthy as the person you'll be at the end." She palms his cheek. "I'm so proud of the man you are. My life was blessed when you entered it. Paul's too. It's about time you accept that you were chosen to be loved by us as you were. Your mama and papa never wanted you to be without a family. So join ours. Let me adopt you once and for all."

Bridger rests his forehead on the side of her bed and gives in to wracking sobs. Benny catches my eye and I don't hesitate. I rise from my chair and cross the room. Standing behind him, I touch his shoulder. He grasps my hand and won't let go.

Finally, he composes himself and peers up at her face. "Okay, Mama. When we get back to California, we'll start that process but not until you get yourself better."

"Then I better hurry it up and get well." Benny faces me.

"And you, Jade dear. You need to remember that your past

doesn't define you. Learn from my namesake, Queen Berenice. Heaven knows she had a scandalous history. But when her people were under threat, she put her life on the line to save them. Our lives, our purpose, can pivot on a dime. Your past brought you to this moment. I hope you'll pave your own future now."

I slowly nod while choking down a sob of my own. "I can do that."

"Good," Benny says. "Now I know you don't have your fancy camera or microphones, but if you don't mind, I'd like to tell you the rest of my story now."

Chapter 45

1956
Benny

The morning after the wrap party, I walked into the car dealership and drove out in a red-on-white Pontiac Star Chief convertible, just like the one in *I Love Lucy*. But rather than driving west to California, I drove east to Albuquerque. I'd promised my parents I would look in on Louie as often as I could until he was released. Maybe I could even arrange a transfer to a California mental hospital. Then at least I'd have someone dear to me close by. If only I could have two someones . . .

That thought was still going through my head when I pulled my Pontiac into the parking lot of Sandia Ranch and paused at the sight of a familiar Chevy '55. What was Paul doing here? What had his mother said? That he was paving a future for himself. Did that include Louie—the same Louie who hated him for reporting his war crime?

A honk startled me. I looked in the rearview mirror.

"Are you gonna take that spot or not?" a man yelled.

I cleared the tears from my eyes and turned into the empty spot next to Paul. Everything in me wanted to hop out of the car and run into the hospital. I settled for a half walk, half skip. The sign-in process took far too long, and I was about to burst when the orderly finally brought me to Louie's room. I peeked in and saw Louie, unrestrained, and Paul playing cards at a table. When the door opened, they both looked my way. Paul and I locked eyes, even as Louie hurried over to hug me. Paul stood from his seat but kept his distance.

"Benny," Louie said, "I didn't know you were coming to visit."

"Filming wrapped." I broke my gaze away from Paul's to take in the sight of my brother. There were no longer dark circles beneath his eyes, and he was clean-shaven. "You look good, Louie. I like these overalls they've got you in."

He hooked his thumbs around the straps where they met the bib. "They're great for my job. Did you see the gardens when you drove in? That's what I do. I'm a gardener."

"I did. You'll have to teach me your tricks one day when I have a home of my own."

"I will. It'll have to be when I get out of here though."

"Have they told you when that will be?"

"No. That's okay. I'm starting to like it here. They're helping me sort out all the thoughts in my head." He stepped to the side and gestured at Paul. "He's been spending time here with me. We've been talking about stuff we saw and stuff we went through over in Korea. The doctors say it's good for both of us."

"I'm sure it is." I swallowed hard. "Hello, Paul."

"Hello, Benny." His arms hung at his sides, straight and loose, but his fingers fidgeted a bit.

"We were playing rummy," Louie said. "Would you like to join?"

"Yes, I would like that very much."

Paul offered his chair to me while the orderly fetched another. I accepted, noting the way Paul's hand grazed my shoulder as I sat. Louie dealt the cards, and I worked to keep my breath steady, even as I slid my foot next to Paul's and let my shoe rest against his.

I'm not sure how many hands we played before it was dinnertime for Louie. I made my brother a promise that day, to always consider him moving forward. Paul and I bid him goodbye and walked with a nurse back to the front of the hospital.

"I called your mother," I said once we got outside. "She didn't tell me you were here this whole time."

"I wanted to make things right with Louie. I don't think I knew how much of a toll that situation took on me. And I wanted to be close to you in case . . ."

"In case of what?"

"I'm not sure. I couldn't abandon you in New Mexico and go back home."

"Why?"

He paused by the back fender of the Chevy. "Because I love you, Benny. Even if I couldn't be with you, I needed to know you were safe. That you were happy."

My heart pummeled my sternum. "You make me happy, Paul. That's what I want. To be happy with you. And I know I can be immature and rash and—"

"Funny and caring and adventurous—"

"And bullheaded." I laughed. "I'm sorry for getting so angry for reporting what you witnessed. You know, we started this journey west so I could show you there are good people in this world, and I found you. You are a good man, and I'm not sure you even knew that when we started out. Your goodness rubs off on other people. It rubbed off on me. Last night, I made a courageous decision to help someone even if it costs me. Four months ago, I wouldn't have done that."

Paul smiled the most genuine smile I'd ever seen. Knowing he was proud of me was the icing on the cake. I could live for years on that.

"Paul, maybe we don't need Hollywood, but maybe Hollywood needs us. More good people like Clyde and Charlie Irving. I could move to California alone, but I don't want to." I rushed forward and kissed him. It was warm and natural and in it I felt a sense of home. "I love you, Paul Alderidge. Now let's go pave that future together."

Chapter 46

Present Day
Jade

"We went to the courthouse the next day and got married. Our honeymoon was a lazy drive across Route 66, him in the Chevy, me in the Pontiac, stopping perhaps too often to stay the night—and sometimes the day—at a motel in Kingman or Needles or San Bernadino. Eventually, we made it to the coast, and you could say we lived happily ever after."

I quietly blow my nose into a tissue. I'm a weepy mess but I don't care. "That's a beautiful story, Benny."

"Thank you, sweetheart." Benny's yawn tells me it's time to leave.

I kiss her cheek and say goodbye. Tomorrow, if all goes well, an ambulance will take her and Bridger back to Los Angeles where she will enter Swallow's Nest's rehabilitation wing. Then, once she has recovered physically, she'll move into the memory care wing. Bridger will stay at the hospital tonight, so it's time for our goodbye as well.

"I'm going to walk Jade downstairs," he tells Benny.

I debate what to say as we approach the elevator. The doors open, and he waits for me to go in first. When they close, he finally speaks. "You know, Benny's story got me thinking."

"Got you thinking what?"

Bridger captures my lips with his, stealing my breath and every logical thought. His kiss feels the way a 55 Chevy's engine purrs, and I can't explain that. I'm not sure how long we stay in the back of that elevator, but there are many dings, sliding doors, awkward laughs from strangers, and a few times where my stomach lifts, then drops, then lifts, and drops. Finally, it lifts again.

I hear someone clear their throat.

"Uh, I think this is your floor," a man in a lab coat says.

Bridger laces his fingers through mine and escorts me out into the hospital lobby, then the visitors' lot. My father's tow truck towers above all the other vehicles, so it isn't difficult to spot.

We pause before we reach the passenger door.

"What's next for you?" he asks.

"I'm not sure. I'll stay at the Tecoma Springs Motel as long as they'll let me. Maybe Glynda will let me work at the tavern until I have enough for a bus ticket."

"Where will that bus ticket go?"

"God only knows."

"Maybe play 'Hotel California' on repeat for some inspiration." When he winks, I melt.

"I will."

"What about your dad?"

I shrug. "I can only be responsible for my own actions, my own words. I may never know why things happened the way they did. I have to be okay with that." I look to the heavens. "I *will* be okay with that. Now what about you? What will you do?"

"I'll try to salvage what I can of the documentary. I need to turn it into something I'm proud of. But the main priority is getting Benny settled in."

I nod and look down at our intertwined fingers. "If I hear anything about the car, I'll call.

"Until then . . ." I can't finish the sentence with how thick my throat feels.

"Until then . . ." He combs my wild, tangled curls behind my ear and kisses my forehead. Then he helps me into my father's truck.

"It was nice to meet you, Mr. Jessup." Bridger reaches across me to shake my father's hand.

"Take it easy, young man," my father says.

"No doubt. I've got a peaceful, easy feeling." After one last glance, he steps down and shuts my door.

I watch Bridger shrink in the side mirror as we drive. Then we turn, and he's gone.

"You really seem to like him," my father says.

My blush must speak louder than the words that get stuck in my throat.

"Does he treat you better than that Gregory did?"

I shift to face him. "How do you know about Gregory?"

"You're still my daughter, Ba—I mean, Jade. I've tried to keep up on your life from afar. You don't know how many times I wanted to reach out . . ."

"Why didn't you?" My voice is sharp, and I don't care. How dare he say this now?

"There's something you said earlier that's been eating away at me all this time I've been sitting here." He fights to clear his throat. "I never wanted you gone. I've always wanted you with me. Since the moment I found out your mom was pregnant. Thing is, I'm not a good influence. Everything I touch turns to rot. Even people. Look at your mom and Glynda. I don't want to do the same with you."

"Is that why you pushed me away?"

"Partly," he concedes. "After I . . . went after Hank, I should've left you there with your mom. I shouldn't have taken you with me."

"No, you should have taken me farther away. To Mexico or

South America. You wouldn't have been caught, and I wouldn't have gone back. Mom wasn't nice to me. She was bitter and hateful. I guess I can understand why, even if it wasn't right. What I can't understand is why you cut me out of your life."

I wait for him to answer the question I've been asking myself for so long. It isn't until we enter the Tecoma town limits that he speaks.

"You blamed yourself for what happened with Hank. You fought hard to tell everyone that I was only guilty of trying to protect you. It consumed you."

"And you hated me for reminding you that you killed an innocent man."

"No." He glances at me, incredulous. "No, Jade. I never hated you. It was the opposite. You were so consumed with guilt that it was eating away at you." His jaw juts back and forth. "I did it for your own good."

I scrub a hand over my clavicle, the pain of those lost years hastening through every bone in my body.

"If there was another way, I didn't know it. I followed your career, and I was so proud of you. You were doing it. The green-eyed girl helping the whole village feed their families and such. When I saw you yesterday, I worried you were going to tear yourself apart on account of me again. I never thought you'd get it in your head I hated you. You're the only one I've ever loved, Baby Jade." He steers the tow truck onto the road beside his garage. "And I do regret going after Hank. But I tell you what, I'd do it all again if I thought I was protecting you."

"You were." The words erupt from my throat. Our wheel hits a pothole, and my stomach roils.

"What d'you mean?"

I wait for him to park the truck before I unload on him. "The thing is, Dad, I lied."

"I know. You told me."

"No. That day when we got ice cream, I told you Hank was

mean to me so you'd want me to live with you. But that's not the truth. He was the opposite, always buying me gifts, sneaking me candy when Mom wasn't looking. He always wanted to cuddle me. On nights when Mom would work, he'd climb into my bed."

My father stares hard through the windshield. The rays of the setting sun color his face red and orange as he processes the secret Hank warned me to keep. His knuckles strain on the steering wheel.

"It wasn't until a couple years ago, when I was meeting with a counselor, that I realized what he'd been doing. Grooming me for something much worse."

My father thunked the back of his skull against the headrest. "So Hank never . . . ?"

"No." I will him to look at me, but he doesn't. "It could have been worse. For many children, it is. But I wanted you to know that your actions, even though you didn't mean to kill him, it did save me in at least one way. So thank you."

"And you've had to carry this alone?" He turns to face me. The sunset turns his green eyes gold, and I know the same is true for mine.

Desperados. We've both become exactly what we were running from. I think back to Benny's words in the bar. Yes, people travel Route 66 for all kinds of reasons, but it isn't just travelers on that specific road who are running. In our own way, we're all running from or running to something. The lucky ones get to do that with someone they love at their side.

I smile. "Not anymore. Do you think it might be possible to make up for lost time now?"

"I'd like that, Baby Jade." He shakes his head and clears his throat. "I mean, Jade."

"It's okay," I say with a laugh. "I don't mind it so much now."

"Good, because you'll always be my little girl. My good girl."

I lunge across the front seat and squeeze his neck harder than anyone in history, I think. He hugs me right back, and I wonder if this is what it feels like to be wholly and truly loved. I believe so. I only let go when my phone vibrates in the pocket of my shorts. According to the screen, the Tecoma Police are calling.

"This is Jade," I answer.

"Hi, Jade. This is Max. I got good news and bad news. The good news is we've tracked down the car and arrested two men for the theft, including the one messing with you at the tavern."

"And the bad news?" I ask.

"The bad news is the state of the car and its contents. It's all destroyed."

Chapter 47

Like old times, Dad and I belt out the lyrics to "Seven Bridges Road" loud enough for every traveler from Tecoma to Winslow to hear it. Once the song's over, I finish the last bite of the sandwich Glynda made for me. Peanut butter, banana, and honey, I don't have the heart to tell her my tastes are more sophisticated now. After Benny and Bridger returned to California and I came back here, it took three weeks for Glynda to sit in the same room with me, four weeks for her to look me in the eye, six weeks to speak to me, and seven to bring me lunch like she brings for Dad.

I eye the lunch Dad has been too busy to finish. "Want another bite?" I crane my neck to see under the Chevy. At least he can afford jack stands now. That makes undercarriage work much easier, especially when we work side by side.

He slides out on his under-car creeper. I grab one half of his ham and cheese and hold it down for him to take a bit of nourishment.

"You're pushing yourself too hard, Dad. You need to rest and eat."

"I know," he says through a mouthful. "But those Handy brothers did a number on this car. And the sooner we finish the job, the sooner you get to visit California."

"I'm in no rush. Wait." I place the sandwich back on the plate. "Are you sick of me?"

"Not possible. It's just that I see you on those video calls with him. You light up."

I may roll my eyes but I'm smiling just the same.

"I know, I know. But if you ask me, you and Bridger belong together. I'm as sure as Route 66 is long. Any updates on Mrs. Alderidge?"

I brush some crumbs off my shirt. "Still not walking, but her spirits are high as ever. Bridger has her doing chair yoga to get her muscles strong again, so hopefully soon." I stretch my neck one way, then the other. I could use a prayer and yoga sesh myself. "She's having more episodes though. Almost nightly now."

"I'm sorry to hear that. She seems like a real nice lady."

The best, I want to say.

"How's she taking the sale of her house?"

"Better than we expected." I replace a few tools in the tool chest. "Turns out it was purchased by Judy Herron's granddaughter. She promised to take good care of it, the same way Benny took care of Judy when she was younger."

"And that leaves Bridger . . . ?"

"With his brother, Roland, but only temporarily. He said it was rough at first, but I think they're starting to understand each other."

"Nice." My father points behind me. "Grab that other creeper and join me under here. I want to show you something."

I tie the excess fabric of my "Mother Road" T-shirt at my waist. Tecoma doesn't exactly have a Saks to replace my old wardrobe. I also don't have the money or desire to step back into business attire anytime soon. I position myself on the dolly and roll to my father's side where he stares up at not one but two fuel tanks.

"Remember how surprised we were to see that second tank when we first got this up on stands?"

"Yeah."

"Look," he taps the smaller of the two tanks. "This one isn't connected to anything. No fuel line."

I laugh beneath my breath. "I was right. I knew we were only running on eight gallons a tank." I wipe some grease off my thumb. "But why would Paul go through all this trouble to add another tank then not hook it up?"

"Beats me." Dad studies the undercarriage. "Let's take her off and see."

I hold the tank in place while he loosens the clutch head screws. As he does, more and more weight presses down on my palms. "It's heavy. There's something in it."

He helps me keep it in place until it's finally loose. "Okay, let's back this out of here."

Ten minutes later, after Dad removed the cap welded on the filler neck, we kneel on the checkerboard floor with the tank between us. Dad shines a flashlight inside. "What do you see in there?"

I lean over and peer in. All my breath whooshes out of me, and I cover my mouth. The same face I saw in Bridger's coffee cup that fateful day in my office stares up at me now. "It's cash. Open it."

"Okay, Miss Bossy." While he finds something to crack open the tank, I think back on all the conversations I had with Paul as we discussed their finances. About him not trusting the stock market completely, about always wanting a nest egg in case of tragic events. Even the wording of his will that bestowed the Chevy and all of its contents to Bridger.

My phone vibrates in my back pocket, and I jump up. Bridger's name might be the best thing I've ever seen, well, after Ben Franklin's face. I dance my feet in place while I answer.

"Bridger!"

"She's gone, Jade. God took Benny home."

Chapter 48

Behind the wheel of the completely restored Chevy, I drive the remainder of Route 66 in memory of Berenice and Paul Alderidge. The sorrow in my heart is tempered by the clear blue sky and cool, crisp breeze teasing my hair. I can picture Benny and Paul in their twin convertibles playfully passing each other through New Mexico, Arizona, and California, counting down the miles until their next motel stop. Seventy years of that love wasn't enough. They would have loved that way forever. Now, in heaven, they are together again. She found him, finally. A tear slips over my lashes, and the wind wipes it immediately away.

I arrive in Los Angeles with plenty of time, but I don't wish to distract Bridger, Roland, or any family and friends so I wait until the funeral at Our Lady of the Angels Cathedral. According to news reports, thousands have already stopped by the wake to pay their respects to the beloved screen legend. After parking the Chevy, I attempt to sneak through a side door so as not to be seen, but I practically ram into Roland in one of the small parish rooms.

"Roland."

His face burns red, making his blue eyes even more striking.

"Jade. I didn't know if you'd be here."

"I wouldn't miss it. I'm sorry for your loss."

He releases a quiet laugh. "I'm not. Mom was ready. Ready to meet God. Ready to see Dad. She had a full life."

"Yes, she did. Still, I know you'll miss her."

"Every hour, every day," he says. He stares up at the ceiling and sniffles, and I see the tears he's holding back. "Listen, Jade. Amie, Mom, and even Bridger have helped me understand how despicable I've been to you."

"You were looking out for your mom. I can't hold that against you."

He palms the back of his neck. "I haven't been so good to Bridger either. Chalking it up to insecurity and sibling rivalry might be simplifying it too much."

"I don't think so. I've read the parable of the prodigal son, Cain and Abel, Jacob and Esau . . ."

"Those are some harsh examples."

I give him the stink eye, and he holds his hands up in surrender. "I know. I deserve it."

He nods toward a hallway. "If you're looking for him, Bridger's back there."

"I don't want to distract anyone." I wave a dismissive hand although the butterflies in my stomach call my bluff.

"I think that ship has sailed. You've been distracting him since the day he met you." Roland leans in. "Between you and me, I think it would do him good to see you now."

I wait for Roland to disappear, then I slink through the hall. At each doorway, I peek in, until finally I notice a large shadow spread over the floor. He stands with his back to me.

"Bridger?"

Slowly, he faces me. "Jade."

"I need a hug," I say, knowing full well he'll oblige. Bridger would never leave anyone in need. Surely, he learned some of that from Benny, but much of it is simply who he is.

He crosses the room and crushes me against him. "Thank you for coming all this way."

"There's nowhere else I should be."

He plants a kiss on my forehead, and I rest in the familiarity his arms provide. After an extended embrace, I release him and point to the paper in his hand.

"What's that?"

He smiles. "Before she slipped away, Mom filled out my adoption paperwork. Her lawyer just gave this to me. I don't know if it can ever be made official or not, but it's proof she wanted me. My mama."

"Absolutely."

"And funny enough, Roland said that if this doesn't go through, he and Amie will adopt me so I can finally be an Alderidge."

"Oh, Bridger. I love that." I breathe in the scent of him. Salon meets ocean. Clean meets wild. I've missed it so. "I brought the Chevy. It's finished. Dad and I worked nonstop so we could get it done before the funeral."

"Really? I'll be excited to see it when we leave here. But it might raise some brows to drive it, top down, to the cemetery."

"You? Caring about what people think of you?" I jest.

"You're right. I'll take those judgments and stuff 'em in my back pocket."

"That's the Bridger I remember." I limit my smile to a purse of my lips. We are, after all, at the memorial service for one-half of America's most beloved couple. "And there's something else. You know how Paul was concerned about putting all his financial eggs in one basket? Well, we found one of his baskets." I explain about the $2.5 million we found inside the spare gas tank. I hand him the cashier's check and the key to the Chevy. "Leave it to Paul to pull something like this. I guess I won't have to keep crashing at Roland's now."

Bridger simply laughs.

We maintain eye contact for several seconds. "So how's the documentary coming?" I ask.

"I've received several offers. Turns out feel-good stories are on trend. But, you know, I'm not so good with numbers. I may need someone to take a look."

"How convenient. I happen to be very good with numbers."

"Rad." His gaze roams over my face.

Distant organ music begins to play "For the Beauty of the Earth." I can still hear Benny singing.

"I should go," he says. "Pastor Doug will speak first, then Ruthie Irving. I'm up after her."

"Yeah, I should go find a place to stand. I'm sure all the seats are taken. Maybe we can grab coffee or maybe even chili dogs tomorrow."

"I knew I'd convert you." Except the joy on his face is short-lived. "Unfortunately, I can't. I'm heading out on a long trip. I won't be back for a few months."

"Oh, wow. Back up Route 66?" I tease, hoping my own dis-appointment isn't obvious.

"Nah, Samoa. One of the last things Benny said to me was that I should go back to my first home and learn more about where I came from. I've been able to reconnect with an uncle and quite a few of my cousins. Once the adoption goes through, I'm even considering changing my name to Emanuelu Alde-ridge to incorporate my birth name. I never felt like Bridger Rosenblum fit me."

"Emanuelu Alderidge." I let the name roll off my tongue. "I love it. And I love that you've been able to speak to your family. I'm happy for you," I say, even as my voice breaks a bit. "It's everything I could want for you."

"Everything? Really?" He studies me. Then, seemingly learn-ing what he needs to know, he looks away, shifting his weight from one foot to the other. "You know, you could always come with me, in case I need someone to drive me somewhere when it's light. Or dark." He shrugs, and I see a familiar flicker of mischief in the depths of his eyes.

I chuckle under my breath. "I think I can make room in my schedule for that."

"Good." He walks out one door, and I head toward the other. The growing distance between us makes my chest physically ache. "Oh, Jade?"

"Yeah?" I spin a bit too expectantly and see him poke his head back in the room.

"I was thinking that after Samoa, I don't know, maybe we can go to Ohio." He raps his knuckles on the doorframe. "What do you say, Jade? Will you go to Ohio with me?"

I drop my purse and run straight into his arms. We share the kind of kiss that only happens if you truly love someone, and we linger in that moment until I'm unsure if the tears dripping off my jaw are his or mine. He folds himself around me, and I smile, knowing our journey is just beginning.

Author's Note

For most of my life I imagined traveling the glorious stretch of road once called Route 66. My dad often told me how at eighteen years old, he packed his belongings in a 1957 Ford Fairlane Skyliner and took the Mother Road to California, where he met my mother while cruising Main (with an oversize teddy bear in his passenger seat, but that's a whole other story). I read about this historic road in wonder as the Joad family risked all they had, despite immeasurable odds, for a new life in *The Grapes of Wrath*. And then with my children, I spent endless hours on the floor playing with replica toy cars while watching Lightning McQueen find his identity in the neglected Route 66 town of Radiator Springs.

If I ever write a book, I told myself, I'll set it along that road. Fast-forward to 2022 when I experienced one of the greatest joys of my life—solo driving all 2,448 miles of Historic Route 66.

Dear reader, the words in this book cannot adequately describe what it is like to travel cross-country at a slower pace than we're used to living, in and through cities and towns with cultures different than our own, past the neon-lighted businesses that miraculously survived and the skeletal remains of those that succumbed to "progress."

If you do ever travel Route 66 (and I emphatically suggest you do), you'll realize that on that road, time is not linear. On one stretch of pavement, you'll jam to the quintessential traveling song by Nat King Cole. On another, you'll recognize yourself in the drawn faces of those during the Dust Bowl. You'll meet families today that served weary travelers all the way back to 1926. But mostly, you'll find that memories, the indomitable spirit of humankind, and the dreams and fears of those who lived, worked, and moved along this road are alive and well. To put it simply, Route 66 is a beautiful haunt.

I've done my best to preserve the history regarding this road and those places along it. At times, I've adjusted small details for the sake of the story. Such as the Hamons having a pet monkey in 1956. In actuality, the pet monkey lived at the family's home and business in the 1960s. Del's Restaurant in Tucumcari likely did not serve milkshakes when they first opened. And to my knowledge there is no wild burro named Celine near Oatman, Arizona.

Most importantly, I've included a good deal of sensitive topics in this book. Dementia, the Samoan adoption scandal of the early 2000s, the bombing of the Alfred P. Murrah Federal Building in Oklahoma City, the Tulsa Race Massacre and its long-standing cover-up, the realities of Jim Crow and modern-day racism, parental kidnapping, post-traumatic stress disorder as it pertains to veterans of war, war crimes, sexual harassment and assault, and treatment of POWs then and now. Although I have sought the advice of sensitivity readers, I would never be able to understand what it is like to personally or generationally experience such things. If I have gotten anything wrong, I welcome the opportunity to learn more.

You may email me your personal stories and your pictures of Route 66 at janine@janinerosche.com. I'd love to see them!

Turn the page for a sneak peek at another emotional novel from **Janine Rosche**

with

every

memory

one

Lori

Even the best makeup couldn't hide the fact that I'd been raised from death to life. A sound—half chuckle and half sigh—skimmed my lips as I placed my Givenchy powder and brush in my travel case. If Deirdre, my favorite nurse, heard my thoughts, she'd tell me to display my scars proudly, as I was "a walking testimony of the good Lord's mercy and grace." A walking testimony. She'd never caught the slip, and I'd never called attention to it.

I placed the travel case in the basket on the front of my walker and then began my trek to my chair. I'd no sooner caught my breath than a knock sounded at the door. "Come in."

"Good glory, Ms. Lori!" Deirdre sauntered through the doorway like she was wearing a gold-breasted choir robe instead of the same green scrubs all the nurses at the rehab center wore. She spread her arms wide and let the door swing behind her. "Are you excited? It isn't every day you get a second chance at life."

"I am excited. To sleep in my own bed, cook my own food, read with my childr—" I swallowed hard as reality struck. "My daughter."

"That sounds wonderful."

I checked my watch. Nearly nine. "I should make sure I have everything." I readied myself to stand, prompting Deirdre to quickstep to my side and offer her arm as a support. With a flick of my hand, I waved her off. "I must get used to doing all this on my own. May as well start now."

Using the armrests as support, I leaned forward and pushed with my legs. Fire ripped through my quadriceps—a feeling I'd learned to appreciate. Months ago, I'd felt nothing in those muscles at all. After I straightened, I waited for vertigo to come. It didn't, thank heavens. Perhaps it had slept in. Meanwhile I'd been awake since four.

"Don't push yourself too hard now or you're likely to end up right back here." Deirdre watched my slow progress. "Your baby girl may think she's grown, but she still needs her momma."

My lips were too taut for my smile to feel genuine. Deirdre looked over the tray holding my hardly touched breakfast. "Now, now, Ms. Lori. Your hubby might be a feast for the eyes, but you've still got to eat real food."

"I tried. My nerves had other ideas. I'd rather not start my 'second chance' by getting sick all over myself or Michael." With the help of my walker, I shuffled my cashmere-slippered feet over to the large window of my suite—the best money can buy, Michael had called it once. How long ago was that? Was it even Michael who'd said it? I brushed the voile curtain back to see the sunlight sparkling on Denver's South Platte River, yet an even better image caught my attention. In the parking lot below, Michael shut the door to his Lexus. After all his visits to the rehabilitation center, I still expected to see the beat-up Honda since my brain only occasionally acknowledged the eight years prior to our accident.

I closed my eyes and went through my mental checklist: the month and year, the current president, my age, the names of the living members of my family, and the facts of my situation. Each answer tugged harder on my heartstrings, but I wouldn't give in to tears. This was a big day, so I shoved away the consuming sadness and focused on that tall, dark, and handsome man casually walking toward the clinic's entrance.

"Why are you anxious?" Deirdre asked.

My stomach twisted. "Because I know it won't be how it was."

"What if it's better?"

She tried to pat my shoulder, but I shirked away from her touch. "Better? After all I lost, how could it possibly be better?"

"I'm only thinking the Lord's not through with the Mendenhalls yet. With the way you helped us redecorate these rooms to look less like a morgue and more like one of those flippity-flop home shows, I bet you could make quite a name for yourself as an interior designer."

"I don't know. I'm not sure I can handle any more of his plans."

"After all you've accomplished here? 'Course you can. When the hospital transferred you in January, you couldn't walk, talk, or remember your name. Look at you now."

I cast a glance at my reflection in the window's glass. Like I did dozens of times a day, I fussed with the hair near my scar, brushing it forward. Did I have time to grab a scarf from the wardrobe? I had to try. The leg of my walker caught on the chair when I went to turn. It took several jarring shimmies to get it facing the other way.

While Deirdre prattled on about the importance of slow, deliberate movements, I shuffled to the wardrobe as quickly as possible and pulled the door open. Empty.

"Where——"

"We packed most of your stuff yesterday." Deirdre knew better than to add the "remember?" part because, clearly, I didn't. "I'll pack up your toiletries so you two don't linger here one minute longer than you have to. Mr. Handsome is bound to be in a hurry to get you home." She winked at me as she headed to the bathroom.

Warmth flooded my cheeks. My eyes caught something on the top shelf of the wardrobe. I slid the paper toward me and picked it up, finding one of the family photos they'd used for my memory work. My favorite memory. The moment I'd recovered it in therapy had been almost as happy as the day it had occurred. It was Easter Sunday, and the church had set up a backdrop for pictures. Austin and Avery were three. He wore light blue-and-white seersucker overalls with a hand-embroidered turtle on the front pocket. Avery wore a blue dress with pink tights, black Mary Janes, and a sparkly red bow—always the fashionista. They sat together on a bench, holding hands. Austin had insisted on it. And Michael? He was the most dashing man who'd ever dashed. He'd opted for his favorite pose with me. He'd stood behind me, slid his hands over mine, then wrapped me in an embrace.

"Hey."

The voice jolted me, and the photo slipped from my fingers as I looked up. Fifteen years after that photo was taken, Michael stood on the threshold, not an ounce less handsome but much farther away. His gaze wasn't on me but the stack of Michael Kors suitcases he'd had delivered last week. "Are you ready?"

"Yes, I believe so. Deirdre is getting the last of my things from the bathroom."

Finally, his focus found my face, and his eyes widened. He closed the distance between us in only two strides. His fingertips gentled my neck, turning my chin slightly. "When did you get this bruise? What happened?"

"On Sunday," I said, "after visiting hours ended. It was nothing. I thought I could get to the bathroom without my walker, but I fell and bumped my chin on the floor." No need to tell him about the cut on the inside of my bottom lip or the massive headache the fall summoned.

"Why didn't someone tell me?" His glare demanded an answer. "This place is supposed to be the best in Colorado—"

"Michael." I used my softest voice, hoping to recapture his focus. It didn't work the way it used to. Then again, I was no longer the beauty queen he'd fallen for. "I asked them not to call you. It was my fault."

He looked at me from beneath his pinched brow. His hands dropped from my neck and secured my waist in his strong grasp. There was no way I could fall now. "Should you be standing? I can get a wheelchair."

"I'm fine." I wrapped my hands around his upper arms, noticing how much more muscular he was now than in our early years of marriage. When had fitness become so important to him? Since the accident? Or during the part of our life I couldn't remember?

"Don't push yourself too hard, Lori." His eyes, walnut-hued and rimmed by dark lashes, did more than ask me to be careful. They implored me to. The concern radiated through me, stunting my ability to speak.

Instead, I offered a slight nod. Not sure how much more careful I could be than living in a rehabilitation center all this time, never once leaving to go shopping or to get coffee. Maybe the command was meant for when I returned home. Or when I got in the car. With a lifetime of memories swirling about my brain like specks of dust in a tornado, I wasn't sure of anything anymore, except that no place was completely safe. Not even my husband's embrace.

After I assured him I was good to stand on my own, he kneeled and picked up the photograph I'd dropped.

"I nearly forgot that picture when I packed my things," I told him, leaving out how I had no memory of packing at all.

"Hmm," Michael said after a quick examination. "When was this, again?"

"Michael," I said, "I'm the one with a traumatic brain injury."

"You know me and these things. The kids were, what, five here?"

"They were three."

He stared at the picture the way he might analyze stock dividends.

Grief, my therapist had said, is rarely handled in the same manner by everyone, and we must be careful not to judge. That didn't make my heart ache any less.

Deirdre walked into the living area. "Well, Mr. Mendenhall, your queen is ready to leave one castle for the next." She extended the handle on the largest suitcase. "We sure are going to miss her around here."

"Not as much as she'll miss you, I'm sure." Michael's million-dollar smile—another change that had developed in the span of time I couldn't recall—had its effect on Deirdre. She started fanning herself exaggeratedly. When he glanced back at me, though, the smile fell. "I'll go get a wheelchair."

"I told you he'd be in a hurry to get you home," Deirdre said with a chuckle.

"Yes, I'm sure that's it." I fidgeted with my hair again.

After one last check passed from Michael to the clinic's administrator, the fanfare began. Patients and staff who had become my friends lined the third-floor hallway, waving their goodbyes. The ones who could stand offered hugs. Suddenly, I was thankful for the wheelchair. These people had comforted me at my lowest moments, like the day I was informed my son—my precious Austin—hadn't survived the crash that I'd just barely come through. And these people cheered for me every time I relearned something the doctors had said I'd never again do. Saying goodbye was hard.

Still, it wouldn't be as hard as the missing hello back at home.

In the car, Michael was quiet.

"I thought Avery might come with you." I ran my hand over the smooth leather upholstery. This car looked more like a New

York City limousine than a family vehicle. Hadn't he and Avery been doing family things while I'd been at the clinic recovering? Other than visiting me every other weekend, I mean. Avery, it seemed, never enjoyed the visits. It was out of her comfort zone, I told myself each time, which was okay. I was sure the place would have grown on her if I had to stay much longer. Avery wasn't nearly as happy-go-lucky as Austin, but once they had settled into a place or activity, Austin had always helped Avery come around. And when that girl smiled, the sun may as well take a rest. Unfortunately, that was a light I hadn't seen in a long time.

"This is the last day of summer," Michael said. "I thought I'd let her sleep in one more time before the school year starts."

I closed my eyes and willed my brain to work. The current year minus the twins' birth year. That made Avery—

"It's her senior year," Michael whispered as if saying it at a normal volume would embarrass me for not recalling my only surviving child's age.

"Thank you." I unlocked my cell phone and scrolled through the most recent photos that Michael had uploaded of Avery. "I hate that I can't remember."

"That's all right. I'm here to help you, babe." He reached over and patted my knee twice, then settled his hand on my thigh long enough for its heat to burn through my lounge pants. There had been a time when he'd thought I was pretty. Back in my Miss Colorado Teen days. Back when my hair had been the color of the Great Sand Dunes and there wasn't a four-inch-long C scar above my ear.

His hand tensed and his knuckles arched. Then he pulled his arm away entirely. Could I blame him? I looked nothing like the young twentysomething in that Easter Sunday photo.

Michael cleared his throat. "And I've hired the finest home health-care professionals to come over while I'm at work to get you settled in."

"You're going back to work? How soon?"

He kept his eyes on the road. "I have a meeting this afternoon across town. I can cancel it if I need to."

I swallowed my disappointment like it was a chocolate-covered toad. "No, I'll be fine. It's been a tiring morning, so I imagine I'll rest. Maybe read a book." I laughed coarsely. "Do I still like to read?"

"I hope so. I uploaded the latest book from that author you love onto a new e-reader. You know, the one who writes those love stories set in the 1920s. Do you, uh, remember what an e-reader is?"

"Only because one of the nurses had one."

"You loved yours, but it was in your purse when we . . . Anyway, this one has far better features. Top of the line. It's plugged into the charger on your bedside table."

"Michael, thank you."

He stiffly nodded as we headed north on Highway 93 toward Boulder. Funny how I couldn't remember our address, but I knew every hill and curve of this road. Perhaps funny wasn't the best word. I gazed out the windshield at the mountains rising unapologetically from the plains, capturing the focus of anyone looking west and beckoning them toward their cragged beauty. Thank the Lord I could still recall my childhood climbing boulders and befriending foxes outside our cabin, all while promising Mom I wouldn't skin my knees ahead of pageant day.

We passed the neighborhood where our three-bedroom ranch stood. According to Michael, we moved out of our "starter" house four years ago. Was it too much to hope we'd found a quaint home nestled into a secluded mountainside?

My heart leaped when the Lexus turned west onto a road I didn't recognize. Soon, absurdly large homes came into view. The kind in the home decor magazines I used to fawn over after researching the week's best deals on diapers. Michael steered the car between sprawling estates, many of which had horses in adjoining pastures. "Does any of this look familiar?"

My chest tightened, forcing my no out on a breath.

We pulled onto a driveway that led to a sleek home, mountain-style but modern, with sharp eaves, large windows, and textures of lumber and stone. Beautiful and entirely unrecognizable. My eyes stung, and I turned away from Michael.

"Lori, it's okay." His typically deep voice rose in pitch and softened. "Take it one day—"

The car stopped abruptly, and my body pitched forward until the seat belt lashed my chest and neck. I threw my hands up to shield myself from the steel and glass I expected to strike my face. Piercing noise assailed my eardrums as my vision went blindingly white then black.

Acknowledgments

To my publishing team—Your belief in me means the world. Thank you for providing your excellence so this story may reach those who need it in the way it should be told. To my agent, Tamela Hancock Murray, I don't make your job easy, do I? Thanks for all the counseling and encouragement through the years.

Thanks to the many people and businesses along Route 66 that offered inspiration and insight, especially Lucille "Mother of the Mother Road" Hamons' family. It was an honor to learn more about your family legacy. Readers, if you drive Route 66, make sure you stop at Lucille's in Hydro, Oklahoma, and Serenade Music in Grants, New Mexico.

To Tim and Sandy from Syracuse—I absolutely loved running into you repeatedly on the road. I wish you the best retirement full of more travel and endless chili dogs!

To my eleventh grade English teacher who gave me a D on my *Grapes of Wrath* paper—Without that chip on my shoulder, I never would have picked this book up again and discovered what an immensely powerful (and timely) story it remains to be. And yes, I finally understand the symbolism of the turtle.

To those who offered advice on the most sensitive topics—I can't tell you how much I appreciate you, especially Heather Bailey, Brenda Anderson, Miss Ernestine P. Woods, and Joy Massenburge.

Siala Segia Tupu, I'm often changed by what I learn in the research and writing of a book, but never as much as this one, all thanks to you. Your factual input about the Samoan adoption scandal, including your willingness to share what it was like to endure that trauma and loss, made this story (and the character of Emanuelu/Bridger) possible. Not only that but on a personal level, you helped me face unresolved feelings from our own failed international adoption. I pray you'll be able to return to Samoa soon and that people far and wide will hear your story of survival. (Others, visit https://sgirljohnson.wixsite .com/sialatupu to read and watch Siala's story.)

Thanks to my Quotidians for your awesomeness. It's great to be on this roller coaster with you! Janyre and Rachel, bless you for all you help me with on a daily basis.

To my mom—Thanks for reading *The Poky Little Puppy* to me every single day, over and over again, from 1982 to 1986. This writing career is your fault! And thanks for loving on me and my family, especially when I'm stressed with deadlines and whatnot.

George, I don't want to calculate how many sandwiches you made so I could write this book with a roof over my head, a Diet Coke on my desk, Labradors at my feet, and research trips to guide the words. Thanks for appreciating me for who I am and for supporting my calling.

William, Braden, Jonathan, and Corynn, thank you for listening to my stories, acting interested in my travels, and basically for being the best children I could have asked for. Boys, I'll be the Mater to your Lightning McQueen any day. Corynn, even though I wasn't your first mom, I'm so happy to be your second and forever mom. I wish I could always get things right and give you everything you'll ever need in this life, but I know that sometimes my words and actions will fall short. I'll never stop trying though. I love you, girlie.

Lastly, thank you, Jesus, for loving me despite the roads I've taken and how off course I've gotten. You are the God of weary travelers and to you I sing:

Let the sweet hope that Thou art mine,
My life and death attend;
Thy presence thro' my journey shine,
And crown my journey's end.

from "Father, Whatever of Earthly
Bliss" by Anne Steele (1760)

Janine Rosche is the author of *With Every Memory* and the Madison River Romance and Whisper Canyon series of novels. Prone to wander, she finds as much comfort on the open road as she does at home. This longing to chase adventure, behold splendor, and experience redemption is woven into her stories. When she isn't traveling or writing novels, she teaches family life education courses, produces *The Love Wander Read Journal*, and takes too many pictures of her sleeping dogs.

Is the life she can't remember one she'd rather forget?

After a tragic accident robs her of the last nine years of memories, Lori Mendenhall comes home to a family completely different than she remembers. As her memory returns and past secrets resurface, it will take all of them to repair what's been broken and find a new future together.

JANINE ROSCHE

Connect with Janine

Find Janine online at **JanineRosche.com** and sign up for her newsletter to get the latest news and special events delivered directly to your inbox.

Follow Janine on social media!

f JanineRoscheAuthor X JanineRosche ⬛ JanineRosche

Be the First to Hear about New Books from Revell!

Stay up-to-date with our authors and books and discover exciting features like book excerpts and giveaways by signing up for our newsletters at

RevellBooks.com/SignUp

FOLLOW US ON SOCIAL MEDIA

@RevellFiction

@RevellBooks

Revell
a division of Baker Publishing Group
RevellBooks.com

"So twisted and creepy, but absolutely captivating."
—Lauren Christensen, *The New York Times Book Review* (podcast)

"It's excruciating, and almost more than anything that I could imagine—and therefore I read on."
—Pamela Paul, *The New York Times Book Review* (podcast)

"Dazzling . . . A portrait etched in shards of glass."
—*The Boston Globe*

"Brilliantly observed . . . Slimani is brilliantly insightful about the peculiar station nannies assume within the households of working families."
—*The Wall Street Journal*

"Chilling . . . A slim page-turner, *The Perfect Nanny* can be read in a single, shivery sitting . . . It will make a great film."
—*The Economist*

"Grabs us by the throat . . . The story's tension builds relentlessly. . . . Fans of psychological thrillers will find it a perfect start to their 2018 reading list."   —*Minneapolis Star Tribune*

"A deft portrait of bourgeois family life in the 21st century."
—*The Atlantic*

"Like *Gone Girl*, the novel deserves praise for pulling off a tricky plot with nuance. . . . Slimani's focus on race and class certainly elevates the book's crime-drama stakes into something more complicated."   —*The New Republic*

"This brutal chiller has the same compulsive readability as Emma Donoghue's *Room*."   —*The Guardian*

"Devastatingly perceptive . . . [An] unnerving cautionary tale."
—*The New York Times Book Review*

Leila Slimani the first Moroccan woman to win France's most prestigious literary prize, the Goncourt, which she won for *The Perfect Nanny*, one of *The New York Times Book Review*'s 10 Best Books of the Year. Her first novel, *Adèle*, won the La Mamounia Prize, for the best book by a Moroccan author written in French, and her novel *In the Country of Others* won the Grand Prix de l'Héroïne *Madame Figaro*, awarded by France's oldest national daily newspaper to the best novel featuring a female protagonist. A journalist and frequent commentator on women's and human rights, Slimani spearheaded a campaign—for which she won the Simone de Beauvoir Prize for Women's Freedom—to help Moroccan women speak out, as self-declared outlaws, against their country's "unfair and obsolete laws." She is French president Emmanuel Macron's personal representative for the promotion of the French language and culture and was ranked #2 on *Vanity Fair* France's annual list of The Fifty Most Influential French People in the World. Born in Rabat, Morocco, in 1981, she now lives in Paris with her French husband and their two young children.

Acclaim for *The Perfect Nanny*

"A taut page-turner."
—*O, The Oprah Magazine*

"Exquisite . . . In Slimani's hands, the unthinkable becomes art."
—Maureen Corrigan, NPR's *Fresh Air*

"This is a great novel. . . . Incredibly engaging and disturbing . . . Slimani has us in her thrall."
—Roxane Gay, *New York Times* bestselling author of *Bad Feminist* and *Hunger*

THE PERFECT NANNY

A Novel

LEILA SLIMANI

Translated from the French by
SAM TAYLOR

PENGUIN BOOKS

PENGUIN BOOKS
An imprint of Penguin Random House LLC
375 Hudson Street
New York, New York 10014
penguin.com

Originally published in French as *Chanson Douce* by Editions Gallimard, Paris.

LIBRARY OF CONGRESS CATALOGING-IN-PUBLICATION DATA

Names: Slimani, Leïla, 1981– author.
Title: The perfect nanny : a novel / Leïla Slimani.
Other titles: *Chanson douce*. English
Description: New York : Penguin Books, 2018.
Identifiers: LCCN 2017038080 (print) | LCCN 2017046748 (ebook) |
ISBN 9780525503897 (ebook) | ISBN 9780143132172 (paperback)
Subjects: | BISAC: FICTION / Contemporary Women. | Fiction / Literary.
Classification: LCC PQ2719.L56 (ebook) | LCC PQ2719.L56 C4313 2018
(print) | DDC 843/.92—dc233
LC record available at https://lccn.loc.gov/2017038080

Printed in the United States of America

Set in Aldus Nova
Designed by Sabrina Bowers

for Émile

Miss Vezzis came from across the Borderline to look after some children who belonged to a lady until a regularly ordained nurse could come out. The lady said Miss Vezzis was a bad, dirty nurse, and inattentive. It never struck her that Miss Vezzis had her own life to lead and her own affairs to worry over, and that these affairs were the most important things in the world to Miss Vezzis.

—Kipling, *Plain Tales from the Hills*

"Do you understand, dear sir, do you understand what it means when there is absolutely nowhere to go?" Marmeladov's question of the previous day came suddenly into his mind. "For every man must have somewhere to go."

—Dostoevsky, *Crime and Punishment*

THE PERFECT NANNY

The baby is dead. It took only a few seconds. The doctor said he didn't suffer. The broken body, surrounded by toys, was put inside a gray bag, which they zipped shut. The little girl was still alive when the ambulance arrived. She'd fought like a wild animal. They found signs of a struggle, bits of skin under her soft fingernails. On the way to the hospital she was agitated, her body shaken by convulsions. Eyes bulging, she seemed to be gasping for air. Her throat was filled with blood. Her lungs had been punctured, her head smashed violently against the blue chest of drawers.

They photographed the crime scene. They dusted for fingerprints and measured the surface area of the bathroom and the children's bedroom. On the floor, the princess rug was soaked with blood. The changing table had been knocked sideways. The toys were put in transparent bags and sealed as evidence. Even the blue chest of drawers will be used in the trial.

The mother was in a state of shock. That was what the paramedics said, what the police repeated, what the journalists wrote. When she went into the room where the children lay, she let out a scream, a scream from deep within, the howl of a she-wolf. It made the walls tremble. Night fell on this May day. She vomited and that was how the police found her, squatting in the bedroom, her clothes soiled, shuddering like a madwoman. She screamed her lungs out. The ambulance man nodded discreetly and they picked her up, even though she resisted and kicked out at them. They lifted her slowly to her feet and the young female trainee paramedic administered a tranquilizer. It was her first month on the job.

They had to save the other one too, of course. With the same level of professionalism; without emotion. She didn't know how to die. She only knew how to give death. She had slashed both her wrists and stabbed the knife in her throat. She must have lost consciousness, lying next to the cot. They took her pulse and blood pressure. They moved her on to the stretcher and the young trainee applied pressure to the wound in her neck.

The neighbors have gathered outside the building. Women, mostly. It will soon be time to fetch their children from school. They stare at the ambulance, puffy-eyed. They cry and they want to know. They stand on tiptoe, trying to make out what is happening behind the police cordon, inside the ambulance as it sets off, sirens screaming. They whisper to one another. Already the rumor is spreading. Something terrible has happened to the children.

It is a handsome apartment building on Rue d'Hauteville, in Paris's tenth arrondissement. A building where neighbors offer friendly greetings, even if they don't know each other. The Massés' apartment is on the fifth floor. It's the smallest apartment in the building. Paul and Myriam built a dividing wall in the living room when their second child was born. They sleep in one half of that room, a cramped space between the kitchen and the window that overlooks the street. Myriam likes Berber rugs and furniture that she finds in antique stores. She has hung Japanese prints on the walls.

Today she came home early. She cut short a meeting and put off the examination of a dossier until tomorrow. Sitting on a folding seat on a Line 7 train, she thought about how she would surprise her children. During the short walk from the metro station, she stopped at a baker's. She bought a baguette, a dessert for the little ones and an orange cake for the nanny. Her favorite.

She thought about taking the children to the fairground rides. After that, they would buy the food for dinner together. Mila would ask for a toy, Adam would suck on a crust of bread in his stroller.

Adam is dead. Mila will be too, soon.

"No illegal immigrants, agreed?" For a cleaning lady or a decorator, it doesn't bother me. Those people have to work, after all. But to look after the little ones, it's too dangerous. I don't want someone who'd be afraid to call the police or go to the hospital if there was a problem. Apart from that . . . not too old, no veils and no smokers. The important thing is that she's energetic and available. That she works so we can work." Paul has prepared everything. He's drawn up a list of questions and scheduled thirty minutes for each interview. They have set aside their Saturday afternoon to find a nanny for their children.

A few days before this, Myriam was discussing her search with her friend Emma, who complained about the woman that looked after her boys. "The nanny has two sons here, so she can never stay late or babysit for us. It's really not practical. Think about that when you do your interviews. If she has children, it'd be better if they're back in her homeland." Myriam thanked her for the advice. But, in reality, what Emma said had upset her. If an employer had spoken about her or one of her friends in that way, she would have cried discrimination. To her, the idea of ruling a woman out of a job because she has children is terrible. She prefers not to bring the subject up with Paul. Her husband is like Emma. Pragmatic. Someone who places his family and his career above all else.

That morning, they went to the market together, all four of them. Mila on Paul's shoulders, Adam asleep in his stroller. They bought flowers and now they are tidying up the apartment. They want to make a good impression on the nannies who will come here. They pick up the books and magazines that litter the floor around and under their bed, and even in the bathroom. Paul asks Mila to put her toys away in large plastic trays. The little girl refuses, whining, and in the end he piles them up against the wall. They fold the children's clothes, change the sheets on the beds. They clean, throw stuff away, try desperately to air this stifling apartment. They want the nannies to see that they are good people; serious, orderly people who try to give their children the best of everything. The nannies must understand that Myriam and Paul are the ones in charge here.

Mila and Adam take a nap. Myriam and Paul sit on the edge of their bed. Anxious, uncomfortable. They have never entrusted their children to anyone before. Myriam was in her last year at law school when she became pregnant with Mila. She graduated two weeks before the birth. Paul was getting more and more work placements, full of that optimism that had drawn Myriam to him when they first met. He was sure he'd earn enough money for both of them. Certain that, despite the financial crisis, despite budget restrictions, he would forge a career in the music industry.

Mila was a fragile, irritable baby who cried constantly. She didn't put on weight, refusing her mother's breast and the bottles that her father prepared. Leaning over the crib, Myriam forgot that the outside world even existed. Her ambitions were limited to persuading this puny, bawling infant to swallow a few ounces of milk. Months passed without her even realizing. Paul and she were never separated from Mila. They pretended not to notice as their friends got annoyed, whispering behind their backs that a baby has no place in a bar or a restaurant. But Myriam absolutely refused to consider using a babysitter. She alone was capable of meeting her daughter's needs.

Mila was barely eighteen months old when Myriam became pregnant again. She always claimed it was an accident. "The pill is never a hundred percent," she told her friends, laughing. In reality, that pregnancy was premeditated. Adam was an excuse not to leave the sweetness of home. Paul did not express any reservations. He'd just been hired as an assistant in a famous studio, where he spent his days and nights, a hostage to the whims of the artists and their schedules. His wife seemed to be blooming; a natural mother. This cocooned existence, far from the world and other people, protected them from everything.

And then time started to drag; the clocklike perfection of the family mechanism became jammed. Paul's parents, who had got into a routine of helping them after Mila's birth, began to spend more and more time at their house in the country, where they were carrying out major repairs. One month before Myriam's due date, they organized a three-week trip to Asia and didn't tell Paul until the last minute. He took offense, complaining to Myriam of his parents' selfishness, their irresponsibility. But Myriam was relieved. She couldn't stand having Sylvie under her feet. She would smile as she listened to her mother-in-law's advice; she would say nothing when she saw her rummaging inside the fridge, criticizing the food she found there. Sylvie bought organic salads. She made meals for Mila but left the kitchen in a disgusting mess. Myriam and Sylvie never saw eye to eye on anything, and the apartment was filled with a dense, simmering unease that threatened at any moment to break into open warfare. In the end Myriam told Paul: "Let your parents live their lives. They're right to make the most of their freedom."

She didn't realize the magnitude of the task she had taken on. With two children, everything became more complicated: shopping, bath time, housework, visits to the doctor. The bills piled up. Myriam became gloomy. She began to hate going to the park. The winter days seemed endless. Mila's tantrums drove her mad, Adam's first burblings left her indifferent. With each passing day, she felt more and more desperate to go out for a walk on her own. Sometimes she wanted to scream like a lunatic in the street. They're eating me alive, she would think.

She was jealous of her husband. In the evenings, she stood by the door in a frenzy of anticipation, waiting for him to come home. Then she would complain for an hour about the children's screaming, the size of the apartment, her lack of free time. When she let him talk and he told her about epic recording sessions with a hip-hop group, she would spit: "You're lucky." He would reply: "No, you're the lucky one. I would love to see them grow up." No one ever won when they played that game.

At night Paul lay beside her, sleeping the deep, heavy sleep of someone who has worked hard all day and deserves a good rest. Bitterness and regret ate away at her. She thought about the efforts she had made to finish her degree, despite the lack of money and parental support, the joy she had felt when she was called to the Bar, the first time she had worn her lawyer's robes and Paul had taken a picture of her, smiling proudly outside their apartment building.

For months she pretended she was okay. Even to Paul, she didn't dare admit her secret shame. How she felt as if she were dying because she had nothing to talk about but the antics of her children and the conversations of strangers overheard in the supermarket. She started turning down dinner invitations, ignoring calls from her friends. She was especially wary of women, who could be so cruel. She wanted to strangle the ones who pretended to admire or, worse, envy her. She couldn't bear listening to them anymore, complaining about their jobs, about not seeing their children enough. More than anything, she feared strangers. The ones who innocently asked what she did for a living and who looked away when she said she was a stay-at-home mother.

One day, after doing the shopping in Monoprix on Boulevard Saint-Denis, she realized that she had, without meaning to, stolen a pair of children's socks. She'd dropped them in the stroller and forgotten about them. She was a few yards from home and she could have gone back to the shop to return them, but she decided not to. She didn't tell Paul. It was not an interesting subject, and yet she couldn't stop thinking about it. After that incident, she would regularly go to Monoprix and hide things inside her son's stroller: some shampoo or lotion or a lipstick that she would never use. She knew perfectly well that, if the security guards stopped her, she would just have to play the part of a stressed-out mother and they would probably believe her. There was something hypnotic about those pathetic little thefts. Alone in the street sometimes, she would laugh with the feeling that she was taking the whole world for a ride.

When she bumped into Pascal one day, by chance, she saw it as a sign. Her former law-school classmate must not have recognized her at first: she was wearing trousers that were too big for her and an old pair of boots, and she'd tied her unwashed hair up in a bun. She was standing next to the merry-go-round, which Mila refused to come down from. "This is your last go," she repeated each time her daughter, gripping tightly on to a horse, passed her with a wave. She looked up: Pascal was smiling at her, arms outstretched to signify his joy and surprise. She smiled back, hands clinging to the stroller handle. Pascal didn't have much time, but, as luck would have it, his next meeting was close to where Myriam lived. "I have to go home anyway," she told him. "Shall we walk together?" Myriam grabbed hold of Mila, who gave an ear-splitting scream. She refused to budge but Myriam stubbornly kept smiling, pretending that the situation was under control. She couldn't stop thinking about the old sweater she was wearing under her coat and how Pascal must have seen its frayed collar. She frantically rubbed at her temples, as if that were enough to neaten her dry, tangled hair. Pascal seemed oblivious to all this. He told her about the law firm he'd set up with two friends from their year, the difficulties and pleasures of starting his own business. She drank in his words. Mila kept interrupting and Myriam would have given anything to shut her up. Without breaking eye contact with Pascal, she searched in her pockets, in her bag, to find a lollipop, a candy, anything at all that might buy her daughter's silence.

Pascal barely glanced at the children. He did not ask their names. Even Adam, asleep in his stroller, his face peaceful and adorable, did not seem to have any effect on him.

"Here we are." Pascal kissed her on the cheek. He said, "I'm very glad I got to see you again," and he went into the building. The heavy blue door slammed shut, and Myriam jumped. She began to pray silently. There, in the street, she felt so desperate that she could have thrown herself to the ground and wept. She had wanted to hang on to Pascal's leg, to beg him to take her with him, to give her a chance. Walking home, she felt utterly dejected. She looked at Mila, who was playing calmly. She gave the baby a bath and thought to herself that this happiness—this simple, silent, prisonlike happiness—was not enough to console her. Pascal had probably made fun of her. Maybe he'd even called a few of their former classmates to tell them about Myriam's pathetic life and how she "has lost her looks" and "didn't have the brilliant career we all expected."

All night, imaginary conversations gnawed at her brain. The next day, she had just got out of the shower when she heard her phone buzz. A text from Pascal: "I don't know if you have any plans to become a lawyer again. But if you're interested, give me a call." Myriam almost howled with joy. She started jumping around the apartment and kissed Mila, who asked her: "What's going on, Mama? Why are you laughing?" Later Myriam wondered whether Pascal had sensed her despair or whether, quite simply, he couldn't believe his luck: bumping into Myriam Charfa, the most dedicated student he had ever met. Maybe he thought he was doubly blessed, to be able to hire a woman like her and to bring her back to the courtroom, where she belonged.

Myriam spoke to Paul about it and she was disappointed by his reaction. "I didn't know you wanted to work," he shrugged. That made her furious, more than it should have done. The conversation quickly descended into mud-slinging. She called him an egotist; he described her behavior as thoughtless. "You're going to work? Well, that's fine, but what are we going to do about the children?" he sneered, ridiculing her ambitions and reinforcing the impression she had that she was a prisoner in this apartment.

Once they had calmed down, they patiently studied their options. It was late January: there was no point hoping to find a place in day care. They didn't have any connections in the town hall. And if she did start working again, they would be in the worst of all worlds: too rich to receive welfare and too poor to consider the cost of a nanny as anything other than a sacrifice. This, though, was the solution they chose in the end, after Paul said: "If you add in the extra hours, you and the nanny will earn more or less the same amount. But if you think it'll make you happy . . ." That conversation left a bitter taste in her mouth. She felt angry with Paul.

She wanted to do things right. To reassure herself, she went to a nearby agency that had just opened. A small office, simply decorated, run by two women in their early thirties. The shopfront was painted baby blue and adorned with little gold stars and camels. Myriam rang the bell. Through the window, the manager looked her up and down. She got slowly to her feet and poked her head through the half-open door.

"Yes?"

"Hello."

"Have you come to apply? We need a complete dossier. A curriculum vitae and references signed by your previous employers."

"No, not at all. I've come for my children. I'm looking for a nanny."

The woman's face was suddenly transformed. She seemed happy to welcome a customer and equally embarrassed by the contempt she had shown. But how could she have imagined that this tired-looking woman with her bushy, curly hair was the mother of the pretty little girl whining on the sidewalk?

The manager opened a large catalog and Myriam leaned over it. "Please, sit down," she said. Dozens of photographs of women, most of them African or Filipino, flashed past Myriam's eyes. Mila had fun looking at them all. She said: "That one's ugly, isn't she?" Her mother scolded her and, with a heavy heart, returned to those blurred, poorly framed portraits of unsmiling women.

The manager disgusted her. Her hypocrisy, her plump red face, the frayed scarf she wore around her neck. Her racism, so obvious just a minute ago. All this made Myriam want to run away. She shook the woman's hand. She promised she would speak to her husband about it and she never went back. Instead she pinned a small ad to noticeboards in various local shops. On the advice of a friend, she inundated websites with posts marked UR-GENT. By the end of the first week, they had received six calls.

She is awaiting this nanny as if she is the Savior, while at the same time she is terrified by the idea of leaving her children with someone else. She knows everything about them and would like to keep that knowledge secret. She knows their tastes, their habits. She can tell immediately if one of them is ill or sad. She has kept them close to her all this time, convinced that no one could protect them as well as she can.

Ever since her children were born, Myriam has been scared of everything. Above all, she is scared that they will die. She never talks about this—not to her friends, not to Paul—but she is sure that everyone has had the same thoughts. She is certain that, like her, they have watched their child sleep and wondered how they would feel if that little body were a corpse, if those eyes were closed forever. She can't help it. Her mind fills with horrible scenarios and she shakes her head to get rid of them, recites prayers, touches wood and the Hand of Fatima that she inherited from her mother. She wards off misfortune, illness, accidents, the perverted appetites of predators. At night, she dreams about Adam and Mila suddenly disappearing in the midst of an indifferent crowd. She yells, "Where are my children?" and the people laugh. They think she's crazy.

"She's late. Not a good start." Paul is growing impatient. He heads over to the front door and looks through the spyhole. It is 2:15 p.m. and the first applicant, a Filipino woman, still hasn't arrived.

At 2:20, Gigi knocks softly on the door. Myriam goes to open it. She notices immediately that the woman has very small feet. Despite the cold, she is wearing canvas trainers and white, frilly socks. Though nearly fifty years old, she has the feet of a child. She is quite elegant, her hair tied in a braid that falls halfway down her back. Paul coldly points out her lateness and Gigi lowers her head as she mumbles excuses. She expresses herself very poorly in French. Paul tentatively tries to interview her in English. Gigi talks about her experience. About her children, whom she left in her homeland; about the youngest one, whom she hasn't seen for ten years. Paul won't hire her. He asks a few token questions and at 2:30 he walks her to the door. "We'll call you. Thank you."

After that there is Grace, a smiling, undocumented immigrant from the Ivory Coast. Caroline, an obese

17

blonde with dirty hair, who spends the interview complaining about her backache and her circulation problems. Malika, a Moroccan woman of a certain age, who stresses her twenty years of experience and her love of children. Myriam had been perfectly clear. She does not want to hire a North African to look after the children. "It'd be good," people told her. "Try to convince Paul. She could speak Arabic to them since you don't want to." But Myriam steadfastly refuses this idea. She fears that a tacit complicity and familiarity would grow between her and the nanny. That the woman would start speaking to her in Arabic. Telling Myriam her life story and, soon, asking her all sorts of favors in the name of their shared language and religion. She has always been wary of what she calls immigrant solidarity.

Then Louise arrived. When she describes that first interview, Myriam loves to say that it was instantly obvious. Like love at first sight. She goes on about the way her daughter behaved. "It was Mila who chose her," she likes to make clear. Mila had just woken from her nap, dragged from sleep by her brother's ear-splitting screams. Paul went to fetch the baby and came back with the little girl following close behind, hiding between his legs. Louise stood up. As Myriam describes this scene, she still sounds fascinated by the nanny's self-assurance. Louise delicately took Adam from his father's arms and pretended not to notice Mila. "Where is the princess? I thought I saw a princess, but she's disappeared." Mila burst out laughing and Louise continued with her game, searching in the corners, under the table, behind the sofa for the mysteriously vanished princess.

They ask her a few questions. Louise says that her husband is dead, that her daughter, Stéphanie, is grown-up now—"nearly twenty, I can hardly believe it"—and that she is always available. She gives Paul a piece of paper containing a list of her former employers. She talks about the Rouvier family, who are at the top of the list. "I stayed with them for a long time. They had two children too. Two boys." Paul and Myriam are charmed by Louise, by her smooth features, her open smile, her lips that do not tremble. She appears imperturbable. She looks like a woman able to understand and forgive everything. Her face is like a peaceful sea, its depths suspected by no one.

That evening they phoned the couple whose number Louise had given them. A woman answered, a little coldly. As soon as she heard Louise's name, her tone changed. "Louise? You're so lucky to have found her. She was like a second mother to my boys. It was heartbreaking when we had to let her go. To be perfectly honest, I even thought of having a third child at the time, just so we could keep her."

Louise opens the shutters of her apartment. It's just after five in the morning and, outside, the streetlamps are still lit. A man walks along the street, staying close to the walls to avoid the rain. The downpour lasted all night. The wind whistled in the pipes and invaded her dreams. The rain seems to be falling horizontally now so it can hit the building's facade and the windows with full force. Louise likes looking outside. Just across the road, between two sinister buildings, is a little house, surrounded by a bushy garden. A young Parisian couple moved there at the start of the summer, and on Sundays their children play on the swings and help weed the vegetable garden. Louise wonders what they're doing in this neighborhood.

She shivers from lack of sleep. With the tip of her fingernail she scratches the corner of the window. Even though she cleans it zealously twice a week, the glass always looks murky to her, covered in dust and black smears. Sometimes she wants to clean the panes until they shatter. She scratches, harder and harder, with her index finger, and her

21

nail breaks. She puts her finger under water and bites it to stop the bleeding.

The apartment consists of only one room, which Louise uses as both bedroom and living room. She takes care, every morning, to fold up the sofa bed and put the black slipcover on it. She eats her meals at the coffee table, with the television on. Against the wall are piled some cardboard boxes. They contain perhaps the few objects that might give life to this soulless studio flat. To the right of the sofa is the photograph of a red-headed teenager in a sparkly frame.

She has carefully spread out her long skirt and blouse over the sofa. She picks up the ballet pumps that she left on the floor, a pair she bought more than ten years ago but which she's taken such good care of that they still look new. They are patent leather shoes, very simple, with square heels and a discreet little bow on top. She sits down and starts cleaning one, soaking a piece of cotton wool in a pot of makeup remover. Her movements are slow and precise. She cleans with furious care, completely absorbed in her task. The cotton wool is covered in grime. Louise brings the shoe over to the lamp placed on the pedestal table. When she is satisfied with the leather's shine, she puts the shoe down and picks up the second one.

It's so early that she has time to fix the fingernails she broke when she was cleaning. She wraps a plaster around her index finger and paints the other nails with a very discreet pink polish. For the first time, and despite the price, she had her hair dyed at the salon. She ties it in a bun, off her neck. She puts on her makeup and the blue eyeshadow makes her look older. She is so fragile, so slender, that from a distance you would think her barely out of her teens. In fact, she is over forty.

She paces around the room, which seems smaller, more cramped than ever. She sits down then stands up again almost immediately. She could turn on the television. Drink some tea. Read an old copy of the women's magazine that she keeps near her bed. But she is afraid of relaxing, letting the time slip past, surrendering to drowsiness. Waking up so early has left her weak, vulnerable. It wouldn't take much to make her close her eyes for a minute, and then she might fall asleep and she'd be late. She has to keep her mind alert, has to focus all her attention on this first day of work.

She can't wait at home. It's not even six yet—she's going to be much too early—but she walks quickly to the Saint-Maur-des-Fossés suburban train station. It takes her more than a quarter of an hour to get there. Inside the carriage, she sits opposite an old Chinese man, who sleeps curled up, with his forehead pressed against the window. She stares at his exhausted face. At each station, she thinks about waking him. She is afraid that he will be lost, go too far, that he will open his eyes, alone, at the terminus, and that he'll have to double back the way he came. But she doesn't say anything. It is more sensible not to speak to people. Once, a young girl, dark-haired and very beautiful, had almost slapped her. "What are you looking at? Eh? Why the hell are you staring at me?" she yelled.

When she arrives at the Auber station, Louise jumps down on to the platform. It's starting to get busy. A woman bumps into her while she is climbing down the stairs to the metro platform. She chokes on a sickening smell of croissant and burned chocolate. After taking Line 7 toward Opéra, she gets off at the Poissonnière station.

Louise is almost an hour early so she sits at a table on the terrace of the Paradis, a charmless café with a view of the building's entrance. She plays with her spoon. She casts envious glances at the man to her right, who sucks his cigarette with his thick-lipped lecher's mouth. She would like to grab it from his hand and take a long drag. Unable to stand it any longer, she pays her bill and goes into the silent building. She decides to ring the doorbell in a quarter of an hour, and in the meantime she waits on a step between two floors. She hears a noise and barely has time to get to her feet: it's Paul, hurtling downstairs. He's carrying his bike and wearing a pink helmet.

"Louise? Have you been here long? Why didn't you come in?"

"I didn't want to disturb you."

"You wouldn't disturb us. On the contrary! Here, these are your keys," he says, taking a bunch from his pocket. "Go ahead, make yourself at home."

"My nanny is a miracle-worker." That is what Myriam says when she describes Louise's sudden entrance into their lives. She must have magical powers to have transformed this stifling, cramped apartment into a calm, light-filled place. Louise has pushed back the walls. She has made the cupboards deeper, the drawers wider. She has let the sun in.

On the first day, Myriam gives her a few instructions. She shows her how the appliances work. Pointing to an object or a piece of clothing, she repeats: "Be careful with that. I'm very attached to it." She makes recommendations about Paul's vinyl collection, which the children must not touch. Louise nods, silent and docile. She observes each room with the self-assurance of a general standing before a territory he is about to conquer.

In the weeks that follow her arrival, Louise turns this hasty sketch of an apartment into an ideal bourgeois interior. She imposes her old-fashioned manners, her taste for perfection. Myriam and Paul can't get over it. She sews the buttons back on to jackets that they haven't worn for months because they've been too lazy to look for a needle. She hems skirts and pairs of trousers. She mends Mila's clothes, which Myriam was about to throw out without a qualm. Louise washes the curtains yellowed by tobacco and dust. Once a week, she changes the sheets. Paul and Myriam are overjoyed. Paul tells her with a smile that she is like Mary Poppins. He isn't sure she understands the compliment.

At night, in the comfort of their clean sheets, the couple laughs, incredulous at their new life. They feel as if they have found a rare pearl, as if they've been blessed. Of course, Louise's wages are a burden on the family budget, but Paul no longer complains about that. In a few weeks, Louise's presence has become indispensable.

When Myriam gets back from work in the evenings, she finds dinner ready. The children are calm and clean, not a hair out of place. Louise arouses and fulfills the fantasies of an idyllic family life that Myriam guiltily nurses. She teaches Mila to tidy up behind herself and her parents watch dumbstruck as the little girl hangs her coat on the peg.

Useless objects have disappeared. With Louise, nothing accumulates anymore: no dirty dishes, no dirty laundry, no unopened envelopes found later under an old magazine. Nothing rots, nothing expires. Louise never neglects anything. Louise is scrupulous. She writes everything down in a little flower-covered notebook. The times of the dance class, school outings, doctor's appointments. She copies the names of the medicines the children take, the price of the ice creams she bought for them at the fairground, and the exact words that Mila's schoolteacher said to her.

After a few weeks, she no longer hesitates to move objects around. She empties the cupboards completely, hangs little bags of lavender between the coats. She makes bouquets of flowers. She feels a serene contentment when—with Adam asleep and Mila at school—she can sit down and contemplate her task. The silent apartment is completely under her power, like an enemy begging for forgiveness.

But it's in the kitchen that she accomplishes the most extraordinary wonders. Myriam has admitted to her that she doesn't know how to cook anything and doesn't really want to learn. The nanny prepares meals that Paul goes into raptures about and the children devour, without a word and without anyone having to order them to finish their plate. Myriam and Paul start inviting friends again, and they are fed on *blanquette de veau, pot-au-feu,* ham hock with sage and delicious vegetables, all lovingly cooked by Louise. They congratulate Myriam, shower her with compliments, but she always admits: "My nanny did it all."

When Mila is at school, Louise attaches Adam to her in a large wrap. She likes to feel the child's chubby thighs against her belly, his saliva that runs down her neck when he falls asleep. She sings all day for this baby, praising him for his laziness. She massages him, taking pride in his folds of flesh, his round pink cheeks. In the mornings, the child welcomes her with gurgles, his plump arms reaching out for her. In the weeks that follow Louise's arrival, Adam learns to walk. And this boy who used to cry every night sleeps peacefully until morning.

Mila is wilder. She is a small, fragile girl with the posture of a ballerina. Louise ties her hair in buns so tight that the girl's eyes look slanted, pulled toward her temples. Like that, she resembles one of those medieval heroines with a broad forehead, a cold and noble expression. Mila is a difficult, exhausting child. Any time she becomes irritated, she screams. She throws herself to the ground in the middle of the street, stamps her feet, lets herself be dragged along to humiliate Louise. When the nanny crouches down and tries to speak to her, Mila turns away.

She counts out loud the butterflies on the wallpaper. She watches herself in the mirror when she cries. This child is obsessed by her own reflection. In the street, her eyes are riveted to shop windows. On several occasions she has bumped into lampposts or tripped over small obstacles on the sidewalk, distracted by the contemplation of her own image.

Mila is cunning. She knows that crowds stare, and that Louise feels ashamed in the street. The nanny gives in more quickly when they are in public. Louise has to take detours to avoid the toyshop on the avenue, where the little girl stands in front of the window and screams. On the way to school, Mila drags her feet. She steals a raspberry from a greengrocer's stall. She climbs on to windowsills, hides in porches, and runs away as fast as her legs will carry her. Louise tries to go after her while pushing the stroller, yelling the girl's name, but Mila doesn't stop until she comes to the very end of the sidewalk. Sometimes Mila regrets her bad behavior. She worries about Louise's paleness and the frights she gives her. She becomes loving again, cuddly. She makes it up to the nanny, clinging to her legs. She cries and wants to be mothered.

Slowly, Louise tames the child. Day after day, she tells her stories, where the same characters always recur. Orphans, lost little girls, princesses kept as prisoners, and castles abandoned by terrible ogres. Strange beasts—birds with twisted beaks, one-legged bears and melancholic unicorns—populate Louise's landscapes. The little girl falls silent. She stays close to the nanny, attentive, impatient. She asks for certain characters to come back. Where do these stories come from? They emanate from Louise, in a continual flood, without her even thinking about it, without her making the slightest effort of memory or imagination. But in what black lake, in what deep forest has she found these cruel tales where the heroes die at the end, after first saving the world?

Myriam is always disappointed when she hears the door open in the law firm where she works. Around 9:30 a.m., her colleagues start to arrive. They pour themselves coffee, telephones wail, the floorboards creak, the morning calm is shattered.

Myriam gets to the office before eight. She is always the first there. She turns on her desk lamp, nothing else. Beneath that halo of light, in that cave-like silence, she rediscovers the concentration she used to have in her student years. She forgets everything and plunges with relish into the examination of her dossiers. Sometimes she walks through the dark corridor, document in hand, and talks to herself. She smokes a cigarette on the balcony as she drinks her coffee.

The day she started work again, Myriam woke up at the crack of dawn, filled with a childlike excitement. She put on a new skirt, high heels, and Louise exclaimed: "You're very beautiful." On the doorstep, holding Adam in her arms, the nanny pushed her boss out the door. "Don't worry about us," she repeated. "Everything will be fine here."

Pascal gave Myriam a warm welcome. He assigned her the office next to his, with a communicating door that he often left ajar. Only two or three weeks after her arrival, Pascal entrusted her with responsibilities that some of his older employees had never been given. As the months passed, Myriam handled dozens of clients' cases on her own. Pascal encourages her to try her hand at everything and to use her capacity for hard work, which he knows to be immense. She never says no. She does not refuse any of the dossiers that Pascal hands to her, she never complains about working late. Pascal often tells her: "You're perfect." For months, she is weighed down by a mass of small cases. She defends sleazy dealers, half-wits, an exhibitionist, talentless robbers, alcoholics arrested at the wheel. She deals with cases of unpaid debt, credit-card fraud, identity theft.

Pascal counts on her to find him new clients and encourages her to devote her time to legal-aid cases. Twice a month she goes to the Bobigny court and waits in the corridor until 9 p.m. for verdicts to be handed down, eyes glued to her watch, the hands barely moving. Sometimes she gets annoyed, responding brusquely to her disoriented clients. But she gives her all and obtains the best possible deals. Pascal repeats to her constantly: "You have to know each dossier by heart." She takes him at his word. She rereads statements and reports until late at night. She picks out the slightest inaccuracy, spots the smallest procedural error. She works with a fury and in the end she earns her reward. Former clients recommend her to friends. Her name circulates among the prisoners. One young man, who avoided a prison sentence thanks to her, promises to pay her back. "You got me out of there. I won't forget that."

Once, she was called in the middle of the night and asked to report to the police station. A former client had been arrested for domestic violence. And yet he'd sworn to her that he was incapable of hitting a woman. She got dressed in the dark, soundlessly, at two in the morning, and she leaned down to kiss Paul. He grunted and then turned over.

Often her husband tells her that she is working too hard and that drives her crazy. He is offended by her reaction and makes a big show of his benevolence. He pretends to be concerned about her health, to worry that Pascal is exploiting her. She tries not to think about her children, not to let the guilt eat away at her. Sometimes she starts imagining that they are all in league against her. Her mother-in-law tries to persuade her that "if Mila is often ill, it's because she feels lonely." Her colleagues never invite her to go for a drink with them after work and are surprised whenever she works until late. "But don't you have children?" Even the schoolteacher summoned her one morning to talk about a ridiculous incident between Mila and one of her classmates. When Myriam apologized for having missed the latest meetings and for having sent Louise in her place, the gray-haired teacher spread her hands. "If you only knew! It's the modern malaise. All these poor children are left to their own devices while both parents are obsessed by their careers. They're always running. You know what two words parents say most often to their children these days? 'Hurry up!' And of course, we pay the price for all this. The children take out their anxieties and their feelings of abandonment on us."

Myriam had desperately wanted to put the teacher in her place, but she'd been incapable of doing it. Was it because of that little chair, on which she sat uncomfortably, in this little classroom that smelled of paint and plasticine? The setting, the teacher's voice, all of this brought her forcefully back to her childhood, to that age of obedience and obligation. Myriam smiled. She stupidly thanked the woman and promised her that Mila would make progress. She didn't throw the old harpy's misogyny and moralizing back in her face, as she wanted to. She was too afraid that the gray-haired lady would take out her revenge on Mila.

Pascal seems to understand her rage, her vast hunger for recognition, for challenges that measure up to her abilities. Between her and Pascal, a battle begins, and both of them draw an ambiguous pleasure from it. He pushes her; she stands up to him. He exhausts her; she doesn't disappoint him. One evening he invites her to have a drink with him after work. "You've been with us for nearly six months. That's worth celebrating, don't you think?" They walk down the street in silence. He holds the door of the bar open for her and she smiles at him. They sit at the back of the room, on an upholstered bench. Pascal orders a bottle of white wine. They talk about one of their dossiers and then, very quickly, start reminiscing about their student years. The big party their friend Charlotte threw in her mansion in the eighteenth arrondissement. The panic attack, absolutely hilarious, that poor Céline suffered on the day of her orals. Myriam drinks fast and Pascal makes her laugh. She doesn't feel like going home. She would like to have no one she has to call, no one waiting up for her. But there's Paul. And there are the children.

A gently thrilling, lightly erotic tension burns her throat and her breasts. She runs her tongue over her lips. She wants something. For the first time in a long time, she feels a gratuitous, futile, selfish desire. A desire of her own. Although she loves Paul, her husband's body is weighed down by memories. When he penetrates her, it is her motherly womb that he enters, her heavy belly, where Paul's sperm has so often been accommodated. Her belly of folds and waves, where they built their house, where so many worries and joys flowered. Paul has massaged her swollen, purple legs. He has seen the blood spread over the sheets. Paul has held her hair back from her forehead while she's vomited, on her knees. He has heard her scream. He has wiped the sweat from her face covered with angiomas while she pushed. He has delivered her children from her body.

She had always refused the idea that her children could be an impediment to her success, to her freedom. Like an anchor that drags you to the bottom, that pulls the face of the drowned man into the mud. At first, the realization that she was wrong had plunged her into a profound sadness. She thought it unjust, terribly frustrating. She became aware that she could never live without feeling that she was incomplete, that she was doing things badly, sacrificing one part of her life for another. She had made a big deal out of this, refusing to renounce her dream of the ideal balance. Stubbornly thinking that everything was possible, that she could reach all her objectives, that she wouldn't end up bitter or exhausted. That she wouldn't play the role of a martyr or of the perfect mother.

Every day, or nearly every day, Myriam receives a notification from her friend Emma. She posts sepia portraits of her two blonde children on social media. Perfect children who play in a park and go to a school that will allow them to blossom, bringing out the gifts that she already senses in them. She gave them unpronounceable names, taken from Nordic mythology, whose meanings she enjoys explaining. Emma is beautiful too, in these photographs. Her husband never appears in any of them, eternally devoted to taking pictures of an ideal family to which he belongs only as a spectator. He does his best to enter the frame, though. That bohemian bourgeois man with his beard and natural wool pullovers, who puts on tight, uncomfortable trousers to go to work.

Myriam would never dare tell Emma this thought that fleetingly crosses her mind, this idea that is not cruel but shameful, and that she has as she observes Louise and her children. We will, all of us, only be happy, she thinks, when we don't need one another anymore. When we can live a life of our own, a life that belongs to us, that has nothing to do with anyone else. When we are free.

Myriam heads to the door and looks through the spyhole. Every five minutes she repeats: "They're late." She is making Mila nervous. Sitting on the edge of the sofa in her hideous taffeta dress, Mila has tears in her eyes. "You think they're not coming?"

"Of course they're coming," Louise answers. "Give them time to get here."

The preparations for Mila's birthday party have taken on ludicrous proportions. For the past two weeks, Louise has talked about nothing else. In the evenings, when Myriam comes home from work, exhausted, Louise shows her the party streamers she has made herself. In a hysterical voice, she describes the taffeta dress that she found in a boutique and that will, she feels sure, make Mila ecstatic. Several times, Myriam has had to force herself not to tell Louise to forget the whole thing. She is tired of these ridiculous preoccupations. Mila is so young! Myriam doesn't see the point in putting her daughter in a state like this. But Louise stares at her with her wide-open little eyes. Just look at Mila—she is giddy with happiness.

That's all that counts, the pleasure of this little princess, the wonderland of her birthday celebration. Myriam swallows her sarcastic response. She feels as if she's been caught in the wrong, and ends up promising that she will do her best to be there for the party.

Louise decided to hold it on a Wednesday afternoon, when the children are off school. She wanted to be sure that everyone would be in Paris, and available to come. Myriam went to work that morning, swearing that she would come back after lunch.

When she got home, early in the afternoon, she almost cried out in surprise. She didn't recognize her own apartment anymore. The living room was literally transformed, dripping with glitter, balloons, paper streamers. But most of all, the sofa had been removed to allow the children to play. Even the oak table, so heavy that they'd never moved it since their arrival, had been pushed to the other side of the room.

"But who moved the furniture? Did Paul help you?"

"No," Louise replies. "I did all that myself."

Myriam, incredulous, wants to laugh. It must be a joke, she thinks, observing the nanny's match-thin arms. Then she remembers that she has already been taken aback by Louise's strength. Once or twice, she was impressed by the way she picked up heavy, bulky parcels while carrying Adam in her arms. Concealed behind that frail, narrow physique, Louise has the power of a colossus.

All morning Louise blew up balloons, twisted them into the shapes of animals and stuck them all over the apartment, from the entrance hall to the kitchen drawers.

She made the birthday cake herself, an enormous red fruit charlotte covered with decorations.

Myriam regrets having taken the afternoon off. She would have been so much happier in the calm of her office. Her daughter's birthday party makes her anxious. She is afraid that the other children will be bored, impatient. She doesn't want to have to deal with the ones who fight or console the ones whose parents are late to pick them up. Chilling memories of her own childhood come back to her. She sees herself on a thick, white wool carpet, isolated from the group of little girls playing with a doll's tea set. She had let a piece of chocolate melt on the carpet and then she'd tried to hide her misdeed, which had only made things worse. Her host's mother had told her off in front of everyone.

Myriam holes up in her bedroom, closing the door and pretending to be absorbed in reading her emails. She knows that, as always, she can depend on Louise. The doorbell starts to ring. The living room swells with the noise of children. Louise has put music on. Myriam sneaks out of her room and watches the little guests, massed around the nanny. They spin around her, completely captivated. She has prepared songs and magic tricks. She disguises herself as they watch in disbelief and the children, who are not at all easy to deceive, know that she is one of their own. She is there, vibrant, joyful, teasing. She hums songs, makes animal noises. She even carries Mila and one of her friends on her back, and the other kids laugh until they cry, begging her to let them take part in the rodeo as well.

Myriam admires this ability that Louise has to really play. When she plays, she is animated by that omnipotence that only children possess. One evening, coming home, Myriam finds Louise lying on the floor, her face painted. On her cheeks and forehead are the thick black lines of a warrior's mask. She has made an Indian headdress out of crêpe paper. In the middle of the living room she has built a misshapen tepee out of a sheet, a broomstick and a chair. Standing in the half-open doorway, Myriam feels troubled. She watches Louise as she twists her body and makes wild noises, and she is horribly embarrassed. The nanny looks like she's drunk. That is the first thought that comes to mind. Seeing Myriam there, Louise stands up, red-faced and staggering. "I've got pins and needles," she explains. Adam is clinging to her calf and Louise laughs, with a laugh that still belongs to the imaginary world in which their game is taking place.

Perhaps, Myriam reassures herself, Louise is simply a child too. She takes very seriously the games she plays with Mila. For example, if they play cops and robbers,

Louise lets herself be locked up behind invisible bars. Sometimes she plays the forces of law and order and runs after Mila. Each time, she invents a precise geography that Mila has to memorize. She creates costumes and develops a scenario filled with plot twists. She prepares the set with meticulous care. Occasionally the little girl gets tired of this. "Come on, let's start!" she begs.

Myriam doesn't know this, but Louise's favorite game is hide-and-seek. Except that nobody counts and there are no rules. The game is based on the element of surprise. Without warning, Louise disappears. She nestles in a corner and lets the children search for her. She often chooses hiding places where she can continue to observe them. She hides under the bed or behind a door and doesn't move. She holds her breath.

And so Mila understands that the game has begun. She hollers like a mad girl and claps her hands. Adam follows her lead. He laughs so hard that he can hardly stand, and several times he falls on to his bottom. They call her name, but Louise does not respond. "Louise? Where are you?" "Watch out, Louise, we're coming, we're going to find you."

Louise says nothing. She does not come out of her hiding place, even when they scream, when they cry, when they fall into despair. Crouching in the shadows, she spies on Adam as he panics, lying on his back and sobbing. He doesn't understand. He calls out "Louise," swallowing the last syllable, snot dribbling over his lips, his cheeks purple with rage. Mila, too, ends up being scared. For a moment, they start to believe that Louise has really gone, that she has abandoned them in this apartment where night will soon fall, that they are alone and she will not come back. The anguish is unbearable and Mila begs the nanny. She says: "Louise, this isn't funny. Where are you?" The child becomes annoyed, stamps her feet. Louise waits. She watches them as if she's studying the death throes of a fish she's just caught, its gills bleeding, its body shaken by spasms. The fish wriggling on the bottom of the boat, sucking the air through its exhausted mouth, the fish that has no chance of surviving.

Then Mila starts uncovering the hiding places. She has realized that she must open doors, lift up curtains, squat down to look under the bed. But Louise is so slim that she always finds new lairs where she can take refuge. She crawls into the laundry basket, under Paul's desk, or to the back of a cupboard, where she covers herself with a blanket. Sometimes she hides in the shower cubicle, in the darkness of the bathroom. So, Mila searches in vain. She sobs and Louise remains motionless. The child's despair does not make her yield.

One day, Mila doesn't cry anymore. Louise is caught in her own trap. Mila stays silent, pacing around the hiding spot and pretending not to know that the nanny is there. She sits on the laundry basket and Louise feels as if she will suffocate. "Truce?" whispers the child.

But Louise doesn't want to surrender. She just sits there, knees pressed to her chin, not saying a word. The little girl's feet tap softly against the wicker laundry basket. "Louise, I know you're in there," she says, laughing. Suddenly Louise stands up, knocking Mila to the floor. Her head bangs against the bathroom tiles. Dazed, the child cries and then, seeing the triumphant, resuscitated

Louise standing above her, staring down at her from the heights of her victory, Mila's terror is transformed to hysterical joy. Adam runs to the bathroom and joins in the girls' jig of delight, the three of them giggling until they can hardly breathe.

STÉPHANIE

At eight years old, Stéphanie knew how to change a nappy and prepare a baby's bottle. Her movements were sure and her hand did not tremble as she slipped it under the fragile neck of a newborn and lifted it up from the cot. She knew they had to be laid down on their backs and never shaken. She gave them baths, holding them firmly by the shoulder. The screams and cries of babies, their laughter and their tears were the soundtrack to her memories as an only child. They thought she was exceptionally maternal and devoted for such a young girl.

When Stéphanie was a child, her mother, Louise, ran a day care at home. Or rather in Jacques's home, as he always insisted on pointing out. In the mornings, the mothers dropped off their children. She remembers those women, rushed and sad, standing with their ears glued to the door. Louise taught her to listen for their anxious footsteps in the corridor of the apartment building. Some of them went back to work very soon after giving birth and they handed their tiny newborns over to Louise. They also gave her—in opaque bags that Louise put in the fridge—the milk they'd pumped during the night. Stéphanie remembers those little containers arrayed on the shelf of the fridge with the children's names written on them. One night she got up and opened the bag belonging to Jules, a red-faced baby whose sharp nails had scratched her cheek. She drank it all without pausing. She never forgot that taste of rotting melon, that sour taste which stayed in her mouth for days afterward.

On Saturday evenings she would sometimes accompany her mother to vast-seeming apartments where they would babysit. Beautiful, important women passed her in the corridor, leaving a lipstick trace on their children's cheeks. The men didn't like to wait in the living room, embarrassed by the presence of Louise and Stéphanie. They hopped up and down on their heels, smiling stupidly. They scolded their wives then helped them put their coats on. Before leaving, the woman would crouch down, balanced on her thin stilettos, and wipe the tears from her son's cheeks. "Don't cry anymore, my love. Louise is going to tell you a story and give you a hug. Aren't you, Louise?" Louise would nod. She held those children as they struggled and screamed that they wanted their mothers. Sometimes, Stéphanie hated them. She was horrified by the way they hit Louise, the way they talked to her like little tyrants.

While Louise put the children to bed, Stéphanie would rummage through drawers and in boxes left on pedestal tables. She pulled out photograph albums hidden under coffee tables. Louise cleaned everything. She did the washing-up and wiped the kitchen countertops with a sponge. She folded the clothes that madam had tossed on her bed before leaving, hesitating over which outfit to wear. "You don't have to do the washing-up," Stéphanie would repeat. "Come and sit with me." But Louise adored that. She adored observing the parents' delighted faces when they came home and realized that they'd had a free cleaning lady as well as a babysitter.

The Rouviers, for whom Louise worked for several years, took them to their country house. Louise worked and Stéphanie was on vacation. But she wasn't there, like the hosts' children, to sunbathe and stuff herself with fruit. She wasn't there to bend the rules, to stay up late and learn to ride a bicycle. If she was there, it was because no one knew what else to do with her. Her mother told her to be discreet, to play silently. Not to give the impression that she was taking advantage of the situation. "I know they said this was sort of our vacation too, but if you have too much fun they'll take it badly". At the table, she sat next to her mother, away from the hosts and their guests. She remembers that the other people talked and talked while she and her mother lowered their eyes and swallowed their meals in silence.

The Rouviers found it hard to deal with the little girl's presence. It embarrassed them; it was almost physical. They felt a shameful antipathy toward that dark-haired child, in her faded swimsuit, that clumsy child with her blank face. When she sat in the living room, next to little Hector and Tancrède, to watch television, the parents couldn't help feeling annoyed. They always ended up asking her to do them a favor—"Stéphanie, be a sweetie, go and fetch my glasses from the entrance hall"—or telling her that her mother was expecting her in the kitchen. Thankfully, Louise forbade her daughter from going near the pool, without the Rouviers even having to say anything.

On the second-to-last day of the vacation, Hector and Tancrède invited some neighbor kids to play with them on their brand-new trampoline. Stéphanie, who was hardly any older than the boys, did some impressive tricks. Some risky jumps and somersaults that brought shouts of enthusiasm from the other children. In the end Mrs. Rouvier asked Stéphanie to get down, to let the little ones play. She went over to her husband and, in a compassionate voice, said to him: "Maybe we shouldn't invite her again. I think it's too hard for her. It must be tough, seeing all the things she's not allowed to do." Her husband smiled with relief.

Myriam has been waiting for this evening all week long. She opens the front door of the apartment. Louise's handbag is on the armchair in the living room. She hears children's voices singing. A song about a green mouse and boats on the water, something turning and something floating. She moves forward on tiptoes. Louise is kneeling on the floor, leaning over the edge of the bath. Mila dunks the body of her Russian doll into the water and Adam claps his hands as he sings. Delicately, Louise picks up balls of foam and places them on the children's heads. They laugh at these hats that fly off when the nanny blows on them.

In the metro, on her way home, Myriam had felt as impatient as a lover. She hadn't seen her children all week and tonight she had promised herself she would devote herself entirely to them. Together, they would slip into the big bed. She would tickle them and kiss them, she would squeeze them against her until they were dizzy. Until they struggled.

Hidden behind the bathroom door, she watches them

and she takes a deep breath. She feels a frenzied need to feed on their skin, to plant kisses on their little hands, to hear their high-pitched voices calling "Mama." She feels suddenly sentimental. This is what it's like, being a mother. It makes her a bit silly sometimes. The most banal moments suddenly seem important. Her heart is stirred by the smallest things.

This week she came home late every night. Her children were already asleep and, after Louise left, she would sometimes lie nuzzled up to Mila, in her little bed, breathing in the delicious smell of her daughter's hair, a chemical odor of strawberries. Tonight she will allow them to do things that are normally forbidden. They will eat chocolate sandwiches under the covers. They will watch a cartoon and fall asleep late, all snuggled up. In the night she'll get a few kicks in the face and she'll sleep badly because she's so worried about Adam falling off the bed.

The children come out of the water and run, naked, into their mother's arms. Louise starts cleaning up the bathroom. She wipes the tub with a sponge and Myriam tells her: "Don't bother, there's no need. It's late already. You can go home. You must have had a tough day." Louise pretends not to hear. Squatting down, she continues scrubbing the edge of the bath and tidying up the toys that the children have tossed around.

Louise folds the towels. She empties the washing machine and makes the children's beds. She puts the sponge back in a kitchen cupboard and takes out a saucepan, which she puts on the stove. Helplessly, Myriam watches her work. She tries to reason with her. "I'll do it, don't worry." She tries to take the saucepan from her, but Louise grips the handle tightly in her palm. Gently, she pushes Myriam away. "Go and rest," she says. "You must be tired. Enjoy your children. I'll make their supper. You won't even see me."

And it's true. As the weeks pass, Louise becomes ever better at being simultaneously invisible and indispensable. Myriam no longer calls to warn her that she's going to be late and Mila no longer asks when Mama is coming home. Louise is there, single-handedly holding up this fragile edifice. Myriam lets herself be mothered. Every day she abandons more tasks to a grateful Louise. The nanny is like those figures at the back of a theater stage who move the sets around in the darkness. She picks up a couch, pushes a cardboard column or a wall with one hand. Louise works in the wings, discreet and powerful. She is the one who controls the transparent wires without which the magic cannot occur. She is Vishnu, the nurturing divinity, jealous and protective; the she-wolf at whose breast they drink, the infallible source of their family happiness.

You look at her and you do not see her. Her presence is intimate but never familiar. She arrives earlier and earlier, leaves later and later. One morning, coming out of the shower, Myriam finds herself naked in front of the nanny, who does not even blink. "Why should she care about my body?" Myriam reassures herself. "She's not prudish like that."

Louise encourages the couple to go out. "You should make the most of your youth," she repeats mechanically.

Myriam listens to her advice. She thinks Louise wise and kindly. One evening Paul and Myriam go to a party thrown by a musician whom Paul has just met. The musician lives in an attic apartment in the sixth arrondissement. The living room is tiny and low-ceilinged, and the guests are crammed close together. There's a very happy atmosphere and soon everyone starts dancing. The musician's wife—a tall blonde with fuchsia lipstick—passes around joints and pours shots of vodka into ice-cold glasses. Myriam doesn't know these people at all, but she talks with them and laughs loudly, her head thrown back. She spends an hour in the kitchen, sitting on the countertop. At three in the morning, the guests say they're starving and the beautiful blonde makes a mushroom omelet that they eat bent over the frying pan, their forks clinking.

When they go home, about 4 a.m., Louise is dozing on the sofa, her legs folded up under her chest, hands joined together. Paul delicately spreads a blanket over her. "Don't wake her up. She looks so peaceful." And Louise starts sleeping there, once or twice a week. It's never clearly stated—they don't talk about it—but Louise patiently builds her nest in the middle of the apartment.

At times, Paul worries about the nanny's long hours. "I don't want her to accuse us of exploiting her one day," Myriam promises to take control of the situation. Naturally so rigid, so strict, she blames herself for having let things slide. She is going to talk to Louise, get everything out in the open. She is at once embarrassed and secretly thrilled that Louise takes it upon herself to do so much housework, that she accomplishes what she's never been asked to do. Myriam is constantly apologizing. When she gets home late, she says: "I'm sorry for abusing your kindness." And Louise always replies: "That's what I'm here for. Don't worry about it."

Myriam often gives her presents. Earrings that she buys in a discount boutique near the metro station. An orange cake, the only sweet treat that Louise seems to like. She gives the nanny clothes that she doesn't wear anymore, even though for a long time she thought there was something humiliating about that practice. Myriam does everything she can to avoid wounding Louise, to avoid making her jealous or upset. When she goes shopping, for herself or for her children, she hides the new clothes in an old cloth bag and only opens them once Louise has gone. Paul congratulates her on being so tactful.

Everyone in Paul and Myriam's inner circle ends up knowing about Louise. Some of them have seen her in the neighborhood or in the apartment. Others have only heard about the feats of this legendary nanny, who seems to have sprung straight from the pages of a children's book.

"Louise's dinners" become a tradition, an unmissable experience for all the couple's friends. Louise is aware of each person's tastes. She knows that Emma shrewdly conceals her anorexia behind a vegetarian ideology. That Patrick, Paul's brother, is a connoisseur of meat and mushrooms. The dinners generally take place on Friday evenings. Louise spends all afternoon cooking while the children play at her feet. She tidies the apartment, makes a bouquet of flowers and sets the table so it looks pretty. She goes all across Paris to buy a few yards of material, which she uses to hand-stitch a tablecloth. When the places have been set, the sauce reduced and the wine decanted, she slips out of the apartment. Sometimes she bumps into some of the guests in the building's lobby or near the metro station. She replies shyly to their congratulations and their knowing smiles, to the way they pat their stomachs and lick their lips.

One night Paul insists that she stays. This is no ordinary day. "We have so many things to celebrate!" Pascal has given Myriam a very big case, which she is well on her way to winning thanks to an astute, aggressive defense. Paul is also very happy. One week ago, he was in the studio, working on his own music, when a well-known singer came into the producer's booth. They talked for hours, about their shared tastes, the arrangements they imagined for the songs, the incredible material they could get their hands on, and in the end the singer asked Paul to produce his next album. "There are years like that, where everything goes perfectly. You have to know how to enjoy it," Paul declares. He grabs Louise by the shoulders and smiles at her. "Whether you like it or not, tonight you are eating dinner with us."

Louise takes refuge in the children's bedroom. She spends a long time lying next to Mila, caressing her temples and her hair. In the blue glow of the nightlight, she observes Adam's face, surrendered to sleep. She can't make up her mind to leave the room. She hears the front door open and laughter in the corridor. A bottle of champagne is popped open, a chair is pushed against the wall. In the bathroom, Louise reties her bun and puts on some mauve eyeshadow. Myriam never uses makeup. Tonight she is wearing a pair of straight-leg jeans and one of Paul's shirts with the sleeves rolled up.

"I don't think you've met, have you? Pascal, allow me to introduce our Louise. You know everyone is jealous of us for finding her!" Myriam puts her arm around Louise's shoulders. Louise smiles and turns away, slightly embarrassed by the familiarity of the gesture. "Louise, this is Pascal, my boss."

"Your boss? Oh, give me a break! We work together. We're colleagues." Pascal laughs loudly as he shakes Louise's hand.

Louise is sitting at one end of the sofa, her fingers with their long polished nails tensed around her glass of champagne. She is as nervous as a foreigner, an exile who doesn't understand the language being spoken around her. She shares embarrassed, welcoming smiles with the other guests on either side of the coffee table. They lift their glasses to Myriam's talent and to Paul's singer, one of whose melodies someone hums. They talk about their jobs, about terrorism and property prices. Patrick describes his plans for a vacation in Sri Lanka.

Emma, who is sitting next to Louise, talks to her about her children. Louise knows how to talk about that. Emma has worries, which she explains to the reassuring nanny. "I've seen that lots of times, don't worry," Louise repeats. Emma, who has so many anxieties and to whom no one listens, envies Myriam for being able to depend on this Sphinx-like nanny. Emma is a sweet woman, her feelings betrayed only by her constantly wringing hands. She is smiling but envious, a neurotic flirt.

Emma lives in the twentieth arrondissement, in a part of the neighborhood where the squats have been transformed into an organic day care. She lives in a small house, decorated with such taste that it almost makes you un-easy. You have the impression that her living room, crammed with knickknacks and cushions, is designed to provoke envy rather than for its inhabitants' comfort.

"The local school is a disaster. The children spit on the ground. When you walk past it, you hear them calling each other 'whores' and 'queers.' Now, I'm not saying that nobody ever says 'fuck' in their private school. But they say it in a different way, don't you think? At least they know that they're only supposed to say it when no grown-ups are around. They know it's bad."

Emma has even heard that, at the public school, the one in her street, some parents turn up in pajamas, half an hour late, to drop off their children. That one mother, in a veil, refused to shake hands with the headmaster.

"It's a sad thing to say, but Odin would have been the only white kid in his class. I know we shouldn't give up, but I don't think I'd handle it well if he came back to the house talking about God and speaking Arabic." Myriam smiles at her. "You know what I mean, don't you?"

They stand up, laughing, and move to the table. Paul seats Emma next to him. Louise hurries into the kitchen and she is greeted by bravos when she enters the living room, carrying the meal. "She's blushing," Paul says, amused, in a too-shrill voice. For a few minutes, Louise is the center of attention. "How did she make this sauce?" "Ginger—what a good idea!" The guests vaunt her prowess and Paul starts talking about her—"our nanny"—the way people talk about children and old people in their pres-ence. Paul serves the wine, and the conversations soon rise high above such earthly considerations as food. They speak louder and louder. They stub out their cigarettes in their plates and the butts float in puddles of sauce. No one has noticed that Louise has withdrawn to the kitchen, which she is energetically cleaning.

Myriam shoots an irritated look at Paul. She pretends to laugh at his jokes, but he gets on her nerves when he's drunk. He becomes salacious, tactless, he loses all sense of reality. When he's had too much to drink, he issues invitations to horrible people, makes promises he can't keep. He tells lies. But he doesn't seem to notice his wife's annoyance. He opens another bottle of wine and taps on the edge of the table. "This year, we're going to give ourselves a treat and take our nanny with us on vacation! You have to enjoy life, right?" Louise, a pile of plates in her hands, smiles.

The next morning, Paul wakes up in a crumpled shirt, his lips still stained by red wine. In the shower, fragments of the evening flash up in his memory. He remembers his proposal and the dark look his wife shot him. He feels stupid and tired in advance. He'll have to fix his mistake now. Or pretend he never mentioned it, let time pass, wait for it to be forgotten. He knows that Myriam will make fun of him, of his drunken promises. She will blame him for his financial recklessness and the thoughtless way he treats Louise. "Because of you, she'll be disappointed, but she's so kind, she won't even dare to say anything." Myriam will hold their bills in front of his eyes, bring him back to reality. "It's always like that when you drink," she will conclude.

But Myriam does not seem angry. Lying on the sofa, with Adam in her arms, she smiles at him so sweetly that he can't believe it. She's wearing men's pajamas, too big for her. Paul sits next to her and nuzzles her neck. He loves its heather-like smell. "Is it true what you said last night?" she asks. "You think we can take Louise with us this summer? That'll be so great! For once, we'll have a real vacation. And Louise will be so happy. I mean, what else could she do that'd be better than that?"

It's so hot that Louise has left the window of the hotel room half-open. The shouts of drunkards and the screeching of car brakes do not wake Adam and Mila, who snore, mouths open, one leg dangling out of bed. They are spending only one night in Athens and Louise is sharing a tiny room with the children, to save money. They spent the whole evening laughing. They went to bed late. Adam was happy: he danced in the streets, on the cobblestones of Athens, and old people clapped their hands, captivated by his ballet. Louise did not like the city, which they walked through all afternoon despite the sweltering sun and the whining of the children. She is only thinking about tomorrow, about their trip to the islands, whose myths and legends Myriam has recounted to the children.

Myriam isn't good at telling stories. She has a slightly irritating way of articulating the complicated words and finishes all her sentences with "You see?," "You understand?" But Louise listened, like a studious child, to the story of Zeus and the goddess of war. Like Mila, her favorite was

63

Aegeus, who gave his blue to the sea, the sea on which she will ride in a boat for the first time.

In the morning, she has to drag Mila out of bed. The little girl is still asleep when the nanny undresses her. In the taxi on the way to the port of Piraeus, Louise tries to remember some ancient gods, but they are all gone from her memory. She should have written the names of those heroes down in her flowered notebook. She would have thought about them again afterward, alone. At the entrance to the port, a huge bottleneck has formed and some policemen are trying to direct traffic. It's already very hot and Adam, sitting on Louise's knees, is soaked with sweat. Massive luminous signs point the way to the docks where the boats for the islands are moored, but Paul doesn't understand them. He gets angry, becomes agitated. The taxi driver makes a U-turn, shrugging with resignation. He doesn't speak English. Paul pays him. They get out of the car and run to their quay, dragging their suitcases and Adam's stroller behind them. The crew are about to raise the bridge when they see the family, frenzied and disheveled, waving their arms about. They were lucky.

No sooner are they on the boat than the children fall asleep, Adam in his mother's arms and Mila with her head resting on Paul's knees. Louise wants to see the sea and the contours of the islands. She goes up on to the bridge. On a bench, a woman is lying on her back. She is wearing a bikini: a thong and a strip of material around her chest that barely hides her breasts. She has very dry platinum-blonde hair, but what strikes Louise is her skin. It is purplish and covered with large brown stains. In places—inside her thighs, on her cheeks, just above her breasts—her skin

64

is blistered and raw, as if she's been burned. She is immobile, like the corpse of a flayed torture victim, left out as a warning to the others.

Louise is seasick. She takes deep breaths. She closes her eyes then opens them, unable to quell the dizziness. She can't move. She sits on a bench, her back to the bridge, far from the edge of the boat. She would like to look at the sea, to remember it, and those white-shored islands that the tourists are pointing at. She would like to memorize the shapes of the sailing boats that have anchored in the sea and the slim figures diving into the water. She would like to, but she feels nauseated.

The sun grows hotter and hotter and now there is a crowd of people staring at the woman on the bench. She has covered her eyes and the sound of the wind probably prevents her from hearing the stifled laughter, the remarks, the whispers. Louise can't stop looking at that scrawny body, streaming with sweat. That woman consumed by the sun, like a piece of meat thrown on the embers.

Paul has rented two bedrooms in a charming guesthouse in the island's hills, above a beach where the children spend a lot of time. The sun sets and a pink light envelops the bay. They walk toward Apollonia, the capital. The roads they take are lined with cactuses and fig trees. At the bottom of a cliff is a monastery visited by tourists in swimsuits. Louise is completely entranced by the beauty of the place, by the calmness of the narrow streets, the little squares where cats sleep. She sits on a wall, her feet dangling, and she watches an old woman sweep the courtyard outside her house.

The sun has sunk into the sea, but it isn't dark yet. The light has just taken on shades of pastel and the details of the landscape are still visible. The outline of a bell on the roof of a church. The aquiline profile of a stone bust. The sea and the bushy shore seem to relax, plunged into a languorous torpor, offering themselves to the night, very softly, playing hard to get.

After putting the children to bed, Louise can't sleep. She sits on the terrace outside her room, from where she can contemplate the rounded bay. The wind begins to blow in the evening, a sea wind, in which she can almost taste salt and utopias. She falls asleep there, on a deck-chair, with a shawl covering her like a thin blanket. The cold dawn wakes her and she nearly cries out at the spectacle of the new day. A pure, simple, obvious beauty. A beauty within the reach of every heart.

The children wake too, enthusiastic. The only word on their lips is the sea. Adam wants to roll around in the sand. Mila wants to see fish. As soon as they've finished breakfast, they go down to the beach. Louise wears a loose orange dress, a sort of djellaba that makes Myriam smile. It was Mrs. Rouvier who gave it to her, years before, after telling her: "Oh, you know, I've worn it a lot."

The children are ready. She has smeared them in sun cream and they run straight for the sand. Louise sits with her back to a stone wall. In the shade of a pine tree, knees bent, she watches the sunlight glimmer on the sea. She has never seen anything so beautiful before.

Myriam lies on her front and reads a novel. Paul, who ran four miles before breakfast, is dozing. Louise makes sandcastles. She sculpts an enormous turtle that Adam keeps destroying and she keeps patiently rebuilding. Mila, overwhelmed by the heat, pulls her by the arm. "Come on, Louise, let's go in the sea." The nanny resists. She tells Mila to wait. To sit down with her. "Why don't you help me finish my turtle?" She shows the child some seashells that she's collected and that she places delicately on the shell of her giant turtle.

The pine tree no longer gives enough shade and the heat is growing ever more oppressive. Louise is pouring with sweat and she can no longer think of any argument to oppose the begging child. Mila takes her by the hand and Louise refuses to stand up. She grabs the little girl's wrist and pushes her away so brusquely that Mila falls backward. Louise shouts: "Will you leave me alone?"

Paul opens his eyes. Myriam rushes over to Mila and consoles her weeping daughter. They glare at Louise, furious and disappointed. The nanny retreats, ashamed. They are about to ask her for an explanation when she whispers, slowly: "I didn't tell you this before, but I can't swim."

Paul and Myriam remain silent. They signal Mila, who has started to giggle, to be quiet. Mila mocks her: "Louise is a baby. She doesn't even know how to swim." Paul is embarrassed, and that makes him angry. He blames Louise for having brought her poverty, her frailties all the way here. For having poisoned their day with her martyr's face. He takes the children swimming and Myriam dives back into her book.

The morning is spoiled by Louise's sadness and when they eat lunch on the terrace of a little bar, no one speaks. They have not finished eating when, suddenly, Paul stands up and takes Adam in his arms. He walks to the little shop on the beach. He comes back, hopping, because the sand is burning the soles of his feet. He is holding a packet that he waves in front of Louise and Myriam. "Here you go," he says. The two women do not respond and Louise docilely holds up her arm so Paul can slide an inflatable armband past her elbow. "You're so thin, you can even wear children's armbands!"

All week long, Paul takes Louise swimming. The two of them get up early, and while Myriam and the children stay by the guesthouse swimming pool, Louise and Paul go down to the still-deserted beach. As soon as they reach the wet sand, they hold hands and walk through the water for a long time, toward the horizon. They advance until their feet gently lift up from the sand and their bodies start to float. At that instant, Louise is invariably seized by a feeling of panic that she cannot hide. She cries out and Paul knows that he has to hold her hand even more tightly.

To begin with, he is embarrassed by having to touch Louise's skin. When he teaches her to float on her back, he puts one hand under the back of her neck and the other beneath her bottom. An idiotic thought flashes through his mind and he laughs inwardly: "Louise has a bottom." Louise has a body that trembles under Paul's palms and fingers. A body he had not seen or even suspected before, having considered Louise as part of the world of children or the world of employees. Probably he didn't see her at all. And yet, Louise is not unpleasant to look at. Abandoned to

71

Paul's hands, the nanny resembles a little doll. A few strands of blonde hair escape from the swimming cap that Myriam bought her. Her light tan has brought out tiny freckles on her cheeks and nose. For the first time, Paul notices the faint blonde down on her face, like the fur on newborn chicks. But there is something prudish and child-like about her, a reserve, that prevents Paul feeling anything as brazen as desire for her.

Louise looks at her feet, which sink into the sand and are licked by the sea. In the boat, Myriam told them that Sifnos owed its past prosperity to the gold and silver mines under its earth. And Louise convinces herself that the sparkles she can see through the water, on the rocks, are shards of those precious metals. The cool water covers her thighs. Now her sex organs are submerged. The sea is calm, translucent. Not a single wave surprises Louise or splashes against her chest. There are babies sitting close to the edge of the sea, watched serenely by their parents. When the water reaches her waist, Louise can't breathe anymore. She looks at the sky, dazzling, unreal. She pats the yellow-and-blue armbands on her thin arms, with drawings of a lobster and a triton-snail shell on them. She stares at Paul, imploringly. "There's no risk," Paul promises. "As long as you can stand up, there's no risk at all." But Louise seems petrified. She feels she's about to tip over. That she's going to be snatched by the currents below, her head held underwater, her legs kicking at air, until she can't struggle anymore.

She remembers how, when she was a child, one of her classmates fell in a pond during the village outing. It was a small expanse of muddy water, with a smell in the summer that sickened her. The children went there to play, despite their parents' warnings, despite the mosquitoes drawn there by the stagnant water. Here, in the blue of the Aegean Sea, Louise thinks about that black, stinking water, and about the child found with his face buried in the mire. Ahead of her, Mila kicks her legs. She is floating.

They're drunk and they are climbing the stone stairs that lead to the terrace next to the children's bedroom. They laugh and Louise sometimes clings to Paul's arm to climb up a step that is higher than the others. She gets her breath back, sitting under the bright-red bougainvillea, and looks down below at the beach where young couples drink cocktails and dance. The bar has organized a party on the beach. A "Full Moon Party" for the round, red rock that has shone down on them all evening, with all the guests commenting on its beauty. Louise had never seen a moon like that before, a moon so beautiful it was worth lassoing. Not a cold, gray moon, like the moons of her childhood.

On the terrace of the restaurant in the hills, they contemplated the bay of Sifnos and the lava-colored sunset. Paul pointed out the lacy clouds. The tourists took photographs and when Louise wanted to stand up too to get a snapshot of it with her mobile phone, Paul gently pulled her arm to make her sit down again. "It won't capture it. Better just to remember what it looks like."

For the first time, the three of them eat dinner together. The guesthouse owner offered to look after the children. They are the same age as his and they have been inseparable since the start of the vacation. Myriam and Paul were caught unprepared. Louise, of course, began by refusing. She said she couldn't leave them alone, that she had to put them to bed. That it was her job. "They've been swimming all day, they won't have any trouble falling asleep," the owner said in bad French.

So they walked to the restaurant, in a slightly awkward silence. At the table, they all drank more than usual. Myriam and Paul were dreading this dinner. What could they talk about? What would they have to say to one another? But they were convinced that it was the right thing to do, that Louise would be content. "I want her to know that we value her work, you understand?" So they talk about the children, the landscape, the morning swim, Mila's progress with the breaststroke. They make conversation. Louise wants to tell them something—doesn't it matter what, something about her—but she doesn't dare. She inhales deeply, moves her face forward to say something then draws back, tongue-tied. They drink and the silence grows peaceful, languorous.

Paul, who is sitting next to her, puts his arm around her shoulders. The ouzo has made him jovial. He squeezes her shoulder with his big hand, smiles at her like she's an old friend, like they're friends forever. She stares, enchanted, at the man's face. His tanned skin, his large white teeth, his hair turned blond by the wind and the salt. He shakes her a little bit, the way you do with a friend who's shy or sad, with someone you want to relax or get a grip.

If she dared, she'd put her hand on Paul's hand, she'd grip it with her slender fingers. But she doesn't dare.

She is fascinated by Paul's easy assurance. He jokes around with the waiter, who brings them each a *digestif.* In a few days he has already learned enough Greek to make the shopkeepers laugh or give him a discount. People recognize him. On the beach, he's the one that the other children want to play with. Laughing, he bows to their desires. He carries them on his back, he jumps in the water with them. He eats with an incredible appetite. Myriam seems irritated by this, but Louise is touched by his love of food, which drives him to order everything on the menu. "We'll take that too. We have to try it, right?" And he picks up the pieces of meat or pepper or cheese with his fingers and swallows them with innocent joy.

Back on the guesthouse terrace, the three of them burst out laughing into their hands and Louise puts a finger to her lips. Mustn't wake the little ones. This flash of responsibility suddenly strikes them as ludicrous. They play at being children, these adults whose whole day has been spent straining toward the same child-centered objective. Tonight a new lightheartedness blows over them. Their intoxication relieves the accumulated anxieties and tensions that their progeny has insinuated between them, husband and wife, mother and nanny.

Louise knows how fleeting this moment is. She sees Paul staring greedily at his wife's shoulder. Against her pale-blue dress, Myriam's skin appears even more golden. They start to dance, swaying from side to side. They are clumsy, almost embarrassed, and Myriam giggles as if it's been a long time since anyone held her around the waist like this. As if she felt ridiculous to be desired in this way. Myriam puts her cheek on her husband's shoulder. Louise knows that they are going to stop, say good-bye, pretend to be sleepy. She would like to hold them back, to cling to them, scratch her nails in the stone floor. She would like to put them under glass, like two dancers, frozen and smiling, stuck to the pedestal of a musical box. She thinks that she could stare at them for hours without ever getting bored. That she would be content to watch them live, working in the shadows so that everything was perfect, so that the mechanism never jammed. She has the intimate conviction now, the burning and painful conviction that her happiness belongs to them. That she is theirs and they are hers.

Paul giggles. He whispers something, his lips deep in his wife's neck. Something that Louise doesn't hear. He keeps a firm hold of Myriam's hand and, like two polite children, they wish Louise good night. She watches them climb the stone staircase that leads to their bedroom. The blue line of their two bodies blurs, fades, the door slams shut. The curtains are drawn. Louise sinks into an obscene daydream. She hears, without wanting to, while refusing to, despite herself. She hears Myriam's wailing, her doll-like moans. She hears the rustle of sheets and the headboard banging against the wall.

Louise opens her eyes. Adam is crying.

ROSE GRINBERG

Mrs. Grinberg will describe this little journey in the elevator at least a hundred times. Five stories, after a brief wait on the ground floor. A journey of less than two minutes, which has become the most poignant moment of her life. The fateful moment. She could—as she will never cease repeating—have altered the course of events. If she'd paid more attention to Louise's breath. If she hadn't closed her windows and shutters to take her nap. She will cry over the telephone and her daughters will not be able to reassure her. The police will become irritated that she is giving so much importance to herself and her tears will fall more heavily when she tells them coldly: "Well, *you* couldn't have done anything, anyway." She will tell everything to the journalists who are following the trial. She will speak about it to the defendant's lawyer, whom she will find arrogant and sloppy, and repeat it in the courtroom, when she is summoned to testify.

Louise, she will say each time, was not her normal self. Usually so smiling and friendly, she stood motionless in front of the glass door. Adam, sitting on a step, was screaming loudly and Mila was jumping, knocking into her brother. Louise did not move. Only her lower lip trembled slightly. Her hands were joined and her eyes lowered. For once, the noise of the children did not seem to affect her. Though normally so concerned for the neighbors and keeping up appearances, she did not say a word to the little ones. It was as if she couldn't hear them.

Mrs. Grinberg liked Louise a lot. She could even say she admired this elegant woman who took such good care of the children. Mila, the little girl, always had her hair tied in tight braids or a bun held in place by a knot. Adam seemed to adore Louise. "Now she's done what she did, maybe I shouldn't say this. But at that moment I thought they were lucky."

The bell rang and the ground-floor light came on. Louise grabbed Adam by the collar and dragged him into the elevator. Mila followed, singing to herself. Mrs. Grinberg hesitated before getting in with them. For a few seconds she wondered if she should go back into the lobby and pretend to check her letterbox. Louise's pale face made her uneasy. She feared that the five-story journey would feel interminable. But Louise was holding the door for the neighbor, who got in and stood against the wall of the elevator, her shopping bag between her legs.

"Did she appear drunk?"

Mrs. Grinberg had no doubt. Louise appeared completely sober. She couldn't have let her go up with the children if she'd thought for a second that . . . The gray-haired female lawyer mocked her. She reminded the court that Rose suffered from dizzy spells and had vision problems. The former music teacher, who would soon celebrate her sixty-fifth birthday, couldn't see very well anymore. Not only that, but she lived in the dark, like a mole. Bright light gave her terrible migraines. That was why Rose closed the shutters. That was why she didn't hear anything.

That lawyer practically insulted her, in front of the whole court. Rose desperately wanted to shut her up, to break her jaw. Wasn't she ashamed? Didn't she have any decency? From the first days of the trial, the lawyer had portrayed Myriam as an "absent mother," an "abusive employer." She'd described her as a woman blinded by ambition, selfish and indifferent to the point where she pushed poor Louise too far. A journalist seated near Mrs. Grinberg in the courtroom explained to her that there was no point getting upset; that it was merely a "defense tactic." But Rose thought it was disgusting, full stop.

No one talks about it in the apartment building but Mrs. Grinberg knows that everyone is thinking it. That at night, on every floor, eyes remain open in the darkness. That hearts race, and tears fall. She knows that bodies toss and turn, unable to fall asleep. The couple on the third floor have moved away. The Massés, of course, never came back. Rose has stayed despite the ghosts and the overpowering memory of that scream.

That day, after her nap, she opened the shutters. And that was when she heard it. Most people live their whole lives without ever hearing a scream like that. It is the kind of scream heard during war, in the trenches, in other worlds, on other continents. It is not a scream from here. It lasted at least ten minutes, that wordless scream, almost without a pause for breath. That scream that became hoarse, that filled with blood, with snot, with rage. "A doctor" was all that Mrs. Massé ended up articulating. She didn't cry for help, she merely repeated—in the rare moments when she flickered back into consciousness—"A doctor."

One month before the tragedy, Mrs. Grinberg had met Louise in the street. The nanny had looked worried and in the end she'd talked about her money problems. About her landlord who was harassing her, about the debts she'd accumulated, about her bank account, constantly in the red. She'd talked the way a balloon deflates, more and more quickly.

Mrs. Grinberg had pretended not to understand. She'd lowered her chin and said, "Times are hard for everyone." And then Louise had grabbed her by the arm. "I'm not begging. I can work, in the evening or early in the morning. When the children are asleep. I can clean the apartment, iron clothes, whatever you want." If she hadn't gripped her wrist so tightly, if she hadn't stared at her with those dark eyes, like an insult or a threat, Rose Grinberg might have accepted. And, no matter what the police say, she would have changed everything.

The flight was delayed for a long time and it is early evening when they land in Paris. Louise solemnly says goodbye to the children. She hugs them tight and doesn't let go. "See you on Monday, yes, Monday. Call me if you need anything at all," she says to Myriam and Paul, who dive into the elevator that will take them to the airport parking lot.

Louise walks to the overground train station. The carriage is empty. She sits leaning against a window and curses the landscape, the platforms where gangs of youths hang around, the peeling facades of apartment buildings, the balconies, the hostile faces of security guards. She closes her eyes and summons memories of Greek beaches, sunsets, dinners overlooking the sea. She invokes these memories the way mystics call upon miracles. When she opens the door to her studio flat, her hands start to shake. She wants to tear apart the sofa's slipcover, to punch the window. A sort of shapeless, painful magma burns her insides and it takes an effort of will to stop herself screaming.

On Saturday she stays in bed until 10 a.m. Lying on

the sofa, hands crossed over her chest, Louise looks at the dust that has accumulated on the green ceiling lamp. She would never have chosen something so ugly. She rented the apartment already furnished and has not changed any of the decor. She had to find somewhere to live after the death of her husband, Jacques, after her expulsion from the house. After weeks of wandering, she needed a nest. She found this studio, in Créteil, through a nurse in the Henri-Mondor hospital who became fond of her. The young woman assured her that the landlord wouldn't ask for too much in the way of security and that he'd accept cash payments.

Louise stands up. She pushes a chair underneath the ceiling lamp and grabs a cloth. She starts scrubbing the lamp, holding it with such force that she almost rips it off the ceiling. She is on tiptoes and the dust falls in big gray flakes into her hair. By eleven, the whole apartment has been cleaned. She's washed the windows, inside and out, and she's even wiped the shutters with a soapy sponge. Her shoes are lined up along the wall, polished and ridiculous.

Perhaps they will call her. On Saturdays, she knows, they sometimes eat lunch at a restaurant. Mila told her that. They go to a café where the little girl is allowed to order anything she wants and where Adam tries tasting a bit of mustard or lemon from the end of a spoon, under his parents' tender gaze. Louise would like that. In a packed café, surrounded by the din of clanking plates and waiters' shouts, she would be less afraid of the silence. She would sit between Mila and her brother and she'd straighten the large white napkin on the little girl's lap. She'd feed Adam, spoon after spoon. She'd listen to Paul and Myriam speak. It would all go too fast. She would feel good.

She puts on a blue dress, the one that comes down to her ankles and that buttons, up the front, with a row of little blue pearls. She wants to be ready, in case they need her. In case she has to meet them somewhere, quickly, because they've undoubtedly forgotten how far away she lives and how long it takes her, every day, to get to their apartment. Sitting in the kitchen, she drums the Formica table with her fingernails.

Lunchtime comes and goes. The clouds move in front of the clean windows, the sky darkens. The plane trees shake in the wind and it starts to rain. Louise becomes agitated. They're not going to call.

It is too late now to leave the apartment. She could go and buy some bread or get some fresh air. She could just walk. But there is nothing she wants to do in these deserted streets. The only café in the neighborhood is full of drunks, and even at three in the afternoon men sometimes brawl there near the railings of the empty garden.

She should have made her mind up earlier, rushed down into the metro, wandered around Paris, surrounded by parents buying school supplies. She'd have got lost in the crowd and she'd have followed beautiful, busy women as they walked past department stores. She'd have hung around near Madeleine, brushing past the little tables where people drink coffee. She'd have said "Sorry" to the ones she bumped into.

Paris is, in her eyes, a giant shop window. Best of all, she likes to walk in the Opéra neighborhood, going down Rue Royale and turning on to Rue Saint-Honoré. She walks slowly, observing the passersby and the shopfronts. She wants everything. The buckskin boots, the suede jackets, the snakeskin handbags, the wrap dresses, the camisoles overstitched with lace. She wants the silk blouses, the pink cashmere cardigans, the military jackets. She imagines a life where she would have enough money to possess it all. Where she would point out to an unctuous saleswoman the items that she liked.

Sunday arrives, an extension of her boredom and anxiety. A dark, miserable Sunday sunk deep in her sofa bed. She fell asleep in her blue dress and its synthetic material, horribly creased, made her sweat. Several times during the night, she opened her eyes, unsure if an hour had passed or a month. If she was sleeping at Myriam and Paul's apartment or next to Jacques in the house in Bobigny. Then she closed her eyes again and slid back into a brutal, frenzied sleep.

Louise really hates weekends. When they still lived together, Stéphanie used to complain that they never did anything on Sundays, that she wasn't allowed any of the activities Louise organized for the other children. As soon as she could, she started fleeing the house. On Fridays she would be out all night with the neighborhood teenagers. She'd come back in the morning, face pale, eyes red with rings around them. Starving. She'd walk across the small living room, head lowered, and aim straight for the fridge. She would eat, leaning against the fridge door, without even sitting down, digging with her fingers into the boxes that Louise had prepared for Jacques's lunches. Once, she dyed her hair red. She had her nose pierced. She started disappearing for entire weekends. And then, one day, she didn't come back. Nothing now could keep her at the house in Bobigny. Not school, which she'd left a long time ago. And not Louise either.

Her mother reported her disappearance, of course. "Kids that age, running away, it happens a lot. Wait a bit and she'll be back." That was all they said to her. Louise didn't search for her. Later she found out from neighbors that Stéphanie was in the South of France, that she was in love. That she moved around a lot. The neighbors couldn't get over the fact that Louise didn't ask them for details, didn't ask any questions, didn't want them to repeat the little information they had.

Stéphanie had disappeared. All her life, she had felt like an embarrassment. Her presence disturbed Jacques, her laughter woke the children Louise was looking after. Her fat thighs, her heavy figure pressed against the wall in the narrow corridor to let the others pass. She feared blocking the passage, being bumped into, sitting on a chair that someone else wanted. When she spoke, she expressed herself poorly. She laughed and she offended people, no matter how innocent her laughter. She had ended up developing a gift for invisibility, and logically, without fanfare, without warning, as if that had been her manifest destiny all along, she had disappeared.

On Monday morning Louise leaves her apartment before daybreak. She walks to the train station, changes at Auber, waits on the platform, walks up Rue Lafayette then takes Rue d'Hauteville. Louise is a soldier. She keeps going, come what may, like a mule, like a dog with its legs broken by cruel children.

September is hot and bright. On Wednesdays, after school, Louise shakes up the children's stay-at-home indolence and takes them to play in the park or to watch the fish in the aquarium. They go boating on the lake in the Bois de Boulogne and Louise tells Mila that the algae floating on the surface is in reality the hair of a deposed, vengeance-seeking witch. At the end of the month it is so warm that Louise, excited, decides to take them to the botanical gardens.

Outside the metro station, an old North African man offers to help Louise carry the stroller down the stairs. She thanks him and picks up the stroller single-handed with Adam still sitting inside it. The old man follows her. He asks how old the children are. She is about to tell him that they are not hers. But he is already leaning down to the children's level. "They're very beautiful."

The metro is the children's favorite thing. If Louise didn't hold them back, they'd run along the platform, they'd jump into the carriage, standing on people's feet, just so they could sit next to the window, tongues lolling, eyes wide open. They stand inside the carriage and Adam imitates his sister, who is holding on to a metal bar and pretending to drive the train.

In the gardens, the nanny runs with them. They laugh and she spoils them, buying them ice creams and balloons. She takes a picture of them, lying on a carpet of dead leaves, bright yellow and blood red. Mila asks why certain trees have turned that luminous shade of gold while others, the same kinds of trees, planted next to them, look like they're rotting, going straight from green to dark brown. Louise is incapable of explaining. "We'll ask your mama," she says.

On the fairground rides, they howl with terror and joy. Louise feels dizzy and she holds Adam tight in her lap when the train rushes into the dark tunnels and hurtles down the slopes. In the sky, a balloon flies away: Mickey has become a spaceship.

They sit on the grass to picnic and Mila makes fun of Louise, who is afraid of the large peacocks a few yards from them. The nanny has brought an old wool blanket that Myriam had rolled up in a ball under her bed and that Louise cleaned and mended. The three of them fall asleep on the grass. Louise wakes up, with Adam pressed against her. She's cold: the children must have pulled the blanket off. She turns around and doesn't see Mila. She calls her. She starts to scream. People turn to stare. Someone asks: "Is everything all right, madam? Do you need help?" She doesn't answer. "Mila, Mila," she screams as she runs, with Adam in her arms. She goes around all the rides, runs in front of the rifle range. Tears well in her eyes. She wants to shake the passersby, to push the strangers who are hurrying along, holding their children firmly by their hands. She turns back to the little farmhouse. Her jaw is trembling so much that she can't even call Mila's name anymore. Her head is killing her and she feels as if her knees are about to give way. In an instant, she will fall to the ground, incapable of making the slightest movement, mute, completely helpless.

Then she spots her, at the end of a path. Mila is eating an ice cream on a bench, a woman leaning toward her. Louise throws herself at the child. "Mila! Have you gone mad? Why on earth did you go away like that?"

The stranger—a woman in her sixties—holds the little girl protectively. "It's a disgrace. What were you doing? How could she end up alone? I could easily ask this little girl for her parents' number. I'm not sure they would be too happy about it."

But Mila escapes the stranger's embrace. She pushes her away and glares at her, before throwing herself at Louise's legs. The nanny bends down and picks her up. Louise kisses her frozen neck, she strokes her hair. She looks at the child's pale face and apologizes for her negligence. "My little one, my angel, my sweet." She cuddles her, covers her with kisses, holds her tight against her chest.

Seeing the child curled up in the arms of the little blonde woman, the old lady calms down. She no longer knows what to say. She observes them, shaking her head reproachfully. She was probably hoping to cause a scandal. That would have distracted her. She'd have had something to tell people if the nanny had got angry, if she'd had to call the parents, if threats had been made and then carried out. Finally the stranger gets up from the bench and leaves, saying: "Well, next time, be more careful."

Louise watches the old lady leave. She turns around two or three times and Louise smiles at her, grateful. As her stooped figure moves away, Louise holds Mila more and more strongly against her. She crushes the little girl's torso until she begs: "Stop, Louise, I can't breathe." The child tries to free herself from this embrace—she wriggles and kicks—but the nanny holds her firmly in place. She sticks her lips to Mila's ear and says to her, in a cold, composed voice: "Never do that again, you hear me? Do you want someone to kidnap you? A nasty man? Next time, that's what will happen. And even if you shout and cry, no one will come. Do you know what he'll do to you? No? You don't know? He'll take you away, he'll hide you, he'll keep you for himself and you'll never see your parents again." Louise is about to put the child down when she feels a terrible pain in her shoulder. She screams and tries to shove the little girl away from her. Mila is biting her. Her teeth are sunk in Louise's flesh, tearing it, drawing blood, and she clings to Louise's arm like a rabid animal.

That night, she doesn't tell Myriam about her daughter running away, nor about the bite. Mila, too, remains silent, without the nanny warning or threatening her. Now Louise and Mila each have a grievance against the other. This secret unites them as never before.

JACQUES

Jacques loved telling her to shut up. He couldn't stand her voice, which grated on his nerves. "Shut it, will you?" In the car, she couldn't help chatting. She was frightened of the road and talking calmed her. She launched into insipid monologues, barely taking a breath between sentences. She jabbered away blandly, listing names of streets, rolling out old memories.

She felt good when her husband yelled at her. She knew that it was to shut her up that he turned up the volume on the radio. That it was to humiliate her that he opened the window and began to smoke, while humming. Her spouse's anger scared her, but she had to admit that, sometimes, it excited her too. She enjoyed making him writhe, working him up into such a state of rage that he was capable of parking on the roadside, grabbing her by the throat and quietly threatening that he would shut her up for good.

Jacques was heavy, noisy. As he got older, he became bitter and vain. In the evenings, coming home from work, he would rant on for at least an hour about his grievances with this or that person. According to him, everyone was trying to steal from him, manipulate him, take advantage of his condition. After his first redundancy, he took his employer to an industrial tribunal. The trial cost him time and a huge amount of money, but his final victory gave him a feeling of such power that he got a taste for disputes and courtrooms. Later he thought he could make his fortune by suing his insurance company after a car accident. Next he went after the first-floor neighbors, the town hall, the building's management company. Whole days were spent writing illegible, threatening letters. He would go through legal-aid websites in search of any article of law that might play in his favor. Jacques was irascible and utterly hypocritical. He envied the success of others, denying them any merit. Sometimes he would even spend all afternoon at the commercial court, just to binge on others' sufferings. He enjoyed seeing people ruined, the blows of fate.

"I'm not like you," he told Louise proudly. "I'm not a doormat, a slave content to clean up the shit and puke of little brats. Only black women do work like that now." He thought his wife excessively docile. And while that excited him at night, in their conjugal bed, it exasperated him the rest of the time. He was forever giving Louise advice, which she pretended to listen to. "You should tell them to reimburse you, and that's it"; "You shouldn't agree to work one minute more without being paid"; "Just call in sick—what do you think they can do about it?"

Jacques was too busy to look for a job. His legal battles took up all his time. He hardly set foot outside the apartment, spreading his case files over the coffee table and leaving the television on. During that period, the presence of children became unbearable to him and he ordered Louise to work in her employers' apartment. He was irritated by the sound of their coughs and wails, even their laughter. Louise, most of all, revolted him. Her pathetic preoccupations, which always centered on kids, put him in a veritable rage. "You and your bloody women's things," he would repeat. He believed that such matters should not be talked about. Just let them get on with it, somewhere out of sight; we don't need to know anything about all this stuff with babies or old people. They were bad times, those ages of servitude, of repeating the same actions. Those ages when the body—monstrous, shameless, a cold and foul-smelling machine—took over everything. Bodies that craved love and liquid. "It's enough to make you disgusted at being a man."

During that period, he bought—on credit—a computer, a new television and an electrically powered chair that gave massages and that could be inclined when he wanted to take a nap. He would spend hours in front of the computer's blue screen, his asthmatic wheezes filling the room. Sitting on his new chair, facing his brand-new television, he would frantically press the buttons on his remote control, like an overexcited kid.

It was probably a Saturday, since they ate lunch together. Jacques was ranting, as always, but with less vigor than usual. Under the table, Louise had put a bowl of ice water in which Jacques was soaking his feet. In her nightmares, Louise can still see Jacques's purple legs, his swollen diabetic's ankles, which he would constantly ask her to massage. For the past few days, Louise had noticed, his complexion had been waxy, his eyes dull. He'd been having difficulty finishing a sentence without pausing for breath. She cooked an osso buco. After his third mouthful, as he was about to speak, Jacques threw it all over his plate. It was projectile vomit, like a baby's, and Louise knew it must be serious. That he wouldn't get better. She stood up and, seeing Jacques's bewildered expression, she said: "Don't worry, it's nothing." She talked constantly, accusing herself of having put too much wine in the sauce, which had made it acidic, spouting idiotic theories about heartburn. She talked and talked, gave advice, blamed herself and asked for forgiveness. Her quavering, incoherent logorrhea only succeeded in intensifying the panic that had taken hold of Jacques, a fear akin to missing the top step of a staircase and seeing himself tumbling down, headfirst, his spine crushed, his flesh bloody. If she'd shut up, perhaps he could have wept, maybe he'd have asked for help or even a bit of tenderness. But as she cleared the table, as she cleaned the floor, she talked, ceaselessly.

Jacques died three months later. He dried up like a piece of fruit forgotten in the sun. It was snowing on the day of his funeral and the light was almost blue. Louise found herself alone.

She nodded as the notary explained, in an apologetic voice, that Jacques had left her only debts. She stared at the goiter crushed under his shirt collar and pretended to accept the situation. All she had inherited from Jacques were failed lawsuits, pending trials, unpaid bills. The bank gave her a month to leave the little house in Bobigny, which would be repossessed. Louise boxed everything up herself. She carefully collected the few things that Stéphanie had left behind. She didn't know what to do with the piles of documents that Jacques had accumulated. She thought about setting fire to them in the little garden, imagining that, with a bit of luck, the blaze might spread to the house, the street, even the whole neighborhood. In that way, this entire part of her life would go up in smoke. She would feel no sorrow if it did. She would stay there, motionless, discreet, to watch the flames devour her memories, her long walks in the dark empty streets, her bored Sundays with Jacques and Stéphanie.

But Louise picked up her suitcase, she double-locked the door and she left, abandoning in the entrance hall of the little house those boxes of memories, her daughter's clothes and her husband's schemes.

That night she slept in a hotel room, where she paid for a week's stay in advance. She made sandwiches and ate them in front of the television. She sucked fig biscuits, letting them melt on her tongue. Solitude was like a vast hole into which Louise watched herself sink. Solitude, which stuck to her flesh, to her clothes, began to model her features, making her move like a little old lady. Solitude leaped at her face at dusk, when night fell and the sounds of family lives rose from the surrounding houses. The light dimmed and the murmur grew louder: laughter, panting, even sighs of boredom.

In that room, on a street in the Chinese quarter, she lost all notion of time. She felt lost, crazed. The whole world had forgotten her. She would sleep for hours and wake up swollen-eyed, her head aching, despite the cold that seethed through the room. She only went out when she absolutely had to, when her hunger became too painful to ignore. She walked in the street as if it were a cinema set and she were not there, an invisible spectator to the movements of mankind. Everyone seemed to have somewhere to go.

Solitude was like a drug that she wasn't sure she wanted to do without. Louise wandered through the streets in a daze, eyes so wide open that they hurt. In her solitude, she started to see other people. To really see them. The existence of others became palpable, vibrant, more real than ever. She observed, in minute detail, the gestures of couples sitting on terraces. The sideways glances of torpid old people. The self-conscious expressions of students who sat on benches and pretended to revise. In squares, outside metro stations, she would recognize the strange parade of the impatient. Like them, she waited for someone. Every day, she would encounter companions in madness: tramps, lunatics, talking to themselves.

The city, back then, was full of madmen.

Winter comes, and the days blur into each other. November is rainy and cold. Outside, the sidewalks are covered with black ice. Impossible to go out. Louise tries to entertain the children. She invents games, she sings songs. They build a house out of cardboard. But the day seems to last forever. Adam has a fever and he won't stop whining. Louise holds him in her arms; she rocks him for nearly an hour, until he falls asleep. Mila, pacing around the living room, grows fractious too.

"Come here," Louise tells her. Mila approaches and the nanny takes from her handbag the little white vanity case that the child has so often daydreamed about. Mila thinks Louise is the most beautiful woman she knows. She looks like the flight attendant—blonde, with lots of makeup—who gave her candies on a trip to Nice. Even though Louise is constantly on the move, doing the washing-up and running from the school to the house, she always looks perfect. Her hair is meticulously tied back. Her black mascara, of which she applies at least three thick coats, makes her look like a surprised doll. And then there are her hands, which are soft and smell of flowers. And her nail polish that never flakes or peels.

Sometimes Louise paints her nails in front of Mila and the little girl, eyes closed, breathes in the smell of the remover and the cheap polish that the nanny spreads with quick, lively gestures, never getting any on her skin. Fascinated, the child watches Louise wave her hands in the air and blow on the fingers.

When Mila allows Louise to kiss her, it is so she can smell the talcum powder on her cheeks, so she can get a closer look at the glitter that sparkles on her eyelids. She likes to watch her put lipstick on. With one hand, Louise holds a mirror—always perfectly clean—in front of her, while she pulls her face into a strange grimace that Mila tries to reproduce afterward in the bathroom.

Louise rummages around in her vanity case. She holds the little girl's hands and coats them with rose-scented cream, which she takes from a tiny pot. "Smells nice, doesn't it?" Under the child's astonished eyes, Louise puts polish on her little nails. A vulgar pink polish that smells very strongly of acetone. For Mila, this is the smell of femininity.

"Take off your socks, would you?" And she paints the toenails of her chubby little feet with nail polish. Louise empties out the contents of the vanity case on the table. The air fills with orange dust and the smell of talc. Mila laughs suddenly, jubilantly. Louise is putting lipstick on her now, then blue eyeshadow, then a sort of orange paste on her cheeks. She asks her to lower her head and she backcombs her hair—too straight and too fine—until it looks like a mane.

They laugh so hard that they don't hear Paul as he closes the front door behind him and enters the living room. Mila smiles, mouth open, arms spread wide.

"Look, Papa. Look what Louise did!"

Paul stares at her. He had been so pleased to get home early, so happy to see his children, but now he feels sick. He has the feeling that he has walked in on something sordid or abnormal. His daughter, his little girl, looks like a transvestite, like a ruined old drag queen. He can't believe it. He is furious, out of control. He hates Louise for having done this. Mila, his angel, his little blue dragonfly, is as ugly as a circus freak, as ridiculous as a dog dressed up for a walk by its hysterical old-lady owner.

"What the hell is this? What did you do to her?" Paul yells. He grabs Mila by the arms and stands her on a stool in the bathroom. He tries to wipe the makeup off her face. The little girl cries out: "You're hurting me." She sobs and the rouge just smears, ever thicker, ever stickier, over the child's diaphanous skin. He has the impression that he is disfiguring her even more, soiling her, and his rage grows.

"Louise, I'm warning you: I never want to see this again. This kind of thing disgusts me. I have no intention of teaching such vulgar behavior to my daughter. She's far too young to dress up like a . . . You know what I mean."

Louise stands in the bathroom doorway, holding Adam in her arms. Despite his father's anger, despite the agitation, the baby doesn't cry. He glares at Paul coldly, suspiciously, as if to make it clear that he is on Louise's side. The nanny listens to Paul. She does not lower her eyes or apologize.

Stéphanie could be dead. Louise thinks about this sometimes. She could have prevented her from ever living. No one would have known. No one would have blamed her. If Louise had eliminated her, society would perhaps even have been grateful to her today. She would have proved herself clear-headed, a good citizen.

Louise was twenty-five years old and she woke up one morning with heavy, painful breasts. A new sadness had come between her and the world. She felt certain that there was something wrong. Back then, she was working for Mr. Franck, an artist who lived with his mother in a mansion in the fourteenth arrondissement. Louise did not really understand Mr. Franck's paintings. In the living room, on the walls of the corridor and the bedrooms, she would stand in front of the immense portraits of disfigured women—bodies crippled with pain or paralyzed in ecstasy—that had made the artist famous. Louise wasn't sure they were beautiful, but she liked them.

Geneviève, Mr. Franck's mother, had fractured the

neck of her femur getting down from a train. Unable to walk, she had lost her mind on the platform. She spent her life lying down—naked, most of the time—in a light-filled ground-floor bedroom. It was so difficult to dress her—she fought with such ferocity—that they just laid her on an open diaper, her breasts and genitals exposed. The sight of that abandoned body was appalling.

Mr. Franck had begun by hiring qualified, very expensive nurses. But they complained about the old woman's tantrums. They stuffed her full of tranquilizers. The son found these nurses cold and brutal. What he wanted for his mother was a friend, a nanny, a tender-hearted woman who would listen to her ravings without rolling her eyes, without sighing. Louise was young, admittedly, but she had impressed him with her physical strength. On the first day, she had come into the bedroom and, by herself, had managed to lift that body, as heavy as a concrete slab. She had cleaned the old woman, talking constantly, and for once Geneviève had not screamed.

Louise slept with Geneviève. She washed her. She listened to her rant all night. Like a baby, the old woman dreaded dusk. The fading light, the shadows, the silences made her scream with fear. She begged her own mother—who'd been dead for forty years—to come and fetch her. Louise, who slept next to the medical bed, tried to calm her down. The old woman spat insults at her, called her a whore, a bitch, a peasant. Sometimes she would try to hit her.

Louise started sleeping more deeply than ever. Geneviève's cries didn't disturb her anymore. Soon she was no longer capable of turning the old woman over or putting her in her wheelchair. It was as if her arms had atrophied, and she had terrible backache. One afternoon, when darkness had already fallen and Geneviève was mumbling heartrending prayers, Louise went up to Mr. Franck's attic to explain the situation to him. To Louise's surprise, the artist became enraged. He banged the door shut and walked over to her, his gray eyes boring into hers. For an instant, she thought he was going to hurt her. And he started laughing.

"Louise, women like you—single women who hardly earn enough money to live—do not have children. To be perfectly honest with you, I think you're completely irresponsible. You turn up here with your big round eyes and your stupid smile, to tell me that. What do you expect me to do? Open a bottle of champagne?" He was pacing around the large room, hands behind his back, surrounded by unfinished paintings. "You think it's good news? Don't you have any common sense at all? I'll tell you one thing: you're lucky you have an employer like me, who's willing to try to help you improve your situation. I know plenty who would kick you out the door, quick as a flash. Listen, I entrust you with my mother, who is the most important person in the world for me, and I can tell that you're completely brainless, incapable of making a good decision. I couldn't care less what you do with your free evenings. Your light morals are none of my business. But life is not a party. What would you do with a baby?"

In reality, Mr. Franck did care what Louise did with her Saturday evenings. He started asking her questions, increasingly insistent. He wanted to shake her, to slap her face until she confessed. He wanted her to tell him what she did when she wasn't there, at Geneviève's bedside, where he could keep an eye on her. He wanted to know from what caresses this child had been conceived, in which bed Louise had abandoned herself to pleasure, to lust, to laughter. He asked her over and over again who the father was, what he looked like, where she'd met him and what his intentions were. But Louise, invariably, responded to his questions by saying: "He's no one."

Mr. Franck took charge of everything. He said he would drive Louise to the doctor himself and wait for her during the procedure. He even promised her that once it was over, he would have her sign a proper contract, that he would pay money into a bank account in her name, and that she would have the right to paid vacations.

The day of the operation, Louise overslept and missed the appointment. Stephanie took over her life, digging inside her, stretching her, tearing apart her youth. She grew like a mushroom on a damp piece of wood. Louise did not go back to Mr. Franck's house. She never saw the old lady again.

Locked up in the Massés' apartment, she sometimes feels she is going mad. For the past few days there have been red blotches on her cheeks and her wrists. Louise has to put her hands and her face under cold water to soothe the burning sensation. During the long winter days, a feeling of immense solitude grips her. In a panic, she leaves the apartment, closes the door behind her, faces up to the cold and takes the children to the park.

Parks. on winter afternoons. The drizzle scatters dead leaves. The icy gravel sticks to the children's knees. On benches, on narrow paths, you see those people the world doesn't want anymore. They flee cramped apartments, sad living rooms, armchairs sunk with the imprint of boredom and inertia. They prefer to shiver outside, shoulders hunched and arms crossed. At 4 p.m., idle days seem endless. It is now, in the middle of the afternoon, that you notice the wasted time, that you worry about the coming evening. At this hour, you are ashamed of your uselessness.

Parks, on winter afternoons, are haunted by vagabonds, drifters, tramps, the elderly and unemployed, the sick, the vulnerable. Those who do not work, who produce nothing. Those who do not make money. In spring, of course, the lovers return; clandestine couples find shelter under lime trees, in flowered nooks; tourists photograph statues. But in winter, it's something else altogether.

Around the icy slide there are nannies and their army of children. Wrapped up in cumbersome padded jackets, the toddlers run like fat Japanese dolls, noses trickling snot, fingers violet. They breathe out white steam and stare at it, fascinated. In strollers, babies held tight under straps contemplate their elder siblings. Perhaps some of them feel melancholic, impatient. They probably can't wait to be able to get warm by crawling up the wooden climbing frame. They are eager to escape the surveillance of these women who catch them with a sure or rough hand, their voices calm or furious. Women wearing boubous on this freezing winter day.

There are mothers too, mothers staring into space. Like the one who gave birth recently and now finds herself confined to the world's edge; who, sitting on this bench, feels the weight of her still flabby belly. She carries her body of pain and secretions, her body that smells of sour milk and blood. This flesh that she drags around with her, which she gives no care or rest. There are smiling, radiant mothers, those extremely rare mothers, gazed at lovingly by all the children. The ones who did not say good-bye this morning, who didn't leave them in the arms of another. The ones set free by a day off work, who have come here to enjoy it, bringing a strange enthusiasm to this ordinary winter's day at the park.

There are some men too, but closer to the benches, closer to the sandpit, closer to the little ones, the women form a solid wall, an impassable barrier. They are suspicious of men who come near, who take an interest in this world of women. They drive away the men who smile at the children, who stare at their plump cheeks and their little legs. The grandmothers deplore this: "All those pedophiles around nowadays! That didn't exist, in my day."

Louise does not let Mila out of her sight. The little girl runs from the slide to the swings. She never stops, because she doesn't want to get cold. Her gloves are soaked and she wipes them on her pink coat. Adam sleeps in his stroller. Louise has wrapped him up in a blanket and she gently strokes the skin on the back of his neck, between the top of his sweater and the bottom of his woolly hat. The metallic glare of an icy sun makes her squint. "Want one?"

A young woman sits next to her, legs apart. She holds out a little jar in which honey candies are stuck together. Louise looks at her. She can't be more than twenty-five and there is something vulgar about the way she smiles. Her long black hair is dirty and unkempt, but you can tell that she could be pretty. Or attractive, anyway. She has sensual curves, a slightly round belly, thick thighs. She chews her candies with her mouth open and noisily sucks her honey-covered fingers.

"No, thank you." Louise refuses the offer with a wave of her hand.

"Where I come from, we always share our food with strangers. It's only here that I've seen people eating on their own." A boy of about four comes over to the young woman and she sticks a candy in his mouth. The little boy laughs.

"It's good for you," she tells him. "But it's a secret, okay? We won't tell your mother."

The little boy is called Alphonse, and Mila likes playing with him. Louise comes to the park every day and every day she refuses the fatty pastries that Wafa offers her. She tells Mila she mustn't eat any either, but Wafa doesn't take offense. The young woman is very chatty and on that bench, her hip pressed against Louise, she tells the nanny her life story. Mostly she talks about men.

Wafa reminds her of a big cat, not too subtle but very resourceful. She doesn't have her official papers yet, but doesn't seem worried about it. She arrived in France thanks to an old man to whom she used to give massages in a seedy hotel in Casablanca. The man became fond of her hands, so soft, then of her mouth and of her buttocks and, finally, of her entire body, which she offered him, following both her instinct and her mother's advice. The old man brought her to Paris, where he lived in a shabby apartment and received welfare. "He was scared that I'd get pregnant and his children pressured him into kicking me out. But the old man, he wanted me to stay."

Faced with Louise's silence, Wafa talks as if she's confessing to a priest or the police. She tells the nanny the details of a life that will never be recorded. After leaving the old man's apartment, she was recruited by a woman who signed her up for dating sites aimed at young Muslim women who were illegal immigrants. One evening a man arranged to meet her in a local McDonald's. The man thought she was beautiful. He made advances. He even tried to rape her. She managed to calm him down. They started talking money. Youssef agreed to marry her for twenty thousand euros. "That's cheap for getting your French papers," he explained.

She found this job—a godsend—with a French-American couple. They treat her well, even if they're very demanding. They rented her a studio just around the corner from where they live. "They pay my rent, but in exchange I can never say no to them."

"I adore this kid!" she says, staring greedily at Alphonse. Louise and Wafa fall silent. An icy wind sweeps through the park and they know that they will soon have to leave. "Poor little boy. Look at him, he can hardly move cos I've wrapped him up so warm. If he catches a cold, his mother will kill me."

Wafa sometimes feels afraid that she will grow old in one of these parks. That she'll feel her knees crack on these old frozen benches, that she won't be strong enough to lift up a child anymore. Alphonse will grow up. Soon he won't set foot in a park on a winter afternoon. He'll follow the sun. He'll go on vacation. Perhaps one day he'll sleep in one of the rooms of the Grand Hotel, where she used to massage men. This boy she raised will be serviced by one of her sisters or her cousins, on the terrace with its yellow and blue tiles.

"You see? Everything turns around and upside down. His childhood and my old age. My youth and his life as a man. Fate is vicious as a reptile. It always ends up pushing us to the wrong side of the handrail."

The rain starts to fall. Time to leave.

For Paul and Myriam, the winter flies past. During those few weeks, they see very little of each other. They meet in bed, one joining the other in sleep. Their feet touch under the sheets; one kisses the other's neck and laughs at hearing the other mumble like an animal disturbed in its sleep. They call each other during the day, leave messages. Myriam writes loving Post-it notes that she sticks to the bathroom mirror. In the middle of the night, Paul sends her videos of his rehearsals.

Life has become a succession of tasks, commitments to honor, appointments to keep. Myriam and Paul are snowed under with work. They like to repeat this as if their exhaustion was a portent of success. Their life is full to bursting; there's hardly even time for sleep, never mind thinking. They rush from one place to another, change shoes in taxis, have drinks with people who are important for their careers. The two of them have become the heads of a booming business, a business with clear objectives, an income stream, expenses.

All over the apartment, there are lists that Myriam

has written—on a paper napkin, on a Post-it, on the last page of a book. She spends her time looking for them. She is afraid to throw them away as if this might make her lose track of all the tasks she has to accomplish. She has kept some really old ones and, rereading them, she feels a nostalgia that is only intensified when she can no longer remember to what those obscure notes refer.

Pharmacy
Tell Mila Nils's story
Reservations for Greece
Call M.
Reread all my notes
Go back to that shop. Buy the dress?
Reread Maupassant
Get him a surprise?

Paul is happy. His life, for once, seems to be living up to his appetite for it, his insane energy levels, his joie de vivre. The boy who grew up in the great wide open is finally able to spread out. In a few months, his career has changed beyond all recognition, and for the first time in his life he is doing exactly what he wants. He no longer spends his days serving others, obeying and keeping silent, confronted with a hysterical producer, a group of infantile singers. Gone are his days of waiting for artists who turn up six hours late without bothering to warn him. Gone those recording sessions with aging MOR singers or the ones who need liters of alcohol and dozens of lines before they can play a note. Paul spends his nights at the studio, avid for music, new ideas, hysterical laughter. He doesn't leave anything to chance, spends hours correcting the sound of a snare drum, a drum arrangement. "Louise is there!" he always tells his wife when she worries about their absences.

When Myriam first got pregnant he was thrilled, but he told his friends that he didn't want his life to change. Myriam thought he was right, and she looked at her man—so sporty, so handsome, so independent—with even more admiration. He had promised her he would make sure that their life remained luminous and full of surprises. "We'll travel and we'll take the kid with us. You'll become a great lawyer, I'll produce records by acclaimed artists, and nothing will change." They pretended; they tried.

In the months that followed Mila's birth, life turned into a rather sad act. Myriam concealed the rings around her eyes and her melancholy. She was afraid of admitting to herself that she was sleepy all the time. Around that period, Paul started asking her: "What are you thinking about?" and each time she felt like crying. They invited friends to their apartment and Myriam had to force herself not to throw them out, not to knock the table over, not to lock herself in her bedroom. Their friends laughed; they raised their glasses and Paul refilled them. They argued and Myriam worried about her daughter being woken. She could have screamed from tiredness.

After Adam's birth it was even worse. The night they came home from the maternity ward, Myriam fell asleep in the bedroom, the transparent cradle next to her. Paul couldn't sleep. It seemed to him that there was a strange smell in the apartment. The same smell as in pet stores, on the docks, where he sometimes took Mila on weekends. A smell of secretion and confinement, of dried piss in a litter tray. That smell sickened him. He got up and took the trash outside. He opened the window. And then he realized that it was Mila who had thrown everything she could find in the toilets, which were now overflowing, spreading that foul wind throughout the apartment.

During that period Paul felt trapped, overwhelmed by obligations. He became a pale shadow of his usual easygoing, optimistic self, the tall blond man with the booming laugh who made girls turn to watch him as he passed without him even noticing. He stopped having mad ideas, suggesting weekends in the mountains and trips in the car to eat oysters on the beach. He tempered his enthusiasms. In the months that followed Adam's birth he started avoiding the apartment. He invented meetings and drank beer, alone, in hiding, in a quarter far from home. His friends had become parents too, and most of them had left Paris for the suburbs, the provinces or warmer lands in the south of Europe. For a few months Paul became childish, irresponsible, ridiculous. He kept secrets and harbored desires of escape. And yet he made no allowances for himself. He knew just how banal his attitude was. All he wanted was not to go home, to be free, to live again. He realized now—too late—that he hadn't lived very much before this. The clothes of a father seemed at once too big for him and too sad.

But it was done now, and he couldn't say that he didn't want it anymore. The children were there—loved, adored, unconditionally—but doubt was insinuating itself everywhere. The children, their smell, their gestures, their desire for him: all of this touched him to a degree that he would never be able to describe. Sometimes he wanted to be a kid too, to put himself in their shoes, to dissolve into childhood. Something was dead and it wasn't only youth or the feeling of being carefree. He wasn't useless anymore. They needed him and he was going to have to deal with that. By becoming a father, he had acquired principles and certainties, things he had sworn never to have. His generosity had become relative. His passions had grown tepid. His world had shrunk.

Louise is there now and Paul has started arranging dates with his wife again. One afternoon he sent her a message. "Place des Petits-Pères." She didn't reply and he found her silence wonderful. Like a form of politeness; a lover's silence. His heart was racing when he arrived in the square, slightly early, slightly worried. "She'll come. Of course she'll come." She came and they walked on the docks, like they used to do, before.

He knows how much they need Louise, but he can't stand her anymore. With her doll's body, her irritating habits, she really gets on his nerves. "She's so perfect, so delicate, that sometimes it sickens me," he admitted to Myriam one day. He is horrified by her little-girl figure, that way she has of dissecting every little thing the children do or say. He despises her dubious theories on education and her grandmotherly methods. He ridicules the photographs she has started sending them from her mobile phone, ten times a day, showing the children smiling as they lift up their empty plates, with the caption: "I ate it all."

Since the incident with the makeup, he talks to her as little as possible. That evening he even thought about firing her. He called Myriam to discuss the idea with her. She was in the office, and she didn't have time. So he waited until she got home and when his wife came through the door, about 11 p.m., he told her what had happened, the way Louise had looked at him, her icy silence, her arrogance.

Myriam reasoned with him. She played down the episode. She blamed him for having been too hard on the nanny, for having hurt her feelings. But then, they are always in league against him, like two bears. When it comes to the children, they sometimes treat him with a haughtiness that makes him bristle. They act like mothers, treat him like a child.

Sylvie, Paul's mother, made fun of them. "You act like the big bosses with your governess. Don't you think you're overdoing it?" Paul became annoyed. His parents had raised him to detest money and power, and to have a slightly mawkish respect for those "below" him. He had always been relaxed in his job, working with people with whom he felt equal. He had always called his boss *tu*, not *vous*. He had never given orders. But Louise had turned him into a boss. He hears himself giving his wife despicable advice. "Don't make too many concessions, otherwise she'll never stop asking for more," he says, widening his hands apart.

In the bath, Myriam is playing with her son. She holds him between her thighs, presses him against her and cuddles him so tightly that Adam ends up struggling and crying. She can't stop herself kissing him all over his chubby, perfect cherub's body. She looks at him and feels a gust of hot maternal love blow over her. She thinks that soon she won't dare to be like this with him, the two of them naked and close together. That it won't happen anymore. And then, faster than seems possible, she will be old and he—this laughing, pampered child—will be a man.

As she was undressing him, she noticed two strange marks, on his arm and at the top of his back. Two red scars, almost vanished, but where she can still make out what look like tooth marks. She gently kisses these wounds. She holds her son against her. She asks him to forgive her and belatedly consoles him for the sadness he felt at her absence.

The next morning, Myriam talks to Louise about it. The nanny has just entered the apartment. She hasn't even had time to take off her coat before Myriam is holding out

Adam's bare little arm toward her. Louise does not appear surprised.

She raises her eyebrows, hangs up her coat and asks:

"Has Paul taken Mila to school?"

"Yes, they just left. Louise, did you see? That's a bite mark, isn't it?"

"Yes, I know. I put a bit of cream on it to help it heal. It was Mila who bit him."

"Are you sure? Were you there? Did you see it?"

"Of course I was there. The two of them were playing in the living room while I made dinner. And then I heard Adam screaming. He was sobbing, poor thing, and to start with I couldn't work out why. Mila bit him through his clothes; that's why I didn't know straightaway."

Louise sighs. She lowers her head. She looks as if she's hesitating.

"I don't understand," Myriam says, kissing Adam's hairless head. "I asked her several times if it was her. I even told her I wouldn't punish her. She swore to me that she didn't know where that bite came from."

"I promised not to say anything, and I really don't like the idea of breaking a promise I made to a child."

She takes off her black cardigan, unbuttons her shirt-dress and exposes her shoulder. Myriam leans in close and is unable to hold back a gasp of surprise and disgust. She stares at the brown mark that covers Louise's shoulder. It's an old scar, but she can clearly see the shapes of the little teeth that bit into the flesh, lacerating it.

"Mila did that to you?"

"Listen, I promised Mila I wouldn't say anything. Please don't talk to her about it. If the bond of trust between us was broken, I think she'd be even more disturbed. Do you see?"

"Ah."

"She's a bit jealous of her brother. That's completely normal. Leave me to deal with it, okay? You'll see, everything will be fine."

"Yeah. Maybe. But honestly, I don't understand."

"You shouldn't try to understand everything. Children are just like adults. There's nothing to understand."

How gloomy she looked, Louise, when Myriam told her that they were going to the mountains for a week to stay with Paul's parents! Myriam thinks about it again now, and she shivers. A storm flickered behind Louise's dark glare. That evening the nanny left without saying good-bye to the children. Like a ghost, monstrously discreet, she banged the door shut behind her and Mila and Adam said: "Mama, Louise has disappeared."

A few days later, on the eve of their departure, Sylvie came to fetch them. Louise had not been prepared for this. The cheerful, eccentric grandmother shouted as she came into the apartment. She threw her bag on the floor and rolled in the bed with the children, promising them a week of parties, games and gluttony. When she turned away, Myriam laughed at her mother-in-law's tomfoolery. Standing in the kitchen, Louise watched them. The nanny was deathly pale and her eyes, encircled by dark rings, looked sunken. She seemed to be mumbling something. Myriam moved toward her but Louise crouched down to

123

fasten a suitcase. Later Myriam told herself that she must have been imagining things.

Myriam tries to calm herself. She has no reason to feel guilty. She doesn't owe her nanny anything. And yet, without being able to explain it, she has the feeling that she is tearing the children away from Louise, refusing her something. Punishing her.

Perhaps Louise was upset at being informed so late, not having time to organize her vacations. Or maybe she's just annoyed that the children are spending time with Sylvie, whom she doesn't like at all. When Myriam complains about her mother-in-law, the nanny tends to lose her temper. She takes Myriam's side with excessive zeal, accusing Sylvie of being mad, hysterical, of being a bad influence on the children. She encourages her boss not to let it happen; or, worse, to distance the grandmother from the poor children. In those moments, Myriam feels simultaneously supported and slightly uneasy.

As he is about to start the car, Paul takes off the watch from his left wrist.

"Can you put this in your bag, please?" he asks Myriam.

He bought this watch two months ago, paying for it with the money received from a contract with a famous singer. It's a secondhand Rolex that a friend found for him at a very reasonable price. Paul agonized before acquiring it. He really wanted it—he thought it was perfect—but he felt slightly ashamed of this fetishism, this frivolous desire. The first time he wore it, the watch seemed both beautiful and enormous. He found it too heavy, too flashy. He kept pulling down the sleeve of his jacket to conceal it. But very soon he got used to this weight at the end of his left arm. Really, this piece of jewelry—the first he'd ever possessed—was fairly discreet. And anyway, he had a right to treat himself. He hadn't stolen it from anyone.

"Why are you taking off your watch?" Myriam asks him, knowing how fond of it he is. "Has it stopped working?"

"No, it works fine. But you know my mother. She wouldn't understand. And I don't feel like spending the whole evening being told off for that."

It is early evening when they arrive. The house is freezing, and half of its rooms are still being renovated. The kitchen ceiling looks like it's about to collapse and there are bare electrical wires in the bathroom. Myriam hates this place. She is fearful for the children. She follows them all over the house, eyes full of panic, hands ready to stop them from falling. She prowls. She interrupts their games. "Mila, come and put another sweater on." "Adam's breathing strangely, don't you think?"

One morning, she wakes up numb. She breathes on Adam's frozen hands. She worries about Mila's paleness and forces her to keep her hat on in the house. Sylvie prefers not to say anything. She would like to give the children the wildness and whimsy that they are forbidden. There are no rules with her. She doesn't shower them with foolish gifts, like parents trying to compensate for their absences. She doesn't pay attention to the words she uses and she is constantly reprimanded for this by Paul and Myriam.

To annoy her daughter-in-law, she compares the children to "little birds fallen out of their nest." She likes to feel sorry for them having to live in a city, having to put up with rudeness and pollution. She would like to widen the horizons of these children doomed to become sensible, middle-class people, at once servile and authoritarian. Doomed to be cowards.

Sylvie bites her tongue. She does her best not to broach the subject of the children's education. A few months before this, the two women had argued violently. The kind of argument that time does not erase, its words still echoing inside them for a long time afterward whenever they see each other. Everyone had been drinking. Way too much. Myriam, feeling sentimental, had sought a compassionate ear from Sylvie. She complained about never seeing the children, about suffering from this frantic existence where no one ever gave her an easy ride. But Sylvie did not console her. She did not put her hand on Myriam's shoulder. On the contrary, she launched an all-out attack on her daughter-in-law. Her knives, apparently, were well sharpened, ready to be used when the occasion presented itself. Sylvie reproached her for devoting too much time to her job, despite the fact that she herself had worked all the way through Paul's childhood and had always boasted about her independence. She called her irresponsible and selfish. She counted on her fingers the number of work trips that Myriam had made even while Adam was ill and

Paul was finishing the recording of an album. It was her fault, Sylvie said, if her children had become unbearable, tyrannical, capricious. Her fault and also the fault of Louise, that phony nanny, that fake mother on whom Myriam depended, out of complacency, out of cowardice. Myriam started crying. Paul, stunned, did not say a word, and Sylvie waved her arms in the air as she shouted: "Go ahead and cry! Look at her. She cries and we're supposed to feel sorry for her because she's incapable of hearing the truth."

Every time that Myriam sees Sylvie, the memory of that evening oppresses her. That night, she felt as if she were being assaulted, thrown to the ground and stabbed repeatedly with a dagger. Myriam lay there, her guts slashed open, in front of her husband. She didn't have the strength to defend herself against those accusations, which she knew were partly true but which she considered as her lot and that of many other women. Not for an instant was there even a hint of clemency or gentleness. Not a single piece of advice was offered from mother to mother, from woman to woman.

Over breakfast, Myriam stares fixedly at her telephone. She tries desperately to check her emails, but the service is too slow and she gets so furious that she wants to throw her phone at the wall. Hysterical, she threatens Paul that she will go back to Paris. Sylvie raises her eyebrows, visibly exasperated. She had always hoped that her son would find a different kind of woman, more outdoorsy, more whimsical. A girl who loved nature, hiking in the mountains; a girl who wouldn't complain about the discomforts of this charming house.

For a long time Sylvie used to ramble on, always telling the same stories about her youth, her past political commitments, her revolutionary comrades. With age, she learned to tone this down. Essentially, she realized that no one cared about her nebulous theories on this world of sellouts, this world of arrant morons addicted to electronic screens and slaughtered animals. When she was their age, her only dream was of revolution. "We were a bit naïve, though," suggests Dominique, her husband, who is saddened to see her unhappy. "Naïve? Maybe, but we weren't as stupid as them." She knows that her husband doesn't understand her ideals, which are mocked by everyone. He listens kindly as she unloads her disappointments and anxieties. She laments what her son has become—"He was such a carefree little boy, you remember?—a man trapped under his wife's thumb, a slave to her lust for money and her vanity. For a long time, she believed that a revolution led by both sexes would give birth to a very different world, where her grandchildren would grow up. A world where there would be time to live. "Darling, you're naïve," Dominique tells her. "Women are capitalists, just like men."

Myriam paces around the kitchen, phone in hand. To soothe the tension, Dominique suggests they go for a walk. Myriam, calming down, wraps up her children in three layers of sweaters, scarves and gloves. Outside in the snow, Mila and Adam run around, ecstatic. Sylvie has brought two old sledges, which belonged to Paul and his brother Patrick when they were children. Myriam makes an effort not to worry and she watches, breath held, as the little ones speed down a slope.

They'll break their necks, she thinks, and I'll cry about it. She constantly tells herself: Louise would understand how I feel.

Paul is enthusiastic. He encourages Mila, who waves at him and says: "Look, Papa. Look, I'm sledging!" They eat lunch at a pleasant inn, a fire crackling in the hearth. They sit near the window, and shafts of dazzling sunlight shine on the children's pink cheeks. Mila is talkative and she makes the adults laugh with her silliness. Adam, for once, eats heartily.

That evening Myriam and Paul take the exhausted children up to their bedroom. Mila and Adam are calm, their limbs weak, their souls filled with happiness and new discoveries. The parents linger near them. Paul sits on the floor and Myriam on the edge of Mila's bed. She gently tucks her in, caresses her hair. For the first time in a long time, Myriam and Paul sing a lullaby together. They learned the words to it when Mila was born and they used to sing it to her in a duet when she was a baby. The children's eyes are closed, but the grown-ups keep singing for the pleasure of accompanying their dreams. So they don't have to leave them.

Paul doesn't dare say this to his wife but, that night, he feels relieved. Since coming to his parents' house, a weight seems to have lifted from his chest. Half-asleep, numb with cold, he thinks about going back to Paris. He imagines his apartment as an aquarium invaded by rotting seaweed, an airless pit where animals with balding fur prowl endlessly, groaning.

Back home, these dark thoughts are quickly forgotten. In the living room, Louise has arranged a bouquet of dahlias. Dinner is ready, the sheets smell clean. After a week in freezing beds, eating chaotic meals at the kitchen table, they are happy to return to their family comforts. It would be impossible, they think, to manage without her. They react like spoiled children, like purring cats.

A few hours after Paul and Myriam's departure, Louise retraces her footsteps and goes back up Rue d'Hauteville. She enters the Massés' apartment and opens the shutters that Myriam had closed. She changes all the sheets, empties the cupboards and dusts the shelves. She shakes out the old Berber rugs that Myriam refuses to get rid of, and vacuums the floors.

Her chores accomplished, she sits on the sofa and dozes. She doesn't leave the apartment all week and spends each day in the living room, with the television on. She never sleeps in Paul and Myriam's bed. She lives on the sofa. In order not to spend any money, she eats whatever she finds in the fridge and makes a start on the reserves in the pantry; Myriam probably has no idea what's in there anyway.

Cookery programs give way to the news, game shows, reality TV shows, a talk show that makes her laugh. She falls asleep in front of a true-crime show called *Enquêtes Criminelles*. One evening she watches an episode about a man found dead in a house on the outskirts of a small

131

mountain town. The shutters were closed for months, the letterbox was overflowing, and yet no one wondered what had become of the house's owner. It was only when the neighborhood was being evacuated that some firemen finally opened the door and discovered the corpse. The body was practically mummified, due to the cold, stale air. Several times the voice-over mentions that it was possible to calculate the date of the man's death only because of some yogurts found in the fridge that were several months past their expiration date.

One afternoon Louise wakes with a start. She had been in one of those sleeps so heavy that they leave you feeling sad, disorientated, your stomach full of tears. A sleep so deep, so dark, that you see yourself dying, that you wake up soaked with cold sweat, paradoxically exhausted. In a panic, she sits up, slaps her own face. Her head aches so badly that she can hardly open her eyes. She can almost hear the sound of her heart thudding. She looks for her shoes. She slips on the floorboards, weeps with rage. She is late. The children will be waiting for her; the school will call; the nursery will notify Myriam of her absence. How could she have fallen asleep? How could she have been so careless? She has to leave, she has to run, but she can't find the apartment keys. She looks everywhere and finally spots them by the fireplace. In the stairway, the front door bangs shut behind her. Outside, she has the feeling that everyone is staring at her and she sprints along the streets, out of breath, like a madwoman. She puts her hand on her side;

she has a stitch and it's killing her, but she doesn't slow down.

There's no one to help her cross the road. Normally there's always someone in a fluorescent vest, holding a little sign. Either that young man with bad teeth whom she suspects has just got out of prison, or that tall black woman who knows all the children's names. There's no one outside the school either. Louise stands there alone, like an idiot. A bitter taste stings her tongue. She wants to throw up. The children aren't there. She walks with her head lowered now, in tears. The children are on vacation. She's alone; she'd forgotten. She hits her own forehead anxiously.

Wafa calls her several times a day, "just for a chat." One evening she asks if she can come around to see Louise. Her bosses are away on vacation too and for once she is free to do what she wants. Louise wonders what Wafa wants from her. She finds it hard to believe that anyone could be so desperate for her company. But she is still haunted by her nightmare from the day before and she agrees.

She arranges to meet her friend outside the Massés' apartment building. In the lobby, Wafa talks loudly about the surprise that she has for Louise, hidden inside the large woven-plastic bag she is carrying. Louise shushes her. She is afraid that someone will hear them. Solemnly she climbs the stairs and opens the door to the apartment. The living room strikes her as heartbreakingly sad and she presses her palms to her eyes. She wants to retrace her steps, to get rid of Wafa, to return to the television which spits out its reassuring swill of images. But Wafa has put her plastic bag on the kitchen countertop and she takes from it some packets of spices, a chicken and one of the glass jars containing her honey candies. "I'm going to cook for you, okay?"

For the first time in her life, Louise sits on the sofa and watches someone make her a meal. Even as a child, she doesn't remember ever seeing anyone do that, just for her, just to make her happy. As a little girl, she used to eat other people's leftovers. She was given lukewarm soup in the morning, a soup that was reheated day after day until every last drop of it was gone. She had to eat all of it despite the cold fat stuck to the sides of the bowl, despite that taste of sour tomatoes, gnawed bones.

Wafa pours her a vodka mixed with ice-cold apple juice. "I like alcohol when it's sweetened," she says, clinking her glass against Louise's. Wafa is still standing. She picks up the ornaments, looks at the shelves of the bookcase. A photograph catches her eye.

"Is that you? You're pretty in that orange dress." In the photograph Louise is smiling, her hair loose. She is sitting on a low wall, holding a child in each arm. Myriam insisted on putting that picture in the living room, on one of the shelves. "You're part of the family," she told the nanny.

Louise remembers clearly the moment when Paul took that photograph. Myriam had gone into a ceramics shop and she was struggling to make up her mind. Louise was looking after the children in the street lined with shops.

Mila stood on the wall. She was trying to catch a gray cat. That was when Paul said: "Louise, kids, look at me. The light's perfect." Mila sat next to Louise and Paul called out: "Now, smile!"

"This year," Louise says, "we're going back to Greece. There, to Sifnos," she adds, pointing at the photograph with her painted fingernail. They haven't talked about this yet, but Louise is certain that they will return to their island, swim in the clear sea and eat dinner on the port, by candlelight. Myriam makes lists, she explains to Wafa, who sits on the floor, at her friend's feet. Lists that she leaves in the living room, even in the sheets of their bed, and she wrote on those lists that they will go back there soon. They will go for walks in rocky inlets. They will trap crabs, sea urchins and sea cucumbers that Louise will watch shrinking at the bottom of a bucket. She will swim, farther and farther out, and this year Adam will join her.

And then, the end of the vacation will draw closer. The day before they return to Paris, they will probably go to that restaurant that Myriam loved so much, where the boss had let the children choose which fish they wanted. There they will drink a bit of wine and Louise will announce her decision not to go back with them. "I'm not going to catch the plane tomorrow. I'm going to live here." Of course, they will be surprised. They won't take her seriously. They'll start laughing, because they'll have had too much to drink or because they're feeling ill at ease. And then, faced with the nanny's resolve, they will start to worry. They will try to talk her around. "Come on, Louise, that makes no sense. You can't stay here. And how will you make a living?" And then it will be Louise's turn to laugh.

"Obviously, I thought about winter." The island must look very different then. These dry rocky hills, these oregano bushes, these thistles must look quite hostile in the November gloom. It must be dark, up there, when the first rains fall. But she won't change her mind: no one will persuade her to return to France. She'll move to a different island, perhaps, but she will never go back.

"Or maybe I won't tell them anything. I'll just disappear, like that," she says, snapping her fingers.

Wafa listens to Louise talk about her plans. She has no trouble imagining those blue horizons, those cobbled streets, those morning swims. She feels terribly homesick. Louise's words awaken memories, the salty smell of the Atlantic in the evening from the coast road, the sunrises greeted by the whole family during Ramadan. But Louise suddenly starts laughing, shattering Wafa's sweet daydream. She laughs like a shy little girl who hides her teeth behind her fingers and she reaches out her hand to her friend, who sits next to her on the sofa. They raise their glasses and make a toast. They look like two young girls now, two schoolmates sharing a private joke, or a secret. Like two children, lost in an adult world.

Wafa has maternal or sisterly instincts. She thinks about getting Louise a drink of water, making her coffee, making her something to eat. Louise stretches out her legs and crosses her feet on the table. Wafa looks at Louise's dirty sole next to her glass, and she thinks that her friend must be drunk to act like that. She has always admired

Louise's manners, her prim politeness, which could pass for that of a real bourgeois lady. Wafa puts her bare feet on the edge of the table. And in a salacious voice, she says: "Maybe you'll meet someone on your island? A handsome Greek man, who'll fall in love with you . . ."

"Oh, no," replies Louise. "If I go there, it's so I don't have to look after anyone anymore. So I can sleep when I want, eat whatever I like."

To begin with, the plan was not to do anything for Wafa's wedding. They would just go to the town hall, sign the documents, and each month Wafa would pay Youssef what she owed him until she had her French papers. But her future husband ended up changing his mind. He suggested to his mother, who was only too willing to comply, that it would be more decent to invite a few friends. "I mean, it is my wedding. Anyway, you never know, it might help convince the immigration services."

One Friday morning they arrange to meet outside the town hall in Noisy-le-Sec. Louise, who is a witness for the first time, wears her sky-blue Peter Pan collar and a pair of earrings. She signs at the bottom of the sheet that the mayor hands her and the wedding seems almost real. The hoorays, the cries of "Here's to the happy couple!," the applause . . . all of it sounds sincere.

The little group walks to the restaurant, La Gazelle d'Agadir, run by a friend of Wafa's, and where she has sometimes worked as a waitress. Louise observes the other guests, who stand around gesticulating, laughing and slapping one another on the shoulder. Outside the restaurant, Youssef's brothers have parked a black sedan with dozens of gold plastic ribbons attached to it.

The restaurant owner has put music on. He's not worried about the neighbors; on the contrary, he thinks it will be good publicity for his restaurant, that people passing in the street will look through the window at the elegantly set tables, that they will envy the guests' happiness. Louise observes the women; she is particularly struck by their broad faces, their thick hands, their wide hips accentuated by belts tied too tight. They speak loudly, they laugh, they call across the room at one another. They surround Wafa, who is sitting at the table of honor and who, Louise gathers, is not allowed to move.

Louise has been seated at the end of the room, far from the window that overlooks the street, next to a man whom Wafa had introduced her to this morning. "I told you about Hervé. He did some work in my studio. He works quite nearby." Wafa deliberately seated her next to him. He is the kind of man she deserves. A man no one wants but who Louise will take, the way she takes old clothes, secondhand magazines with pages missing, even waffles half-eaten by the children.

She is not attracted to Hervé. She is embarrassed by Wafa's knowing looks. She hates this sensation of being spied on, trapped. And besides, this man is so ordinary. There is so little about him to like. For a start, he is barely any taller than Louise. His legs are muscular but short and his hips are narrow. Hardly any neck. When he speaks, he sometimes pulls his head back into his shoulders, like a shy turtle. Louise keeps staring at his hands as they rest on the table: they are a working man's hands, a poor man's hands, a smoker's hands. She has noticed that he has teeth missing. He is not distinguished. He smells of cucumber and wine. The first thing she thinks is that she would be ashamed to introduce him to Myriam and Paul. They would be disappointed. She is sure that they would think this man isn't good enough for her.

Hervé, on the other hand, stares at Louise with the eagerness of an old man for a young woman who has shown a bit of interest in him. He finds her so elegant, so delicate. He notes the slenderness of her neck, the lightness of her earrings. He observes her hands as they writhe in her lap, her little white hands with pink fingernails, her hands that look as if they have not suffered, not been worked to the bone. Louise reminds him of those porcelain dolls he's seen sitting on shelves in the apartments of old ladies where he has gone to do a favor or do some work. Like those dolls, Louise's features are almost motionless; sometimes her frozen expression is absolutely beautiful. She has a way of staring into space that makes Hervé want to remind her of his existence.

He tells her about his job. He's a delivery driver, but not full-time. He also does odd jobs, repairs things, helps people move house. Three days a week he works as a security guard in the parking lot of a bank, on Boulevard Haussmann. "It gives me time to read," he says. "Thrillers mostly, but not always." She doesn't know what to say when he asks her what she reads.

"What about music, then? Do you like music?"

He is mad about it and, with his little purple fingers, he pretends to pluck the strings of a guitar. He talks about life before, in the old days, when people listened to music all the time, when singers were idols. He used to have long hair and worship Jimi Hendrix. "I'll show you a photo," he says. Louise realizes that she has never listened to music. She never got a taste for it. All she knows are nursery rhymes, simple rhyming songs passed on from mother to daughter. One evening, Myriam heard her humming a tune with the children. She told her she had a very nice voice. "It's a shame, you could have been a singer."

Louise has not noticed that most of the guests are not drinking alcohol. In the center of each table there is a bottle of soda and a large carafe of water. Hervé has hidden a bottle of wine on the floor, to his right, and he pours more into Louise's glass whenever it's empty. She drinks slowly. She ends up getting used to the deafening music, the yelling of the guests, the incomprehensible speeches of the young men who talk with their lips too close to the microphone. She even smiles as she watches Wafa and she forgets that all of this is nothing but a masquerade, a fool's game, a hoax.

She drinks and the discomfort of living, the shyness of breathing, all this anguish dissolves in the liquid she sips. The banality of the restaurant, and of Hervé . . . it is all transformed. Hervé has a soft voice and he knows when to shut up. He looks at her and he smiles, eyes lowered to the table. When he has nothing to say, he says nothing. His little lashless eyes, his sparse hair, his purplish skin, his manners no longer displease Louise so much.

She lets Hervé walk her to the metro station. She says good-bye and walks down the steps without turning around. On the way home, Hervé thinks about her. She inhabits him like a catchy song in English, a language he doesn't understand at all, and in which, despite all those years spent listening to music, he continues mangling his favorite choruses.

At 7:30, as she does every morning, Louise opens the front door of the apartment. Paul and Myriam are standing in the living room. They look as if they've been waiting for her. Myriam resembles a half-starved animal that has been prowling its cage all night. Paul turns on the television and, for once, lets the children watch cartoons before they go to school.

"Stay here. Don't move," he orders Mila and Adam, who stare hypnotized, mouths hanging open, at a group of hysterical rabbits.

The adults lock themselves in the kitchen. Paul asks Louise to sit down.

"Shall I make you a coffee?" the nanny asks.

"No, thanks, I'm fine," Paul replies coldly. Behind him, Myriam stares at the floor; her hand touches her lips. "Louise, we received a letter that has put us in a difficult position. I have to admit that we are very upset by what we learned. There are certain things that cannot be tolerated." He says all this in a single breath, his eyes riveted to the envelope in his hands.

Louise stops breathing. She can't even feel her tongue anymore and has to bite her lip to prevent herself crying. She wants to act like a child would: cover her ears, scream, roll on the floor, anything to avoid having this conversation. She tries to identify the letter that Paul is holding, but she can't make out anything: not the address, nor the contents.

Suddenly she feels sure that the letter is from Mrs. Grinberg. The old harpy was probably spying on her while Paul and Myriam were away, and now she is telling them everything. She's written a poison-pen letter, denouncing Louise, insulting her, as a way of distracting herself from her solitude. Undoubtedly she has told them how Louise spent her vacation here. That she invited Wafa. Maybe she even sent the letter anonymously, to add to the mystery, the malice. And besides, she probably invented things, covering the paper with all her old-lady fantasies, her lewd, senile delusions. Louise won't be able to stand it. No, she won't be able to stand the disgusted look on her boss's face, the idea that Myriam will believe that she slept in their bed, that she made fun of them behind their backs.

Louise stiffens. Her fingers are tensed with hate and she hides her hands behind her knees so Paul and Myriam won't see them shaking. Her face and throat are pale. In a rage, she puts her fingers through her hair. Paul, who was waiting for a reaction, goes on.

"This letter is from the tax office, Louise. They're asking us to take from your wages the sum that you owe them—and have apparently owed them for months. You've never replied to single reminder letter!"

Paul could swear he saw relief in the nanny's face.

"I'm well aware that this is humiliating for you, but it's not very pleasant for us either, you know."

Paul hands the letter to Louise, who does not move.

"Look."

Louise takes the envelope and removes the sheet of paper from it, her hands clammy and trembling. Her vision is blurred. She pretends to read the letter, but she doesn't take in a word of it.

"If it's got to this point, it's their last resort, you understand? You can't act so negligently," Myriam explains.

"I'm sorry," she says. "I'm sorry, Myriam. I'll take care of this, I promise."

"I can help you, if you need help. You'll have to bring me all the documents so we can find a solution."

Louise rubs her cheek, palm open, eyes vacant. She knows she ought to say something. She would like to hug Myriam, to ask for her help. She would like to say that she is alone, completely alone, and that so many things have happened, so many things that she hasn't been able to tell anyone, but that she would like to tell her. She is upset, shaky. She doesn't know how to behave.

In the end Louise puts a brave face on it. She claims it is all a misunderstanding. Says something about a change of address. She blames Jacques, her husband, who was so careless and so secretive. She denies it, against all reality, against all the evidence. Her speech is so confused and pathetic that Paul rolls his eyes. "Okay, okay. It's your business, so deal with it. I don't ever want to receive this type of letter again."

The letters had pursued her from Jacques's house to

her studio flat and, finally, here, to her domain, in this household that is held together only by her. They sent her the unpaid bills for Jacques's treatment, the property tax and the fines for its late payment, and some other debts that she doesn't even recognize. She had thought naively that they would just give up if she didn't reply. That she could just play dead. She doesn't represent anything, after all, doesn't possess anything. What can it matter to them? Why do they need to hunt her down?

She knows where the letters are. A pile of envelopes that she has not thrown away, that she has kept under the electric meter. She wanted to burn them. In any case, she doesn't understand any of those interminable sentences, those tables that cover entire pages, those columns of numbers with a total that keeps increasing. It was like when she used to help Stéphanie do her homework. When it came to helping her with math questions, her daughter would laugh and taunt her: "What the hell do you know about it, anyway? You're stupid."

That evening, after putting the children in pajamas, Louise lingers in their bedroom. Myriam stands rigid in the entrance hall, waiting for her. "You can go now. We'll see you tomorrow." Louise wishes she could stay. She wishes she could sleep here, at the foot of Mila's bed. She wouldn't make any noise; she wouldn't disturb anyone. Louise doesn't want to go back to her studio. Every evening she gets home a little later, and when she walks in the street she keeps her eyes lowered, her chin covered by a scarf. She is afraid of bumping into her landlord, an old man with red hair and bloodshot eyes. A miser who only trusted her "because renting to a white in this neighborhood is practically unheard of." He must be regretting his decision now.

On the train, she grits her teeth to stop herself crying. An icy, insidious rain soaks into her coat, her hair. Heavy drops fall from porches and slide down the back of her neck, making her shiver. At the corner of her street, even though it's empty, she feels she is being watched. She turns around, but there's no one there. Then, in the darkness, between two cars, she spots a man squatting on his haunches. She sees his two naked thighs, his huge hands resting on his knees. In one hand he holds a newspaper. He looks at her. He does not appear hostile or embarrassed. She recoils, feeling suddenly nauseated. She wants to scream, to make someone else witness the spectacle. A man is shitting in her street, under her nose. A man who apparently has no shame left and must have got used to doing his business without any modesty or dignity.

Louise runs to the door of her building. She is trembling as she climbs the stairs. She cleans her entire apartment. She changes the sheets. She would like to wash herself, to stand under a jet of hot water for a long time, until she's warmed up, but a few days ago the shower collapsed—the rotten floorboards under the cubicle gave way—and now it is out of order. Since then she has been washing herself in the sink, with a washcloth. She shampooed her hair three days ago, sitting on the Formica chair.

Lying on her bed, she is unable to fall asleep. She can't stop thinking about that man in the shadows. She can't help imagining that, soon, that will be her. That she'll be on the street. That she will have to leave even this vile apartment and that she will shit in the street, like an animal.

The next morning, Louise can't get up. All night she's been feverish, to the point that her teeth chattered. Her throat is swollen and full of ulcers. Even her own saliva seems impossible to swallow. It's just after 7:30 when the telephone starts to ring. She doesn't answer. And yet she sees Myriam's name on the screen. She opens her eyes, reaches out to the phone and hangs up. She buries her face in the pillow.

The telephone rings again.

This time Myriam leaves a message. "Hello, Louise, I hope you're well. It's nearly eight o'clock. Mila has been ill since last night—she has a fever. I have a very important case today, as I told you, and I need to be in court. I hope everything's all right, and that nothing has happened. Call me back when you get this message. We're expecting you." Louise throws the phone to the foot of the bed and rolls herself up in the bedcovers. She tries to forget that she is thirsty and desperate to urinate. She doesn't want to move.

She has pushed her bed against the wall, closer to the feeble warmth of the radiator. Lying like this, her nose is almost pressed up to the windowpane. Eyes turned to the skeletal trees in the street, she can find no way out. She has the strange certainty that all struggle is futile. That all she can do is let events carry her away, wash over her, overwhelm her, while she remains passive and inert. The day before, she gathered all the envelopes. She opened them and tore up the letters, one by one. She threw the pieces in the sink and turned on the tap. Once they were wet, the scraps of paper stuck together, forming a foul paste that she watched disintegrate under the trickle of hot water. The telephone rings, again and again. Louise has covered it with a cushion, but the shrill ringing stops her falling back asleep.

In the apartment, Myriam paces around in a panic, her lawyer's robes draped on the stripy chair. "She's not coming back," she tells Paul. "This won't be the first time that a nanny has just vanished overnight. I've heard lots of stories like that." She tries calling her again, but in the face of Louise's silence she feels completely helpless. She blames Paul. She accuses him of having been too harsh, of treating Louise like a mere employee. "We humiliated her," she says.

Paul tries to reason with his wife. Perhaps Louise has a problem; something probably happened. She would never dare abandon them like this, without an explanation. And she's so attached to the children, she couldn't leave them without saying good-bye. "Instead of coming up with crackpot theories, you should find out her address. Look on her contract. If she doesn't answer in the next hour, I'll go to her apartment."

Myriam is crouched on the floor, going through the drawers, when the telephone rings. In a barely audible voice, Louise makes her excuses. She is so ill that she hasn't managed to get out of bed. She fell asleep this morning and didn't hear her phone ringing. At least ten times she repeats, "I'm sorry." Myriam is caught out by this simple explanation. She feels slightly ashamed not to have even thought of it: a straightforward health problem. As if Louise were infallible, her body immune to fatigue and illness. "I understand," Myriam replies. "Get some rest. We'll find another solution."

Paul and Myriam call friends, colleagues, family. Finally someone gives them the number of a female student who "can help out if you're desperate," and who, thankfully, agrees to go to their apartment straightaway. The girl—a pretty blonde of twenty—does not inspire much confidence in Myriam. After entering the apartment, she slowly takes off her high-heeled ankle boots. Myriam notices that she has a hideous tattoo on her neck. To every recommendation that Myriam makes, she replies "Yeah" without really seeming to understand, as if she just wants to get rid of this nervous, nagging boss. With Mila, who is dozing on the sofa, she overdoes the solicitude, acting like a worried mother when the truth is she is still a child herself.

But it's in the evening, when she goes home, that Myriam is overwhelmed. The apartment is in chaos. Toys are scattered all over the living-room floor. The dirty dishes have been tossed in the sink. There are dried-out mashed-carrot stains on the little table. The girl gets to her feet, as relieved as a prisoner freed from her cell. She

153

stuffs the cash in her pocket and runs to the door, mobile in hand. Later Myriam finds a dozen hand-rolled cigarette stubs on the balcony and, on the blue chest of drawers in the children's bedroom, some chocolate ice cream that has melted, damaging the paintwork.

For three days Louise has nightmares. She doesn't sink into sleep but into a sort of perverse lethargy, where her thoughts become scrambled and her unease is intensified. At night she is inhabited by a silent screaming inside her that tears at her guts. Her blouse stuck to her chest, her teeth grinding, she hollows out a furrow in the sofa bed's mattress. She feels as if her face is being crushed under a boot heel, as if her mouth is full of dirt. Her hips twitch like a tadpole's tail. She is totally exhausted. She wakes up to drink and go to the toilet, then returns to her nest.

She emerges from sleep the way you might rise up from the depths after you have swum too far, when you are oxygen-deprived, the water is a black sticky magma, and you are praying that you still have enough air, enough strength to reach the surface and breathe in, greedily, at last.

In her little notebook with the flower-patterned cover, she noted the term used by a doctor at the Henri-Mondor hospital. "Delirious melancholia." Louise had thought that was beautiful; it seemed to bestow a touch of poetry and

155

escape on her sadness. She wrote it down in her strange handwriting, all twisted, slanting capital letters. On the pages of that little notebook, the words resemble those shaky wooden constructions that Adam builds with blocks purely for the pleasure of watching them collapse.

For the first time, she thinks about old age. About her body, which is starting to malfunction; about the movements that make her ache deep in her bones. About her growing medical expenses. And then the fear of growing old and sick, bedridden, terminal, in this apartment with its dirty windows. It has become an obsession. She hates this place. She can't stop thinking about the smell of damp coming from the shower cubicle. She can taste it in her mouth. All the joints, all the cracks are filled with a greenish mold, and no matter how furiously she scrubs at them, they grow back during the night, thicker than ever.

Hate rises up inside her. A hate that clashes with her servile urges, her childlike optimism. A hate that muddies everything. She is absorbed by a sad, confused dream. Haunted by the feeling that she has seen too much, heard too much of other people's privacy, a privacy she has never enjoyed herself. She has never had her own bedroom.

After two nights of anguish, she feels ready to start work again. She has lost weight and her girlish face, pale and gaunt, looks as if it's been beaten into a narrower shape. She does her hair and makeup. She calms herself with layers of mauve eyeshadow.

At 7:30 a.m, she opens the front door of the apartment on Rue d'Hauteville. Mila, in her blue pajamas, runs at the nanny and jumps into her arms. She says: "Louise, it's you! You came back!"

In his mother's arms, Adam struggles. He has heard Louise's voice, he has recognized her smell of talc, the light sound of her footsteps on the wooden floor. With his little hands, he pushes himself away from his mother's chest. Smiling, Myriam hands her child into Louise's loving arms.

In Myriam's refrigerator, there are boxes. Very small boxes, piled neatly on top of one another. There are bowls, covered in aluminum foil. On the plastic shelves are little slices of lemon, a stale cucumber end, a quarter of an onion whose smell pervades the kitchen as soon as you open the fridge door. A piece of cheese with nothing but the rind remaining. In the boxes Myriam finds a few peas that are no longer round or bright green. Three bits of ravioli. A spoonful of broth. A shred of turkey that wouldn't feed a sparrow, but which Louise carefully kept anyway.

Paul and Myriam joke about this. This mania of Louise's, this phobia of throwing away food, makes them laugh at first. The nanny scrapes out the last morsels from jam jars; she makes the children lick out their pots of yogurt. Her employers find this ludicrous and touching.

Paul makes fun of Myriam when she takes out the trash bags in the middle of the night because they contain leftover food or a toy of Mila's that they can't be bothered to fix. "You're scared of being told off by Louise—admit it!" he laughs, following her into the stairwell.

They find it amusing to watch Louise study, with great concentration, the junk mail from local shops that is delivered to their letterbox and which they are used to throwing away without a thought. The nanny collects coupons and proudly presents them to Myriam, who is ashamed to find this behavior idiotic. In fact, Myriam uses Louise as an example when she lectures her husband and children. "Louise is right. It's bad to waste food. There are children who have nothing to eat."

But after a few months, Louise's obsession becomes the subject of tension. Myriam complains about the nanny's inflexible attitude, her paranoia. "Let her search through our garbage if she wants! I don't have to justify myself to her," she tells Paul, who is convinced that they have to free themselves from Louise's power. Myriam stands firm. She refuses to let Louise give the children food that is past its expiration date. "Yes, even if it's only one day past. That's it, end of discussion."

One evening, not long after Louise has returned to work following her illness, Myriam comes home late. The apartment is in total darkness and Louise is waiting at the door, wearing her coat and holding her handbag. She mumbles good-bye and rushes downstairs. Myriam is too tired to think about this or feel troubled by it.

Louise is sulking? Oh, who cares!

She could collapse on the sofa and fall asleep fully dressed, with her shoes still on. But she moves toward the kitchen, to get herself a glass of wine. She feels like sitting in the living room for a moment, drinking some very cold white wine, smoking a cigarette and relaxing. If she wasn't afraid that she would wake the children, she might even take a bath.

She enters the kitchen and turns on the light. The room looks even cleaner than usual. There's a strong smell of soap in the air. The fridge door has been cleaned. Nothing has been left on the countertop. The extractor hood over the cooker is free of grease stains, and the handles on the cupboard doors have been sponged off. As for the window facing her, it is spotlessly, dazzlingly clean.

Myriam is about to open the fridge when she sees it. There, in the middle of the little table where the children and their nanny eat. A chicken carcass sits on a plate. A glistening carcass, without the smallest scrap of flesh hanging from its bones, not the faintest trace of meat. It looks as if it's been gnawed clean by a vulture or a stubborn, meticulous insect. Some kind of repulsive animal, anyway.

She stares at the brown skeleton, its round spine, its sharp bones, its smooth vertebrae. Its thighs have been torn off, but its twisted little wings are still there, the joints distended, close to breaking point. The shiny, yellowish cartilage resembles dried pus. Through the holes, between the small bones, Myriam sees the empty insides of the thorax, dark and bloodless. No meat remains, no organs, nothing on this skeleton that could rot, and yet it seems to Myriam that it is a putrescent carcass, a vile corpse that is festering and decaying before her eyes, here in the kitchen.

She is sure of it: she threw away that chicken this morning. The meat was no longer edible; she didn't want her children to get ill from eating it. She remembers clearly how she shook the plate over the trash can and how the creature fell, covered in gelatinous fat. It landed with a wet thud at the bottom of the trash and Myriam said, "Ugh." That smell, so early in the morning, made her feel sick.

Myriam moves closer to the creature, but she doesn't dare touch it. Louise can't have done this by mistake or out of forgetfulness. And certainly not as a joke. No, the carcass smells of washing liquid and sweet almond. Louise washed it in the sink; she cleaned it and put it there as an act of vengeance, like a baleful totem.

Later Mila told her mother exactly what happened. She was laughing and jumping around as she explained how Louise had taught them to eat with their fingers. Standing on their chairs, she and Adam had scratched away at the bones. The meat was dry and Louise let them drink big glasses of Fanta as they ate, so they wouldn't choke. She was very careful not to damage the skeleton and she never took her eyes off the creature. She told them that it was a game and that she would reward them if they followed the rules exactly. And when it was over, they were allowed to eat two lemon drops as a special treat.

HECTOR ROUVIER

It's been ten years, but Hector Rouvier vividly remembers Louise's hands. That was what he touched most often, her hands. They smelled like crushed petals and her nails were always polished. Hector squeezed those hands, held them against him; he felt them on the back of his neck when he watched a film on television. Louise's hands plunged into hot water and rubbed Hector's skinny body. They massaged soap bubbles in his hair, slid under his armpits, washed his penis, his belly, his bottom.

Lying on the bed, face buried in his pillow, he would lift up his pajama top to let Louise know that he was waiting for her to caress him. She would run her fingernails down his back and his skin would get goosebumps, and he'd shiver, and fall asleep, soothed and slightly ashamed, with a vague understanding of the strange excitation into which Louise's fingers had sent him.

On the way to school, Hector would hold very tight to the nanny's hands. As he got older and his palms grew bigger, he felt increasingly worried that he might crush Louise's bones, her biscuit-like, porcelain bones. The nanny's knuckles would crack inside the child's palm, and sometimes Hector thought that the was the one holding Louise's hand, helping her to cross the road.

No, Louise was never harsh. He doesn't remember ever seeing her get angry. He's sure of that; she never lifted a hand to him. Despite all the years he spent with her, his memories are vague, blurry. Louise's face seems distant to him; he isn't sure he would recognize her today if he happened to pass her in the street. But the feel of her cheek, soft and smooth; the smell of her powder, which she put on every morning and evening; the sensation of her beige tights on his child's face; the strange way she had of kissing him, sometimes using her teeth, biting him as if to signify the sudden savagery of her love, her desire to completely possess him. Yes, all this he remembers.

He hasn't forgotten her culinary talents either. The cakes she would bring with her when she met him at the school gates and the way she would rejoice in the little boy's gluttony. The taste of her tomato sauce; the way she would pepper the steaks that she hardly cooked at all; her creamy mushroom sauce . . . these are memories that he often evokes. A mythology linked to his childhood, of the world before frozen meals eaten in front of his computer screen.

He also remembers—or, rather, he thinks he remembers—that she was infinitely patient with him. With his parents, the ceremony of bedtime often went wrong. Anne Rouvier, his mother, would lose patience when Hector cried, begged her to leave the door open, asked for another story, a glass of water, swore that he'd seen a monster, that he was still hungry.

"I'm the same," Louise had confessed to him. "I'm afraid of falling asleep too." She indulged him when he had nightmares and sometimes she would stroke his temples for hours, her long, rose-scented fingers accompanying him on his journey toward sleep. She had persuaded her boss to leave a light on in the child's bedroom. "There's no point in terrifying him like that."

Yes, her departure had been a wrench. He missed her terribly, and he hated the young woman who replaced her, a student who would pick him up from school, who spoke English to him, who—in his mother's words—stimulated him intellectually." He blamed Louise for abandoning him, for not keeping the impassioned promises she had made, for betraying those solemn oaths of everlasting love, after swearing to him that he was the only one and that no one could ever take his place. One day she wasn't there anymore and Hector didn't dare ask any questions. He wasn't able to mourn the woman who had left him because, even though he was only eight, he intuitively knew that this particular love was laughable, that people would make fun of him, and that anyone who felt sorry for him would be pretending.

Hector lowers his head. He stops talking. His mother is sitting on a chair next to him, and she puts her hand on his shoulder. She tells him: "You did well, darling." But Anne is nervous. Facing the police, she looks guilty. She is trying to find something to confess, some sin she committed long ago, for which they want to punish her. She has always been like this, innocent and paranoid. She has never gone through a security check without sweating. One day, sober and pregnant, she blew into a breathalyzer test, convinced that she was about to be arrested.

The captain, a pretty woman with thick brown hair tied back in a ponytail, is sitting on her desk, facing them. She asks Anne how she came into contact with Louise and the reasons she chose to hire her as her children's nanny. Anne replies calmly. All she wants is to satisfy the policewoman, to help her with her enquiries, and—most of all—to find out what Louise is accused of.

Louise was recommended to her by a friend, who spoke very highly of her. And, for that matter, she herself was always satisfied with her nanny. "Hector, as you can tell, was very attached to her."

The captain smiles at the teenage boy. She goes back behind her desk, opens a file and asks: "Do you remember the phone call you got from Mrs. Massé? Just over a year ago, in January?"

"Mrs. Massé?"

"Yes, try to remember. Louise gave you as a reference and Myriam Massé wanted to know what you thought of her."

"That's right, I remember now. I told her that Louise was an exceptional nanny."

They have been sitting for more than two hours in this cold, featureless room. The desk is very neat. There are no photographs on it. There are no wanted posters on the wall. Occasionally the captain stops in the middle of a sentence, apologizes and leaves the office. Anne and her son see her through the window, talking on her mobile phone, whispering in a colleague's ear or drinking a coffee. They have no desire to speak to each other, not even to relieve the boredom. Sitting side by side, they avoid each other, pretending that they have forgotten they are not alone. Sometimes they sigh or stand up and walk around a bit. Hector checks his phone. Anne cradles her black leather handbag. They are bored stiff, but they are too polite and too fearful to show any sign of irritation to the policewoman. Exhausted, submissive, they wait to be released.

The captain prints some documents and hands them to mother and son.

"Sign here and here, please."

Anne bends over the sheet of paper and, without looking up, she asks in a hollow voice: "What did she do? Louise, I mean. What happened?"

"She is accused of killing two children."

There are dark rings around the captain's eyes. Swollen, purplish bags that give her a solemn look and, oddly, make her even prettier.

Hector walks out into the street, into the June heat. The girls are beautiful and he wants to grow up, to be free, to be a man. His eighteen years weigh heavily on him; he'd like to leave them behind, like he left his mother at the door of the police station, dazed and numb. He realizes that what he first felt earlier, when the policewoman told them, was not shock or surprise but an immense and painful relief. A feeling of jubilation, even. As if he'd always known that some menace had hung over him, a pale, sulfurous, unspeakable menace. A menace that he alone, with his child's eyes and heart, was capable of perceiving. Fate had decreed that the calamity would strike elsewhere.

The captain had seemed to understand him. Earlier she had examined his impassive face and she had smiled at him. The way you smile at survivors.

All night long Myriam thinks about that carcass on the kitchen table. As soon as she shuts her eyes, she imagines the animal's skeleton, right there, next to her, in her bed.

She gulped down her wine, one hand on the little table, watching the carcass from the corner of her eye. She was revolted by the idea of touching it. She had the strange feeling that something might happen if she did, that the creature might come back to life and jump at her face, cling to her hair, push her against the wall. She smoked a cigarette by the living-room window and went back into the kitchen. She put on a pair of plastic gloves and threw the skeleton in the trash. She also threw away the plate and the tea towel that had been lying next to it. She hurried downstairs with the black bags and banged the building's front door behind her when she came back in.

She goes to bed. Her heart is pounding so hard in her chest that she finds it hard to breathe. She tries to sleep and then, unable to bear it any longer, she calls Paul and in tears tells him this story of the chicken. He thinks she's overreacting. It's like the script of a bad horror film, he laughs. "Surely you're not going to get into a state like this because of a chicken?' He tries to make her laugh, to make her question the gravity of the situation. Myriam hangs up on him. He tries to call her back but she doesn't answer.

Her insomnia is haunted by accusatory thoughts and then by guilty thoughts. She starts by hurling abuse at Louise. Then she thinks that the nanny must be mad. Maybe dangerous. That she nurses a sordid hatred for her employers, an appetite for vengeance. Myriam blames herself for not having guessed at the violence of which Louise is capable. She had already noticed that the nanny gets angry about this kind of thing. Once, Mila lost a cardigan at school and Louise threw a fit about it. Every day she talked to Myriam about that blue cardigan. She swore she would find it; she harassed the teacher, the caretaker, the dinner ladies. One Monday morning she saw Myriam dressing Mila. The little girl was wearing the blue cardigan.

"You found it?" the nanny asked, looking ecstatic.

"No, but I bought another one."

Louise became uncontrollably angry. "I can't believe I tried so desperately to find it. And what does that mean? You get robbed, you don't take care of your things, but it doesn't matter because Mama will buy Mila a new cardigan?"

And then Myriam turns these accusations against herself. It's my fault, she thinks. I went too far. It was her way of telling me that I was wasteful, frivolous, casual.

Louise must have been offended that I threw away that chicken, when I know that she has money problems. Instead of helping her, I humiliated her.

She gets up at dawn, feeling as if she's hardly slept. When she gets out of bed, she immediately sees that the kitchen light is on. She comes out of her bedroom and sees Louise, sitting in front of the little window that overlooks the courtyard. The nanny is holding her cup of tea—the cup that Myriam bought her for her birthday—in both hands. Her face floats in a cloud of steam. Louise looks like a little old lady, like a ghost trembling in the pale morning. Her hair and her skin are drained of all color. Myriam has the impression that Louise always wears the same clothes nowadays. She feels suddenly sickened by that blue blouse with its Peter Pan collar. She wishes she didn't have to speak to her. She wishes she could make her disappear from her life, with no effort, with a snap of the fingers or a blink of the eyes. But Louise is there; she smiles at her.

In her thin voice, she asks: "Shall I make you a coffee? You look tired."

Myriam reaches out and takes the hot cup.

She thinks about the long day that awaits her; she has to defend a man in court. In her kitchen, face-to-face with Louise, she considers the irony of the situation. She, Myriam Massé—whose pugnacity everyone admires; whose courage when confronting her adversaries Pascal always praises—is terrified by this little blonde woman.

Some teenagers dream of movie sets, football pitches, concert halls packed with fans. Myriam always dreamed of courtrooms. Even as a student, she tried to go as often as she could to watch trials. Her mother didn't understand how anyone could be so passionate about sordid accounts of rapes, about precise, deadpan descriptions of seedy murders or cases of incest. Myriam was preparing for the Bar exam when the trial of the serial killer Michel Fourniret began. She followed the case closely. She'd rented a room in the center of Charleville-Mézières and every day she would join the group of housewives who had come to observe the monster. Outside the courthouse an immense tent had been put up, where the crowd could watch the trial broadcast live on a giant screen. She stood slightly apart from the others. She didn't speak to them. She felt uneasy when these red-faced, short-haired women with their close-cut fingernails would greet the van containing the accused with screamed insults and gobs of spit. Myriam, so full of her principles, so rigid sometimes, was fascinated by that spectacle of open hate, by those calls for vengeance.

Myriam takes the metro and reaches the courthouse early. She smokes a cigarette, her fingertips holding the red string that encircles her huge dossier. For more than a month Myriam has been helping Pascal prepare for this trial. The defendant, a twenty-four-year-old man, is accused of committing a hate crime—along with three accomplices—on two Sri Lankan men. Under the influence of alcohol and cocaine, they beat up the two illegal immigrants, who were employed as cooks. They hit them again and again, hit them until one of the men died, hit them until they realized they had got the wrong men; that they had got their darkies mixed up. They weren't able to explain why. They weren't able to deny the charge either, as they'd been caught in the act by surveillance cameras.

During the first meeting, the man told his lawyers his life story, an account littered with obvious lies and exaggerations. On the threshold of life imprisonment, he tried to charm Myriam. She did all she could to keep a "good distance." That was the expression that Pascal always used; the basis, he said, of a successful case. She sought to disentangle truth from falsehood, methodically, with the evidence to back her up. In her teacher's voice, choosing simple but sharp words, she explained that lying was a poor defense technique and that he had nothing to lose now by telling the truth.

For the trial, she bought the young man a new shirt and advised him not to tell his sick jokes, and to wipe that smug smirk off his face. "We have to prove that you, too, are a victim."

Myriam manages to concentrate, and the work allows her to forget her night of horror. She questions the two experts who stand in the dock to talk about her client's psychological profile. One of the victims gives evidence, with the aid of a translator. The testimony is laborious but the public's emotion is palpable. The accused keeps his eyes lowered, his face impassive.

During a pause in proceedings, while Pascal is on the telephone, Myriam sits in a corridor, staring into space, seized with a sudden panic. She was probably too high-handed in the way she dealt with that issue of Louise's debts. Out of discretion or indifference, she didn't look at the letter from the tax office in much detail. She should have kept the documents, she thinks. Dozens of times she asked Louise to bring them to her. To start with, Louise said she had forgotten them, that she'd think about it tomorrow, she promised. Myriam tried to find out more. She questioned her about Jacques, about those debts that seemed to go back years. She asked her if Stéphanie was aware of her difficulties. But these questions, asked in a gentle, understanding voice, elicited nothing from Louise but an impenetrable silence. It's modesty, Myriam thought. A way of maintaining the frontier between our two worlds. So she gave up trying to help her. She had the awful feeling that her questions were like the lashes of a whip on Louise's fragile body, that body which for the previous few days had seemed to be turning pale, withering, fading away. In this dark corridor, filled by a nagging murmur of voices, Myriam feels bereft, prey to a deep and heavy exhaustion.

This morning Paul called her back. He was gentle and conciliatory. He apologized for having reacted so stupidly. For not having taken her seriously. "We'll do what you want," he told her. "In these circumstances, we can't keep her." And, pragmatic, he added: "We'll wait for the summer. We'll go on vacation, and when we get back we'll make it clear to her that we don't really need her anymore."

Myriam replied in a hollow voice, without conviction. She thinks again of how thrilled the children were when they saw the nanny again after she had been ill for a few days. Of the sad look that Louise had given her. Of her moonlike face. She hears again her hazy and slightly ludicrous excuses, her shame at having failed in her duty. "It won't happen again," she said. "I promise."

Of course, all she has to do is put an end to it. But Louise has the keys to their apartment; she knows everything; she has embedded herself so deeply in their lives that it now seems impossible to remove her. They will drive her away and she'll come back. They'll say their good-byes and she'll knock at the door, she'll come in anyway; she'll threaten them, like a wounded lover.

STÉPHANIE

Stéphanie was very lucky. When she started secondary school, Mrs. Perrin—Louise's employer—offered to enroll the young girl in a Parisian school, one with a much better reputation than the school in Bobigny she was due to attend. The woman had wanted to do a good deed for poor Louise, who worked so hard and was so deserving.

But Stéphanie did not repay this act of generosity. The troubles began only a few weeks after the start of the school year. She disturbed the class. She couldn't stop laughing, throwing objects across the classroom, swearing at her teachers. The other pupils found her simultaneously funny and tiresome. She hid from Louise the notes in her parent-teacher contact book, the warnings, the meetings with the headmaster. She started bunking off and smoking joints in the morning, lying on a bench in a little park in the fifteenth arrondissement.

One evening Mrs. Perrin summoned the nanny to tell her how disappointed she was. She felt betrayed. Because of Louise, she had been humiliated. She had lost face with the headmaster, whom she had spent so long persuading and who had been doing her a favor by accepting Stéphanie. A week later Stéphanie was summoned to the disciplinary council, which Louise was also expected to attend. "It's like a court," her boss explained coldly. "You will have to defend her."

At 3 p.m., Louise and her daughter entered a round, poorly heated room with large windows made of green and blue glass that spread a churchlike light. A dozen people—teachers, counselors, parent-teacher representatives—were sitting around a large wooden table. They all spoke in turn. "Stéphanie is a misfit, undisciplined and rude." "She's not a bad girl," someone added. "But once she gets started, there's no reasoning with her." They are surprised that Louise never reacted, given the scale of this problem. That she didn't respond to the teachers' requests for meetings. They had called her on her mobile. They had even left messages, but she never called them back.

Louise begged them to give her daughter another chance. She explained, in tears, how well she took care of her children; how she punished them when they didn't listen. How she didn't allow them to watch television while doing their homework. She said she had strong principles and a great deal of experience in the education of children. Mrs. Perrin had warned her: this was a trial, and she was the one being judged. Her, the bad mother.

Around the large wooden table, in this freezing room where they all kept their coats on, the teachers tilted their heads sideways. They repeated: "We are not questioning your efforts, madam. We are certain that you are doing your best."

A French teacher—a slim, gentle woman—asked her: "How many brothers and sisters does Stéphanie have?"

"She doesn't have any," replied Louise.

"But you were talking about your children, weren't you?"

"Yes, the children I look after. The ones who stay with me every day. And believe me, my boss is very pleased with the education that I give her children."

They asked her to leave the room so they could deliberate. Louise stood up and smiled at them in a way that she imagined made her look like a woman of the world. In the school corridor, opposite the basketball court, Stéphanie kept laughing idiotically. She was too fat, too tall, and she looked ridiculous with that ponytail on the top of her head. She was wearing printed leggings that made her thighs look enormous. She did not seem intimidated by the formal nature of this meeting, merely bored. She wasn't afraid; on the contrary, she kept smiling knowingly, as if these teachers in their nerdy mohair sweaters and their old-lady scarves were just bad actors.

As soon as she left the meeting room, her good mood returned, along with her dunce's swagger. In the corridor she collared some friends who were coming out of class. She jumped up and down and whispered secrets in the ear of a shy girl who suppressed a laugh. Louise wanted to slap her, to shake her as violently as she could. She wished she could make her understand how humiliating and exhausting it was bringing up a daughter like her. She wished she could rub Stéphanie's nose in her sweat and her anxieties, could wipe that stupid, carefree smile off her face. She wanted to rip apart what remained of her childhood.

In that noisy corridor, Louise forced herself not to tremble. She gradually reduced Stéphanie to silence by tightening her fingers' grip around her daughter's chubby arm.

"You can come back in."

The headmaster poked his head through the doorway and beckoned them to return to their seats. The deliberation had taken only ten minutes, but Louise didn't realize that was a bad sign.

Once the mother and daughter had sat down again, the headmaster began to speak. Stéphanie, he explained, was a disruptive element that all of them had tried and failed to control. They had used every educational method they knew, but nothing had worked. They had exhausted every possibility. They had a responsibility and they simply could not allow her to take an entire class hostage. "Perhaps," he added, "Stéphanie would be more comfortable in a neighborhood closer to home. In an environment more suited to her, where she would have more points of reference. You understand?"

This was March. It still felt like winter. It seemed as if the cold weather would never end. "If you need help with the administrative aspects, there are people for that," the career adviser reassured her. Louise did not understand. Stéphanie was expelled.

On the bus home, Louise stayed silent. Stéphanie

giggled; she looked through the window, earbuds stuck in her ears. They walked up the gray street that led to Jacques's house. They passed the market and Stéphanie slowed down to look at the stalls. Louise felt a surge of hate for her; for her offhand reaction, her adolescent self-ishness. She grabbed her by the sleeve and dragged her away with incredible strength and abruptness. Anger filled her, an anger that grew ever darker and more heated. She wanted to dig her nails into her daughter's soft skin.

She opened the small front door. Barely had she closed it behind them than she started showering Stéphanie with blows. She hit her on the back to start with, heavy punches that threw her daughter to the floor. The teenager curled up in a ball and cried out. Louise kept hitting her. She summoned all her colossal strength. Again and again her tiny hands slapped Stéphanie's face. She tore her hair and pulled apart the girl's arms, uncovering her head. She hit her in the eyes. She insulted her. She scratched her until she bled. When Stéphanie didn't move anymore, Louise spat in her face.

Jacques heard the noise and he went up to the window. He watched Louise punishing her daughter but made no attempt to separate them.

The silences and misunderstandings have infected everything. In the apartment, the atmosphere grows heavier. Myriam tries not to let the children perceive it, but she is more distant with Louise. She speaks to her in a clipped voice, giving her precise instructions. She follows Paul's advice, which she repeats to herself: "She's our employee, not our friend."

They no longer drink tea together in the kitchen, Myriam sitting at the table and Louise leaning on the countertop. Myriam no longer pays her compliments: "Louise, you're an angel" or "You're the best nanny in the world." She no longer offers, on Friday nights, to share a bottle of rosé, forgotten at the back of the fridge. "The children are watching a video. Why don't we have some fun too?" Myriam used to say. Now, when one of them opens the door, the other closes it behind her. They are hardly ever in the same room anymore, the two of them avoiding each other's presence in a perfectly synced choreography.

Then spring comes, dazzling and sudden. The days grow longer and the first buds brighten the trees. The good weather sweeps away their winter habits; Louise takes the children outside, to parks. One evening she asks Myriam if she can finish earlier. "I have a date," she explains, her voice trembling slightly.

She meets Hervé in the neighborhood where he works. Together they go to the cinema. Hervé would rather have gone for a drink on the terrace of a café, but Louise insisted. And she likes the film so much that they go back to see it again the following week. Next to her in the darkness, Hervé dozes discreetly.

In the end she agrees to have a drink with him on a terrace, outside a bar on one of the Grands Boulevards. Hervé is a happy man, she thinks. He smiles as he talks about his plans. The vacations they could take together in the Vosges. They would go skinny-dipping in the lakes; they would sleep in a mountain chalet belonging to a man he knows. And they would listen to music all the time. He would play her his record collection and he is sure that, very soon, she wouldn't be able to live without music. Hervé is ready to retire and he can't imagine enjoying those years of rest and relaxation on his own. His marriage ended in divorce fifteen years ago. He has no children and solitude weighs heavily on him.

Hervé tried every ploy in the book before Louise finally agreed, one evening, to go home with him. He waits for her at the Paradis, the café opposite the Massés' apartment building. They take the metro together and Hervé puts his red-skinned hand on Louise's knee. As she listens to him, her eyes are fixed on that hand, that man's hand which settles, starts to move, wants more. That discreet hand which tries to hide its intentions.

They make love clumsily, him on top of her, their chins sometimes banging together. Lying on her, he grunts, but she doesn't know if it's a grunt of pleasure or because his joints are hurting and she's not helping him. Hervé is so short that she can feel his ankles against hers—his thick ankles, his hairy feet—and, to her, this contact seems more incongruous, more intrusive than the man's sex organ inside her. Jacques was so tall and he made love like he was punishing her, angrily. After this embrace, Hervé emerges relieved, as if a heavy weight has been lifted from him, and he acts more familiarly toward her.

It was here, in Hervé's bed, in his council house in the Porte de Saint-Ouen, with the man asleep beside her, that she thought about a baby. A tiny baby, just born, a baby completely enveloped in that warm smell of life just beginning. A baby abandoned to love, which she would dress in pastel-colored romper suits and which would be passed from her arms to Myriam's and then to Paul's. A newborn that would bind them more closely to one another, bringing them together in the same surge of tenderness. That would erase all the misunderstandings, the dissensions, that would give meaning to their daily habits. She would rock this baby on her knees for hours in a little room, illuminated only by a nightlight that would project boats and islands on to the wall. She would caress its bald head and gently insert her little finger into its mouth. The child would stop crying then, sucking her polished fingernail with its swollen gums.

The next day she makes Paul and Myriam's bed more carefully than usual. She moves her hand over the sheets. She searches for a trace of their lovemaking, a trace of the child she is now sure is going to arrive. She asks Mila if she would like a little brother or a little sister. "A baby we could look after together—what do you think?" Louise hopes that Mila will talk about this to her mother, that she will whisper this idea into her ear and from there it will enter her mind and grow stronger. And one day the little girl asks Myriam, under Louise's delighted gaze, if she has a baby in her belly. "Oh, God, no, I'd rather die!" Myriam laughs.

Louise thinks that is bad. She doesn't understand Myriam's laughter, the lighthearted way she answers this question. Myriam is saying that, she thinks, to ward off bad luck. She feigns indifference, but she thinks about it all the same. In September, Adam too will start school; the house will be empty, and Louise will have nothing to do. Another child has to arrive to fill the long winter days.

Louise listens to conversations. It's a small apartment—she isn't doing it deliberately—but she ends up knowing everything. Except that, recently, Myriam has been speaking more quietly. She closes the door behind her when she talks on the phone. She whispers, her lips just above Paul's shoulder. They look as if they are keeping secrets.

Louise talks to Wafa about this child that will soon be born. About the joy it will bring, and the extra work. "With three children, they won't be able to do without me." Louise has moments of euphoria. She has the vague, fleeting sense of a life that will grow bigger, of wider open

186

spaces, a purer love, voracious appetites. She thinks about the summer, which is so close, and their family vacations. She imagines the smell of plowed soil and olive pits rotting by a roadside. The vault of fruit trees under a moonbeam and nothing to carry, nothing to cover up, nothing to hide.

She starts cooking properly again; in the past few weeks her meals have become almost inedible. For Myriam, she makes cinnamon rice pudding, spicy soups and all sorts of dishes reputed to increase fertility. She observes the young woman's body as attentively as a jealous husband. She examines the fairness of her complexion, the weight of her breasts, the shine of her hair: all, she believes, signs of pregnancy.

She takes care of the laundry with the concentration of a witch, a voodoo priestess. As always, she empties the washing machine. She stretches Paul's boxer shorts. She washes Myriam's lingerie by hand; in the kitchen sink, she runs cold water over the lace and silk of her bras and knickers. She recites prayers.

But Louise is always disappointed. She doesn't need to rip open the trash bags. Nothing escapes her. She saw the stain on the pajama bottoms left by Myriam's side of the bed. On the bathroom floor this morning, she noticed the tiny drop of blood. A drop so small that Myriam didn't clean it, and which was left to dry on the green-and-white tiles.

The blood returns ceaselessly; she knows its odor, this blood that Myriam cannot hide from her and that, each month, announces the death of a child.

Euphoria gives way to days of dejection. The world seems to shrink, to retract, to weigh down on her body, to crush it. Paul and Myriam close doors on her and she wants to smash them down. She has only one desire: to create a world with them, to find her place and live there, to dig herself a niche, a burrow, a warm hiding place. Sometimes she feels ready to claim her portion of earth and then the urge wanes, she is overcome by sorrow, and she feels ashamed even to have believed in something.

One Thursday evening, around 8 p.m., Louise goes back to her studio flat. The landlord is waiting in the dark corridor. He stands beneath the bulb that no longer works. "Ah, there you are." Bertrand Alizard practically pounces on her. He aims the light from his phone screen at Louise's face and she covers her eyes with her hands. "I was waiting for you. I've come here several times, in the evenings and afternoons. I never found you." He speaks smoothly, his upper body leaning toward Louise, as if he is about to touch her, take her arm, whisper in her ear. He stares at her with his gummed-up eyes, his lashless eyes that he rubs after taking off his glasses, which are attached to a string around his neck.

She opens the door to her flat and lets him in. Bertrand Alizard is wearing a pair of beige trousers that are too big for him. Observing him from behind, Louise notices that the belt has missed two loops and that his trousers hang loose at his waist and beneath his backside. He looks like an old man, stooped and frail, who has stolen a giant's clothing. Everything about him seems harmless: his bald-ing head, his wrinkled cheeks covered in freckles, his trem-bling shoulders . . . everything except his huge, dry hands, with their thick nails like fossils; his butcher's hands, which he rubs together to warm up.

He enters the apartment in silence, slowly and care-fully, as if he were discovering the place for the first time. He inspects the walls, runs his finger over the spotless skirting boards. He touches everything with his calloused hands, caresses the sofa's slipcover, strokes the surface of the Formica table. To him, the apartment appears empty, uninhabited. He would have liked to make a few remarks to his tenant, to tell her that in addition to paying her rent late, she is failing to take care of the flat. But the room is exactly as it was when he left it to her, the day she visited the studio for the first time.

He stands with one hand on the back of a chair and looks at Louise. He waits, staring at her with his yellow eyes that don't see much anymore but that he is not ready to lower. He waits for her to speak, or to rummage in her handbag for the rent money she owes. He waits for her to make the first move, to apologize for not having replied to his letters or the messages he left on her phone. But Louise doesn't say a word. She remains standing against the door, like one of those little dogs that bite you when you try to calm them down.

"You've started packing up, by the looks of it. That's good." Alizard points, with his thick finger, at a few boxes in the entrance hall. "The next tenant will be here in a month."

He takes a few steps and tentatively pushes open the door of the shower cubicle. The porcelain bowl has sunk into the ground, and the rotten planks beneath it have given way.

"What happened here?"

The landlord squats down. He mutters to himself, takes off his jacket and drops it on the floor, then puts on his glasses. Louise stands behind him.

Mr. Alizard turns around and says in a louder voice: "I asked you what happened!"

Louise jumps. "I don't know. It happened a few days ago. The shower's old, I think."

"No, it's not! I built this shower cubicle myself. You should think yourself lucky. Before, people used to wash in the bathroom on the landing. It was me, on my own, who put the shower in this studio."

"It collapsed."

"You didn't look after it, obviously. Surely you don't think I'm going to pay for this to be repaired when you're the one who let it rot?"

Louise stares at him and Mr. Alizard cannot guess what that closed, silent look means.

"Why didn't you call me? How long have you been living like this?" Mr. Alizard squats down again, his forehead covered in sweat.

Louise does not tell him that this studio is merely a lair, a parenthesis where she comes to hide her exhaustion. That she lives somewhere else. Every day she takes a shower in Myriam and Paul's apartment. She undresses in their bedroom and delicately places her clothes on the couple's bed. Then, naked, she crosses the living room to reach the bathroom. Adam sits on the floor and she walks past him. She looks at the babbling child and she knows he will not betray her secret. He will not say anything about Louise's body, its marble whiteness, her mother-of-pearl breasts, which have seen so little sunlight.

She leaves the bathroom door open so she can hear him. She turns on the water and for a long time—as long as possible—she remains motionless under the burning jet. She doesn't get dressed again straight away. She sinks her fingers into the pots of cream that Myriam hordes and she massages her calves, her thighs, her arms. She walks barefoot through the apartment, her body wrapped in a white towel. Her own towel, which she hides every day under a pile in a cupboard.

"You noticed the problem and you didn't try to fix it? You'd rather live like a gypsy?"

Crouching in front of the shower, Alizard hams it up. This studio in the suburbs, he only kept it out of sentimentality. He exhales loudly and puts his hands to his forehead. He touches the black foam with his fingertips and shakes his head, as if only he could possibly understand the gravity of the situation. Out loud, he calculates the cost of the repair work. "That's going to cost about eight hundred euros. At least." He dazzles her with the science of DIY, using technical words, claiming that it will take him more than two weeks to repair this disaster. He tries to impress the little blonde woman, who still says nothing.

She can pay for it out of her deposit, he thinks. When she moved in, he insisted that she pay him two months' rent in advance, as a form of security. It's sad, but the truth is you can't trust people. As far as the landlord can remember, he has never had to pay back that sum to any of his tenants. Nobody is careful enough: there is always something to be found, a defect to be highlighted, a stain somewhere, a scratch.

Alizard has a head for business. For thirty years he drove a lorry between France and Poland. He slept in his cab, barely ate, lied about his rest time, resisted every temptation. He consoled himself for all of this by calculating the money he'd saved. He felt pleased with himself, proud of his ability to make such sacrifices in preparation for his future fortune.

Year after year he bought studio flats in the Paris suburbs and renovated them. He rents them out, at an exorbitant price, to people who have no alternative. At the end of each month he goes around to all of his properties to pick up his rent. He pokes his head through doorways; sometimes he goes inside, to "have a look around," to "make sure everything's in order." He asks indiscreet questions, to which the tenants reply grudgingly, desperate for him to leave, to get out of their kitchen, to take his nose out of their cupboard. But he stays there and in the end they offer him something to drink, which he accepts and slowly sips. He tells them about his backache ("Thirty years driving a lorry, it messes you up"). He makes conversation.

He likes to rent to women, because they're more conscientious and less likely to cause trouble. He particularly favors students, single mothers, divorcees—but not old women, who can move in and stop paying and still have the law on their side. And then Louise arrived, with her sad smile, her blonde hair, her lost-waif expression. She was recommended by one of Alizard's former tenants, a nurse at the Henri-Mondor hospital who had always paid her rent on time.

Bloody sentimentality. This Louise had nobody. No children and a dead husband. She stood there in front of him, a wad of euros in her hand, and he thought she was pretty, elegant in her blouse with its Peter Pan collar. She looked at him, docile and grateful. She whispered: "I was very ill," and in that moment he was eager to ask her questions, to ask her what she'd done after her husband's death, where she had come from and what pain she had suffered. But she didn't give him time. She said: "I've just found a job, in Paris, with a very good family." And the conversation ended there.

Now Bertrand Alizard wants to get rid of this mute, negligent tenant. He's no longer fooled. He won't put up with any more of her excuses, her shifty behavior, her late payments. He doesn't know why, but the sight of Louise makes him shiver. Something in her disgusts him: that enigmatic smile, that excessive makeup; that way she has of looking down on him, her mouth tight-lipped. Not once has she ever responded to one of his smiles. Not once has she made the effort to notice that he's wearing a new jacket and that he's brushed his sad few strands of red hair to the side.

Alizard heads over to the sink. He washes his hands and says: "I'll come back in a week with the parts and a plumber to do the work. You should finish packing."

Louise takes the children for walks. They spend long afternoons in the park, where the trees have been pruned, where the lawn—green once again—attracts the local students. Around the swings, the children are happy to see one another again, even if they don't know anyone's names. For them, nothing else matters but this latest fancy-dress costume, this new toy, this miniature stroller in which a little girl has nestled her baby.

Louise has only one friend in the neighborhood. Apart from Wafa, she speaks with nobody. She offers nothing more than polite smiles, discreet waves. When she first arrived, the other nannies in the park kept their distance. Louise was like a chaperone, a quartermaster, an English governess. The others disliked her haughty airs, her ludicrous *grande dame* pose. There was something sanctimonious about the way she didn't have the decency to look away when another nanny, phone glued to her ear, forgot to hold a child's hand as they crossed the road. Sometimes she would even make a point of telling off unsupervised children who stole toys from others or fell off a guardrail.

As the months passed, the nannies—sitting on those benches for hours on end—gradually got to know one another, almost despite themselves, as if they were coworkers sharing an open-air office. Every day after school they would see one another, in the supermarket, at the doctor's or by the merry-go-round in the little square. Louise remembers some of their names and countries of origin. She knows the apartment buildings where they work, their bosses' occupations. Sitting under the barely flowering rose bush, she listens to the interminable conversations that these women have on their phones as they nibble chocolate biscuits.

Around the slide and the sandpit she hears snatches of Baoulé, Dyula, Arabic and Hindi, sweet nothings whispered in Filipino or Russian. Languages from all over the world contaminate the babbling of the children, who learn odd words and repeat them to their enchanted parents. "He speaks Arabic, I swear! Listen to him." Then, with the passing years, the children forget. And as the face and the voice of the now-vanished nanny fade from memory, nobody in the house recalls how to say "Mama" in Lingala or the name of the exotic dishes that the nice nanny used to make. "That meat stew, what did she call it again?"

Around the children—who all look alike, often wearing the same clothes bought in the same shops, with their names written on the labels by their mothers to avoid any confusion—buzzes this swarm of women. There are young women in black veils, who have to be even gentler, cleaner and more punctual than the others. There are the ones who change wigs every week. The Filipinos who beg the children, in English, not to jump in puddles. There are the old ones, who have worked in the neighborhood for years, who are on familiar terms with the school headmistress; the ones who see teenagers in the streets who they used to look after when they were little and persuade themselves that the teenager recognized them, that he would have said hello if he wasn't so shy. There are the new ones, who work for a few months and then vanish without saying good-bye, leaving trails of rumors and suspicions behind them.

About Louise, the nannies know very little. Even Wafa, who seems pretty close to her, has been discreet about her friend's life. They have tried asking her questions. The white nanny intrigues them. How many times have the other parents used her as a benchmark, vaunting her qualities as a cook, her total availability, mentioning the complete trust Myriam puts in her? They wonder who she is, this fragile, perfect woman. Who did she work for before she came here? In which part of Paris? Is she married? Does she have children who she picks up in the evening, after work? Are her bosses good to her?

Louise does not respond—or hardly—and the nannies understand this silence. They all have shameful secrets. They hide awful memories of bent knees, humiliations, lies. Memories of barely audible voices on the other end of the line, of conversations cut off, of people who die and are never seen again, of money needed day after day for a sick child who no longer recognizes you and who has forgotten the sound of your voice. Some of them, Louise knows, have stolen—just little things, almost nothing at all—like a tax levied on the happiness of others. Some conceal their real names. It never even crosses their minds to blame Louise for her reserve. They are wary, that's all.

In the park, they don't talk much about themselves, or only by allusion. They don't want the tears to well in their eyes. Their bosses are fodder enough for animated conversations. The nannies laugh at their obsessions, their habits, their way of life. Wafa's bosses are stingy; Alba's are horribly suspicious. The mother of little Jules has a drinking problem. Most of them, the nannies complain, are manipulated by their children; they see very little of them and constantly give in to their demands. Rosalia, a very dark-skinned Filipino woman, chain-smokes cigarettes. "The boss surprised me in the street last time. I know she's spying on me."

While the children run around on the gravel, while they dig in the sandpit (the rats that lived there having recently been exterminated by the local authorities), the women turn the park into a cross between a recruitment office, a union headquarters, a claims center and a classified-ads listing. Here there is talk of job offers and disputes between employers and employees. The women come to complain to Lydie, the self-proclaimed president, a tall woman in her fifties from the Ivory Coast who wears fake-fur coats and has thin red-pencil eyebrows.

At 6 p.m., groups of youths invade the park. The nannies know them. They're from the Rue de Dunkerque, from the Gare du Nord. The nannies know that these youths leave broken crack pipes by the edge of the playground, that they piss in flowerbeds, go looking for fights. Seeing them, the nannies quickly pick up children's coats and toy excavators covered in sand, they hang their handbags from the handles of the strollers, and they leave.

The procession goes through the park's gates and the women go their separate ways: some walk up toward Montmartre or Notre-Dame-de-Lorette; others, like Louise and Lydie, head down toward the Grands Boulevards. They walk side by side. Louise holds hands with Mila and Adam. When the sidewalk is narrow, she lets Lydie walk ahead of them, bent over her stroller with a baby asleep inside it.

"A young pregnant woman came by yesterday. She's going to have twins in August," Lydie tells her.

Everyone knows that some mothers—the most sensible and conscientious ones—come here nanny-shopping, the way people used to go down to the docks or to the end of an alley to find a maid or a warehouseman. The mothers prowl around the benches, observing the nannies, examining the faces of the children when they go running to the thighs of these women, who brusquely blow their nose or console them after a fall. Sometimes the mothers ask questions. They investigate.

"She lives on Rue des Martyrs and she's due at the end of August. She's looking for someone, so I thought of you," Lydie concludes.

Louise looks up at her with her doll-like eyes. She hears Lydie's voice, as if from far away; the sound echoes inside her head but the words are a blur and she doesn't grasp their meaning. She leans down, takes Adam in her arms and puts her hand under Mila's armpit. Lydie raises her voice; she repeats something. She thinks that perhaps

Louise didn't hear her, that she's distracted, her mind wholly occupied by the children.

"So what do you think? Shall I give her your number?"

Louise does not reply. She gathers speed and pushes past, brutal, silent. She cuts in front of Lydie and as she makes her escape, she knocks over the stroller with a sudden gesture, waking the baby, which starts to scream.

"What the hell is wrong with you?" shouts the nanny as all her shopping falls into the gutter. Louise is already far away. In the street, people gather around Lydie. They pick up mandarins that have rolled along the sidewalk; they throw the soaked baguette in a trash can. They worry about the baby, who is fine, thankfully.

Lydie will recount this incredible story several times, and each time she will swear: "No, it wasn't an accident. She knocked over the stroller on purpose."

Her obsession with the child spins endlessly in her mind. She thinks of nothing else. This baby, which she will love madly, is the solution to all her problems. Once it's on its way, it will shut up the harpies in the park, it will drive away her horrible landlord. It will protect Louise's place in her kingdom. She feels sure that Paul and Myriam don't have enough time to themselves. That Mila and Adam are an obstacle to the baby's arrival. It's the children's fault if their parents are never alone together. Paul and Myriam are exhausted by their tantrums; Adam wakes up too often in the night, cutting short their lovemaking. If the children weren't constantly under their feet—whining, demanding cuddles—Paul and Myriam would be able to forge ahead and make a child for Louise. Her desire for that baby is fanatical, violent, blindly possessive. She wants it in a way she has rarely wanted anything; so badly it hurts, to the point where she is capable of choking, burning, destroying anything that comes between her and the satisfaction of her desire.

One evening, Louise waits impatiently for Myriam.

When her boss finally opens the door, Louise practically jumps on her, eyes ablaze. She is holding Mila by the hand. The nanny appears tense, concentrated. She looks as if she's making a great effort to contain herself, not to hop up and down or yell something. She has been thinking about this moment all day long. Her plan seems perfect to her, and now all she needs is for Myriam to agree, to let her do it, and to fall into Paul's arms.

"I'd like to take the children to eat at a restaurant. That way, you'll be able to have a nice dinner with your husband."

Myriam puts her handbag on the chair. Louise watches her; she moves closer, stands next to her. Myriam can feel the nanny's breath on her; her presence makes it impossible for Myriam to think. Louise is like a child whose eyes are saying "So?," whose entire body is stiff with impatience, exaltation.

"Oh, I don't know. We haven't planned anything. Maybe another time." Myriam takes off her jacket and starts walking to her bedroom. But Mila holds her back. The child enters the scene, following the nanny's script to perfection. In a sweet voice, she begs: "Mama, please. We want to go to a restaurant with Louise."

At last Myriam gives in. She insists on paying for their meal and begins to rummage in her handbag for cash, but Louise stops her. "Don't. Please. Tonight, I want to take them out."

Inside her pocket, against her thigh, Louise holds a banknote, which she caresses sometimes with her fingertips. They walk to the restaurant. She spotted this little bistro a while ago; its customers are mostly students, who come here to drink its three-euro beer. But tonight the bistro is practically empty. The owner, a Chinese man, sits behind the bar, in the neon light. He wears a garishly patterned red shirt and he is chatting with a woman who sits in front of a glass of beer, socks rolled up over her fat ankles. Out on the terrace, two men are smoking.

Louise pushes Mila inside the restaurant. The air is thick with the smell of stale tobacco, meat stew and sweat, and it makes the little girl want to throw up. Mila is very disappointed. She sits down and looks around the empty room, her eyes searching the dirty shelves with pots of ketchup and mustard on them. This is not what she had been imagining. She expected to see pretty ladies; she thought there would be noise, music, lovers. Instead of which, she slumps over the greasy table and stares at the television screen above the bar.

Louise, with Adam in her lap, says she doesn't want to eat. "I'll choose for you, okay?" Without giving Mila time to reply, she orders sausages and chips. "They'll share it," she explains. The Chinese man barely responds. He takes the menu from her hands.

Louise also orders a glass of wine, which she sips very slowly. She tries to make conversation with Mila. She has brought some pencils and sheets of paper, which she puts on the table. But Mila has no desire to draw. She's not very hungry either and hardly touches her meal. Adam has gone back inside his stroller. He rubs his eyes with his little fists.

Louise looks through the window. She looks at her watch, at the street, at the bar where the owner leans his elbows. She bites her nails, smiles, then her eyes turn vague, absent. She would like to find something for her hands to do, focus her mind on one single idea, but her thoughts are like broken glass, her soul weighed down by rocks. Several times, she passes her folded hand over the table, as if to sweep away invisible crumbs or smooth the cold surface. A jumble of unrelated images fills her head; visions that flash past ever faster, connecting memories to regrets, faces to unfulfilled fantasies. The smell of plastic in the hospital courtyard where they took her for walks. The sound of Stéphanie's laughter, at once blaring and muffled, like the noise a hyena makes. The faces of forgotten children; the softness of hair, stroked with her fingertips; the chalky taste of an apple turnover that had dried out at the bottom of a bag, but that she'd eaten anyway. She hears Bertrand Alizard's voice, his lying voice, which mingles with other voices, the voices of all those who gave her instructions, advice, orders; the surprisingly gentle voice of that female bailiff whose name, she remembers, was Isabelle.

Louise smiles at Mila. She wants to console her. She can tell that the little girl is on the verge of tears. She recognizes that feeling, that weight on the chest, that discomfort at being there. She also knows that Mila is restraining herself, that she has self-control, bourgeois manners, that she is capable of a thoughtfulness beyond her age. Louise orders another glass of wine. While she drinks, she watches Mila stare at the television screen, and she can make out, very clearly, her mother's features beneath the mask of childhood. Those innocent, little-girl gestures are the bud containing the woman's edginess, the boss's severity.

The Chinese man picks up the empty glasses and the half-full plate. He puts the bill—scribbled on a scrap of graph paper—on the table. Louise doesn't move. She waits for the time to pass, for the sky outside to grow darker; she thinks about Paul and Myriam, enjoying their time alone, about the empty apartment, the meal she left for them on the table. They've eaten by now, she imagines, standing up in the kitchen, the way they used to do before the children were born. Paul pours his wife more wine and finishes his own glass. His hand slides over Myriam's skin and they laugh. That's the kind of people they are: they laugh with love, with desire, shameless.

At last Louise stands up. They leave the restaurant. Mila is relieved. Her eyelids are heavy; she wants to go to bed now. In his stroller, Adam has fallen asleep. Louise straightens his blanket. As soon as night falls, the winter cold returns from its hiding place, sneaking under their clothes.

Louise holds the little girl's hand, and for a long time they walk through city streets where all the other children have disappeared. In the Grands Boulevards, they pass theaters and packed cafés. They head down streets that become ever darker and narrower, sometimes emerging into a little square where young people lean against trash cans, smoking joints.

Mila does not recognize these streets. A yellow glow illuminates the sidewalks. To her, these houses, these restaurants seem very far from home and she looks up at Louise with anxious eyes. She waits for a reassuring word. A surprise, perhaps? But Louise just keeps walking and walking, breaking her silence only to mutter: "Come on—aren't you coming?" The little girl twists her ankles on the cobblestones. Her stomach is racked with anxiety. She feels sure that, if she complained, it would only make things worse. She senses that a tantrum would do no good. In Rue Montmartre, Mila observes the girls smoking outside bars, the girls in high heels, who shout too loud, causing the bar owner to bark at them: "Shut up, will you? We've got neighbors here." Mila is completely lost; she doesn't know if this is even the same city, if she can see her house from here, if her parents know where she is.

Abruptly, Louise stops in the middle of a busy sidewalk. She glances up, parks the stroller next to a wall and asks Mila: "What flavor do you want?"

Behind the counter a man waits wearily for the child to make up her mind. Mila is too small to see the trays of ice cream, so she stands on tiptoes and then answers nervously: "Strawberry."

One hand holding Louise's, the other gripping her cone, Mila walks back the way they've come through the darkness of the night, licking her ice cream, which gives her a terrible headache. She squeezes her eyes shut to make the pain go away, trying to concentrate on the taste of crushed strawberries and the little pieces of fruit that get stuck between her teeth. Inside her empty stomach, the ice cream falls in heavy flakes.

They take the bus home. Mila asks if she can put the ticket in the machine, as she does whenever they take the bus together. But Louise shushes her. "We don't need a ticket at night. Don't worry about it."

When Louise opens the door of the apartment, Paul is lying on the sofa. He is listening to a record, eyes closed. Mila rushes over to him. She jumps in his arms and buries her frozen face in her father's neck. Paul pretends to tell her off for coming home so late, going out and having fun at a restaurant, like a big girl. Myriam, he tells them, took a bath and went to bed early. "She was exhausted by work. I didn't even see her."

A sudden melancholy chokes Louise. So all that was for nothing. She is cold, her legs ache, she spent the last of her cash, and Myriam didn't even wait for her husband before she went to sleep.

She feels alone with the children. Children don't care about the contours of our world. They can guess at its harshness, its darkness, but they don't want to know anything more. Louise tells them about it and they turn away. She holds their hands, crouches down so they are at the same level, but already they are looking elsewhere: they've seen something. They've found a game that gives them an excuse not to hear. They don't pretend to feel sorry for those less fortunate than them.

She sits next to Mila. The little girl is squatting on a chair, drawing pictures. She is capable of staying focused on her sheets of paper and her pile of felt-tip pens for nearly an hour. She colors the picture carefully, attentive to the smallest details. Louise likes to sit next to her, to watch as the colors are spread over the paper. She observes, in silence, the blooming of giant flowers in the garden of an orange house where people with long hands and tall, slender bodies sleep on the lawn. Mila leaves no empty spaces. Clouds, flying cars, hot-air balloons fill the densely shimmering sky.

"Who's that?" Louise asks.

"That?" Mila puts her finger on a huge, smiling figure, lying on the lawn and covering more than half of the page. "That's Mila."

Louise can no longer find any consolation in the children. The stories she tells them get stuck in a rut and Mila points this out to her. The mythical creatures have lost their vivacity, their splendor. Now her characters have forgotten what they are fighting for, and her tales are just descriptions of long, broken, confused wanderings; impoverished princesses, sick dragons; selfish soliloquies that the children don't understand and of which they soon grow weary. "Think of something else," Mila begs her, but Louise can't. She is sinking into her own words as into quicksand.

Louise doesn't laugh as much anymore. She puts less enthusiasm into their pillow fights and games of ludo. And yet she adores these two children, whom she spends hours observing. It's enough to make her cry sometimes, the looks they give her when they want her approval or her help. Most of all, she loves the way Adam looks around at her, wanting her to notice his improvements, his joys, to show her that in everything he does there is something that is meant for her, and her alone. She would like to drink in their innocence, their excitement, until she is intoxicated. She would like to see through their eyes when they look at something for the first time, when they understand the logic of a mechanism, expecting it to repeat itself infinitely without ever thinking of the weariness that will one day slow it down.

All day long Louise leaves the television on. She

watches apocalyptic news reports, idiotic shows, games whose rules she doesn't fully understand. Since the terrorist attacks, Myriam has forbidden her to let the children watch television. But Louise doesn't care. Mila knows she must not tell her parents what she has seen. That she mustn't say the words "hunt," "terrorist," "killed." The child watches the news in rapt silence. Then, when she's had enough, she turns to her brother. They play, they fight. Mila pushes him against the wall and the little boy turns red before retaliating.

Louise does not look around. She stays where she is, eyes glued to the screen, her body completely immobile. The nanny refuses to go to the park. She doesn't want to talk to the other women or see the old neighbor, whom she humiliated herself with by offering her services. The children get cranky and pace around the apartment. They beg her; they want to go outside, to play with their friends, to buy a chocolate waffle at the top of the street.

The children's cries irritate her; she's ready to scream too. The children's nagging whines, their foghorn voices, their "why?"s, their selfish desires seem to split her skull. "When is tomorrow?" Mila asks, hundreds of times. Louise can't sing a song without them begging her to do it again; they want the eternal repetition of everything—stories, games, funny faces—and Louise can't stand it anymore. She has no patience now for their tears, their tantrums, their hysterical excitement. Sometimes she wants to put her fingers around Adam's neck and squeeze until he faints. She shakes her head to get rid of these thoughts. She manages to stop thinking about it, but a dark and slimy tide has completely submerged her.

Someone has to die. Someone has to die for us to be happy.

Morbid refrains echo inside Louise's head when she walks. Phrases that she didn't invent—and whose meaning she is not sure she fully grasps—fill her mind. Her heart has grown hard. The years have covered it in a thick, cold rind and she can barely hear it beating. Nothing moves her anymore. She has to admit that she no longer knows how to love. All the tenderness has been squeezed from her heart. Her hands have nothing left to caress.

I'll be punished for that, she hears herself think. I'll be punished for not knowing how to love.

There are photographs of that afternoon. They have not been printed but they exist, somewhere, deep inside an artificial memory. The pictures are mostly of the children. Adam, half-naked, lying in the grass. He is staring absently to the side, with his big blue eyes, his expression almost melancholic despite his tender age. In one of those images, Mila is running down a broad, tree-lined path. She is wearing a white dress with a butterfly design. She is barefoot. In another photo, Paul is carrying Adam on his shoulders and Mila in his arms. Myriam is behind the lens. Her husband's face is blurred, his smile hidden by one of Adam's little feet. Myriam laughs too; she doesn't think to ask them to keep still. To stop wriggling for a moment. "Please? I'm trying to take a picture."

She is fond of these photographs, though. She takes hundreds of them and looks at them in melancholy moments. In the metro, between two meetings, sometimes even during a meal, she scrolls through portraits of her children. She also believes it is her duty as a mother to immortalize these instants, to possess the proof of past joys.

One day she will be able to show them to Mila or Adam. She will recount her memories and the image will awaken old sensations, details, an atmosphere. She has always been told that children are just an ephemeral happiness, a fleeting vision, a restlessness. An eternal metamorphosis. Round faces that are gradually imbued with seriousness without us even realizing. So, every chance she gets, she looks at her children from behind the screen of her iPhone. For her, those small beings are the most beautiful landscape in the world.

Paul's friend Thomas invited them to spend the day at his country house. He goes there, alone, to write songs and nurse his alcoholism. Thomas keeps ponies at the bottom of his garden. Picture-book ponies, with short legs and hair as blonde as an American actress. A little stream runs through the vast garden, whose borders even Thomas doesn't know. The children eat lunch on the grass. The parents drink rosé and in the end Thomas puts the box of wine on the table and helps himself to glass after glass. "We're among friends, aren't we? Let's just get stuck in."

Thomas has no children, and it doesn't even cross Paul or Myriam's mind to bother him with their worries about the nanny, the kids' education or family vacations. During this beautiful May day, they forget their anxieties. Their preoccupations appear to them as they are: minor everyday concerns, mere vagaries. All they think about now is the future, their plans, their ripening happiness. Myriam is sure that Pascal will ask her to become a partner in September. She will be able to choose her cases, delegate the drudgery to interns. Paul looks at his wife and his children.

He thinks to himself that the hardest work is over, that the best is yet to come.

They spend a glorious day running around and playing. The children ride ponies and feed them apples and carrots. They pull weeds from what Thomas calls the vegetable garden, even though not a single vegetable has ever grown there. Paul grabs a guitar and makes everyone laugh. Then everyone falls silent when Thomas sings and Myriam harmonizes. The children stare wide-eyed at these calm adults singing in a language that they don't understand.

When it's time to go home, the children howl in protest. Adam throws himself on the ground and refuses to leave. Mila, who is also exhausted, sobs in Thomas's arms. Almost as soon as they're inside the car, the children fall asleep. Myriam and Paul are silent. They watch the fields of rapeseed lying stunned in the fawn sunset that paints the motorway rest areas, the industrial zones, the gray wind turbines with a touch of poetry.

The motorway is blocked by an accident and Paul, who has a particular hatred of traffic jams, decides to take the next exit and return to Paris on a B-road. "I just have to follow the GPS." They rush down long dark streets lined with ugly bourgeois houses, their shutters closed. Myriam nods off. The leaves of trees shine under the streetlights like thousands of black diamonds. Occasionally she opens her eyes, anxious that Paul, too, might have slipped into a dream. He reassures her and she falls back asleep.

She is woken by the blare of car horns. Eyes half-closed,

her brain still fogged by sleep and too much rosé, she does not at first recognize the avenue where they are stuck in traffic. "Where are we?" she asks Paul, who doesn't reply, who has no idea, and who is busy trying to understand what is blocking them. Myriam turns her head to the side. And she would have fallen back asleep had she not seen—there, on the opposite sidewalk—the familiar figure of Louise.

"Look," she tells Paul, pointing. But Paul is concentrated on the traffic jam. He is thinking about how to get out of it, perhaps by making a U-turn. He is at a crossroads where the cars, coming from all directions, are no longer moving. Scooters wind between the cars; pedestrians brush past the hoods. The traffic lights change from red to green in a few seconds. No one moves.

"Look over there. I think it's Louise."

Myriam sits up a bit in her seat to get a better look at the face of the woman walking on the other side of the crossroads. She could lower the window and call out to her, but she would feel ridiculous and the nanny probably wouldn't hear her anyway. Myriam sees the blonde hair, tied up in a bun at the back of her neck; she recognizes Louise's inimitable gait, agile and trembling. The nanny, it seems to her, is walking slowly, staring at the shop windows. Then she moves out of sight, her slender frame concealed by other pedestrians, disappearing behind a group of people who are laughing and waving their arms around. And she reappears on the other side of the zebra crossing, as if in the faded images of an old film, in a Paris rendered unreal by the darkness. Louise looks incongruous, with her eternal Peter Pan collar and her too-long skirt, like a character that has ended up in the wrong story and is doomed to roam endlessly through a foreign world.

Paul honks the horn furiously and the children are startled awake. He puts his arm through the open window, looks behind him and speeds down a side street, cursing loudly. Myriam wants to calm him down, to tell him that they are not in a rush, that there is no point getting so angry. Nostalgically she continues staring, until the last possible moment, at a chimerical, almost hazy Louise, motionless under a streetlamp, who appears to be waiting for something, at the edge of a frontier that she is about to cross and behind which she will vanish.

Myriam sinks into her seat. She looks ahead again, troubled, as if she had just seen a memory, a very old acquaintance, a childhood sweetheart. She wonders where Louise is going, if it was really her, what she was doing there. She would have liked to continue observing her through that window, to watch her live. The fact of having seen her on that sidewalk, by chance, in a place so far from their usual haunts, makes her desperately curious. For the first time she tries to imagine, in a corporeal sense, everything Louise is when she is not with them.

Hearing his mother pronounce the nanny's name, Adam, too, had looked through the window.

"It's my nanny!" he shouted, pointing at her, as if unable to understand that she might live elsewhere, alone, that she might walk without pushing a stroller or holding a child's hand. "Where is Louise going?" he asked.

"She's going home," Myriam replied. "To her own house."

Captain Nina Dorval keeps her eyes open as she lies on her bed in her apartment on Boulevard de Strasbourg. Paris is deserted this rainy August. The night is silent. Tomorrow morning, at 7:30—the time when Louise used to see the children every day—they will remove the police tape from the apartment on Rue d'Hauteville and they will begin the reconstruction. Nina has informed the investigating judge, the prosecutor, the lawyers. "I will play the nanny," she said. Nobody dares contradict her. The captain knows this case better than anyone. She was the first to reach the crime scene after the phone call from Rose Grinberg. The music teacher screamed: "It's the nanny! She killed the children."

That day, the policewoman parked outside the apartment building. An ambulance had just left. They were taking the little girl to the closest hospital. Already the street was filled with onlookers, fascinated by the screaming of sirens, the urgency of the medics, the paleness of the police officers' faces. Passersby pretended to wait for something; they asked questions as they stood in the doorway of the baker's or under a porch. A man, lifting his arm above the crowd, took a photograph of the building's entrance. Nina Dorval had him removed.

In the stairwell the captain walked past the medics who were evacuating the mother. The accused was still upstairs, unconscious. In her hand she held a small white ceramic knife. "Take her through the back door," Nina ordered.

She entered the apartment. She assigned each person a role. She watched the forensics experts working in their baggy white overalls. In the bathroom she took off her gloves and leaned over the bathtub. She began by dipping her fingertips into the cold, murky water, tracing ripples, setting the water in motion. A pirate ship was taken by the waves. She couldn't make up her mind to remove her hand; something was drawing her into the depths. She submerged her arm up to her elbow and then up to her shoulder, and that was how the forensics officer found her: crouching down, sleeve soaked. He asked her to leave; he was going to make an inspection.

Nina Dorval wandered around the apartment, Dictaphone pressed to her lips. She described the premises, the smell of soap and blood, the noise of the television and the name of the program that was on. No detail was omitted: the open glass door of the washing machine, with a crumpled shirt hanging out of it; the full sink; the children's clothes strewn across the floor. On the table were two pink plastic plates containing the dried-out remains of lunch. The police photographer took a picture of the pasta shells and the pieces of ham. Later, when she knew more about Louise, when she'd heard all the stories about the obsessively tidy nanny, Nina Dorval was surprised by the disorder of the apartment.

She sent Lieutenant Verdier to the Gare du Nord to meet Paul, who was coming back from a business trip. He'll know how to deal with the situation, she thought. He's an experienced man; he'll find the right words; he'll manage to calm him down. The lieutenant got there very early. He sat sheltered from the drafts of air and watched the trains arrive. He wanted to smoke. Passengers jumped down from a carriage and started running, in clusters. They probably had to catch a connecting train. The lieutenant watched as they passed, this crowd of sweating people: women in high heels, clutching their handbags to their chests; men shouting, "Get out of the way!" Then the London train arrived. Lieutenant Verdier could have walked to the carriage where Paul was sitting but he preferred to stand at the end of the platform. He watched the father of the dead children coming toward him, headphones covering his ears, carrying a little bag. He didn't move to intercept him. He wanted to give him another few minutes. Another few seconds before abandoning him to an endless night.

The policeman showed him his badge. He asked Paul to follow him, and at first Paul thought it was a mistake.

Week after week, Captain Dorval went over the course of events. Despite the silence of the nanny, who did not come out of her coma, despite the corroborating testimonies about this perfect nanny, she told herself she would find the flaw. She swore she would understand what had happened in this warm, secret world of childhood, behind closed doors. She summoned Wafa to police headquarters and questioned her. The young woman couldn't stop crying; she didn't manage to articulate a single word and in the end the policewoman lost patience. She told her that she couldn't care less about her situation: her papers, her work contract, Louise's promises, Wafa's naivety. All she wanted to know was whether she had seen Louise that day. Wafa said that she'd gone to the apartment in the morning. She'd rung the doorbell and Louise had half-opened the door. "As if she was hiding something." But Alphonse had run in. He'd slid between Louise's legs and he'd joined the children, still in their pajamas, sitting in front of the television. "I tried to persuade her. I told her we could go out for a walk. It was a nice day and the children would get bored in the apartment." Louise had refused to listen. "She wouldn't let me in. I called Alphonse, who was very disappointed, and we left."

But Louise did not remain in the apartment. Rose Grinberg is categorical on that point: she saw the nanny in the building's lobby, one hour before her nap. One hour before the murder. Where was Louise coming from? Where had she been? How long had she stayed outside? The police went around the whole neighborhood, showing people the photograph of Louise. They questioned everyone. Some of them—the liars, the lonely ones who make things up to pass the time—they had to tell to shut up. They went to the park, to the Paradis café. They walked through the covered arcades off Rue du Faubourg-Saint-Denis and questioned the shopkeepers. And then they found that supermarket CCTV video. The captain must have watched that recording a thousand times. She watched Louise walk calmly down the aisles until she felt sick. She observed her hands—her very small hands—pick up a carton of milk, a packet of biscuits and a bottle of wine. In these images the children run from one aisle to another, ignored by the nanny. Adam knocks some packets off the shelf; he bumps into the knees of a woman pushing a trolley. Mila tries to reach some chocolate eggs. Louise is calm; she doesn't open her mouth, doesn't call them. She heads for the till and the children follow her, laughing. They cling to her legs and Adam pulls at her skirt, but Louise pays no attention. Her irritation is betrayed only by a few little signs, spotted by the policewoman: a slight contraction of her lips, a furtive glance downward. Louise, the captain thinks, looks like one of those duplicitous mothers in a fairy tale, abandoning her children in the darkness of a forest.

At 4 p.m., Rose Grinberg closed the shutters. Wafa walked to the park and sat on a bench. Hervé finished his shift. It was at this time that Louise headed toward the bathroom. Tomorrow Nina Dorval will have to repeat the same movements: turning on the tap, leaving her hand under the trickle of water to test the temperature, as she used to do for her own sons when they were still little. And she will say: "Come on, children. Time to take a bath."

She had to ask Paul if Adam and Mila liked water. If they were usually reluctant to get undressed. If they enjoyed splashing around, surrounded by their bath toys. "There might have been an argument," the captain explained. "Do you think they might have been suspicious, or at least surprised, to be taking a bath at four in the afternoon?" They showed the father the photograph of the murder weapon. An ordinary kitchen knife, but so small that Louise could probably have partly hidden it in her palm. Nina asked him if he recognized it. If it was theirs or if Louise had bought it; if her act was premeditated. "Take your time," she said. But Paul hadn't needed time. That knife was the one that Thomas had brought them back from Japan as a gift. A ceramic knife, extremely sharp. Merely touching it to your skin was enough to cut into the flesh. A sushi knife, in return for which Myriam had given him a euro, to ward off bad luck. "But we never used it for cooking. Myriam put it in a cupboard, high up. She wanted to keep it out of the children's reach."

After two months investigating this woman, night and day, two months tracing her past, Nina started to believe that she knew Louise better than anyone. She summoned Bertrand Alizard. The man shook as he sat in the chair in her office. Drops of sweat ran over his freckles. He was so afraid of blood, of nasty surprises, that he stayed out in the corridor while the police searched Louise's studio flat. The drawers were empty, the windows spotless. They didn't find anything. Nothing but an old photograph of Stéphanie and a few unopened envelopes.

Nina Dorval plunged her hands into Louise's rotting soul. She wanted to know everything about her. She thought she could smash down the walls of silence within which the nanny had locked herself. She questioned the Rouvier family, Mr. Franck, Mrs. Perrin, the doctors at the Henri-Mondor hospital, where Louise had been admitted for mood disorders. She spent hours reading the notebook with the flower-patterned cover and at night she dreamed of those twisted capital letters, those unknown names that Louise had written down with the seriousness of a solitary child. The captain tracked down some neighbors from when Louise lived in the house in Bobigny. She asked questions of the nannies in the park. Nobody seemed able to figure her out. "It was hello, good-bye, that was all." Nothing to report.

And then she watched the accused sleep on her white bed. She asked the nurse to leave the room. She wanted to be alone with the aging doll. The sleeping doll, with thick white bandages on her neck and hands, instead of jewelry. Under the fluorescent lights, the captain stared at the pale eyelids, the gray roots at her temples and the weak throb of a vein beating under her earlobe. She tried to read something in that devastated face, on that dry and wrinkled skin. The captain did not touch the immobile body but she sat down and she spoke to Louise the way you speak to children who are feigning sleep. She said: "I know you can hear me."

Nina Dorval has experienced it before: reconstructions are sometimes revelatory, like those voodoo ceremonies where the trance state causes a truth to burst up from the pain, where the past is illuminated in a new light. Once you are there, a detail appears, a sort of magic can occur: a contradiction finally makes sense. Tomorrow she will enter the apartment building on Rue d'Hauteville, outside which a few bouquets of flowers and children's drawings are still fading. She will make her way past the candles and take the elevator. The apartment—where nothing has changed since that day in May, where nobody has been to fetch their things or even pick up their papers—will be the scene of this sordid theater. Nina Dorval will knock three times.

There, she will let herself be engulfed by a wave of disgust, by a hatred of everything: this apartment, this washing machine, this still-filthy sink, these toys that have escaped their boxes and crawled under the tables to die, the sword pointed at the sky, the dangling ear. She will be Louise, Louise pushing her fingers in her ears to stop the shouting and the crying. Louise who goes back and forth from the bedroom to the kitchen, from the bathroom to the kitchen, from the trash to the tumble dryer, from the bed to the cupboard in the entrance hall, from the balcony to the bathroom. Louise who comes back and then starts again, Louise who bends down and stands on tiptoe. Louise who takes a knife from a cupboard. Louise who drinks a glass of wine, the window open, one foot resting on the little balcony.

"Come on, children. Time to take a bath."

THE PERFECT NANNY

When Myriam decides to return to work after having children, she and her husband look for the perfect nanny. They never dreamed they would find Louise: a quiet, polite, devoted woman. But as the couple and the nanny become more dependent on one another, jealousy, resentment, and suspicions mount. Building tension with every page, *The Perfect Nanny* is a riveting exploration of power, class, race, domesticity, motherhood, and madness.

ADÈLE

Adèle appears to have the perfect life: She is a successful journalist in Paris who lives in a beautiful apartment with her surgeon husband and their young son. But underneath the surface, she is bored-and consumed by an insatiable need for sex. Suspenseful, erotic, and electrically charged, *Adèle* is a captivating exploration of addiction, sexuality, and one woman's quest to feel alive.

SEX AND LIES

True Stories of Women's Intimate Lives in the Arab World

Leila Slimani was in her native Morocco promoting her novel *Adèle*, about a woman addicted to sex, when she began meeting women who confided the dark secrets of their sexual lives. *Sex and Lies* combines vivid, often harrowing testimonies with Slimani's passionate and intelligent commentary to make a galvanizing case for a sexual revolution in the Arab world.

Ⓟ PENGUIN BOOKS

Ready to find your next great read? Let us help. Visit prh.com/nextread

P.O. 0005399783 20231020